ALSO BY HAYDEN SMITH

Tom O'Banion Mystery Series

Nine Expensive Funerals

Vengeance Served Cold

Intrigue in Paris

PRAISE FOR HAYDEN SMITH'S VENGEANCE SERVED COLD, THE SECOND IN HIS TOM O'BANION MYSTERY SERIES

This is the long awaited second book in the Tom O'Banion Mystery Series; and Hayden Smith has written another winner. Not only is this book tightly written and plotted, as was its predecessor, *Nine Expensive Funerals*, but Smith has moved beyond the thriller genre to write a novel about community, friendship, love—both agape and eros—compassion, and respect for elders and institutions. This time around, Smith adds food writing to his repertoire. Readers are treated to many mouth-watering fried perch dinners (with French fries and onion rings) from the Doo Drop Inn in Muskegon, as well as pizza and beer in front of the fire, charcuterie boards, chocolate mousse, Maria's delicious lasagna, and cabernet sauvignon. There's naps, conspiracy, duplicity, local politics, and murder in these pages.
In other words, everything anyone would want from a
master thriller writer. *Charles W. Brice*

I was born on Muskegon's East side in 1936. I grew up in that wonderful town. As I read this gripping tale of scheming and murder I was constantly pleasantly surprised by the local content of streets, restaurants, factories, businesses, and landmarks, some now gone but not forgotten. … Thank you, Hayden, for a great read and re-kindled memories. *Lou Schulist*

I enjoyed the book very much. Couldn't put it down, powered through it in a day and a half. So naturally you would have to say it held my interest. I usually like protagonists to have flaws which must be overcome to get a satisfactory conclusion.
I think Tom fits the bill here. *Philip Smith*

Smith's use of a clean narrative style will sweep you through a couple's surprising journey. *Bear River Review, Monica Rico – Editor-in-Chief*

I bought the book, read it, and loved it – to the extent that I ignored my dog, the phone calls, any chores that needed doing, and about everything else …. I really liked Tom and the two sets of in-laws who supported about every decision he made. The good guys were people of honor and integrity, the "bad guys" appropriately evil and amoral. *Dr. Carol Thompson*

INTRIGUE IN PARIS

TOM O'BANION MYSTERY SERIES
BOOK 3

HAYDEN SMITH

First Trade Paperback Edition published August 2025
First e-book Edition published August 2025
Cover by: Rocking Book Covers
Lighthouse logo by: VendeDesign
Author photo by: Kenny Hekhuis Photography

ISBN 978-1-7359983-5-0 (Trade paperback)
ISBN 978-1-7359983-6-7 (e-book)
Library of Congress Control Number: 2025916310

Published in the United States of America by: The McKinley Company

This book is dedicated to my children, grandchildren, and great-grandchildren.

You are my joy, my raison d'être.

A NOTE TO MY READERS

You will remember from the first books in the Tom O'Banion mystery series that Tom knows enough French to delight Maria with French phrases when they are courting. In fact, they plan a honeymoon in Paris. When the honeymoon is delayed, they work to improve their French so they can talk with the people of France when they go. This story is based mostly in Muskegon, Michigan as the other books are. But it begins and ends in France.

For those of you who are not well versed in the French language, I have included a glossary of the occasional French words used in the book. To make it easy to find, it is the last section of the book and is arranged in alphabetical order by the French word followed by the English word.

It is, I hope, accurate and will help you come to know the French words and phrases scattered throughout the book. After a word is used a number of times, you will come to know it and have to look less often. I have worked hard to make it accurate. I hope you will like learning a little French while you enjoy the story.

For example, you might see:
Je m'appelle Hayden. (My name is Hayden.)

Have fun with it. Enjoy the read.

1

———

The knock startled Tom and Maria. Relaxing in their Hotel La Louisiane suite before venturing out for a late Parisian dinner, they weren't expecting room service or a visitor. Tom raised an eyebrow at Maria who shook her head, "I'm not expecting anything."

Tom grabbed his robe and strode to the door. Peering through the peephole, he didn't see anyone. Opening the door, he saw an envelope on the floor outside their room. Looking left and right, he saw the hallway was empty. He scooped up the envelope, closed and locked the door.

"My dear friends" was on the front of the envelope. Tom turned it over. Nothing else written on the envelope. He showed it to Maria. "Curious. Maybe it got delivered to the wrong room? I'll call the front desk."

"*Non, monsieur.* A gentleman asked to have the letter delivered to your room. It is not a mistake."

Tom gingerly opened the note.

`You have a reservation, 7:30 p.m. tonight at La Citrouelle. Your hotel will know where it is. You will be seated at the table near the picture of Edith Piaf, the chanteuse of France. Please leave the seat facing the front of the restaurant open for me. You will be served by a waiter named Chabon. You'll like him.*

Order three Kir Royale cocktails and tell Chabon you have someone joining you. I would be most happy if you would accept my request to join me. Forgive me if I overstep, but the correct French expression is 'veuillez le faire' –' please do it' en français. See you soon, mes amis. Oh yes, and dress for the occasion.

If you think I resemble someone from your past, please allow me my fun and don't indicate that you know me. Be assured all will be revealed.

Maria said, "Why didn't they sign the note? Who could this be? Someone we met on a tour? That couple from Australia?"

"Maybe, but I have a hunch." Tom murmured. "The phrase *'mes amis'* is significant. Doug has used that with us. I think we should go and see what this is about. What do you suppose 'dress for the occasion means? Capes and masks?"

Maria laughed and said, "No, silly. I think it only means dress appropriately."

Maria, a little skittish after being shot by an assassin in her hometown of Muskegon, Michigan added, "Suppose it's someone who wants to do us harm? I'm not sure we should do this."

Tom took Maria in his arms and said, "It will be okay. We'll be in a busy restaurant with lots of people around. Nothing will happen. It's probably just someone we ran into who wants to have dinner with us and they forgot to sign the card. If the restaurant looks sketchy or you get uncomfortable, we'll just leave."

Maria changed into a soft beige wool dress and low-heeled tan shoes. Over her shoulders, she threw her new scarf from Galleries Lafayette, the huge French department store, and draped it in what she hoped looked somewhat Parisian. Tom added his tweed sport coat to his grey slacks and long sleeve white shirt. After checking with the front desk for directions, they walked down the Rue de Buci bustling with restaurants and cafés to the bistro. They didn't notice the man with the full beard watching them from across the street, checking to see if they were being followed.

La Citrouelle was an intimate little bistro with perhaps twenty tables. One wall was rough stone, lined with pictures and the other wall, mirrored atop rough timbers. Hearing Tom's name, the host seated them near the picture of Edith Piaf just as it was supposed to happen. Their waiter, Chabon, introduced himself and asked, "May I get you something to drink?"

"We are waiting for someone. We would like to have three Kir Royales." As they waited for the drinks, a tall man with a full beard and mustache and dressed in a Saville Row pin stripe suit approached and asked if he could join them.

Tom responded as instructed, *"veuillez le faire."*

The man took the seat with a view of both the front door and the rear exit. He said, "As I recall, you are American, so can we speak English?"

"We can," answered Maria. "Didn't we meet on our tour of Giverny?" She took another look and knew in spite of his disguise who it was. She was about to stand up and hug him but the man shook his head.

"We did indeed." He lowered his voice. "And we've met many times before. Do you know who I am? If you do, just nod. I thought I caught you. Maria, looking at me quizzically earlier as if you thought you should know me," he said sotto voce.

Maria nodded. She looked at Tom to make sure he recognized their old friend, Doug, from their hometown, Muskegon, Michigan. He nodded.

"Please allow me to introduce myself. My name is Sir Douglas McDermott from Ireland, but please, you must call me Doug." He continued in a loud enough voice that anyone eavesdropping could hear. "I am here on business for a couple of days in Paris and I enjoy finding dinner companions who speak English. Is this your first trip to Paris?"

Playing along, Tom introduced himself and his lovely wife, Maria. "Yes, it's our first trip to Paris. We're here on a month-long honeymoon and we've been here just a week." He murmured so just Doug could hear, "Good to see you, Doug."

Doug smiled mischievously and asked, "Ahh, Kir Royales. How did you know this is one of my favorite drinks? Let's toast to a great honeymoon trip for the two of you. Tell me about your trip so far."

Tom said, "We arrived in Paris just a week ago. Friends told us that mid-September is the best time for sightseeing, not so hot but pleasantly warm, and just the right time to see France's stunning fall foliage."

Maria, excited, jumped in, putting her acting skills on display. "We're here on our much-delayed honeymoon trip. We're staying in the bridal suite at La Louisiane just a few blocks from here – which you already know since you invited us to dinner. You must have overheard us telling the Australian couple?" Doug nodded.

Maria continued, "Our hotel is in the eclectic 6th arrondissement giving us a perfect central location to see all the sights on our list. This historic hotel is right in the intellectual and literary center of Paris. Writers like Hemingway, Satre, Simone de Beauvoir, and Antoine de Saint Exupery loved the location. Simone de Beauvoir said upon discovering the Hotel La Louisiane that she 'never lodged anywhere that fulfilled her dreams' as that place did. She once said she would have happily stayed there for the rest of her life."

Tom said, "I love the fact that many of my favorite jazz musicians like Miles Davis, John Coltrane, Dizzy Gillespie, Billie Holiday, and Charlie Parker also stayed at La Louisiane. The hotel is not fancy, but it was good enough for Jean-Paul Sartre and George Sand so it is good enough for us. And the location couldn't be better — just a couple of long Paris blocks to the famous literary cafés — Les Deux Magots, Café de Flore, and Brasserie Lipp — as well as the beautiful church, Église Saint Germaine de Prés."

Doug started to speak, but…Maria interrupted, "We spent the first week doing the things first time visitors to Paris do. We started with a tour on a double-decker bus for a look at the places we wanted to return to. The museums were superb — The Louvre, Jeu de Paume, and L'Orangerie covering both classical and Impressionist art. On a memorable walking tour of the Montmartre district and Sacré Coeur Cathedral, we had a great lunch at a lovely pink deco restaurant, La Maison Rose, a favorite of many artists."

She sipped her Kir Royale and continued. "On Wednesday morning we toured Notre Dame and then wandered around Île Saint Louis. We lunched at La Brasserie de l'Isle Saint Louis and finished the meal with delicious Berthillon ice cream. Such delights for the visual pleasures and palates."

Doug inserted, "There is nothing better than Berthillon ice cream. Did you have spéculos, praline amaretto, pistachio, or salted caramel?"

Maria laughed, "You sound like a regular!"

Doug smiled, "They know me by name there."

Tom carried on "This morning as you know we took a bus tour to Giverny and Monet's gardens. It was such a joy seeing firsthand his magnificent gardens, the lily pads, and the bridge, and more, that we had only seen before in prints of his art. His home told another story -- at least until the staff threatened to remove us for taking so many pictures. By this evening, we were pleasantly exhausted. We were just relaxing when we received your invitation for dinner."

"You are most welcome," Doug said loudly. "As I said, I enjoy having the opportunity to speak English with fellow travelers. Do you feel that you have experienced Paris fully?"

"We feel we've done almost all of what we had wanted to of the sights of Paris. The French people know how to preserve things. Still more sights to discover for sure, but now, we want to see another side of Paris, the real Paris with its neighborhood bistros, and get some feeling for the people. "

Doug interrupted with, "I can see the excitement on your faces and the sparkle in your eyes. I'm so happy that you are having this experience."

Maria exclaimed, "Sir Doug, I mean, Doug, it is exciting, so much to see and learn. We have been the typical first-time tourists so far, going to all the well-known places. This restaurant is the first new experience for us as we begin to get to know the real Paris. My French is not as good as Tom's but we're trying to learn it by being immersed in it."

"That is the best way. Now I think it is time for me to tell you why I looked you up ..."

Just then, Chabon returned to take their orders and said, "Ah, Sir McDermott, *bienvenue ce soir*. Welcome."

Tom said, "You have been here before."

"*Oui*," Doug said, "many times. This is one of my favorite restaurants in Paris. I highly recommend the *soupe de poisson* — fish soup — as a starter. And for your main course — *le magret de canard* — duck —

or the *poulet fermier* — roast chicken — or *moules marinières* — mussels — are all delicious."

Tom selected the roast chicken and fish soup while Maria chose the mussels and French onion soup. Doug started with the fish soup and selected the duck. He ordered a bottle of Beaujolais for the table.

"*Merci.* I'll bring you a basket of bread." Chabon left to take the orders to the kitchen.

Doug scanned the room and did not see anyone paying particular attention to them. He continued quietly, "I need your help, both of you. I remember what a valuable asset you were in solving the mystery of the group of nine in your hometown of Muskegon, MI. From what I remember you were a major factor in that solution. This time, I need more eyes to help me watch over an entourage from the States that is important to current events back home."

He hesitated and looked around again, "The Sûreté Nationale doesn't want anything to happen to this United States high ranking official or his contingent of five staff while they are in Paris. So even though we're on the same side, they don't want me interfering with their job. I'm working 'off the books' so to speak. I can introduce you as a team I have worked with before.. You were here on a vacation. The agency approved my hiring you to help with security."

He continued quietly, "There are factions from the States watching as well. This official and his contingent are here to meet with President de Gaulle. They will meet at the Palace of Versailles, get President Kennedy's questions answered, and get back home.. Our job is to make sure this happens without problems and they get back home safely."

Doug turned to Maria. "And how do you like your Kir Royale?" He continued softly, "A sightseeing couple will be a great cover for you. Will you help? It should take no more than a day or two. We'll bring you back here so you should leave most of your luggage here and let the front desk know of your plans and that you will return to go on with the rest of your trip. The agency will pick up the tab for another week here in and around Paris."

Tom and Maria looked at each other and turned back together to Doug. "We're in. Let us know what we can do. Can you tell us who it is?"

"I'll tell you who and also fill you in on all the details tomorrow morning."

Doug said, "Here is Chabon with our starters. Let's enjoy our meals and we'll talk more later."

After they were served, Maria asked, "What time will we leave?"

Doug replied, "It will take a little time to finalize the arrangements. I should be able to pick you up by, say 10:00 am, tomorrow. Can you be ready by then?"

Maria smiled, "We can do that. I have a phone call to make in the morning to postpone a visit to an old and dear friend, a pen-pal, in the village of Sucy-en-Brie. I'll just tell her we'll get to see her and her family next weekend."

Their conversation turned to the places they had seen. Doug listened as though he were a new friend learning about their lives. Doug told them stories about his "business" in Ireland. When they finished, Chabon persuaded them to have coffees, along with desserts — profiteroles for Tom and Maria and baba au rhum for Doug.

Doug finished the conversation about the group. "It takes about 45 minutes to get to the Palace. You'll have time for a short tour. I'll pick you up and we'll have some time to talk more on the way down. We will meet the American group and four person French security contingent in front of your hotel so there will be seven of us for the American security group. I know the way but we'll follow them. The key officials are already in the Palace with their own security detail. If the American group wants a short tour of the castle, we'll have to adapt and go with them. Lunch is at 12:30 pm sharp, We will have lunch and conversation. It will give President de Gaulle's group and the American group an opportunity to be comfortable with you around all the time. The meeting of the officials of each nation will take place at 2:00 pm, A state dinner is set for 7:00 pm. That is a rough schedule of our day."

As Chabon arrived with the desserts, Doug stood quickly, moving behind Chabon.

Doug spoke quietly but urgently, "Both of you stand up, right now please, and stand close together. Sûreté officers just came in the front door. I don't think they will know me in this getup. I don't want to take the chance, so I'm leaving through the back door. Chabon is tall, so the three of you will shield me from their sight. The bill is all paid, so stay as long as you want. If the Sûreté officers ask you about me, just tell them we met on our tour to Giverny and we just enjoyed a dinner together. And that your dinner companion was late for another engagement. He had to leave quickly."

Doug finished with, "I'll be in touch. Thanks to you both."

2

———————

Tom and Maria finished their desserts and a quite good French coffee. When they waved to Chabon, he came quickly and said, "You are all set. Have a pleasant stroll back to La Louisiane."

Tom said, 'Chabon, this has been such a wonderful surprise to be here with Doug. We would like to leave a tip for you."

Chabon protested, "Please, *non*. Doug always takes good care of me. I understand you will be visiting the Palace of Versailles for the next two days. When you return, come and see me again."

Together they said, "We will, Chabon. Good food and you made it special. Good evening."

This time of year, mid-September, meant a pleasant but cool evening. Tom asked, "Are you warm enough with just your scarf over your dress?"

Maria smiled at him, "Yes, warm enough but let's move it along. We have to pack for the two days ahead and then you can warm me up." Her smile broadened, "It's going to be more than awhile, so ..."

Tom grabbed her hand and stepped right along. When they reached the hotel, the night manager stopped them. He said, "You had a phone call from your friend Celeste. She asked that you call her back if you are here before 10::00 pm. I can put you through in the little room right over there."

Celeste exclaimed, *"Bonsoir,* Maria, I hope you and Tom had a lovely dinner with your friend."

"Thank you. Doug is a special friend. We've talked about him before. But his presence here means postponing our get together. I was going to call you tomorrow morning to tell you."

"Tomorrow is what I am calling about. Our Alice is not doing well. The doctor said that it won't last long. But it is a bad cold. Our little two-and-a-half-year-old, your goddaughter, will be just fine in a day or two. Étienne and I are so much looking forward to your visit."

Maria answered, "We are as well. We're taking a short trip to Versailles to help out an old friend. You'll remember that I didn't get there when my parents and I came for my graduation trip after college." Maria shared a little about the situation. "Now being needed, in the right place at the right time, worked out well. I will fill you in on the details when we see you. Can we make our date on the weekend, Saturday next?"

Celeste said, "It sounds intriguing. Saturday next will be fine. I look forward to seeing you again along with your Tom and hearing more. Can you make it by 9:00 a.m. or so? And would you like to spend the night with us?"

"Nine will work and an overnight stay will be great. Who would have thought when we started being pen pals so long ago that we would grow so close. I love you, Celeste."

"Je t'aime aussi, Maria. Until then."

Tom thanked the night manager and tipped him well. He asked him to put a note in their file that they would be on a two-day trip to the Palace of Versailles. Tom then said, "We will return and finish our honeymoon trip with La Louisiane as our base. We will pay for the entire month as planned. Thank you for understanding the change."

Tom and Maria headed upstairs to their suite, got packing done, and were off to bed. Tom said, "I'll get up first, shower, and go get our breakfast. How about those French baked eggs, croissants, and lots of hot coffee?"

"I'll be up, final packing done, and waiting for all that."

As they ate their breakfast and sat there enjoying more coffee, they could both feel a frisson of excitement.

Doug picked them up right on time at ten o'clock. Before going up to get them, he spoke with the manager. "I'm sorry about taking them away from you. Don't tell Tom and Maria yet, but I will be picking up the tab for their bridal suite. Mum's the word now until they are ready to go home. I have a phone number on this card for you if something comes up and you need to contact Tom or Maria."

Doug parked at the front door reserved spot behind the US dignitaries' van. They loaded their luggage quickly and crossed the Seine on the Pont des Invalides headed west along the Seine. Doug said, " Everything is all set with La Louisiane for when you return tomorrow. We are following the French protection detail who are traveling with Speaker of the House John W. McCormack, Majority Leader Carl Albert, and Majority Whip Hale Boggs. In the evening we also have a state dinner with this group and Charles de Gaulle, the president of France and members of his foreign policy staff who have been at the Palace since last evening."

3

When Celeste hung up from her call to Maria, Etienne said, "That sort of worked out well didn't it? Do you know anything about what Maria, and maybe Tom as well, are involved in? And who is this Doug that they seem so tight with?"

Celeste replied, "Let me answer the part about Doug first. Maria, Tom, and Doug were all teachers at Muskegon Senior High School. Tom had vocal music and the choirs, Maria was acting and drama, and Doug was band and orchestra conductor. They spent a lot of time together and became fast friends. Tom and Maria's relationship soon blossomed into a romance and now they are married for about a year and a half. They can't have children naturally –Tom had the mumps when he was younger. When Alice was born, you'll recall we asked Maria and Tom to be her godparents."

She continued, "Remember how I told you that Maria and I finally met when her parents brought her to Paris after college graduation. Our letters took on a new meaning after we met. Next week, I will meet Tom for the first time and you will be able to meet both."

Etienne repeated his first question, "So, what are they involved in?"

"Here's the story in brief. Maria told me Doug is older than she and Tom and had another career in his past. He was, in his childhood, quite serious about classical music. Over the years from childhood, he learned to play several band and string instruments, his favorite being the cello. At Western Michigan University, Doug finished his undergraduate degree with a major in music and was first chair cello in the school's symphony orchestra. He signed up for the ROTC program that required some military service. He liked it so well that he enlisted for two years of active duty. He graduated from officers training school, became a second lieutenant, and reupped for four more years. He showed some strong skills that attracted the attention of the OSS (Office of Strategic Services, the USA's intelligence service during World War II) for their SO (Special Operator) group. The OSS later became the CIA (Central Intelligence Agency) during the Truman administration. The CIA with the help of the veterans of the OSS led the way through the Cold War after WWII. Doug passed every test and spent some years training and doing missions for the CIA as an SO with a current rank of Captain. After reaching this rank, the CIA gave him a year off and helped him get his master's degree in band and orchestral conducting. During that time he studied under some of the finest cellists and became very proficient himself. Most of this year was spent at Western Michigan University where it all began. With me so far?

"Doing fine. What's next?

I don't know all the details. Tom and Maria didn't know about his early career until this last year or two. His last move was to become an independent agent for the CIA working on contract doing missions. The story goes that he was tired of it and wanted a break so he took the job at Muskegon High School where he stayed until this last year when he was reactivated as an independent agent. The current mission is only his second assignment and has something to do with the protection of a contingent from the U.S. House of Representatives. Because of their connection at the high school and some detective work on all their parts, Tom and Maria have been recruited to help him. Now you know as much as I do."

Etienne asked, "Are you still certain that Tom and Maria are the right people as godparents?"

"More than ever now. I see two people who will do what is right for Alice. I think when you meet them, you'll see the same qualities in them that I do."

"I'm going to trust your judgement in this, my love. My years as a commodities trader didn't lend itself to learning to evaluate people. I was so lucky when we found each other."

"So was I, Etienne, lucky that is. What your fellow traders may have never seen is how warm and loving you are. They might be surprised if they found out."

Alice woke up from her nap. Since Alice's nanny, Elise, had the day off and wouldn't return until just before Sunday dinner, Celeste went to her crib, changed her, and came back to the sitting room and handed her to Etienne. He loved cuddling with her, he kissed her and put her on his lap. That didn't last long. Alice was starting to roam around the room a lot now. She had walked late but now was so active that they both got down on the carpet with her. She would play with daddy, then play with a toy, and then scurry to Celeste.

Etienne said, "I'm so glad I was older when Alice was born. I love her and enjoy watching her change as she learns. Her vocabulary is growing, but sentences aren't there yet."

Celeste said, "I feel some of that as well. I am only half your age but old enough to see and appreciate the changes. Now at two and a half years, she is growing so fast. I don't want to miss anything. Remember how she quickly learned to call me *'maman'* and you *'papa.'* Any regrets about having her call us that instead of the more formal *'mère'* and *'père?'"*

"I prefer the less formal, *Papa*. How about you?"

"I agree, I like *Maman and Papa.*"

They whiled away the time. Etienne asked, "If you dress her warmly, I'll take Alice for a little stroll around the garden."

"Good! You do that and I'll check with cook on tonight's dinner. I think she is doing *coq au vin* cooked in red wine with bacon, butter, mushrooms, and beef stock. She is serving it with *pommes de terre à la crème* et *haricots français beurrés*. I think that sounds good."

Taking Alice, now bundled up, he said, "I like that. Let's skip dessert and have a digestif. I have a new bottle of cognac I think you'll like."

"I'll let the cook know. Enjoy your garden stroll."

4

———

Etienne and Celeste chatted over their Gand Marnier after Sunday dinner. Etienne asked, "Celeste, I can see how excited you are about this visit."

"Yes, it will be good for us to spend some time here with our daughter's godparents."

"I agree. Now, changing directions, I have another question for you. Do you think Alice is ready to stay with her nanny for an evening?"

"Yes, I think so. What are you up to, Etienne?"

"Well, Wednesday is our fifth anniversary and there is a special place I want to take you?"

Excited, she said, "Where?"

"It will be a surprise. I haven't been there recently, but I think it is the perfect spot for our fifth anniversary."

"What should I wear?"

"How about that lovely red silk gown with the low-cut bodice?"

"Are you sure that extreme decolletage is acceptable in a restaurant?"

"Trust me, it will be perfect. With me in my tux, we'll make a grand appearance!"

Wednesday evening they kissed Alice good night and walked down the front steps to their new all-white Peugeot 403 Saloon. Celeste looked stunning in her sleek red gown, carrying a black velvet shawl against the night coolness. With Etienne in his tux, they made a very handsome couple.

The Tour d'Argent maître d escorted them to a second-floor window table with a view of the back of Notre Dame Cathedral. Their waiter poured their first glass of Dom Perignon champagne as he delivered the fois gras Etienne had pre-ordered.

Etienne took a box from his pocket and said, "Happy Anniversary, my darling." She gasped when she opened it to discover a diamond necklace with a large center stone and five smaller stones on either side. He asked, "May I help you with it?"

"Please do."

He looped it on and fastened it As he returned to his seat, he noticed smiles at nearby tables.

"*Je t'adore,! Merci!*" She handed him a beautifully wrapped gift.

He opened it and found the latest Omega steel watch. "Ah ha, a new watch to treasure! Thank you, Celeste. Now how about a toast?"

They raised their glasses and toasted with arms entwined. He said, "*Voici de nombreuses années heureuses, mon chère.*"

When the moment passed, their champagne glasses were refilled. Foie gras and champagne are a superb combination.

The waiter asked, "Would you like to place your order now, monsieur?"

Etienne replied, "*Oui*, I will have the pressed duck and the lady will have the lamb confit, and a bottle of Domaine de la Romanée-Conti burgundy with our dinner."

The waiter replied, "Thank you. Enjoy your foie gras!"

When they finished the foie gras, the waiter brought the duck and lamb. He opened the wine at the table. Etienne tasted it and said, 'Oh yes, *magnifique.*"

They lingered over Celeste's favorite dessert, Tour d'Argent's praline ice cream, and a pot of fresh pressed coffee. They chatted about their chance meeting at Orly airport. Etienne said, "We need to share that story, get it written up so that Alice will know."

"I have a surprise for you. I have a rough draft of it written. You may have some things to add to the story. We'll do that soon. I want to share it with Maria when we see them."

Etienne beamed, "I look forward to reading it. How about home? Are you ready?"

"Let's go!"

Etienne and Celest left for Sucy. The early part of the trip passed quickly with little traffic. They were enjoying the ride, still basking in the moment. Celeste said, "I love you. It has been a good five years."

Etienne smiled, "And we have more coming. Another child or two, who knows. Are you ready now that your studies are done?"

"Yes, I am. Alice is two and a half now. It's time we had another child."

Etienne smiled, saying "I'll help with that. Let's hurry home."

Celeste said, "Behave now, we're coming up on several sharp turns."

"See those dark clouds. The rain must be coming soon. Let's hope it holds off until we make that switchback right turn at Boissy-Saint-Leger."

A clap of thunder came and the sky opened up. Sheets of rain started. Etienne continued, "Those big semi-trucks taking the exit ramp off had better slow down."

Just as Etienne approached the turn, he saw a large truck coming off the ramp too fast. He said, "Brace yourself, love, I think that truck will hit us."

The truck couldn't stop and t-boned them directly on the driver side front door. Their car skidded then rolled over and over to rest with Celeste's side against a big tree.

EMT's rushed to the scene but the man was dead. They couldn't get to the woman because of the tree. They heard her moans.

"We have a live one here. We need to move fast to get her out." As they rushed toward the Sucy hospital, they found an emergency card with the numbers for their doctor, priest, and attorney. The ICU nurse made the calls, informed all of the urgency, and told them to hurry. Celeste's attorney called the number for the manager of La Louisianne telling him of the urgency and asked him to contact Maria and Tom as quickly as possible.

5

———————

Doug, Tom, and Maria were in the second vehicle. Doug knew the way but decided to follow so they could be ready to deal with any problems that might come up on the way.

Doug said, "Now that you know the Speaker is meeting with President De Gaulle, do you have any questions?"

Tom asked, "Do you know the agenda and is President Kennedy involved?"

"The only thing I know for certain is that the President and the Speaker met the day before the entourage left. The Speaker's foreign policy team are with him and President De Gaulle's foreign policy advisors will be there as well. I'm assuming a discussion of developments in the Far East are on the agenda. We may not know until later. Any other questions?"

Maria said, "It looks like we just do our job and then take a leisurely trip back to Paris and finish our honeymoon."

Doug answered, "You're right. Now, I have a different kind of question for you. I don't know anything about Celeste and Etienne. I'm hoping to meet them some day and I'm curious about them. You've not said much about them."

Maria smiled, "I will be happy to tell you. It is a tale of two pen pals since the summer before ninth grade for me and about the same for her. I think she is a year older than me. Over the years we bonded. I met Celeste in person when my parents brought me to Paris as a college graduation present. My parents were wise after we got to know her and let her show us around Paris. She had some vacation time from her first job out of college so it was perfect. Dad and Mom were close by us but gave us our space. Celeste is an orphan who had been raised by the sisters of a Catholic nunnery. She bonded quickly with Dad and Mom. Ok, so far?"

Both men nodded so she continued, "Celeste is very bright and earned a scholarship. She started out to major in literature and learn to write. She had also done well in high school mathematics and so took some math classes. Her math professors convinced her to major in math. She did a double major in literature and mathematics graduating magna cum laude. While working at her first job, she decided to apply to the University of Michigan's MBA program. The university wanted her to come for an interview. She was waiting at Orly to fly to Michigan when a phone call changed everything."

Continuing, Maria said, "The call was from her priest, Father Lemire. He had been a reference on her application to the University of Michigan. The letter was bad news. The university had budget cuts and couldn't take as large a class so she could not be admitted. They wanted to catch her before she came for her interview. When Father Lemire told her the bad news, she burst into tears and collapsed at the airport phone station."

Doug asked, "So where is Etienne at this point?"

"Patience, Doug. Now comes the beginning of a great love story." Maria told him the story that Celeste had shared with her.

Etienne at this time was already a successful commodities trader in Paris. He also had a partnership with a trader in the U.S. Chicago Commodities market. He was, in fact, waiting for his flight to be called so he could go to the U.S. and have a strategy session with his partner. It was over an hour before flight time.

He had lunched in the Air France lounge and decided to take a walk. When he emerged from the lounge, he almost bumped into a lady walking by. She was lovely, no, beautiful. She was much younger than him but he was smitten and decided to follow her. There was an announcement over the airport system for a Miss Celeste Beaufoy. The lady stopped immediately, looking around for an airport phone. He looked as well and found none. He approached her saying, "Are you Miss Beaufoy?"

She was startled, "Who are you?"

He said, "I noticed your reaction to the request for Celeste Beaufoy to call the airport people at once. There doesn't happen to be one close by but I can help."

"What do you mean, help?"

He smiled, "My name is Etienne Chastain and I am a member of the Air France lounge club and we have such a phone there. I can bring you in as my guest and you can make your call."

She hesitated. He continued, "No strings. Just a fellow traveler and fellow Frenchman offering a hand. Please allow me to help."

She followed and was introduced as a guest. The attendant in charge immediately said, "Of course, Monsieur Chastain, how can we help?"

"Miss Beaufoy was just paged and has to call the airport authorities."

"Of course, please come this way. We have a phone where you will have some privacy."

Celeste entered a small private area, closed the windowed door, and called Father Lemire. When told that she should not come to the University of Michigan, she was no longer being considered for their MBA program. The news so upset her that she collapsed against the windowed door. Etienne opened the door and caught her before she fell to the floor. He called the attendant for some help. They were soon able to revive her and though embarrassed, she said, "I'm alright. Some bad news just caught me by surprise."

They were seated in a private area. Etienne asked if there was something she would like to drink. She smiled and said, "I think I need a glass of wine. Red wine, please."

Etienne motioned to the attendant, ordered wine for them both. When it came, he sat down across from her, raised his glass, and said,

"Here's to better news from your next phone call. If you feel like sharing your story, I'm ready."

She said, "Why would you be interested? You don't even know me."

He said, "Ah, that's unfortunately true, I don't know you. But I would like to change that. You are quite safe here, please tell me what has so upset you."

She told him what had happened. He said, "It is no wonder that you are upset. Getting into the MBA program there would have been a great thing."

"Again, why would you care?"

"I noticed you the instant I stepped out of the lounge. There you were – such a lovely vision who captivated me. I thought, *'I would love to get to know her.'* And so I say again, I would love to get to know you."

"So, you are flirting with me."

He said, "Celeste, not flirting. I have a feeling about us. The only way to see if those feelings are what I believe them to be is to get to know each other better. What do you say?"

"I believe you, Monsieur Chastain … Etienne, what do you suggest we do next?"

"I will cancel my flight, call for my car, and take us to a restaurant where we can have dinner and conversation. I will answer all your questions and ask some for you to answer or not. Then I will take you home or send you home in a cab, your choice."

"Where were you flying to?"

"I was going to Chicago in the U.S. I have a partner on the commodity trading exchange over there. It can be postponed. I am a member of the Bourse de Commerce of Paris, France since I was 27."

"How old are you?"

"You come right to the point, don't you? How old do you think I am?"

"Early 40's, I would think."

He motioned her to go higher. When she started adding years, he finally said, "I will be 50 next year."

"I notice that you didn't ask my age. Are you married?"

"No, not even close. And no, I didn't ask your age. One never asks a lady her age. You'll tell me when you think it is right to do so."

"Why, why not even close?"

"I love your questions. You come right to it, don't you? I have never found anyone who has come anywhere close to what you are and could become to me. I knew it right away. I just didn't know where you would be."

"You're straight out, too. Where are we going to dinner?"

"Let me take care of some things. Flight, car, and reservation, a surprise for you." He left immediately and was back shortly. "We should move downstairs, get our luggage. The car will be here in about 15 minutes."

Maria continued, "That was over seven years ago. They were married six months after the airport encounter. It's quite a love story."

Doug asked, "More children to come?"

'Both of them want more. We'll see."

Doug said, "We are about a half hour from the Palace. We'd better review our roles."

6

House Speaker John McCormack was meeting with President Charles de Gaulle on behalf of President Kennedy. The meeting was to be held at the Palace of Versailles. President de Gaulle, his staff, and his security detail made up of members of the "Garde republican," which is a branch of the National Gendarmerie. The Garde republican is responsible for providing ceremonial and security services to various government officials and institutions, including the president.

President De Gaulle had been in place since yesterday afternoon.

The bulletproof vehicles with the American group arrived a little late because of traffic congestion. There was no time for tours of the Palace. They made their way to the secure dining room in the interior of the Palace. President de Gaulle and his contingent had arrived first and formed a receiving line just inside the dining room doors. Speaker of the House John McCormack, Majority Leader Carl Albert, and Majority Whip Hale Boggs entered and were greeted by President de Gaulle and his foreign affairs staff. They were all seated on one side of the head table with their seconds directly across from them. The Secret Service and the *Garde republican* were then seated at tables forming a semicircle around the head table. When all were seated, President de Gaulle stood and welcomed them all. He then told them he would be calling the names of each person there including their security team. He said, "I like to know who is watching over the meeting principals, including me." He asked each to stand when their names were called so they could be recognized as a member of the "good guys and ladies." They did so and lunch was served. It went well. There was much camaraderie since they were all part of the same congenial team. As the lunch progressed, like clockwork, two members of each security team took their place at each door. The handoff went smoothly so all got lunch and still kept the watch at each door. It ended well. President de Gaulle congratulated them all and said "Let's adjourn to the meeting room.

`All had been briefed as to procedure in the room where the meeting was to take place. An extra guard group including Tom were assigned to the outside door. Maria was stationed inside along with members of President de Gaulle's team as a watcher for anything out of the ordinary and keeping her eyes on the larger picture.

The meeting concluded with a good exchange of views and a decision about what to take back to President Kennedy. The group heard shots in the hallway. The security detail in the hallway retreated in a hurry to the meeting room and bolted it shut. The President's detail chief said, "Mr. President, it's the OAS one more time."

`The Organization armée *secrete* (OAS, "Secret Army Organization") was a far-right French dissident paramilitary and terrorist organization operating during the Algerian War. Its primary motive for existence was opposition to Algerian independence from France. Its operating years were early 1961 to 1962 with some rogue groups still active in 1963. It was officially formed in Madrid, Spain in January 1961, as a response by some French politicians and French military officers to the January 8, 1961, referendum on self-determination. The official movement was organized by President de Gaulle who formed a movement to make Algeria independent against the wishes of the OAS. He naturally became a target. Several attempts were made on his life while they were active.

They rushed the President, the Speaker, and their contingencies through secret passages to their vehicles in a secure garage. Tom guarded the outside door, watching for any OAS. He was about to board when he heard a noise and turned toward it. Some of the OAS had come around from the front. Tom fired several rounds hitting one man, then boarded his vehicle. The OAS fell back taking the wounded man with them. All vehicles went on four different preplanned escape routes. Doug, Tom, Maria, Speaker McCormack, and his group were on the way to the Orly terminal where Doug had left the government plane. President de Gaulle and his contingency of the guard left in one of the two duplicate vehicles to make their way back to his residence in Paris.

Doug turned to Tom and Maria saying, "I know you were looking forward to spending time with your friends in Sucy but I think it would be better if you come back to the States for now."

After they landed at Andrews and met with his handlers for debriefing, his phone rang. It was the manager at La Louisiane who told Doug about the accident and the urgency to get back. He said Celeste may not last long and wanted to see Maria and Tom before she passed. Doug asked his handlers if he could rush them back to Sucy. Upon approval, he asked them to get word to Celeste's attorney about their landing time in Sucy.

Doug hung up, "I need to tell you something. Etienne and Celeste had a terrible accident last night. Etienne is dead. And Celeste has serious injuries and may not live long."

Maria burst into tears, "We have to go back! Can we make it in time?"

"Her doctors give her two days at most." Doug continued, `"I'll get the plane ready. We'll fly directly to Orly airport and will be there tomorrow morning. Let your families know you are okay and will be back soon."

The attorney, Monsieur Lament, picked them up at Orly West for private planes. Twenty-five minutes later they were at Sucy's hospital and the private ICU room.

When they walked in, Celeste was asleep. Her doctor was brought in and gently woke her up, "Celeste, they are here."

Celeste stirred, finally opened her eyes, and saw Maria at her bedside and said, "You made it."

"I'm here, Celeste."

Celeste said, "I don't have long. The adoption papers are ready, just needing your signatures. Will you adopt Alice? Monsieur Lament has already pre-cleared the adoption and permission to take her back the States with you…"

Maria said, "I promised you a long time ago that I would raise your child as my own if something happened to you and I'll keep that promise, so yes, Tom and I will adopt Alice and raise her as our own. Where are the papers?" Tom and Maria signed them.

Celeste said, "One more thing I must tell you. Etienne and I are both orphans. Etienne was a successful commodity trader for over 25 years and made a great deal of money. We have made you heirs. You will get details on all this when you meet later with Monsieur Jean Paul Lament and Father Lemire. They will explain it all. It will help with the expenses of raising Alice and there is enough there for you to accomplish some good things in your hometown. Will you accept it?"

Maria and Tom both said, almost in unison, "We want to raise Alice. We'll do it. We will follow your wishes." They signed the papers, and a notary signed as well.

Celeste took Maria's hand, then Father Lemire's hand, and with a look at them both she said, "Thank you all." and breathed her last.

Monsieur Lament told them, "It may take a few days to get everything arranged. Father Lemire will bring you to my office tomorrow afternoon."

Father Lemire said, "We'll have to think about the service tomorrow."

Doug said, "Don't worry about flights back. I will see that you get home to Muskegon.

Father Lemire said, "Thank God you made it just in time for Celeste to go in peace."

Celeste's doctor took them all to a conference room where they could deal with what comes next. He said to Maria and Tom, "I am so sorry for your loss. Celeste talked about the two of you so much that I feel as if I know you already. Maria, she told me of your long-term correspondence and how you solidified your friendship when you came here after your college graduation. She spoke of you as the sister she never had."

Maria teared up, "We both felt like that. She was an orphan and I am an only child so we bonded. Where is Alice now?"

Father Lemire told her, "She is with her nanny, Elise, at the house. I called the Reverend Mother of our abbey. She and two of the nuns that Celeste knew well have been staying with Elise and Alice. I spoke to them before I came here. They all know Elise well. She is like one of the family. Alice is in good hands for now. As soon as we are done here, we'll go to the house."

Monsieur Lament added, "The funeral director is here to take them both to the funeral home. We can talk to the staff tomorrow. Since Etienne and Celeste were orphans, they made all the arrangements after Alice was born. We'll talk about all that sometime tomorrow."

He continued, "Tonight, we have to let everyone at the house know what has happened. The only one who knows Etienne and Celeste have both passed is the Reverend Mother. We'll break the news to all, have a little snack. We all need some nourishment and we'll answer questions as they come. Alice is asleep of course. We won't wake her.

7

They all made their way over to the house. The Reverend Mother, the nuns, and Elise were waiting. The cook, Madame Lavigne, was right behind them. The butler/handyman, Henri, came out to help with the luggage. Maria and Elise shared a hug and the ladies all went to the living room. The Reverend Mother said, "As soon as the men are here, we'll talk." She turned to the cook, "Madame Lavigne, would you be so kind to pour us some wine?"

The cook said, "I will if you'll call me Belle, or even just 'Cook.'" She served each of them a glass of wine of their choice.

Elise nervously asked, "Maria, how is it you are here? How are Celeste and Etienne?"

The Reverend Mother said, "Patience, child. We'll get to that when all of us are together. It won't be long."

The men brought in the luggage and left it in the foyer. They made it into the living room, led by Henri. After they were all seated, and sipping their wine, Monsieur Lament noted that the Reverend Mother and a nun were seated on either side of Elise, the other nuns were close by Belle. He rose, without his wine saying, "We'll all introduce ourselves shortly, but..."

Elise said, "What's going on? Tell us something..."

Lament continued, "We have some bad news. Celeste passed away about a half hour ago. Etienne died instantly at the scene of a terrible automobile accident. They are both gone. Our dear friends are gone."

Maria had set her glass down and took Elise's glass the minute she started to sob. It didn't take long for everyone in the room to be in tears. The questions started coming – about the accident and what was going to happen to poor Alice now.

When Monsieur Lament composed himself, he asked Belle to top off all their wine glasses. When she had done that, he said, "Let's all adjourn to the *salle à manger*, I mean, the dining room. Belle has put together a light dinner, some charcuterie boards, and two soups. Belle has asked friends to help. When we are settled at the table, I'll take questions."

Elise was first, "Where did the accident happen?"

"As you know, they had been in Paris for a fifth anniversary dinner. They were nearly home and making that switchback right turn at Boissy-Saint-Leger. A big semi-truck took the exit ramp off the N19 too fast, couldn't stop, and t-boned them on the driver side front door. The car skidded then rolled over several times ending up with Celeste's side up against a large tree. Etienne was killed instantly and Celeste passed at the hospital after Maria and Tom arrived. She wanted to hold on until they came."

Elise asked, "When are you going to tell Alice and what will we tell her?"

"We would like to do it tomorrow morning. I plan to be back here early as does the Reverend Mother. Alice is too young to understand much. I would also like to hold the reading of the wills. Can all of you be here in the morning, say 10:00 am?"

Maria changed direction and asked, "When will the service be and where.?"

He answered, "Where is a question best settled when we know how many are coming. The church is not large, and the funeral home is somewhat bigger but still has a limit. They were private people and had only lived here for two and a half years. She was pregnant with Alice when they moved in. There will be some friends from his work. Their wish when we discussed it was that any funeral would be in the church where a full Mass could be held. As to when, it depends on whether his partner can come or not. We'll know more when I can get some calls made. I'm hopeful that it can be held on Saturday. That's only three days away."

Father Lemire said, "I think we can manage more than you know. We have had as many as 150 people in the chapel. Do you think there will be more than that?"

Monsieur Lament indicated that it would not likely be a problem. "We had better wind this up, get home, and get some sleep. We have a busy morning ahead of us. And Reverend Mother, would you bring along two nuns who will care for Alice?"

Elise jumped in, "I can do that. There's no need for them."

He said, "Not tomorrow morning you can't. You have to be at the reading of the wills."

Continuing, "All of you may not know that both Etienne and Celeste were orphans. All of you who need to be here tomorrow are here tonight. Get some rest tonight. We'll get this done."

Elise again jumped in, "Why do Maria and Tom need to be here? They are only godparents."

Monsieur Lament said, "No longer. It was the express wish of both Celeste and Etienne that Maria and Tom adopt Alice and raise her as their own. The codicil to both wills attest to this. The papers are already filed with the authorities. Tom and Maria both agreed and signed both sets of papers with a notary. The papers were messengered to the proper authorities and will take effect immediately."

Elise stood, shouting, "That's not right. I'm leaving."

He said, "Please be here in the morning for the reading. Celeste and Etienne didn't leave you out."

When the door slammed, they all looked at each other in astonishment. Someone said, "I wouldn't have believed it."

Monsieur Lament said, "I knew it was coming. I had her checked out but Etienne wouldn't believe it. Later he came around and hired Elise as a nanny instead of an au pair."

Tom asked, "Did you check us out too?"

"I didn't, but Etienne had his partner do both of you. I hope you are not offended, but he had to know. Celeste never knew that he checked up on the two of you."

He continued, "I see by a little frown that you have not been vetted before. Don't worry, it was done discreetly, and you both came through with flying colors. His partner, Gerald McDowell, said he has never had a rating so high. You are well regarded, my friends."

Tom beamed, "That's good to hear."

Monsieur Lament turned to Madame Lavigne. "Belle, could you ask one of the ladies you had tonight come tomorrow? Some coffee, tea, and petit fours or cookies would be great."

One of the nuns, Sister Mary, said, "We'll be glad to take care of the serving. That way you can focus on what is being said."

Belle smiled, "That is gracious of you both. Thank you."

Monsieur Lament had one more suggestion as he started to leave. "I would recommend that all doors and windows are locked tight. Does Elise have a key to the house?"

Belle said, "No, Monsieur Chastain wouldn't allow it. She objected at first but came around to it after a while here. She had only been their nanny for a few months. They didn't hire her until Alice was eleven months old and suggested to her that eventually she would have a key and become an au pair. Just the same, she might come back later tonight."

Doug said, "This is my expertise. All I need is a blanket, a pillow, and a cot to rest on centrally located. I'll be our watchdog."

After Monsieur Lament and the church contingent left, it was just Maria, Tom, Doug, and Alice … still sleeping.

Maria asked Belle, "Will you show Tom and me how to call back home? We want to call our parents and let them know what has happened."

Maria's dad answered the phone. Maria said, "Hi Dad, please get Mom on the extension so I can give you both some news … Hi Mom, I have some good and sad news. There has been a terrible car accident. Both Celeste and Etienne died, Etienne right away and Celeste after we got to the hospital in Sucy." Maria teared up but quickly got herself back in control to tell them the news about Alice. "Their attorney had the adoption papers approved right away. We have officially adopted her, and she is cleared to come home with us. Everyone says she is a little sweetheart. We all will love her. I have to go now so Tom can call his parents. We won't be home for a few days yet. We will call you when we get to the States. We love you both."

Tom called his parents with a similar message. His dad had a question about money. Tom said, "Doug and the government are taking good care of us. We will be landing at Andrews Air Force Base for fuel and fresh pilots. We will let you know when we are due back in Muskegon. We all love you both. And oh yes, Dad would you call Mark, the chief and let him know we will be delayed getting home? Tell him some of what has happened and I will call him when we get back in a week or so. Thanks Dad."

8

————————

Maria, Tom, and Doug refilled their wine glasses and adjourned to the living room. Tom said, "Belle and Henri, why don't you join us while your ladies clean up?"

Belle replied, "Henri can stay now. I'll get them started on clean-up and coming back tomorrow. Henri and I would like to share something so you won't be surprised tomorrow. We've been with Etienne and Celeste since they moved into this house. That was about three years ago. They had been living in a Paris apartment while it was being built. Celeste was about six months into her pregnancy with Alice when they moved in. I was hired first and Henri followed a month or so later. Both of us were single, a widow and a widower."

Maria jumped in, "And you fell in love and were soon married. I thought I noticed glances and smiles."

"You're very perceptive. Yes, Celeste and Etienne were so happy that we found each other. We had the wedding right here in *le salon*. They paid for the wedding, a dinner that I didn't have to cook, and a honeymoon in Provence. Neither of us had ever been to that part of France. We've been here ever since, just like two members of the family." She took Henri's hand and said, "Oh dear, I wonder what we will do now."

Maria took her other hand, "Don't worry. I'm sure they have taken care of you in the wills. It will be okay."

"Maria, you are such a comfort. You are going to be a great mother for Alice. Let me get the ladies going on clean-up and you and I will look in on Alice."

Tom asked, "Doug, what is your situation? Do you have to get back to the U.S. soon?"

"I was ordered to be a bodyguard for you two until we get you home. Taking care of you here and getting you back home will be my pleasure. The agency I represent is grateful for the responsibility you took to get the Speaker of the House and his entourage out of the country without a problem. It was in large part because of the way you took the lead against the OAS assassins. You can take your time getting things settled here and when you are ready, I will be too."

Henri asked, "Who do you work for, or shouldn't I ask?"

"You shouldn't ask. But I am legitimate. America's tax dollars at work. I had better take a walk around and find the best place to stand guard. Henri, would you help me by walking around with me while I check doors and windows and scout out a place to spend the night?"

"Let's get started."

After their tour and check of all entry points, Doug and Henri rejoined Maria and Belle in the salon. Belle had paid her helpers and sent them home. They had seen to Alice, still sleeping. Belle told Maria that she would likely wake up between seven and eight. She said, "I'll be up and readying breakfast and listening for her. She will ask right away where Maman and Papa are. We should be ready to tell her that her parents are with the angels in heaven. You can meet her then and we'll eventually bring her out where she'll see another familiar face in Henri and then introduce her to Tom and Doug. The nuns will be here and they will see to her care. I know they volunteered to serve but that will only take time in the beginning of the will reading. They can then keep her entertained and get her down for her morning nap."

She continued with, "Doug, I locked both the front door and the dead bolt, er ... at least that is what you call it in English. Do you have suggestions as to improving the security system?"

"Let me think on that a bit. I'll have some ideas put together in a day or so. In view of last night's outburst, I suggest getting new locks installed in the doors, windows, and dead bolts. Will you need to talk with Monsieur Lament about that?"

"He leaves those things to Henri and me, but I'll talk to him about it. He'll approve of that, I'm sure. We have sufficient funds in the household account to cover it, I think. If not, he will add to the fund."

Doug smiled, "Etienne and Celeste had a lot of trust in the two of you. They seem to have thought of everything and then left it to you both."

"They trusted us and knew we would never violate that trust."

Doug sat thinking and after a moment said, "I would like to have met both Etienne and Celeste. It seems that they were special people. I knew a little about Celeste from Maria. Maria and I taught together a number of years at the local high school and when Tom came on the scene as the choral director, We became like D'Artagnan's three Musketeers."

Henri said, "Aha, you know something of our *histoire*. Can you name the musketeers?"

Doug answered with a slight French accent, "But, of course, or as you say, *mais, bien sûr*. Their names are Athos, Porthos, and Aramis."

Belle asked, "So you know our language?"

"Only a little, *un peu*, I think that is right."

Henri said, "It will be a joy for us to have you all around for some time."

Tom added, "We feel the same."

Alice woke at her usual time. When Belle heard her, she said to Maria, "Will you keep an eye on that bacon? I'll change and dress her. When we get down here, she will ask 'where is maman and papa?' And we'll tell her together. It's important that you are here. I'm going to say to her that they are with the angels but that she asked Maria here to be her new maman. What do you think of that approach?"

"That should work and thank you for involving me. Hopefully, that will turn her to me and eventually Tom. Thank you for that. Go! I've got the bacon."

When she brought Alice down and put her in her highchair, sure enough she asked, "*Où est maman et papa?*"

Belle answered, "*Ils sont avec les anges.*" She started to tear up. Belle pointed to Maria and added, "*Ta nouvelle maman?*"

Maria held out her arms. Alice looked at Belle who nodded, then looked at Maria who extended her arms closer. Alice looked up at Belle, Belle nodded, and Alice got down and into Maria's waiting arms. She stayed there through breakfast.

Tom came down about that time and smiled, "Well look here. Aren't you the natural?" He leaned in to kiss Maria and while he was at it, brushed a little kiss on Alice's forehead. Alice smiled.

There was a knock on the door. Henri went to answer. It was the Reverend Mother, two nuns, and Father Lemire. "Bonjour," he said.

Alice jumped down from Maria's lap to greet the nuns.

Belle greeted them. "Welcome to you all. We were about to enjoy a light breakfast. Will you join us?"

"We've already eaten, but we'll have coffee with you.

Henri finished his breakfast quickly. He looked at his watch, and said, "If you will excuse me, I'll be in *le salon* arranging the room as Monsieur Lament told me last night. He'll be here in a few minutes."

Doug said, "Let me help with that. Then I'll join our nun friends in the kitchen with Alice and help with the set-up."

Monsieur Lament came in a few minutes later. He approved the arrangements and said, "Let's get everyone in here and we'll get started. Elise was waiting in her car and should be coming right in."

Once all were seated, Elise stood and said, "Monsieur Lament, may I say something before we start? I regret my behavior last night. I apologize to all of you for the outburst. It won't happen again. Thank you for hearing me out."

Monsieur Lament smiled at her, "Thank you, Elise."

He continued, "This will be quite straight-forward. Etienne and I, and later, Celeste have respect and affection for each of four, five if you count me, for which there will be an inheritance. They accounted for that respect and affection, plus the length of time each of you had been here. They thought of you all as the family they never had as orphans. I will refer to them in the rest of the reading as 'he,' 'her.' 'they' or 'their' Any questions so far? *Non*, good, let's proceed."

"They also were quite firm that each heir, or heir group, would not know what the others received. I have known Etienne over 25 years. A trust and almost brother-like bond had formed. I listened to him as a businessman, and he listened to me regarding legal matters. We've done well together. I concurred with their decision regarding the amount each received and each only knowing theirs."

He pulled a stack of envelopes from his briefcase. "I have something to say to each of the groups. I will then hand you a sealed envelope holding a card in it with the amount of your inheritance. Bank accounts have been established at his bank. You may leave the money in his bank or move to another bank if you wish. If you wish to confer with me about your decision, please think about any questions you might have and make an appointment. There will be no charge for this one-time consultation. When I have said to each of you what they wished me to, you can open the envelope if you wish. All the monies in the first three inheritances for you here are in the new francs just established a brief time ago. You may leave then or stay. Belle's helpers have prepared a light lunch where we can join in a last gesture of affection and respect for both of them. You may then leave if you wish. Everyone is clear on all that. Good."

"I'll start with the Reverend Mother and Father Lemire. He has known the two of you the longest. He bought the land this chateau sits on a long time ago. He had no plans to build right away but wanted to have a presence here in Sucy. He did so by affiliating with your diocese. He was busy building his career in the early days. But he confessed to me once over dinner that he felt he would still like to have a family. A fortuitous meeting at Orly airport brought Celeste and Etienne together. And you married them in your church six months later. Here is what they wished for you to have." They chose not to open it until they were back at the church.

"After he built the house and moved in, he knew quickly that he would need some help. They knew of Belle who was also a member of your parish. She had lost her husband a couple of years before they built the house. They interviewed her, talked with others who knew her. It was a match. You, Belle, came in and took over. They came to love you."

"When the house was finished and the job of landscaping was started, Henri was a member of the crew. They soon discovered he had other skills, and they knew Henri was another winner. Little did they know that Henri had his eyes on Belle and vice versa. Etienne and Celeste were overjoyed when you came to them as a couple and said you wanted to be married. It seems that Celeste noticed the looks and suspected it might have happened before Etienne did. Father Lemire married you right here in the salon. It was their wish that you stayed here, continue your duties, but become the house caretakers. It is hoped that the new owners will want you to stay. Your envelope contains both an inheritance and a new salary arrangement. We'll talk more about that later." They also decided to open their envelope later.

He turned to Elise, the youngest member of the group. "Elise, you were with them the shortest time. You were hired as a nanny for Alice when she was almost one year old. Since Alice is being adopted by Maria and Tom, your situation will change. This will be a challenging time for you since we all know that you and Alice have bonded. They knew about the bond with Alice and loved you for the care you provided. Your envelope contains a letter of recommendation and money sufficient to carry you for at least a year. That should give you enough time to find a new position as a nanny or look for something new." Elise tore open her envelope and frowned.

He pulled a large file from his briefcase and turned to Tom and Maria. "That brings us to the two of you. First, the final adoption approval came by messenger this morning. Alice is now your adopted daughter. You have the blessings of the adoption system to take her back the United States with you, stay here if you should wish, or travel back and forth. Etienne and Celeste know from your conversations and letters that should you take her to the U.S. You promised Celeste that you would be sure that Alice is back here enough to preserve her French beginnings." He paused, "And welcome to your new home. They wanted you both and Alice to own the house, to have a place to be when you bring her back home to France. This file contains the now approved adoption papers, and documents detailing the trust funds for Alice both here in France and in the United States. She will have full control of them when she reaches the age of 21. There is also an inheritance for you which will transfer to the bank of your choice in your hometown and a trust account here in new francs for the care and maintenance of your new home here in Sucy. There is another deposit ready to be made in a trust fund management company in Chicago, Illinois that can be used as seed money to do some of the things that you have indicated by your actions you wish to do. All your monies you receive are in dollars except for the trust account here in Sucy. We have much to talk about in private so would you please factor that in when you think of when you will go back to the States? By the way, I will be with you in Chicago when you go to meet with Etienne's partner."

Tom and Marie were stunned. They took the file and envelope and turned to hug each other, Marie crying softly on Tom's shoulder.

"I know this is a lot for all of you to take in," Monsieur Lament attempted to calm them. "Let's have some lunch and make plans for the service and for our future without our friends."

9

———————

They went into the dining room to a light lunch of French onion soup and cheese boards with a choice of wines. There was a bit of relief now that the reading was done. None except Elise had glanced at the contents of their envelopes. The sadness at losing their friends still weighed heavily on them, but they at least knew something about their futures. When they finished the lunch, Elise asked about the service and was told someone would let her know. She left after promising to call and make an appointment at Monsieur Lamont's office.

Lament had a private moment with the Reverend Mother and Father Lemire. He said, "I see you have still not looked in your envelope. I suspect you will want to do that in the privacy of your church."

Father Lemire said, "*Oui*, we prefer to wait."

Lament wanted them to know that there would be enough to do some of the things they had put off because of money and told them, "Please accept my offer to consult with you as you plan what to do. This will be my pleasure to do for you as my contribution."

After they left, he turned to Tom and Maria. "Why don't you spend some time with Alice and see if you can get her down for her nap? While you do that, I will chat with Belle and Henri. When we are done, at least for now, I'll want a first meeting with Tom and Maria and then we'll rejoin Belle and Henri and wrap things up."

"Belle and Henri, please join me in *le salon*." Once they had settled in, he added, "Now open your envelope please."

The first paper they saw was their inheritance, one million francs. Belle teared up, "This is so much, too much." Lament said, "They didn't think so. You were much loved and they wanted you to have it. Since you were already banking with their bank, the inheritance was put in an investment account until you decide if you want to do something different. Now please look at the next paper."

This one outlined their new positions at the chateau. They had been hired as *gestionnaires de domaine* with a substantial increase in salaries for their new responsibilities if they accept it. "Do you accept?"

They looked at each other, "Of course, we do. What do you have in mind for the kinds of additional duties we will do here?"

Lament said, "I only have a list from Etienne and Celeste, but they want you to have input as well. I have contacts with the government, and I think I can get the chateau set up as a place for visiting dignitaries. If I can, we will likely put in a helicopter landing site out back. You might also want to have wedding receptions here and even weddings outdoors in some seasons. Etienne specifically asked that you give some thought to other kinds of activities you think might work."

Lament continued. "At first you could hire extra help that you have on reserve. As things progress you may need to consider permanent staff members. We'll see."

Belle and Henri looked at each other, shook their heads in awe of what had changed for them. Belle said, "We never thought something like this would come our way."

Lament said, "You'll be just right for it. Take your time thinking about ways to go, what to do. And please keep in mind that Tom and Maria will be coming back here periodically. We may need to set off a suite of rooms for them. Again, we'll see."

Henri asked, "Doug and I took a tour of the chateau and environs yesterday. I asked him if there were additional security elements he could suggest. His immediate response was that all locks should be rekeyed, especially in view of the outburst last night. And in the light of your thought about visiting dignitaries, more security may be needed. What do you think?"

"I think it is fortuitous that he is here. Why don't you call a locksmith you trust and get the rekeying done as quickly as they can? I'll have a chat with Doug sometime before they leave." He continued, "Let me get Maria and Tom in here and I'll have you all together shortly."

When Monsieur Lament got Tom and Maria settled in *le salon*, he told them he had some brandy nearby just in case. They asked, "May we have Doug here with us if he wants to?"

"Are you sure you want to do that?"

"Please ask him."

Lamont did so. Doug said, "Tell them no. They can tell me what they want to later." He relayed the answer to Maria and Tom.

"Why would we need some brandy?

"You'll see. When you open your envelope, you will find you have become not only a new mother and father. As you will see, you are also very wealthy people. Well deserved, I might add. And when I saw the vetting documents from Etienne's partner, Gerald McDowell, I knew they had made a good choice to raise their daughter . It helps that I know that Alice is in good hands."

"Your documents are in an expanding file. These are your copies to take home and keep somewhere safe. I have a second set for you and a copy in my office. Please take out the first one. These are your adoption papers for Alice. All is in order for you to take Alice back home with you. They include travel documents for her as well."

"The second set of papers is the deed to this house and property. The property has been registered with the both of you as well as Alice when she turns twenty-one years old. It was done in that fashion so that if something should happen to the two of you, she will own it free and clear."

"The next two papers are trust accounts for Alice that she can access when she is twenty-one. One is for one million francs and stays here in France. The second is for one million dollars for Alice to be placed in a bank in the United States. These cannot be touched by anyone except Alice or one of you if something happens to her."

"The next two papers are a similar arrangement for you, Tom and Maria. You will have a trust account in your names that you can draw from here. It is one million francs. There is also a maintenance trust fund for the care and management of the property in francs,"

"The next two papers are in dollars. One account is for two million dollars directly to you both that will be placed in a bank of your choice in your hometown. The second account is for over five million dollars that will be placed in a trust company that we need to choose. It will cover your U.S. taxes and the balance will be the seed money for you to do what you have planned for your hometown."

Maria said, "Now I think I'm ready for that brandy!"

Tom said, "I think I'll join you."

Lamont went to the door and asked all the others to come back in,

When they were all together again, Monsieur Lament told them he had spoken with the undertaker as well as Father Lemire. "The service is set for 11:00 a.m. on Saturday and a visitation time before starting at 10:00 a.m. There will be a luncheon after the service and a private committal at the cemetery after that. That will only be for those who were here today. The only thing to settle at this point is who will care for Alice. Father Lemire suggested that if you both approve, there is a novitiate who has bonded with Alice and she has offered to take care of her. What do you think? Maria? Tom?"

Maria said, "Is she reliable and can we trust her?"

"Spoken like a mother," said Lament.

Doug jumped in, "I'll baby sit with her if Father Lemire is okay with that."

Maria said, "Thank you. Uncle Doug to the rescue. You can bring her back to join us when the luncheon gets underway. All that okay, Doug?" They all laughed at how Maria was taking over with Alice.

After the laughter had subsided, Lament said, "I'll stop on my way back to my office and speak to Father Lemire. I'm sure he will approve."

He continued, "You are about a 15-minute drive to the church. We ought to be there no later than 9:45 a.m. A driver will arrive from the funeral home about 9:25 a.m. to take you to the church. I would suggest that you all talk about plans for the house and the possible uses of it when you aren't here. Tom and Maria, you need to be comfortable with the plans. It is your home now."

Tom said, "Maria and I have already talked a little about it. We will be inclined to follow your lead, along with Henri and Belle. We will return here soon to talk about all the ideas and help finalize a plan."

"I have much to do. I'll see you all Saturday. That's only a day and a half away."

10

Saturday dawned bright and sunny and with the promise that it would be a little warmer than usual for late September. All were ready when the car arrived. There had been a quick shopping trip on Friday to get something appropriate to wear for Maria and Alice. They were greeted at the church by Father Lemire, the Reverend Mother, and Monsieur Lament. The caskets were already in place at the front of the chapel.

They all went into the chapel to see the arrangements. Then they were taken to the nursery where the novitiate Caroline, a lovely young lady, and Uncle Doug would be watching Alice. After greetings, Alice spotted Caroline and she ran to her. They talked a little. Maria said to Caroline, "I'll want Alice with me as the visitation starts. When she begins to tire, you and Doug can take her back to the nursery. When the luncheon starts, would you bring her back to eat with us? She will be seated between Madame Lavigne and me. After Doug has finished his lunch, he will bring her back to the nursery. Thank you so much for taking care of her."

Caroline said, "It is my pleasure and privilege to do it."

They made their way to the visitation room. People began to arrive. Monsieur Lament and the Reverend Mother were there to introduce

Tom, Maria, and Alice to the townspeople. So many new faces, but all with warm smiles and loving greetings. By this time, the story of who they were and that they had adopted Alice had spread around town.

Doug could see that Alice was reacting to all this and seemed to be weary of it. He took her from her new mother, met Caroline at the door, and went to the nursery. Alice went to Caroline right away and started to nod. After she was sound asleep, they moved to nearby chairs where they could see the crib. They both got coffee and began to learn about each other.

The townspeople were guided into the chapel and the family to the room for them along with Father Lemire and the Reverend Mother. The service was finished including the high mass by 12:15 p.m.

Caroline, Doug, and Alice were waiting at the door of the dining room. Caroline said, "Thank you for allowing me a last time with Alice. I understand you will be living in Michigan in the United States but will still be coming back on occasion. Doug told me. I hope to be able to see her as she grows. I will take my vows next month. So the next time you are here I'll be a nun. Thank you again for this time."

Maria smiled, hugged her, and said, "You will. I'll see to that. Thank you again. Doug will bring her back to the nursery when he has his lunch."

Tom, Maria, Doug, and Alice made their way to their table. When all were seated, Father Lemire said grace. Maria and Doug went together to get a plate for Alice and Doug. Tom would get theirs later.

It was a somewhat more festive time than you might have thought. The townspeople were anxious to meet these Americans who were new parents. They seemed ready to accept them and welcome them to their new home and country.

Doug finished his lunch and looked at Maria. She nodded and he took Alice back to the door to Caroline. Maria also caught sight of some cookies on a plate that Doug took along and handed to Caroline… and smiled, *cookies for their coffee and Alice's milk.*

When all the townspeople had left, the group gathered to make sure all was in order. Father Lemire said to Tom and Maria, "We would be pleased if you and your daughter would come to Sunday mass. In addition to the homily, I will have some words to say to everyone about Etienne and Celeste as well as introduce you to the church membership. The parishioners will appreciate getting to hear these words and get to know you both a little. The regular nursery staff will be on duty and Doug has agreed to be a part of that group. I would appreciate having the flowers here until after the service. You may want to take some of them home with you tomorrow. Anything else?" When no one asked a question, he continued.

"Then let's have the gravesite service. The funeral home is ready to take us all out there and will take you home after."

After the service and a promise to be at Mass on the morrow, they all went their own way.

When the limo with the new family reached the house, Doug got out first and said, "Please let me check a few things before you come in. I won't be long."

He let himself in with Tom's set of new keys. He then made a quick survey of all possible entry paths, doors, and windows, for disturbed telltale signs. He found none. Similarly, Henri had walked outside around the house and reported the same.

They returned to the limo and said, "All is well. No signs of entry or attempts. Let's go in."

Their driver followed them in. He had a large basket with him. He said, "the Reverend Mother sent this along, knowing that the hour would be late and the day was long. So, Madame Lavigne, you won't have to cook tonight."

After many thanks and a couple of hugs, he took his leave.

11

The next morning Henri Etienne's second car, a sedan just big enough for the five of them and Alice, to the church for mass.

Father Lemire conducted the service as though it was a normal Sunday, ending with mass and communion. His homily was on giving and having gratitude for the gifts we receive. He also spoke of the generosity of Etienne and Celeste. He said, "We will miss our friends, but thanks to their generosity in the wills, their presence will be felt here for a long time. Thanks to them we will be able to do some of the things we have been praying for."

Father Lemire then said, "We have one more thing to do before we have our usual coffee and cookies. Thank you to all who have brought them today." He stepped down to the floor level and motioned Maria and Tom to come there with him.

He continued, "I would like to introduce Tom and Maria O'Banion. They are Alice's new father and mother. Celeste stayed alive after the accident until both came, agreed again to take Alice and raise her as their own. The adoption papers were filed and approved."

He continued, "They have a life in the United States and will be taking Alice back to the States next week. But as they agreed with Etienne and Celeste, they will bring Alice back home to Sucy often so that she won't lose her French ties. They will be back periodically. They told me just yesterday that they will, with our approval, be affiliating with our parish as well as their parish at home. Do we approve?"

Loud applause filled the chapel. When it subsided, he said, "Follow me to the cookies and welcome them."

12

That night, dinner was informal in the kitchen. Belle had been going between the living room and the kitchen. Belle, in the kitchen, laid out the leftovers from the service, and set out wine glasses for all. Alice had her own little wine glass with a sippy top for her grape juice.

Henri and Doug were in their seats. Still in the salon, Maria and Tom were playing with Alice and some of her toys when Belle appeared and said, *"le dîner est servi."*

Alice immediately looked at Maria who picked her up, set her on Tom's shoulders but held on to her. When they reached the kitchen, Maria took her from Tom's shoulders and put her in her chair between them. Tom sat down Maria and went to his seat. Belle poured the Beaujolais for Maria, saying *"pour vous, maman."* Alice looked at Maria who smiled at her and reached over to kiss her on the cheek. Belle put Alice's hand on Maria's cheek saying 'ta maman.' Alice kissed Maria's cheek. Belle did the same for Tom's glass and said, *"pour vous, papa."* And called Tom 'ton papa.' Alice kissed his cheek.

Alice was enjoying the game. When Belle poured for Doug, saying *"pour vous, oncle Doug."* Alice now looked at *oncle* Doug who smiled at her. But Alice let him know that wasn't enough, she touched her cheek and giggled. They all laughed at her. She then looked at Henri and said, "Henri," touching her cheek again giggling. When Belle poured her own, Alice pointed to both cheeks, then held out her arms to Belle. Belle came around to her, kissed her on both cheeks and gave her a little hug.

Belle was seated and they had the blessing together. Maria fixed Alice's plate, and they all raised their glasses, including Alice. Belle smiled at them all and said, "*Mange! Mange!*

It was not long after eating that Alice began to nod. Maria took her to the nursery, changed her, and put on her night clothes. She picked a story that she had been told was one of Alice's favorites. She had only read a page or two and Alice was fast asleep. Maria tiptoed out to the living room where all were having a digestif. She joined them and they toasted the first real progress. Alice, Tom, and Maria had a long way to go yet, but a start had been made.

13

———————

On Monday, Monsieur Lament met with Henri and Doug, then Belle and Henri at his office. He approved the new security measures so that Doug could get materials sent and workers assigned to come and install the system. He said, "Doug, I understand you made arrangements for the plane to be back at Orly West late Tuesday. And you are planning to fly home to the States on Wednesday. Please arrange for my vehicle and a van to be in the hangar."

When he met with Belle and Henri, he said, "Your new salaries started today. You indicated you would leave your personal accounts at Etienne and Celeste's bank. Doug told me that they would all be flying home on Wednesday and that you agreed that would give you enough time to get together Alice's clothing, bedding, and toys plus her new bed just like the one here. There will be two trunks and the new bed in its packing. Doug said there will be enough room for all that luggage. You may want to rent a van to carry Alice's trunks and her new bed on Wednesday. Please see my secretary as you leave to set a time on Thursday to meet me at the bank for some introductions and to set up your investment account with your inheritance."

They all returned home to have lunch. Belle agreed to watch Alice so that Henri could take Maria and Tom in for their appointments with

Monsieur Lament. He welcomed them and asked, "Do you have questions?"

Tom answered, "Only one. Will you still be acting as our attorney?"

Monsieur Lamont smiled and said, "Etienne and Celeste asked me to do that if it were your wish."

"We would like that very much."

"*Très bien. Ou en anglais.* I'm sorry. Habits are strong. In English, all that was 'Very well. Which brings to mind a question for you. How is your French?"

Maria answered, "We both studied French in college. I also had some in high school. Tom is the better speaker *en français*. We want to get better so that we can help Alice to learn more French vocabulary but also learn English. Do you have any suggestions in that regard?"

"I'm glad you are thinking of this. To begin with, you could just be teaching her new, to her, French words, by saying it and then pointing to the object or picture. Then in a few weeks or as soon as possible, I would recommend that you find a person who is truly bilingual, English and French. Such a person should also have a bonafide French accent. Do you live near a four-year university or college?"

"The closest four-year college would be Hope College. I could call them when we are home."

"*Bon!* Please keep me appraised of how you are doing with that. Other questions?"

"We don't know your first name." Tom replied.

"Here are a couple of my business cards. My full name is Jean Paul Lament. Most of my close friends call me Jean or Jean Paul. It is my wish that you could become comfortable in doing so. I would like to be on a first name basis with you in informal settings."

Marie said, "*Bon*, Jean Paul."

He laughed, "I like this wife of yours, Tom. How about you?"

Tom smiled, "*Très bien*, Jean,"

Jean Paul chuckled, "I'm going to like working with you two. Anything else?"

They replied no.

"I have one more thing I have done for you. I won't be able to come to your hometown, Muskegon in Michigan and Chicago Illinois until next week when I will come to Chicago and then Muskegon to settle your inheritances in your current or new accounts. I would like, with your permission, to make an appointment with Gerald McDowell for Tuesday next. That will give you several days to settle back into your home in Muskegon. You will need to drive or fly to Chicago to meet with Gerald McDowell and a trust company. I would like to come back to Muskegon with you to meet with your people, banker and attorney. We can get your major deposit in your local bank and talk about how best to make it work for you."

He paused, "This will take some money, both settling in with Alice, as well as the travel to Chicago and back."

Jean Paul handed them a thick pouch. He said, "This contains $20,000, $15,000 in $100 bills and $5,000 in $20 bills. If you need some of that before you get home, take it out in $20's keeping the balance in your travel carry-on bag instead of luggage. If it sounds like I'm taking care of too much, forgive me. My goal is always to do it right."

Tom asked, "Jean, do we need to begin paying you a retainer or whatever you call it in your world?"

"Music to my ears, Tom. But you don't have to think about that now and maybe never. My annual retainer is paid until Alice turns 21 years. After that if you have legal needs here in France, I would do so on a fee basis. Don't even think about it right now. Thank you for asking."

"One last thing. You may have thought of this already. I would advise you to keep your actual net worth to yourselves and tell your banks, trust company, and attorneys of your wish for your net worth to be private."

14

Wednesday morning dawned bright and sunny. Jean Paul's car with Alice, Maria, Tom, and Belle led the way with Henri and Doug following in the van. At Doug's suggestion, they had driven part of the way to Paris and then to Orly on the A6a. This way it would appear that they had come from Paris. As they approached the entry to Orly West, Doug noticed a green Peugeot sedan that seemed to be following them. He said to Henri, "I think we are being followed. As soon as we get to the private plane terminal, let me off at the office, then follow Jean Paul on to the hangar where our plane is located. After you are inside, have the hangar door closed and locked. I'll stop at the security office and join you later."

Henri asked, "Is there any risk to us?"

Doug replied, "Not at the moment and I will get some help here so that doesn't change." He went into the office and said, "Call security and have them cordon off this area so the green Peugeot behind us can't leave. Our vehicles are going to our hangar. Let them in and lock it."

Showing his CIA ID, he asked for a phone to call the Sûreté. He called them, identified himself, and asked for Director Garnier. He apprised the director of the situation and who was with him at Orly

West and told him, "They had been following us on Highway A6a. I believe them to be members of the OAS group who attacked President de Gaulle at the Palace of Versailles a few days ago. If they are, there could be others on different routes."

The director said, "There is a team on duty waiting for a dignitary. We'll divert them to Orly West and send more. Are you armed?"

Doug said, "I am but I would prefer not to be involved in a gun fight. I have passengers that we are taking back to the States that I must protect. I hear the sirens. Tell them the car has stopped and will likely try to escape."

The director asked Doug to get all his people in one location, the hangar would be good and stay there until he called back. "Oh and say bonjour to my friend, Monsieur Lament."

By this time, the green Peugeot was surrounded by airport security cars. The occupants were still in the car but being ordered to leave their vehicle.

Doug walked to the hangar through the entrance from the office. Once inside, Jean Paul rushed to him and asked, "What is happening?"

Doug told him, "After we turned onto the A6a, I noticed a green Peugeot turn in behind us. There were two vehicles, the second being a black Peugeot. They often switched places but I still spotted them. The green car followed us into Orly West. I called the Sûreté from the airport security office. They now have a standoff situation with the occupants of the green car. We think they are part of the faction OAS who attacked your President at the Palace of Versailles. And by the way, Director Garnier said *bonjour*."

Jean Paul smiled and said, "We are long term friends. I had a chat with him earlier this week regarding our thoughts about making the home a place for visiting dignitaries. He thought it was a great idea."

The phone rang. A staff member answered and said, "Is there someone named Doug here?"

Doug took the phone – it was the director. He said, "We have them in custody along with their companions in the black Peugeot. They all maintain they were only touring, but we are taking them in and impounding their cars. "

The director asked, "When are you leaving?"

"We are ready to go as soon as I know that Jean Paul, Belle, and Henri will get home safely. By the way, I should tell you that the pilots brought a lot of security equipment with them that will need to go back to Sucy. We are sending a crew later to install it."

"Please let me speak with Jean Paul. Tell him August wants to talk with him."

"Thank you for the rescue."

"Jean Paul, can you do without your vehicles for a day or two?"

"We can. What do you have in mind?"

"Is there a helipad in Sucy?"

"Yes, at the hospital."

"*Très bien.* Until we know for certain there are no OAS people floating around the area, I'd rather you did not drive home. I do not want them to know you are located in Sucy. Doug told me how you faked coming in as though from Paris. Let's keep it that way. I'll have the helicopter there for you in about 30 minutes. There will be someone at the hospital to take all of you back home."

"Good, that will give us time to say proper goodbyes. Thank you, August. We'll talk more soon."

Jean Paul told them all what the arrangements were. "We have enough time for proper goodbye for now."

Doug called the office with the pilot and submitted their flight plan. They could fit into the queue.

Goodbyes were made, tears were shed, and they taxied away.

15

Their flight was uneventful, just the kind you like. With the flight time, the fuel stop, and the six-hour time difference, their arrival at Andrews Air Force base was in late morning. A car met them at the plane and took them to the main building to wait for the plane's refueling.

The director of the facility met them at the door and said, "Welcome to Andrews. I'm the director here, please call me Jonathan. Hello Doug, would you introduce your friends?"

"This is Tom and Maria O'Banion. And this little one is Alice, their newly adopted daughter. She speaks very little English."

Jonathan bent down to Alice's level. *"Bonjour Mademoiselle Alice. Bienvenue en Amérique!"*

He continued, "I will take you to the Community Commons room where you can be comfortable. There is even a playroom for your Alice. Oh, and by the way, there is someone there who wants to meet you all."

They entered and knocked on the door. The door opened and they were greeted by the Vice President, Lyndon Johnson. "Do come in," he said.

Jonathan said, "Mr. Vice President, these are Tom and Maria O'Banion and their daughter Alice. And of course you know Doug."

Vice President Johnson said, "My friends call me 'LBJ' – I hope we will be great friends so please call me LBJ. So good to meet you all. Let's sit over here around this table. Hello Doug. We have a little light lunch, some cookies, and there is coffee, tea, and milk for your Alice."

"Please let me tell you why it is me instead of President Kennedy. He wanted to be here to meet you in person but duty called. He is in Cleburne County, Arkansas dedicating the new Greers Ferry Dam. And of course, doing a little campaigning while he is there. One other thing," taking a framed document out of its sleeve. "This is a commendation for your service at the Palace of Versailles. President Kennedy would like you to return to the White House after you are settled back at home. He will present it to you in a more formal ceremony."

They took it, read it, and handed it to Doug. "Thank you Mr. Vice President."

They were served their coffee. Some small sandwich quarters and cookies appeared. LBJ said, "With your permission, I'd like to entice your Alice over to see if she would sit on my lap. May I?"

Maria said, "Of course, sir. She is a little shy when meeting someone the first time." She set Alice down, touched her own cheek. Alice remembered the game and kissed her new Maman on the cheek. Maria then pointed to LBJ and touched Alice's cheek, pointed again to LBJ.

Alice giggled and walked over to LBJ who took her in his lap. Alice pointed to her cheek. LBJ kissed it and then he pointed to his cheek whereupon she kissed him. They both laughed, giggled and when he handed her a cookie, she said, "*Merci beaucoup.*"

They chatted a little longer. LBJ said, "Duty calls. I need to get back to the White House. This has been quite an honor for me to be the one to give you the commendation, Thank you for your service."

Tom and Maria said, "The honor is ours. Thank you."

Doug walked out with them. LBJ said, "Those are some good people you have as friends."

Doug said, "They are very special people. I believe we haven't heard the last of their accomplishments."

While Alice and Maria were in the playroom, Doug and Tom sat talking with Jonathan. He wanted to know more about both of them. He said, "I've seen you as you fly in and out of here, Doug. But I don't know what you do."

Doug said, "I can't say much about what I do. I know you'll understand. By the way, we have a new flight crew coming in."

Jonathan asked, "How about you Tom? Can you tell me about what you do besides help Doug?"

Tom laughed, "I can. My job back home is acting chief of detectives with Muskegon's police department. Doug, Maria, and I were high school teachers there for a number of years until I made this move."

The new pilots came in and said, "We are all refueled and have filed a flight plan for Muskegon, Michigan. We should have you in Muskegon by around 3:00 p.m."

Tom said, "Jonathan, is it possible for me to make a brief long-distance call. I need to let our parents know when we will get in."

"Come with me. I'll dial the number for you."

Tom said, "Dad, we just got into Andrews and we'll be home about 3:00 p.m. this afternoon. Could you spread the word and be ready to take us home and could you find someone with a truck or a small van to bring all our luggage and a new bed to the house?"

"Of course, son. I'll take care of it. How was your trip from France?"

"It was a good flight and Alice did just fine."

"See you soon, Love you Dad." Twenty minutes later they were airborne.

16

———————

The flight was uneventful except for a brief shower over Cleveland. They flew around it and were soon on approach to the slightly off east-west runway. As they pulled up to the private plane terminal, they could see their parents waiting just inside.

Maria had put her sweater on and dressed Alice in a light jacket. The temperature was in the mid-60's and it was only a short walk to get inside. Maria carried Alice, who seemed a little tense with all the people. When she saw Uncle Doug, she held out her arms for him to take her. finally another familiar face. Maria got her hugs from the rest.

Doug said, "You'll recall that the Company agreed to let me stay a week or two while you three get settled in. They reserved a car and a room at the Ramada on Henry Street. I'll pick up my car and get checked in. So why don't you all caravan to your place and I'll see you later."

Maria said, 'Will you come for dinner?"

He replied, "Why don't I bring it? I know it isn't French cooking but I'm hankering for some Doo Drop perch and all the trimmings. How many of you are staying?"

"Everyone. It will be a little homecoming celebration," Tom said.

"Good. What shall I bring for Alice?"

Maria said, "I think they have a broiled chicken breast dinner. Get it with those little diced potatoes, potato bites. I think that will work for her. Maybe some milk or grape juice for her to drink."

Doug smiled, "Good. That will work. I'll be there around six with all the goodies. That should give you enough time to get Alice's bed put together and find some of her toys and books."

Maria laughed at him, "Okay, *Oncle Doug*. We have our marching orders. We'll be ready for Doo Drop. I'll get the champagne chilling and have the wine ready as well."

By this time, the movers had unloaded all the luggage – two trunks, three suitcases, the new bed. and Alice's chair for the table.

Doug started to hand Alice to Tom. She balked, looked around the room, held out her arms and said, "*Je veux maman.*"

Maria teared up and took her into her arms. There were others with tears, including Tom and Doug. Tom said, "Some bonding going on there."

Doug left with the pilots who were going to get a snack at the main terminal. Doug got an iced tea and talked with them while they ate. Doug told them that he had been authorized to stay for a week or two. He explained that there was some concern about the OAS. He said, "I want to be sure they are all settled in with no problems. I will be traveling with them to Chicago when they go to meet with Etienne's partner and take care of some business there."

"What's next for you?" one asked.

Doug replied, "Well, when I get back to the D.C. area, the first thing I want to do is take you two and the other two pilots who we flew with from Paris to dinner at one of your favorite spots."

"And after that?"

"Then it's back to France and who knows? Wherever I'm needed."

Doug said his goodbyes, picked up his car, and settled in at the Ramada. After a quick shower and shave, he headed for Doo Drop.

Arrival at home was a little hectic. Tom had to move their cars out of the driveway so the van could back in for unloading. Maria unlocked the front door and went in with Alice. While walking around, she said to Alice, "*Notre maison.*" Her parents came in, her dad carrying a rocking chair.

He said, "This the rocker your mother used when you were little. I think it will work for Alice." He set it down for the moment in the living room. Maria sat with Alice in the rocker, but that didn't last long. Alice decided to explore, climbed down, and proceeded to check things out.

Maria said, "Thank you, Dad and Mom. We'll make good use of it."

Maria said, "Everyone keep an eye on her while we move some things out of the storage room, Alice's bedroom to be. It's big enough for her bed, her toy box, the rocker. We'll figure the rest out later."

When the room was empty, the ladies cleaned it and opened the window for some fresh air. The men had unboxed the new bed on the front porch and brought the pieces in as needed. Maria opened the trunk with the toys and bedding. When she brought out Alice's little rocker, Alice marched right over and began to rock in it. Everyone laughed. She did too. She was home. She said, "*Chez moi.*" Maria said, "my home." Then Alice was up and checked out the toy box that Tom had removed from the trunk.

In the meantime, the ladies got her bedclothes out of the other trunk, got her bed made with familiar bedding. Maria sighed and said, "There. The rest of the unpacking can wait until tomorrow. Doug should be here any minute with the perch dinners."

Tom found Alice's chair for the table, unpacked it, and set it between where Tom and Maria would be sitting. Doug would be sitting next to Tom and the four grandparents were on the other side of the long table.

17

———————

There was a knock on the door. Tom said, "That's a Doug knock!" Tom and Doug set the table, put out plates of perch and French fries. Tom popped the cork on the champagne and poured each a glass. Maria in the meantime poured Alice some grape juice in her wine glass shaped sippy cup.

Tom said, "Hold up just a minute for the toast. I would like to say grace." To Alice he said, *"dis les grâce."* Tom then recited their regular Catholic grace, only *en français*. Alice looked at him, unfolded her hands, and whispered to him, *"Papa,"* then turned to Maria and said, *"Maman."*

Doug asked, "May I offer a toast?" After Tom and Maria nodded, Doug continued, "When we got the message about the accident, I wasn't sure we would make it in time, but we did. And when Celeste asked them if they would adopt Alice and raise her as their own, they both said yes. After the adoption papers were signed and on their way to the authorities, Celeste passed peacefully. These two got busy and you have seen how far they have come as new parents. Alice knows it, she shows it to them, you've seen that. And so, to you, Maria and Tom, you are the best. Here's to you and your new family." They clinked glasses as did Alice with her sippy cup to the great joy of all at the table.

Tom's mother said, "She has seemed a little shy around all of us. But now since grace and the toast she seems to be perking up. Did you teach her the toasting or did Celeste and Etienne?"

Maria answered, "Celeste taught her. And their routine was our Catholic *grace en français*. We have continued it trying to keep as many things unchanged as we can."

She continued, "As to her shyness, she is that way with anyone new. That will change the more we are all together. In time, she will open up to you as she sees that you're going to be around. For now we want to be here to bond more with us. It is happening a little more with me but she is getting closer to Tom as time goes on. It will happen with you as well. We had some guidance on this while in Sucy. She is very outgoing, a bright little girl who is very curious, laughs a lot, and will soon be coming to you. Just keep those smiles and looks of love coming. You'll see." Doug and the grandfathers soon had platters of Doo Drop perch, French fries, and onion rings. Maria began to cut up Alice's chicken into little bites and put them on Alice's plate with the potato bites. Everyone started eating as did Alice. While she seemed to like her food, she kept eyeing the perch and fries.

When Maria cut up a small piece of perch, checked for bones and put it on Alice's plate, who looked at it, turned back to Maria, got a smile and a nod from her. Alice tried a small bite of the perch. At first, to everyone's delight, her nose wrinkled up, she frowned, then smiled, and took another bite from Maria. They all laughed. Maria's dad said, "Look at her eating. She's like you, Maria." He smiled at Alice and she back to him with a little shy smile.

Tom served Sauvignon Blanc for the ladies and himself. Doug and the grandfathers preferred beer.

"I have some recipes from Belle. I will be learning some French dishes. It will be good for her to have some food she is familiar with. It will be an education for us too."

Her dad asked, "Now, who is Belle?"

Alice reacted, "*Maman, où est Belle?*"

Maria took Alice to her lap, "*Belle est en France.*"

Maria said, "She will soon fade. It has been a long day for all of us, but I see it in her. I'll spend a little time with her, read her a story, and she'll be off to sleep."

Tom took Alice out of her chair, kissed her on the cheek, and handed her to Maria. Maria faced them all, said, "Bonne nuit." She took Alice's hand and waved it. They all smiled and waved back. Tom walked back with them to her bedroom but soon returned to put the coffee on.

Everyone pitched in and cleaned up. When Maria came out some time later, all had settled in the living room. Tom had a good fire going in the fireplace and all were enjoying coffee, or another glass of wine or a beer.

Maria said, "She went right out after I read her favorite story to her."

Tom's dad said, "You have become her *maman* already. We are all so proud of you."

Her dad said, "You have a long way to go with her. But I'm sure you know that."

Her mother said, "You look tired too. Are you ready for us to leave?"

"It has been a long day. But there are some things we can share tonight."

Tom said, "We have so much more to tell you. But we have some things that need to be done right away. We were given an inheritance and need to go to Chicago in connection with that. We and Jean Paul Lament have an appointment in Chicago next Tuesday with Etienne's partner in this country."

His dad asked, "Will you take Alice with you?"

Maria said, "Yes, we will, We want to keep her close in these early days."

"Another new name. Who is Monsieur Lament?"

Tom answered this one. "Monsieur Lament, Jean Paul, is our attorney of record in France. He has been so good to us and settled everything quickly so that we could get back home as soon as we have. You will meet him before he returns to Sucy in France. We are meeting him in Chicago next Tuesday and he is coming to Muskegon the next day to take care of business up here."

He continued, "Tomorrow, Thursday, we will go to Ettermans to stock up on some groceries and find a place to get some diapers and other things … imagine us buying diapers? After our grocery trip and lunch, I will be seeing Mark at 1:30 pm and let him know I will need some time before I can come back to work. Maria and Alice will take afternoon naps while I'm there. On Friday, we'll have another settling in and bonding day, just the three of us. We might go down to the Ovals and let Alice get a little sand in her shoes. We won't stay long, it may be a little chilly, After naps, we'll have dinner, play time, and off to bed."

He continued, "I know this all sounds very sketchy at the moment but you'll understand after you get the whole picture. We are hoping the four of you can come over again on Saturday. Alice takes her afternoon nap around 2:00 p.m. If you could come about 1:15 p.m. or so, you'd have a little time to interact with Alice. Then we'll have a charcuterie board and something to drink. We'll sit around in front of the fire and we'll tell you the whole story of what happened and why our lives are now changed in more than just having a child. Will that work for you?"

Both sets of parents agreed they could do it. Doug asked if he could be here too. Tom said, "We would like that. You can fill in some details that we might forget. Good, so we'll see all on Saturday."

\

18

—————

Maria and Alice came home from Ettermans, unloaded the groceries, and put some away in the refrigerator. After a quick lunch, Tom said, "I need to get to the office and my meeting with Mark. Are you going to be okay?"

"We'll be fine. We'll both have naps. Go get your business done."

Tom walked into the station right on time. He first greeted Gerri and asked if Mark was ready for him. Mark was the police chief and Gerri was his secretary and aide de camp. She took him in to see Mark.

"Hello Tom. Good to see you. You look a little tired. Long trip home?"

"Yes, it was, but my fatigue is not from the trip, just so much happening. Maria is home taking a nap. She is exhausted. But we'll recover soon and be just like new. Will we have an hour or so to talk?"

"Actually even more if we need it. Would you like something to drink? Coffee or iced tea?"

"Some coffee sounds good for now." Mark asked Gerri to bring it.

"Mark, I'm going to start sort of in the middle of this and then back up to fill in the back story." Mark nodded okay.

Tom continued, "You may remember that Maria had a pen pal in France since her early teens. They finally met when Maria's parents took her to France after college graduation. Maria and Celeste bonded immediately when they met. They were now almost like sisters. Some tragic events that I'll tell you about later happened and as a result our lives have changed. Maria and I are now parents. We have adopted their daughter, Alice, who is two and a half years old." Gerri knocked and as was her habit came on in.

She said, "What's this about a daughter? Oops, I guess I wasn't supposed to hear that."

Tom smiled and said, "It's okay. Just keep it to yourself for now."

"What's her name? How old is she? Where is she now?"

Tom said, "How about that coffee and I'll answer your questions."

Mark said, "Please close the door, Gerri, and sit for a few minutes. Tom, I'd like to know all those answers too."

Tom took a sip of coffee, "Her name is Alice, spelled like our Alice, but pronounced 'Ah-lees.' She'll be three in January." Tom's eye's shone with pride, "She is our little sweetheart, so smart. She already calls us *Maman* and *Papa*. She doesn't speak much English yet. We're working on that."

"Well, where is she now? You are such a proud Papa already."

"I know, I know. But she is… is Alice and she is our daughter." He teared up.

Mark said, "There you are, Gerri."

"But where is she?"

"Home with her Maman, both napping."

Mark, laughed, "Okay now, Gerri."

On her way out, Gerri said, "When do I meet her?"

"As soon as we get some things finished up. Soon!"

Mark poured more coffee, "Now Tom, tell me as much as you can, you know, the short version, because I need to bring someone else in on all this."

"Who?"

"You'll see. Just tell me, Tom."

Tom told him about the accident, Etienne dying immediately, and Celeste not long after. And then about the good people of Sucy, the house, the people of the church. Such a caring group.

Tom said, "So from a lovely first week of a honeymoon, to a job we did with Doug, the accident, the funeral, meeting the church people. From all this to now finally home, now a fairly wealthy family. Oh, and Mark, we want to keep our new wealth private. We still have to figure out what we will do with the money. Both Celeste and Etienne wanted us to use the money to do some of the things we often talked about with Celeste, our town, and its potential. It has been a whirlwind, and we are a long way from coming to understand what has happened to us. You know that we couldn't have children, so Alice is the best part of all this."

He continued, "So I'm asking if I can have a couple of weeks before I come back to work. Can that be worked out?"

"Of course, it can, Tom. By the way, Gene, your protégé for chief of detectives is coming along nicely. And thankfully, things have been pretty quiet here."

"The first thing we have to do is go to Chicago, meet with Etienne's partner and some bankers and attorneys. We also have an attorney of record in France. He is meeting us in Chicago and will come back to Muskegon to help us with the money and bank details here. Oh, and one more thing, both Maria and I were frightened when the OAS caught up with us at Orly. I'm not sure how Maria will cope with that potential threat."

Mark said, "With the OAS business, it's time to bring that someone else in." He beeped Gerri and told her to send him in.

A minute later Doug walked in.

Tom looked up, "I didn't think it would be you. What's up?"

"Forgive me. I had a call from DC early this morning. The boss had a heads-up from the Sûreté. It seems that some members of OAS are here in the US, somewhere on the eastern seaboard. They don't know where we are now, but they have immense resources and might figure it out."

Doug saw the concern in Tom's eyes and face. He said, "There is a team on the way. Pairs of them will be posted at various locations around town. The OAS won't get anywhere near you. We want you to go about your business, like grocery shopping. By the way, I followed you to Ettermans this morning. You see, well protected."

Mark asked, "Tom, what are your immediate plans, other than what you told me about Chicago?"

"We will be visiting, the three of us, on Saturday with all the parents, telling them the whole story. Then Sunday after church we will be planning the Chicago trip."

Mark asked Doug, "When do you think your team will be here?"

Doug said, "On Monday they are flying out one agent who will be my partner. The rest of them are likely not until late Tuesday. They'll drive out. My best guess if the OAS comes this way at all, it won't be until later in the week, Actually our hope is that we will catch them in transit and maybe even stop them before they get this far."

Mark said, "I'll start rounding up some teams, but we'll just stay in the background and step up if you need us to provide some support. Tom, if you need some help while Doug is setting things up, just let me know."

Mark put his hand on Tom's shoulder, "I know you have Doug and your parents here, but if you need someone else to talk to as you decide your future, I'm your guy. Now let me get some work done."

19

Tom and Doug stopped at Gerri's desk. Tom asked, "Is there a phone I could use? I need to call Maria."

"Use the one in your office. Please tell them both hello for me. And Tom, here is my phone number at home if Maria wants to call."

"Hi sweetheart, how are you two doing?"

"We are all doing great. Sara and her little one are here. We are having a good time."

"I bumped into Doug at the station. We'll have a quick bite and see you soon. I'll be home about 2:00 p.m."

Tom and Doug stopped at U.S. 31 Barbecue to get takeout sandwiches, French fries, and lemonade. Sitting at a picnic table, they went over the situation again. Tom said, "I'm feeling a little more secure about this now. Thanks for being here."

"Me too. The agency is taking this seriously, but don't give the OAS much chance of success in finding you. They are taking no chances. A good outcome would be if we could take them, hold them for a while, and see what we can learn. I didn't say anything at the station about the commendation. The reason is if LBJ's staff leaks that to the press, the OAS could pick up on that. The Director called LBJ's office and asked them to hold the publicity about the presentation."

He continued, "Do you want me there when you tell Maria about this new development?"

"Let me talk with her first. I think she'll be okay. I can always call you."

"That's good. Mark loaned us a car with a radio to the station. While you are doing your thing telling her and giving her parents the whole picture, I'll be catching a nap. Getting some sleep when I can is the rule.

By the way, I think you might not want to tell both parents about the possible threat. There will be time later in the week if it becomes necessary. Here's my room number and phone number in my room. See you Saturday."

20

Tom came in the front door to a lovely scene. Two mothers talking over tea with Alice and her new friend scrambling around her toys. "Hi sweetheart." And hugged Maria.

"Hello Sara," He gave her a quick hug. "How are you and Bob doing?"

Before Sara could answer, Tom picked up Alice who said, *"Papa,"* and snuggled up to him. She didn't stay long. She wanted to get back to her toys and her new friend.

Sara said, "We are great. You have a lovely daughter . She was a little shy at first. But these two are going to be good friends. It's been great, Maria. I know you have things to do. I'll be on my way."

"We have things to get settled next week, so maybe soon, we'll have you here for dinner. Bye for now."

Tom asked, "Has Alice had her nap yet?"

"No. Does it have to be now?"

"Yes, we have to talk. It was a good meeting at the station."

"Give me a few minutes. They've been playing hard."

When Maria returned, she said, "Okay. What's up? Your little worry frown gave you away."

"The meeting was mostly good. That will be first. Mark okayed my taking some extra time to get settled in. And Gerri is so excited for us both about Alice. She can't wait to meet her. Mark too, for that matter. They are both happy for us."

Tom continued, "Now as to the worry part. Mark and I talked for some 20 or 25 minutes. I just gave him a quick overview about events and our change in life status. He stopped me and a minute later in walks Doug."

"Why was Doug there?"

"That took another hour and a half to get some strategy plans made. Doug got a call from D.C. early this morning. He was told that the OAS was in the country somewhere on the east coast. No one has seen them yet, but the intelligence on their presence here is solid."

Maria interrupted, "Is there any way the OAS could find out where we live?"

"Doug told me there had been no publicity yet about our role in France and the commendation. The bottom line is that finding us is very unlikely." Tom went on to give Maria the plan, for the D.C. protection teams. "I can see you are concerned even if you are not the worrier I am. By the way, both Doug and Mark suggested no to telling our parents about the possible threat until later."

"Okay for now. I thought about having Sara take care of Alice. But the more thought I gave it, the less we are apart the more comfortable she will be."

"I agree. We have some time to get something worked out. Doug's partner agent will be here Monday afternoon by agency plane. We'll take the plane with Doug and his partner to Chicago. By the time we return Tuesday afternoon late, the whole team will be in place.

"We'll get Doug here Saturday morning and brainstorm it before our parents come."

The next morning, Friday, was to be a special day with just the three of them. Alice called from her bed, *"Maman."*

Maria said, "Your turn. She may be wet."

"But I don't know how to do that."

"That's probably true. But maybe you could learn. I have to get my nighty and robe on I'll be there soon.

Tom went to Alice, took her out of bed, and said, "Yup, a little damp. She will need a fresh one." He called out "Maria, where are the diapers?"

"In the top drawer of her dresser."

"*Maman*," Alice said.

"Help, Maria. I can't make this thing work."

Maria walked in about that time. "Let me … and watch."

Alice said, "*Maman*."

"Did you see how that went? It's easy."

Soon they were at the table enjoying breakfast. Tom had dressed her in her play clothes. Alice was playing on the living room rug while Tom and Maria were having their second and third cup of coffee, When Maria finished her coffee, she got down on the floor to play and read picture books with Alice. Tom soon got the idea and Alice crawled over and sat on his stomach. "Oof," he said.

Alice said, "Oof" back to him.

Maria laughed, then Alice and Tom started in. Tom said, "I'd like to try reading to her. Which one should I read? Not the one you often do." Tom slid over and used the sofa to lean back on. Alice was still on his stomach. Maria got another cup of coffee and sat watching them. Tom would turn to a page with an animal, like a cow. He would point to the animal and say the name first *en français, vache*. He would say the name again, point to Alice and tell her '*tu le dis.*' He would then repeat the process saying 'cow' and 'you say it.' When Alice got it right, he would smile at her and clap his hands in approval. If she didn't get it the first time, he would repeat the process. Then after two or sometimes three words he would go back to a previous animal and ask '*C'est quel animal*?' Another round of applause.

Maria got down on the floor with them and began to clap as well. After a look back for 'cow,' she said to Tom, 'You are great. Where did you learn that technique?"

Tom said, "I watched Belle at first and then you. You were doing so well. It was natural to mimic you two and then add my own twists. I had good teachers."

"You are a natural, so patient." Tom noticed a little tear in the corner of her eye. He brushed it away and put his palm on her cheek.

He leaned to her and kissed her cheek. Alice mimicked her palm on the cheek and kiss on the cheek. That brought on a group hug.

Maria got up and said, "You two keep going. I'll get an early lunch started. Then how about a quick tour of the ovals, a run downtown, maybe a walk in Hackley park? We'll be back in time for her nap."

Tom drove, Maria holding Alice close to the window. They went along Lake Shore Drive, then on to Clay Ave and stopped by the park across from the Masonic Temple and the Muskegon Chronicle. Alice walked between them, her hands in one of theirs until she saw the statue. She wiggled loose and walked faster to the 80 feet tallest statue in the center of the park. Alice stopped in front of the statue, called the 'Victory,' and looked it over. Tom said, "Someday we'll have to bring Alice down here and teach her about the history of these statues."

They took a walk around the park with a statue at each corner and ended back at the car. The next leg of the trip was back on Lake Shore Drive through Lakeside and the Beechwood/Blufton area to the Ovals.

Tom put Alice on one shoulder as they walked to the water's edge. Alice's eyes were big like saucers. Who knew what was going through her head seeing so much water. On the way back to the car, Tom strapped her in a swing and gave her a little ride. She squealed with joy.

Back in the car, they were home in just a few minutes. Alice fell asleep on Maria's lap. She put Alice in her bed and tiptoed out. "She'll have a good nap. I think I will too, I still haven't caught up."

Tom said, "I'll join you in a little bit. I have some work to do to be organized for the meeting tomorrow with our folks and Doug."

He kissed Maria, "Sleep well, sweetheart."

21

———————

Saturday morning Doug knocked on the door on time as usual. He found Tom, Maria, and Alice sitting on the living room floor. They were working together on word skills for Alice, both French and English.

"*Oncle* Doug," she said. He waved to her. She went back to her game with Tom and Maria. Doug watched for a time, then nodded to Tom.

Tom asked Maria, "How do you want to do this?"

Maria said, "We'll keep going on the vocabulary lessons for a while. Then I'll nudge her toward her toys and just keep watching her while I listen to you both. I'll jump in when I can and ask and answer questions as they come to me."

Tom said, "We'll set up on the kitchen table so I can take some notes. When we are done with this, I'll go over them again and may have some questions to ask. We need to be done by one o'clock so I'll have some time before our parents come. My initial thoughts are to be as brief as I can. I may not be able to hold to that. My thought is that our parents are going to want to know more than I think we ought to give. I'm going to call on the two of you to back me up if I get in trouble."

Maria asked, "Tom and Doug, what do you think about the question of telling the parents about the possible threat from OAS?"

Doug said, "You know my position. The reason for it is that if they are frightened by the possibility of OAS finding us and attacking is one of preventing a general sense of fear in the town if the word gets out. You know your parents better than I do. Will they be scared enough to let the word out?"

Maria said, "If they know what your concern about spreading the words is, I think it won't happen. They have been through things like this before. I realize that this is at a different level, but they'll be okay with it because of what they've been through.'

Doug asked, "So you are quite sure they won't panic?"

"I am. They will surprise you."

"What are your thoughts, Tom?"

"I think we should just ask them, 'if there is a possible threat coming, would you help us in keeping it quiet?'"

Maria said, "I like that. You are okay in my book, Mr. O."

Tom laughed, "I haven't heard that since my high school teaching days."

Doug said, "Good. Settled then, and just in time. Here they come."

Tom put all their jackets on their bed.

Both grandmas sat on the couch, not too far apart and close to Alice who was sitting on the floor next to *maman*, Maria. Maria's mother said, "We have been working on names for us and have decided that I will be *grand-mère*."

Tom's mother said, "I will be *grand-maman*. Will you introduce us?"

Maria said, "I think that might work. How about the grandpas?"

Maria's mother said, "We thought they could wait until next time we see Alice."

"I'm not sure she will let you get away with that but let's give it a try. She said to Alice, *"Tu es Alice."* Pointing to her mother, *"C'est grand-mère."* She repeated it.

She then said, *"Tu es Alice."* Pointing to Tom's mother, *"C'est grand-maman."* She repeated that.

"Now let's try something." Pointing to her, *"Tu es ..?"*

Alice said, "Alice" and smiled at *maman*.

Pointing to her mother, "C'est …" Alice said, *"grand-mère."* Everyone clapped including Alice. Maria repeated with Tom's mother, got the same result, an answer of her as *'grand-maman.'* After another round of applause, Maria stood, picked up Alice, saying, *"Je t'aime."* She did a little dance whirl around the living room and hugged her tight. She nodded to the fathers and motioned to the couch. When they were sitting by their wives, she sat down in an easy chair and said, "She is getting a little tired. I think it is nap time."

Alice pointed to the grandfathers but started nodding. Maria said, "She is done for today. I'll go and read a little to her."

Maria said, "Why don't you all gather around the table? We have two charcuterie boards with a variety of cheeses, meats, and crackers. Pick out what you'd like to drink and then we'll tell you what happened to us in France. Please start without me. I won't be long."

22

Maria returned and with a smile said, "I'll have a glass of that lovely sauvignon blanc. We discovered it in France and have found a source here in the States. I have a toast to make."

They raised their glasses and Maria said, "To grandparents who worked out the names for the grandmothers and even though we don't know them yet, grand poppas. We'll get to you next time. And I want to toast Alice who knows you now as *grand-mère* and *grand-maman,* even though she can't know what it means yet. She amazed me with what she did today. I didn't expect her to grasp those names that fast. We have a special little girl. We'll have to learn how to help her. Part of her gifts may have come because she had so many loving adults around her in France. I suspect she inherited a lot of good genes from Celeste and Etienne. So once again, raise your glasses to grandparents and Alice, special people all." They clinked their glasses and sipped their wine or beer. Maria sat down with tears in her eyes.

When they started sampling the boards, Maria's mom said, "You two, … and Doug, you all have the floor. Please tell us."

Tom said, "I'll start it off. Maria and Doug will jump in whenever they want. Questions are welcome."

He continued by telling them of their sightseeing week with Maria as his guide. They were due to see Celeste, Etienne, and Alice that first weekend. That got postponed for two reasons, Alice had a cold and Doug hired them for a job down in Versailles. Their visit was postponed until the next weekend. They accepted Doug's offer and the job came off almost as planned. Doug recommended that we come with him back to the States because of an almost disaster and the need to be debriefed.

"We were being debriefed when a call came from France. There had been a terrible accident, Etienne was killed instantly and Celeste was injured so badly, she wasn't expected to live. We flew back and got to the hospital in Sucy en Brie in time. Celeste affirmed our vow that we would adopt Alice. We were also advised that we would be receiving an inheritance."

Tom's dad asked, "So you did get to talk with Celeste before she passed?"

Maria answered, "We did. She took my hand and asked me and Tom again if we would adopt Alice. Then we had a surprise. I knew Celeste was an orphan but just learned that Etienne was as well. So not only did we become Alice's parents they made us their major beneficiaries. She was gone about 10 minutes or so after we arrived. My friend was just hanging on until we made it back."

Tom took her hand. He knew that she was nearly in tears from just that much. Her mother took her other hand.

He said, "Let me finish now please. The next few days starting with the Wednesday of the accident, almost a week just flew by. The townspeople were gracious, people at their local parish went out of their way to help. It became apparent that Celeste and Etienne were well thought of in the community. Etienne had been very successful in his career as a commodities trader. He shared his good fortune with the city and his church. Neither of us knew of his wealth, made from his trading in commodities and other investments in both France and the States."

"So, quickly, here is where we are. We are owners of the house, almost a chateau (they did this so we would be able to go back often enough so that Alice would not lose her French beginnings.) We have accounts in a bank in Sucy and will have one in our local bank in Muskegon. After our trip to Chicago next Tuesday, we will have money in a Chicago bank, both a standard account and through a trust company a trust account of a size that will allow us to do some things that Celeste and Etienne knew we wanted to do in Muskegon. In short, we are millionaires many times over."

Maria's mother asked, "Are we allowed to know how much?"

Maria said. "Mom, we would rather not tell you. No one else knows. If anyone asks, you can say, 'enough to care for the child.' If anyone gets pushy and wants to know how much, just say 'it's none of my business. We know they will do right by our granddaughter.' They should get the idea, hopefully. I'll let Tom finish it up. Anyone need any more wine or a glass of brandy?" This got a good laugh.

Tom went on, "We are going to do everything we can to keep our wealth private. We plan to buy a house as soon as things settle down. It won't be a big house, just adequate, not ostentatious. And even though we could pay for it, we will do a mortgage. I will go back to work in a few weeks as interim police chief. Mark tells me my protégé is nearly ready. I'll help him to get the job. Then I'll bow out and become a consultant to the department."

Tom's dad asked, "What are you thinking of doing with your future? Have you given it any thought?"

"So much has happened so fast that I can't focus on the future that far out. I would like to do as they suggested and do something for the city. Fred had an amazing vision for Muskegon. Since we were close, I picked up some of his ideas and would like them to become reality. One question is how best to do that, run for mayor and come from that direction or stay in the background and do what I can there. My mind is whirling so I need to get through this period until I figure this out. That is, at least in part, why it is so important to keep our inheritance private. I'll be coming to you for any thoughts you might have about it. Most important is that little girl in there. Maria decided and I agreed that she would not be working on a job until Alice is in school. She may be studying for something new to do as well, we'll see."

Maria said, "We are agreed, Tom and me. Our main focus is Alice. We need to get her settled in her new country, learn the language but keep her native one. We need to think about where to live that will give her the best opportunity to learn."

Maria's dad asked Tom, "What about your music? Will you try to keep that going?"

"Nothing for now. When we look for a house, we want at least three bedrooms, a music room with a new piano, and lots of other things that Maria wants that she knows more about than I do."

Tom's mom asked, "Do you think there are people still in town who don't want what Fred wanted?"

"I think that is likely to be true, so we'll see. I may have to learn some new skills to be able to make anything happen here."

Tom, Maria, and Doug exchanged glances and finally nodded.

Maria's mom asked, "What was that little exchange about? Is there something else?"

"Yes, there is. When we go to Chicago on Tuesday, Doug and one of the agents of the organizations he works with will be going with us. We'll be flying down in the agency private plane that day. By the time we get back to Muskegon, there will be several teams from the agency around town watching."

"Watching for what?"

Doug said, "Let me take over the conversation for a few minutes. Tom may be too modest to tell it all and it is important that you know it all. I can't tell you much about the mission I enlisted them for in France. You may not have known about it but the Speaker of the House made a trip to France at the behest of President Kennedy. The meeting in France was with French President Charle de Gaulle. What you may not know is there was an attempt on their President that might have been successful if Tom and Maria were not there. Maria was not armed so she was inside as another set of eyes on what was happening. It was she who first spotted the OAS, the operation that wanted to assassinate de Gaulle. Tom was armed so he took it upon himself to meet the OAS as they approached the meeting room. He got off several shots, drove them back, and wounded a couple of them. No one other than two OAS people was hurt. The meeting was a success from the standpoint of the international importance."

Doug paused for a moment, "Yesterday, I received an early morning call from the agency that some of the OAS people are in the country on the southeast coastline. They have no idea at this time where any of us are. There is no immediate threat, but the agency isn't taking any chances."

Maria got up to find the commendation. There is something else you should know. Tom won't tell you but I will." Tom shook his head.

"Going on," Doug added, "When we arrived at Andrews Air Force Base, we all met with Lyndon B. Johnson (LBJ) who presented them with a commendation. Tom and Maria were told that they would be brought to the White House for a more formal presentation. We are trying to get that postponed in view of what I just told you. Doing a formal presentation, the press will be there and that might point them right here. They have agreed to postpone it as of yesterday afternoon."

Maria said, "This commendation is a recognition of our contribution. We are pleased and proud to have this unforeseen honor. Again this is one of those things you can't talk about."

Doug continued, "So why did we decide to tell you? For two reasons, one, you are close to Tom and Maria, and two, you won't panic as some of the townspeople might do."

"I emphasize again there is no cause for alarm. We hope to find them, detain them, and use the time to interrogate them."

Maria said, "Uh Oh, I hear a little voice asking for her *maman*. Back in a few with your granddaughter."

"Anything else anyone wants? that shot of brandy?"

They all laughed. Tom's mom said, "No, but it is a lot to take in. We're proud of you both."

Maria came back out with Alice. She said, "Say *au revoir* to grandmas and grandpas."

Alice said, "*Au revoir.*"

It was just the three of them again,

23

———————

Tom called Jean Paul about the security. He got the address where they were to meet both Jean Paul and Gerald McDowell, Etienne's partner. The rest would follow from that.

Doug drove them all to Muskegon's private terminal and they arrived at Midway by 8:30 am. Gerald had arranged a limo that brought them to his office by 8:55 am. Monsieur Lament, Jean Paul, was already there talking with Gerald and his attorney.

Jean Paul took care of the introductions including Alice. Everyone oohed and aahed over her. He then said, "Gerald, could I have a few minutes with my clients before we get started? I haven't seen them since we were together in France. I need to catch up on what has been happening in Muskegon."

"Of course, let us know when you are ready."

Jean said, "I didn't realize you would be bringing Alice. Has something happened that suggested it?"

Maria answered, "Yes, Jean. There are two reasons. After conversations with Alice's new doctor in Muskegon and the psychologist he recommended, we decided to follow their advice. We were told it would be best for Alice to stay close to us so she can bond with us. That, we were told, may take a few weeks of staying close and slowly introduce her to others. No babysitters alone with her for a while. It seems to be working. We can share some of that with you after we get back to Muskegon. If Alice fusses, I will leave the room with her. As to the second reason, Tom and/or Doug can answer that."

Tom began, "Doug and his companion, an agent with the government entity Doug works with are here because elements of the OAS are in the US somewhere along the southeastern coast. There is a team being set up in Muskegon as we speak. The agency does not think there is a real danger, but they are taking this precaution. That team will be in place until the OAS people are captured and deported or held for questioning."

Jean Paul asked, "I can understand why you would want Alice with you. But this other thing is disturbing. How about your job?"

"I am on an extended leave until I am ready. I'm still deciding what my new direction is going to be and will take my time figuring it out."

Jean Paul asked, "Anything else we need to talk about before we ask them back in? Oh, and should we mention the reason for Doug and the agent's being here?"

Doug said, "It wouldn't hurt if they know and might help to ensure the need for keeping the wealth private."

"Let me manage that with them. I will let them in."

As Gerald and his attorney came back, a pot of coffee and some sweet rolls were brought in. Gerald said, "I have taken the liberty of inviting the Northern Trust people to come. They will be here at 11:00 am. We have about 45 minutes left to discuss the accounts you will have and how they will be set up at Northern. Etienne and I, together with our attorneys, chose Northern Trust when we first realized we needed their counsel and expertise. They are an old-line company founded in 1889 to provide trust and banking services for the city's prosperous citizens. They have grown to become one of the world's largest private banks, asset management, and asset services. Etienne and I have been collaborating with them for over 20 years. You and your inheritance will be safe. Do you have questions so far?"

Tom asked, "Are all the funds we will be inheriting in Etienne's investment account?"

Gerald answered, "No. When you work in the commodities, you

need to have ready cash. Some of the purchases need to be made, as Etienne would say, *tout suite*, or 'immediately" in English. We always kept equal amounts in the purchases accounts, in the U.S. account and a similar one in France. We needed to do that so that we could act fast. As each purchase account grew to be more than we needed for transactions, Northern would, on our order, transfer equal amounts in each of our investment accounts. That way we shared in growth here and in France equally. Jean and my attorney set that up early in our partnership. It has worked for many years. That will change now. And by the way, I have just transferred equal amounts into both our investment accounts so you will receive $50,000 more than you thought you would. Now, I have a question for you. Are you interested in becoming active in the commodities business or maybe become a silent, but not active participant?"

Tom said, "My first reaction is to not be active in the commodities business. It would take me a long time to gain the knowledge that you and Etienne have. I am interested and would like to think about being a silent partner. I want to talk with Jean Paul and then get back to you. Would that be okay?"

"That is excellent, Tom. I understand the knowledge base. I would love to have you as a silent partner. The people at Northern and I will work out the details if you decide to do that."

Tom asked, "So, we will have an investment account, checking account and all that, plus the investing expertise to make the money grow. Do I have it right?"

Jean Paul said, "I told you he was a quick study. He has the gist of this relationship with Northern down."

Tom added, "Having the money grow will be more and more important if I pursue doing for the city of Muskegon those things we think it will make it the city we know it can be. It will take some time for us to figure out the best way to make that happen. That could be a year or two before we make a move. Is the market growing at the moment?"

Gerald said, "Oh, it is doing well. They have taken good care to make that happen over the years. The growth has been good."

A knock on the door interrupted. They were told that the Northern Trust people were here.

Gerald took over, introduced them all. Tom and Maria said, "Lots of new names and faces to learn."

Gerald introduced Etienne and Celeste's account manager, Samuel Behrman, to Tom and Maria. He said, "I am pleased to meet you. Etienne, Celeste, and I have been clients and account manager for over ten years now. We will come to know each other well over the years to come unless you would like to choose your own manager?"

Tom looked at Maria, she nodded, and he said, "We have done well so far by accepting people who worked for Etienne and Celeste. We would be pleased if you stay on as account manager for us."

Sam said, "Very well, thank you. I understand you are to have an account for this little one in trust until she is twenty-one. The second one is for the two of you. You'll be interested in hearing that the amount of money in the account has gone up since we talked last. When we get to our facility this afternoon to do the transfers, we'll have the latest figures. You'll be able to talk with our tax people as well. Since you are staying with us, the transfer can be quickly done. No wire transfers needed. You'll have to sign some papers for the accounts and a signature card for general use. When you leave this afternoon you will have all the documents you need to learn about us, all the data for both accounts, and a checkbook for your account with both names. Monsieur Lamont has done a superb job of taking care of all the legalities. My card will be in the folder, and you'll have a direct number to my office. Mrs. Jones, Mary, is my assistant and will get you right to me or set up a time I can get back to you."

Maria asked, "When do we need to be at your offices?"

"If you could be there at 2:30 pm, we can have you on your way by 3:00 or a little later. Will that work?"

Jean Paul said, "That will be fine. All the legalities and account details were discussed yesterday."

Doug said, "I will alert the pilots to be ready for a 4:00 pm or so departure and we'll be back in Muskegon by 6:00 pm their time."

Sam introduced Tom and Maria to the tax lady. After verifying everything about their pertinent data, Tom asked, "When will we know the final figures for taxes?"

She said, "I'll have that for you sometime tomorrow. Here is my card with my direct number. If you give me a call sometime in the afternoon, I will have the figures. Then Sam will get on and answer any other questions you might have."

"Good. We'll be calling you then. Good to meet you all. And Sam, we'll talk about a silent partnership."

Goodbyes were said and they were off in the limo to Midway.

24

By the time they reached the Midway terminal, Alice was sound asleep. Maria asked Doug, "Will she be okay if she stays asleep?"

Doug answered, "She will be just fine. Better asleep than awake. The pressure change on a short hop will not be much, so she will have a good snooze and probably won't wake up until we get to Muskegon."

Doug went up to the cockpit and said, "We are all ready, Take us home. Can you keep the altitude low, so we don't have a big pressure change? The baby is sleeping!"

Doug and the agent found their own little cubbyhole, as did Maria and Alice. Tom and Jean Paul sat across the aisle from Maria so she could hear and contribute the silent partner discussion.

Tom asked, "Jean, do you have any first thoughts about this silent partner decision?"

Jean said, "His offer came as a bit of a surprise to me. I don't have any problem with Gerald. As you know, he and Etienne have worked together as partners for a long time. There has never been a problem with them. They have done well together. His business is going to change in the sense that they share information back and forth so both new about the U.S. market and the European market on commodities.

That lent them a much broader possibility for capitalizing on the combined markets. He may want to take another partner. In fact, if he asks me, I will suggest that he try to find someone new in Etienne's affiliation. That won't have anything to do with your silent partnership. I think that if you trust him, and he takes on a new partner, you might earn better on the commodities market than you do on Northern's portfolio. Combine the two and you should do very well. It still comes down to a matter of trust. I'll take care of the legalities for you if you decide to do that."

Tom asked, "What do you think, Maria?"

She said, "I like Gerald and have the inclination to trust him. I think that is the crucial factor, trust. He knows his business as did Etienne. This could be a good arrangement for us."

Tom added, "That settles it. Let us talk about it again tomorrow after we meet with the Muskegon bankers. Jean, could you stay another day in Chicago to get it set up or will you need more time?"

Jean said, "I can get it started but it will mean another trip back as we put it together. I'll call Gerald and see what he sees as a timetable."

Tom said, "Maybe he would take you on as a silent partner as well. Would you be interested? We need to find some way to compensate you for the extra work you are doing."

"I've said it before, Etienne provided very well for me. Let me sleep on that."

The pilot announced their arrival and asked them to buckle up. He told them they would be on the ground by 6:15 pm.

Maria said, "I'm getting hungry. What are we doing for dinner?"

Tom smiled, "That's my lady. Always hungry. Jean Paul, have you ever had lake perch with all the fixings? And how about you, Agent Jones?"

Both said in unison, "No, but it sounds interesting."

Doug chimed in. "I'll take my car if someone can drive the rest to your house. I'd like Paul to go with you to your house and I'll stop and bring the goodies."

Alice, in Maria's arms, woke up. She said, "Maman."

By the time Doug got to their house with the Doo Drop goodies, Tom had the table set for six and the wine ready to pour. While the food was being laid out, Doug called Chief Mark to tell him they were all back in town. Doug was told that there were no new developments except that the security contingent had arrived and were being organized into teams. Doug thanked him and said he would see him tomorrow.

They toasted a successful day in Chicago. As before, Doug had brought something special for Alice. But she spotted the perch right away and wanted some. It wasn't long before she started to nod. Maria said, "Will you excuse me gentlemen, I'm going to put our baby to bed. See you in a little while."

Tom took Alice, carried her into her bedroom, and kissed her goodnight. He also gave Maria a hug and a kiss along with a promise for later. He went back to the dining area and the men to join the conversation.

Doug told the group what he had learned and said, "Your 24-hour watch teams will start when we leave tonight." Maria came back and joined them with another glass of wine. All left as soon as Doug welcomed the first watch. He reminded them all that there was an appointment with Mr. John Strahan of New Shores Bank at 10 am tomorrow morning and that he would pick them up.

25

Next morning, Tuesday, Doug, Agent Jones, and Jean Paul picked up Tom, Maria, and Alice for the short ride downtown to the New Shores Bank. Tom had arranged the meeting last week when he knew what Jean Paul's schedule was. Mr. Strahan's executive assistant, Mrs. Arnson, was waiting outside of their suite of offices when the group entered. She recognized Tom and Maria who were customers of the bank. She introduced herself and waved to the chief teller that this was the group so she could alert Mr. Strahan.

Mr. Strahan came out of his office to greet Tom and Maria. He said, "I didn't remember that you would have your little one with you. Why don't we step into our conference room?"

He asked Tom whom he had met to make the introductions. Tom did so starting with Alice, Maria, and Doug. Mr. Strahan shook hands with Doug saying, "I seem to remember you."

Doug said, "I was a part of the team working with the police on the Group of Nine case. That's likely where we met. This gentleman is Agent Paul Jones, my partner. Tom can tell you as much as he sees fit about why we are here. We'll leave now and be out in the lobby." Mrs. Arnson escorted them out and showed them where they could get coffee if they wanted it.

When they left, Tom said, "This gentleman is one I spoke to you about. Allow me to introduce you to Monsieur Jean Paul Lament. Jean Paul is our attorney of record in France. Jean Paul, this is John Strahan, president of the bank."

After a little chit-chat over coffee, Mr. Strahan said, "Tom, you were quite mysterious when we talked last week. Can you enlighten me now?"

Tom said, "I'd love to." Tom told him in a shortened version of some of the events and what they had led to. He continued, "This little one, Alice, is now our daughter, adopted in France and come to live with us in Muskegon. We knew if something happened to Celeste and/or Etienne that we would be raising her. Celeste and Maria made this commitment a long time ago and I became part of the promise. What we didn't know until just before Celeste passed that we had an inheritance coming. We didn't know how much until the wills were read. The reality is still sinking in with us."

Mr. Strahan said, "I have three questions. Why is Monsieur Lament here? Why here and not another bank here in town, and how much money are we talking about?"

Tom said, "Jean Paul was Etienne's attorney, and later both his and Celeste's attorney for over 25 years. Their relationship is one of the most unique I have ever seen. It has paid off handsomely for both of them. As I said earlier he is now our attorney of record for our affairs in France, our new home in Sucy en Brie, France, and Alice's affairs as well.

"As to why your bank, it is a combination of many things. We both, Maria and I, had accounts here beginning when we became teachers at Muskegon Senior High school. I was part of the investigation team who took down the Group of Nine over the last year or so. I was impressed with your commitment to helping us several times. And finally, Jean Paul and the people at Northern Trust investigated your bank. By the way, all reports said you were the bank we should use."

Mr. Strahan interrupted, "Why did you go to all that trouble, checking us out with Northern Trust and Monsieur Lament?"

Tom smiled, "Maria and I personally and me as I said earlier from what I learned about you during that investigation of the Group of

Nine gave us all we needed to choose you and your bank. And of course, Jean Paul is not going to let us do anything wrong. That comes to the third question. We are talking about several million dollars, three million of which we want to put into your bank. That will be one million dollars in an investment account for Alice, our names on it too." Jean Paul handed him a certified check for the one million made out to New Shores Bank. "The other two million will go into our account or maybe split between an investment account and our current joint account we have here. We'll talk later and lean to you as to how to make the split." Jean Paul handed him a certified check for the two million dollars.

Mr. Strahan said, "I think I need something more than a cup of coffee, but we don't do that on premises. You kept this pretty quiet."

Maria spoke up, "Jean Paul asked us if we wanted a spot of brandy before we were told about the terms of the will. We took him up on it afterwards." Maria speaking made Alice stir from her nap though she went right back to sleep.

Tom said, "By the way, we were in Chicago yesterday, meeting Etienne's partner in their joint endeavors in commodities and the people at Northern Trust. They have only good words about you and your bank.'

"That's good to hear. We do a fair amount of business with them."

Tom said, "There is one request we have for you. We want our newfound wealth to be our and your business, only ours and your bank. Can you do that, Mr. Strahan?"

"We can and will. We can have all accounts marked so that nothing is revealed. Do you need that to be true for your checking and savings accounts as well? And I have a question or two for you?"

Tom said, "We would like to keep it quiet except for our regular accounts. I will be returning soon to my job as interim chief of detectives at the Muskegon police department. I will be there at least several weeks, maybe up to three or four months. I haven't yet figured out what I want to do with the rest of my life but we need some time to settle into a new life with our daughter. Toward that end, we need to buy a house with a little more room than we have in the house we have been renting. We have lived there since we got married but now with Alice we need more room. I have some extra money from our time in France and cash that we took out of our Sucy account. I want to put that in our joint savings account for use as the down payment on a house. Then I hope we can get a mortgage through your bank. We want to look like any other citizen and not like anyone with money. Again, can you help us keep it quiet?"

"We can and we will, Tom. Count on it. By the way, do you have a realtor yet?"

Tom said, "Not yet. Is there someone you could recommend?"

"Let me make a phone call. We have a firm we dealt with when we bought our home. She might be a good person to start with. I'll call you in the next day or so."

"Good. Thank you. Now what other questions do you have, Mr. Strahan?"

"First of all, my name is John Strahan, John. I would be pleased if you would call me John in our private meetings. I suspect there will be a few of those down the line."

"John, I would be pleased to do that."

"And how about you, Monsieur Lament?"

"Of course, John. And please call me Jean Paul."

John asked, "How long will you be in Muskegon, Jean Paul?"

He said, "At most another day. I need to confer some more with Tom and Maria. And if I might, if our discussions involves the bank may I call on you again?"

John said, "Just give me a call and I'll arrange some time. Now, I have one more question. My wife and I would like to invite you all to our home tonight. We will have some caterers come in and prepare a meal. We'll enjoy some wine, good food and a good time. What do you think?"

After checking with everyone else, all of whom nodded yes, Tom said, "we would love to."

"Let me confer with my wife so she can get the catering arranged. How many will there be?"

"Five if you include Doug and Agent Jones, plus Alice."

"I'll be right back."

When he returned, he said, "We're on at six. Martha said we even have a highchair for Alice. And if you wish, maybe you can clue me in a little as to why you need the security?"

Tom said, "Why don't I share a little about that now and we can keep tonight light. You see, on our recent trip to Paris, we were on Doug's team to help protect President Charles de Gaulle when he met with our Speaker of the House. During the encounter with a group who tried to assassinate De Gaulle, I shot someone in the group of assassins and some of them are in the states. Doug's agency believes they are here for revenge. The agency has a large force here to make sure they don't get close. We don't want the general public to know as it might create some panic. The agency believes they will take them into custody before they get anywhere close."

"So, if you will, no talk of this tonight. Thank you for making time for us. We'll be prompt tonight." They left and drove to the police station as he had promised when he talked to Chief Mark.

After Mark was introduced to Alice, he asked Gerri if she would spend some time with Alice and Maria. He then took Tom, Doug, and his partner Paul into his office where they were surprised to find special agent Alec Hall of the Detroit FBI office. After introductions were made, Doug asked, "Alec, how is it you are in charge of this protection operation?"

Alec said, "The agency that you contract with wanted us to be involved since any possible action that comes up will be on American soil. There is a combined total of 40 plus people from the two agencies. Mark has many others that can be called in if needed. The order to do a combined force came directly from President Kennedy."

Mark said, "I heard about your activities in France. And Tom, you didn't tell me about all this and your commendation. Congratulations!"

"Sorry Mark, I would have gotten to it soon. Is there any more news about the OAS in the states?"

Alec answered, "We have a BOLO on for the entire eastern half of the country. We now have pictures of four of them but there have been no sightings yet. With twenty teams floating around town, we feel we are ready for them if they come this way."

Mark said, "We are good for now. Let us see how the ladies are getting along. Tom, before you leave, can I have a few minutes with you?"

Gerri had brought in some toys for Alice. She and Maria were having a good meeting as they kept watching Alice. Alice related quickly to Gerri. She had already offered some baby-sitting time when Maria became ready to allow that to happen. Doug waited with them while Tom and Mark talked.

In Mark's office, Tom asked, "Is my protégé Gene ready to work with me?"

"He is still in training with the state police school investigating course. He should be finished with that by the end of October. He will be here full-time. Can you be ready to spend some time with him after that?"

Tom said, "That will give us enough time to buy a new house. We're hoping to find something in the Beechwood or Bluffton area. During that time I could be available for consultation. And then when he is here full time, would one to two months of full-time work with him be enough to get him ready?"

"It should be enough. Have you come any closer to what you will do long term?"

"Nothing firm yet, but some new opportunities and offers have come along. I should be solid on it in the next few weeks. And, of course, I would like to remain available to you in a consulting relationship for as long as I can. The one thing I will be doing, no question, is to figure out how I can help Muskegon become what Fred and I talked so much about. I'll know better after what a role for me in that might be. I'm not at all sure that being involved in city politics is a good thing for me. I'll get it all figured out soon."

"There is one other thing that plays into what I do. We have discovered that Alice is a pretty special little girl. Maria hasn't decided how that will affect her work. She has decided she is ready to become a full-time Mom until Alice is well established in school. We'll be talking a lot about these things when we get practical things done. A new home for us is a high priority right now. We owe Celeste and Etienne the best we can give Alice. We will find our way soon."

Mark asked, "Have you thought about your possible involvement if the OAS makes it here?"

"We'll see when and if that time comes."

26

———————

Doug took Tom, Maria, and Alice back home. He introduced them to the day shift of their protection team. He said, "I have to meet with Alec and some others. I'll lend Jean Paul my rental car so he can come here for your time with him. I'll give you a call tomorrow but if you need to talk before that, you know how to get me. See you soon."

Maria said to Tom, "It is getting close to her nap time. While I change her, would you get out the lunch I fixed this morning? We'll feed her, get her to sleep, and have a chance to talk before Jean Paul comes."

Tom said, "Just the three of us!" They shared their lunch and got Alice off to sleep.

Maria said, "She will be out for a while. Do you want anything to drink?"

"No, we'll have some wine when Jean Paul comes. You seem to have something on your mind. So let's talk about it. I've sensed that you have some notions about how we both will change."

"A part of your role is already solved. You've said you will be working in the police department for at least a few months. We could also go ahead with hanging out our shingle as a two-person private detective agency. After your time as acting chief, we could use the agency as cover, you take on any consulting arrangement that Mark might have. And to keep up the façade, we might even promote the agency a bit. That's sort of what we were planning while I completed my training. If we don't get any jobs right away, even for a year or more, that's okay. New businesses are like that."

"You've done a bit of thinking about it. I think it will work. I could use some of the time to make contacts with potential clients. So my role, besides being a new father, is pretty well set. I suspect you have another path for yourself that I don't know about yet."

"Yes, Tom. I have been thinking about that. To the world outside of our home, er, our new home, I'm doing studies to qualify to be a full-fledged detective and partner. Just as we had planned before. But I'm not really going to be doing that."

Tom sat still, not saying anything, knowing Maria had more to say.

She continued, "I've been watching new mothers, talking with them, reading about my new role, and here's what I've come to. We have a perfect situation for what we both know we have to do. So here it is. I want to be a full-time mother at least until Alice starts first grade and is in school all day. I'll be doing some studying but I don't know yet on what. Maybe to become a detective, maybe something else. But from this time forward, until we, together, know that the time is right, I want me to be a full-time mother and you a full-time father. Now that we know a little about what a special little girl Alice is, we can best do what Celeste and Etienne asked us to do by being full-time at it. I'm ready to make that commitment. I'll know when the right thing comes along for me to do. I suspect you will find that too, even though like me, you don't know what that might be yet. So, Tom…"

Tom sat, stunned for just a few seconds, then reached for Maria. "You are amazing. You have found a path for us. How did you do this in such a short time?"

"I started thinking about it in Sucy. I talked to Belle who was, I think, more tuned in to how smart Alice is than we knew at that point. The best part of this is that we can do this together."

Tom, excited now, said, "You have helped me to make a decision of my own. You'll remember that Gerald mentioned that if I wanted to, he would tutor me and teach me the business. I was uneasy about that and now I will tell him no. We should talk with Jean Paul today about becoming a silent partner.

He continued, "Hey, you know what else we could do together? We could hire someone who could teach Alice English while at the same time we learn French. You've talked before about finding someone at Hope College or Grand Valley State College. Maybe there is someone in town here at one of the local high schools. We could get some children's books and teach her the names of things in both languages."

He laughed, "I'm getting ahead of myself here."

"I love it when you do. I think our highest priority right now should be getting into another house. I think we ought to take as much as we can of the furniture we have to start with so Alice doesn't have to cope with another big change all at once. We can then replace items over the next few years."

The phone rang. Tom grabbed it quickly so it didn't wake Alice. It was John Strahan. He said, "I have a realtor's name for you. I wanted to call you myself and if you agree, I'll ask her to call you. "

Tom said, "Thank you, John. Could you ask her to call us tomorrow morning? Jean Paul is coming any time now for our last talk with him for a while. Would that be okay?"

John said, "That will be fine. You can expect a call in the morning."

Tom said, "John, we want to thank you again for last night. It was a lovely time, meeting your wife and children. Also for all the quick arrangements you made at the bank."

"You're welcome. We enjoyed your visit. Martha especially enjoyed meeting Alice. Our children are much older, but we have no grandchildren yet. I'll be in touch soon for another meeting at the bank."

"We'll see you soon."

Tom prepared the charcuterie board and opened a highly recommended Beaujolais. Alice stirred, Maria went to her, changed her, and brought her out, putting her down on the rug in front of the sofa for some play time.

Jean Paul identified himself to the protection team. He knocked. Tom let him in saying, "Welcome to our home, come in. There is a friend here who will want to see you and talk with you."

Alice saw Jean Paul and went to him when he sat on the sofa. He said, *"Bonjour, Mademoiselle Alice."* He held out his arms and Alice climbed up on his lap. They shared a hug. Alice seemed happy to see him.

When Tom set the charcuterie board on the coffee table, Maria took her, put her in her new movable chair with a tray for food or whatever. She locked the wheels and put some pieces of cheese on the tray. Tom poured the Beaujolais for the three of them along with some grape juice for Alice. When they raised their glasses in a toast, Alice did too. Jean Paul said, "A toast to a new family in a new place. Everything is coming together for you." They touched glasses, Alice as well, as she looked each in the eyes. He continued, "She picked up on that so quickly. She is so bright."

Maria said, "We were just talking about that." She told Jean Paul about their new plans to be into the house quickly and start as full-time parents for Alice.

Jean said, "Celeste and Etienne would be so pleased with your plans. I am. You could do nothing better. I hope you can find someone quickly to help with the languages for all of you."

Tom told him about John's call and their meeting with the realtor soon. Jean said, "I'm also pleased that you will not becoming a commodities trader. Not that you couldn't. It seems to me that your talents lie elsewhere. Now, a silent partnership with Gerald is something else. Do you have other thoughts about that?"

Tom said, "We are considering it. If we do it, there are decisions to be made about how much we invest. Our expectation is that Northern will do very well for us. We don't want to upset our new relationship with Northern."

Jean said, 'Why don't you let me negotiate that with them? I'm thinking about doing the same. I'm sure we can work it out with Northern. I'm going to spend most of tomorrow with Sam, your Northern representative, and Gerald. I'll call you to discuss it tomorrow afternoon. If you approve, we can get it all set up before I fly out the next morning for home. By the way, I would like to have them copy me on your status with them at the end of each month. Are you okay with that?"

Tom looked at Maria, she nodded, so he said, "That will work fine. We'll be meeting tomorrow morning with a real estate person that John has recommended."

Maria asked, "Do you have any reservations about John?"

Jean Paul smiled, "No. Not at all. I think you are in good hands with him. I hope you realize that keeping your new wealth private will become more difficult as you, Tom, become active in the community."

Tom answered, "I'll be taking it slowly. Alice's needs are first, getting settled into another home is next. When I can, I'll begin exploring things with old friends in the city and see what develops. We can keep the wealth private as I move slowly into what is happening in the city and in the city government. For some time, we'll just be a new family settling in. I'll keep you posted."

"Do you have any thoughts yet about your first time back in Sucy?"

Maria answered, "We haven't talked about that yet. It seems to me that it ought to be sometime next spring. We'll see how Alice is coming and make our decision later."

Jean said, "So much depends on how Alice is doing. I think your focus on her and settling in here should be your first concern. You'll know when it is right. I should be getting back. Doug and Alec want to have a chat tonight over dinner. Doug has kindly arranged to have the agency plane fly me to Chicago and then they will continue back to D.C. My flight back home from Chicago leaves the next morning. Thank you for the excellent wine and cheeses." He had a hug for Maria and Alice, then a hug and handshake for Tom. "I'm going to miss all of you. I've become very fond of you three."

Tom walked him to his car. When he came back in, he found Maria with tears in her eyes. She said, "He is such a friend, I don't know how we could have done all this without him."

27

Next morning they were roused by Alice saying "*Maman.*" Maria shook Tom and asked, "How about a little three-way cuddle time? We haven't done that in a while."

Tom reached for her and gave her a kiss. He said, "I'll get my pjs back on while you go get her."

Maria changed Alice, put on a dry gown, came back in, and handed her to Tom, saying, "*Voici, Papa.*"

Tom took her with both hands, held her up high at arm's length and said, "*Un câlin pour papa?*" He brought her down, they shared a hug, and Tom put her between them.

Alice turned to Maria and said, "*Maman, un câlin?*" They hugged. Maria giggled followed by Alice.

Tom asked, "Do you suppose *câlin* is a new word for her?"

"I don't know. That is a 'hugging' bunch in Sucy. We can count it as a new word if we want to."

The phone rang. Tom said, "That may be the realtor. I'll get it."

"Hello and good morning."

"Good morning to you. Is this Tom O'Banion?"

"Yes, who am I speaking with?"

"This is Jeanne Hanley of Fagan Realty. John Strahan asked me to call you. I understand you are looking for a house and want to move quickly on it."

"We are all of those things. When could we meet with you?"

"Will this morning work?"

"It would be better if you could come here this afternoon. We have an almost two-and-a-half-year-old and she has her nap in the early afternoon, so around 2:00."

"I can do that. Do you have some idea of where you want to live?"

"We live in a rented home in the Bluffton area. We are hoping to stay in this area or maybe somewhere in the Beech St. area." He gave her their address.

"I'll be there. If you could have some tea, I'll bring some of my homemade scones."

"That would be wonderful. We'll be ready for you. By the way, does your car have a realty sign on it and what color is it?"

"It does. Why do you ask?"

"I'll explain when you are here. We are on the right after you turn on to our street. See you soon, Mrs. Hanley."

She arrived a little early. The protection team didn't pay her any attention. Tom had alerted them and told them she was expected. She came with a cookie tin and a collection of listings. When she knocked, Tom was right there to let her in. He introduced himself and Maria and said, "Why don't we sit at our dining table so we can spread things out and still enjoy our coffee or tea and your scones? Thank you for bringing them."

"John said you would be right on top of things. And here's the proof. Thank you. I like this arrangement but usually have to set it up myself. Let's get to it. And please call me Jeanne."

"We're Tom and Maria."

"Now that I've met you, I know where it was that I had seen you. When I walked in, I was sure I knew you from somewhere. It was at St Mary's. That's our home church. But we've never met. You said Bluffton or Beechwood area. Do you have a preference for either?"

"We are in the Bluffton area now but I'm not sure we're going to find what we want here."

"Can you give me a list of what you might need? You only have the one child but are you planning for more?"

Maria said, "Let me explain. We've only been married about a year and a half. We can't have children of our own. We were eventually planning to adopt in a couple of years. But some recent events in France changed all that. Alice is nearly three and we just adopted her. She is French but is just building a vocabulary now and knows no English other than what we have taught her in the last three weeks. We had a covenant with her parents that we would raise Alice if something happened to her parents. And now here we are, learning how to be parents and to a little French girl at that. We're loving it already but we have a long way to go with her."

Jeanne said, "I can't wait to meet her. Her name is lovely. How is it spelled?"

"It is spelled like the American 'Alice' but is pronounced 'Ahlese.' And already we are *Maman* and *Papa*."

Maria continued, "Tom has a list of what we think we need."

"Here is a copy for you. Just follow me down the list. Please. We want a living room somewhat larger than this one, a fireplace is a must, a dining room, a larger kitchen than we have here, and we think four bedrooms, two full baths, a laundry room, and a two-car garage. Did I miss anything, Maria?"

"No, except for lots of closets. And, oh yes, a breakfast bar in the kitchen. We both enjoy cooking but are used to electric so we would prefer that. And finally a big back yard for Alice."

Jeanne exclaimed, "Oh, my. John said you would be looking for something far bigger than what you were currently living in. But what your list tells me is that most of the listings I brought won't work for you. May I ask, why four bedrooms? Three bedrooms is more common around here."

"We need a master bedroom for us. A smaller one but big enough for Alice. Tom will very shortly be working mostly from home, doing consulting work so he'll need an office, and finally a spare bedroom for guests. In addition, we need a place for a piano. Tom is a pianist and choir conductor."

Jeanne looked at Tom and Maria. "I know another place where I have seen you two. You, Tom, did choir concerts at Muskegon High School. And you, Maria, were the drama teacher and director in the drama program. And I saw you perform Anna in Muskegon Civic Theatre's production of *The King And I*. You are terrific!"

"Uh Oh, we're busted." And they all laughed.

Jeanne asked, "What about schools?"

Maria explained, "We don't know yet what we will have to do about schools. We began to see in France that Alice is a special child, very bright. We have seen things since we came back home that tells us we have underestimated her. We may have to find a special school but we don't know if we should go that route. We would like her to have as normal a life as other children but to be able to reach her potential."

Tom poured some more coffee and brewed Jeanne some more tea.

Jeanne looked from one to the other and finally said, "I sense that you already know how much of a job you have with your child. I agree with that assessment. But we need to get you into a house that fits your needs right now. That has to be our priority. I have a house that could work. It is on the edge of the Bluffton area – an older home. We just got the listing and I haven't shown it yet. It is expensive, over \$100,000. These folks are moving to Florida and have already bought a house there so they might come down from their asking price. They are down there moving in as we speak. Rather than tell you more about it, I'd like to take you to see it. You can judge for yourselves. Do you have time tomorrow?"

Maria looked at Tom, 'Do you have anything going tomorrow morning?"

"No, I don't. What do you have in mind?"

Turning to Jeanne, Maria asked, "How about 10:00 in the morning?"

Jeanne replied, "That will be good. The house is on Beech St. Do you want to ride over with me or follow me there?"

"Would you mind coming here again? We'll follow you over. We're due to see both our parents and need to be back here between noon and 1 p.m."

"That will work. I'll be here about 15 minutes early. So good to have met you both. I'm looking forward to meeting Alice tomorrow. I don't have any French. How should I answer when we are introduced?"

"Just say, *bonjour* Alice. She will love it that you do."

When they were alone, Tom said, "This is really happening fast. I think we should postpone things with the folks and reschedule when we know we can make it work." They each called their parents, explained that they were looking at a house that might work for them and that they would call them later and set something else up. It was okay with each.

28

———————

Tom was out talking with their protection team when Jeanne arrived. Tom introduced them. Maria and Alice came out. Tom said, "Here she is, Jeanne. Alice, *voici Mme*. Hanley."

"*Bonjour*, Alice." Alice smiled,

Jeanne said, "What a lovely child!"

They drove as if going to the Ovals but turned left driving on Beech St. past the water filtration plant and continued on with a sand dune on their left and a beach on Lake Michigan on their right. Beech St. then curved left away from the lake and then right just after Beechwood Park, Jeanne turned into a driveway, and they followed in. Alice hadn't missed a thing sitting in Maria's lap. She was excited and pointing at everything that was new to her.

They entered at the front door to a small foyer with the living room to the right and the dining room to the left. Maria turned Alice loose on the living room carpet and she set out to explore. Jeanne said, "Let her roam, we'll follow her and we'll see it all."

Tom said, "I like that fireplace at the other end of the living room. The free-floating dark wood mantel is gorgeous. And see how that stone just leads you up to the mantel. " Jeanne didn't say anything. Tom was doing what she hoped, selling himself and Maria.

Alice led them into the kitchen and both Maria and Tom were oohing and aahing. Both of them cooked. But Maria was checking it out. She said, "It is almost as though it was made for us, there is a breakfast nook with room enough for a small table and chairs and a breakfast bar on the other side." She picked up Alice and sat her on one of the highchairs at the breakfast bar and stayed there with her. Alice wasn't having it. She wanted to explore.

It seemed as though it was meant for them, everything they wanted and more. After they had found all the other rooms, they checked the big back yard that would need to be fenced in. When Maria said, "I'd like some different chairs and table for the breakfast nook," Jeanne knew they wanted the house. She took them to the basement that housed the gas furnace and water heater on one side and was unfinished on the other side.

Jeanne said, "They told me they had given away everything on the unfinished side. They left the ping pong table thinking a buyer might want it."

Maria asked, "Can we go back upstairs and talk?"

Tom said, "It sounds like your mind is made up."

"You know me too well. How about you?"

"Jeanne, let's get somewhere we can talk. Maybe back at our house? What do you think?"

Jeanne said, "I am pleased that it works for you. You haven't said anything about an offer. While I would like to get their price for them, I want to make sure you get the best price for you. While we are driving back, why don't you think about all you have to do and what you might like to offer?"

When they were back in the house, Maria said, "Alice was so busy over at the new house, she seems exhausted. I'll get her a snack and put her down for a nap. Maybe the two of you could get our questions answered." Tom and Jeanne settled again at the dining room table with more coffee and tea. She also had the house data book ready for Tom. By the time Maria got back, all of Tom's questions were answered.

Maria asked Tom if he was satisfied and ready to buy. Tom said, "I am satisfied and yes I'm ready."

She turned to Jeanne and said, "We want the house. We're ready to pay their price."

Jeanne said, "I'd be willing to bet they would come down. I've looked it over carefully and I'll leave it here so you can do the same. But my best guess is that they would be willing to drop the price a bit for a quick sale and cash. They are asking $120,000 but I bet they would take $115,000. Why don't you offer $110,000, and let them come back to you? I bet I can sell that to them."

Maria shook her head, "We don't want to lose it, They might want to see what someone else might pay."

"I don't think they will do that. Let me call John. Between the two of us, we can close it quickly. John said that you have the down payment and are preapproved for the mortgage. Let him work his magic."

Maria said, "But don't forget we are willing to pay their price."

When the phone rang, Tom answered quickly so it wouldn't wake Alice. It was Doug who said, "We're on our way with a bigger crew. We're about five minutes out. Three OAS people are in town and we think heading to your house. We'll have a welcoming committee inside your house and others hidden around it. We also have teams headed for both sets of parents." Tom tried to ask a question, but Doug said, "Don't delay, Tom. We're about three minutes away And make sure your guys watching now don't know where you are going. Don't let them see what direction you are going. If they push, you might say we're going out for a bite to eat with Doug."

Tom said, "We have to leave in a couple of minutes. Get Alice wrapped. I'll grab her go bag, some snacks for us, and my weapon. Jeanne, could we go back to our house-to-be? No one but the three of us know where that house is, right?"

`"That's right Tom, I didn't tell John. My realty office knows but I can call them after we get there. Their phone is still hooked up until Monday. I won't say anything about what is happening. We're just going back for another look at some things."

"We'll follow Jeanne to the house."

Doug pulled into the driveway. Tom, Maria, and Alice got into the middle seat that had just been vacated. Three other agents were in the back seat and Doug had one with him in the front seat. There was one other agent in Jeanne's car with her.

The second and third vans followed Doug in and dropped several agents off. The drivers left to park several blocks away. The agents took the regular day shift protection unit into Tom and Maria's house and left two new agents in their car. They intended to surround the OAS men and get them under arrest without gun fire.

The vehicles with Jeanne in the lead headed down Lakeshore Drive as though they were looking for a restaurant. But they turned at McCracken St. instead then down to Sherman. They turned right and approached the new house from there, hiding both vehicles in the double garage.

29

The team led by Alec, the FBI agent in charge, had nine men inside the house, two at the sides of each door, front, back, and garage. He had stationed a man hidden in the garage, a man in the main bedroom, and a man in the bathroom. All were expected to play a surprise once the six near the doors had engaged the OAS. Per Alec's instructions, lights were on in the living room and music was playing softly.

He also had two vans located at houses covering two routes to the house. Each had three men in them including the driver. Finally there was a sedan following the OAS vehicle at a long distance. There were other cars with local police further out. This vehicle had sent a double-click signal that the OAS was nearly at the turn, When they turned into the house, they stopped to look around. Seeing nothing amiss, they moved slowly to stop just outside the driveway where Tom's car was parked. Two of the men exited the car with their guns ready and started walking toward the front door and the garage door. The third man held back but was focused on the house and didn't see the two men exit from Tom's car. They waited, watching for things to start.

Both the front door and the garage door exploded from the charges they had placed. The front door went first. The man stepped in only to have a gun placed first on his right side and then on his left side when he reacted. The procedure was the same at the garage door. Two OAS men were subdued and down on the floor cuffed. The man outside could see the front door man on the floor. He turned to go back to their car but was confronted by two men with guns trained on him. One said, "Drop your gun." He turned toward the man at the front of the car, lifted his gun, and was shot by the man at the back of the car.

"All clear inside, both men down and secured. What happened out there?" sounded on their walkie talkies.

"It is okay to come out. The outside man is down and bleeding badly. We're going to need some medical help. They will call for medical help and then come in to transport our captives to their lockup."

When all had gathered outside the house, Alec said, "Thank you all for a near perfect capture. None of the good guys were hurt, that's important. One of the OAS was shot but he'll heal. Best of all, Doug and his charges are fine. I need to call Doug on the police phone and let him know what happened. Two men, Muskegon police, will soon be here and guard the premises until those doors get fixed so our friends can move back in."

"The men who were assigned to Tom and Maria's said they would stay but were told we didn't need them here right now. I would like to get all our people back on regular assignment as soon as possible. We need the whole team until we get our first interrogation finished and we are certain there are no more OAS in this country. Our hope is these three are the only ones here. In the meantime, please be patient. We'll get you back to your home base as quickly as we can. Until then, please stay at the hotel. There will be a meeting at the police department for all of us from each agency for a debriefing. We'll let you know when."

Alec called Doug on the walkie talkie system, gave him a quick rundown, and told him that it was ok for them to come home when the doors were fixed, that it was safe for the O'Banions now, and asked him to come over for a quick talk.

Doug gave Tom, Maria, and Jeanne a quick synopsis of what had happened. He said, "I need to go over there and check it out before I can let you go back. The good news is that you are safe."

Maria asked, "Do you know for certain that there is not another team of them?"

"I don't know that for certain right now. My first thought is they only sent this one group. That's the way they operate. We'll know more after we get done questioning them both here and back in the DC area."

She asked, "Will you keep some sort of force here?"

Doug continued, "We will. And when you close on this house, our agency will set it up with security like we have at your home in Sucy."

Tom said, "We can pay for that."

"Our agency will cover it. You put your life on the line in France and we take care of our own, even though you will no longer be directly involved.

"Let me get over there and I will be back within an hour and we'll see where we go from now.

After Doug left, Jeanne said, "I want to give my office a call to let them know that I'll be along soon. And with damage to your home that may keep you from staying there, I'd like to talk with John about how we can get you in here faster. I have a question. Tom, how much can I tell John about your activities in France, your commendation, and your ties with the agencies?"

"You don't know the whole story yet. There are some things that I can't tell you. But you can tell him what you know. What do you have in mind?"

"Let me talk with John first. Maybe there is a way to get you here as early as tomorrow. When John and I have a plan, I'll get back to you."

Tom asked, "Do you feel comfortable being out and about again?"

"I do. And I can call you today on this phone. There is no connection there that ties back to your home. I'll be in touch soon."

Alec filled Doug in on his plan and how well it worked. He told me that he was sorry about the doors but that he didn't anticipate OAS blowing them out. Doug said, "I'm glad you were on this job. There are so many things that could have gone bad. I'd like to be there for that first questioning of the three OAS men."

Alec said, "I don't want to have you where they can see you. Does the department have a one-way window with sound piped to you?"

"It does. That would work. Can you be there yet this afternoon?"

"I only need to stop for a few minutes to make sure Tom and Maria's protection detail is there and then I can be right over. Maybe a half hour."

30

When Doug knocked on the door, Tom was on the phone with Jeanne, their realtor. Maria let him in and got a hug from him. Doug asked, "What is happening with the house?"

She answered, "Hang on for a few minutes and Tom can tell you."

Tom said to Jeanne, "That is good news. And we can stay here tonight?"

Jeanne replied," John worked it all out with them for $115,000. I'll be there in about a half hour with papers for you to sign showing your $20,000 down payment. Mr. and Mrs. Anderson are doing a set of papers. John is arranging all the details to be done by tomorrow afternoon late. And the Andersons said you can stay here tonight. By the way, since you may not be able to move much over tonight, my husband, Bud, suggested that we bring camp cots and a crib if that's okay with you."

Tom exclaimed, "Thank you, Jeanne. You made some magic happen. We'll treat this as an adventure for the three of us. See you soon."

He repeated everything to Maria and Doug. She had a tear when she asked, "So the house is ours?"

Tom said, "It is ours, sweetheart. We'll get some things from the old house and get a mover going tomorrow to get everything else."

Doug said, "I'll wait until they get here so I can meet them. I'll also work out another protection team for the trip to the other house. I shouldn't be more than an hour for the first questioning of the OAS men. That should put me here around five."

They heard the car doors and soon a knock on the door. Tom let Jeanne and Bud in and they were all introduced. Bud asked, "Where's that little girl of yours? Jeanne can't stop talking about her."

Maria said, "She fell asleep. She had a busy time showing us the house."

They all heard, "*Maman. Maman.*"

"There she is now. She is on the carpet, the only soft place here for now." She cuddled Alice close. Alice spotted Jeanne and smiled.

Jeanne said, "Alice, this is Bud."

Bud took her hand, kissed it, and said, "*Bonsoir, Alice. Comment va tu?*"

Suddenly shy, Alice cuddled closer to Maria, then looked back, said, "*Bonsoir*, Bud." and smiled.

Jeanne laughed, "Ah, ha. Another woman in your life."

Doug said, "Good to meet you both." To Tom and Maria, he said, "I'll be back in about an hour with some food." Then to Jeanne and Bud, he asked, "Would you like to join us for a pickup dinner?"

Jeanne smiled, "Thank you, but our children are here for a visit and are waiting at home. It's taco night, their favorite. How about a rain check?"

Tom said, "You have a deal."

Doug left. Tom, Bud, and Jeanne made quick work of putting the cots and sleeping bags in the living room. Jeanne took the time to tell them about the deal that John had negotiated. She had them both sign the papers. When done, she said, "Welcome to your new home!"

They said, "Thank you Jeanne." And then shared a group hug.

Jeanne added, "The phone company said, if you call them tomorrow, you can change the account to your name. You might want to see what Doug thinks about an unlisted number. And John asked if you would give him a call in the next day or two."

Bud said, "Let us know when you are done with the cots and such. We'll come and get them."

Maria said, "Thank you both so much."

"I have to change Alice and get her ready for bed."

Maria said, 'I think we should call our parents and let them know what happened. They'll be anxious because they have protection details, too."

They did so with both parents promising to stay in touch.

Tom heard Doug drive up. He opened the door before the knock. Doug said, "A little anxious to know what we found, are we? We didn't get many facts. They're quite cagey, but after a little time, we got more. They are telling us that there are no others here. I'll give you a little more when Maria is here."

Sure as could be, Doug had brought perch and the fixings from Doo Drop Inn. He said, "I know all of you, including Alice, like them. I even brought a six pack of beer and a bottle of wine. No fancy glasses, but paper cups will work for tonight." The four of them settled into the breakfast nook. It wasn't long before Alice was full and starting to nod off.

When she was asleep, Doug started over. Then he added, "I'm convinced that there are no other cells here from the OAS. In fact, I believe these three are mercenaries playing the role of OAS. I'm not telling anyone about my theory. I want to wait and see what the third man, in the hospital, has to say. And then the investigators at the agency will go after the three together when we get them to DC. They are better than I am at this."

He continued. "If I'm right, and I'm pretty sure I am, it says to me that the OAS doesn't want to come to the U.S. I don't know why but I believe we'll get it figured out."

"Now, how does this affect you three? It means we may be able to put OAS out of business and you are home free. So when I get to DC, observe their investigation, and hear their conclusions, we can reaffirm that. You can have a normal life again."

"In the meantime, I'm having a team come and put in the same security standard that you have in your house in Sucy. Alec and his team did a great job of it at the old house. We'll fix the doors and all you'll have to do over there is get it ready for the next tenant. I'm going to miss that place, Lots of good times there."

Maria said, "How can we ever repay you?"

"Just stay best buddies and do what I know you can do for Alice and for the city of Muskegon."

They clinked glasses of wine –er, paper cups don't clink. But it was a new bonding for these three.

31

Next morning they left a message for Doug saying that they would be at the old house having breakfast. Their protection team would be with them. They removed one of the temporary doors and hung a blanket over it. Tom told them he would fix breakfast for all of them and call them when it was ready.

A half hour later, they all were at the dining table having scrambled eggs, bacon, and pancakes with maple syrup. Tom said, "I'll be right back and we'll have the blessing and enjoy." He took some coffee to the protector outside. Tom told him a replacement would soon come and that he could come in and have breakfast.

When Doug arrived, he slipped in past the blanket and said, "Well now isn't this a fine gathering."

Alice said, "*Bonjour, Oncle* Doug."

He replied, "*Bonjour,* Alice." He took his place at the table and started eating. Tom made some fresh scrambled eggs and pancakes. He gave the inside protector a big mug of coffee and said, "Send your buddy in please."

When he was out the door, Doug said, "You're taking a little liberty here, Tom."

Tom answered, "After our last conversation last night, I thought it was safe enough."

"You are right. But we still don't want a connection between the two houses for a while yet. So let's get you moved, and you can relax even more. There is a crew of retired policemen with pickup trucks and some protection staff who will be here soon with a van and finish up the job."

"That's terrific, Doug," Tom said. He added, "Things happened so fast." When the crew got there, Tom and Maria had the kitchen all cleaned and everything from the kitchen packed in boxes. "I had better call our landlord and tell him we're moving. He'll understand and be okay when we pay next month's rent and forfeit our deposit. We'll have to do the doors later."

Doug said, "I've already talked to him. There is a crew coming after we're done with the move. They'll have it done late this afternoon."

Tom and Maria smiled, "You think of everything, don't you?"

Doug said, "Tom, you, and Maria, have been doing the right thing for so long, we are just following your example."

By two p.m. or so, the job was done. Everything was out of the old house and in the new one. Maria had gone back with the first load and directed where each item was to go. Beds were put together in the master bedroom and Alice's bedroom. Alice was so busy walking all around and making new friends that she soon tired. When Tom, Doug, and the crew finally left, she was sound asleep in her bed. Everyone loved her and learned to work around her. One of the consistent comments from all was 'you don't have enough furniture.'

Maria said, "All of you are right. But we didn't want to take the time to buy furniture. We want to live here a little until the furniture we want will become obvious to us. We'll get there in a while and when we do, we'll have an open house in a few weeks so you can all see what we have done. Then there is another more important reason. Alice has been through enough that we wanted furniture she was used to. We'll get the new things slowly so she can make the adjustment. Thank you all so much for what you have done for us."

She continued, "Tom just got back from a trip to Ettermans and has prepared cheese plates, or charcuterie boards, as we call them in France. We don't have enough places to seat you so some may have to sit on the floor or stand. There's also beer and wine. I know you are former policemen, but you are not on duty now, so have a drink. You are here on a labor of love. Thank you again. Dig in!"

A fun time was had by all. Lots of camaraderie. They all knew each other so it was like old home week. Each promised to come to the open house and bring their spouses. They insisted in a final cleanup, so the house was spic and span when they were all gone.

Doug said, "How about a celebration glass of wine? You're in your new home! And then I'm off to plan tomorrow's interview with the man in the hospital."

Tom built a fire with wood from the old place. The fireplace worked well. Soon they were enjoying a good blaze and had some jazz music going. Doug said, "Here's to your new home and a good life to come in it."

Tom added, "Here's to a best friend. We couldn't have gotten it done without you and your team."

Maria added, "Here's to so many new friends, good new friends, people who cared enough about us that they dropped everything and got our move made."

Tom asked, "When will the surveillance teams be done?"

"If nothing new comes up and the man in the hospital verifies what the others said, we'll be out of your lives so you can get to what you want to. Mark has promised a drive-by several times a day. This is Wednesday. I'll need to get a walk through and get a layout of the house from Jeanne. I want to work with the tech team about your Level Three security. They'll be flying out Monday and so I can walk them through it and then I'll leave them to get back and be debriefed."

"How about your prisoners? How will you get them to DC?"

"There is a prisoner transport on its way. It will come with a four-man team, one for each prisoner and two drivers. They will likely leave sometime on Monday to drive back. By rotating drivers, they'll make it a one-day trip each way. We should be able to have them with the interrogators sometime Tuesday."

Maria asked, "His wounds will allow him to travel so soon?"

Doug smiled, "They were just superficial wounds. He lost some blood but he wasn't seriously injured."

"What are you two up to tomorrow?"

"We will have to get in a good supply of food. Our shelves are larger here and we were a little low at the old house. We need to get our parents over here soon or we'll have a problem with them. They were told we were okay but they'll have to see for themselves, you know. Say, we'll likely have a potluck tomorrow night, as they had planned when the trouble started. I'm sure they would love to see you before you go back."

"That sounds great. What time?"

"Can you be here by 5:30 for Kir Royales before dinner?"

"I can. See you then."

Maria and Tom saw him off. They refilled their wine glasses and cozied up by the fire. For the first time in a while they shared a deep kiss and did an arm wrap toast, "To the three of us, in our new home."

"Let's call the folks. You first."

Maria's mother answered, "I didn't know the number but I just knew it was you. Where are you and what's going on?"

Maria said, "Hi Mom. We're in our new house. A big group of retired policemen from all areas came and before we knew it we were here, not settled in yet but soon, We were wondering if we could have a potluck over here tomorrow night, say about 5:30 pm. Whatever you and Tom's mother can work out since our things are still in boxes. We'll have something to add and have Kir Royale's to celebrate. We'll fill you in tomorrow on so much. Uh oh, I hear a *maman* from her bedroom. Alice has been taking a nap. Tom will call his parents and then you can get together on the menu. Love you Mom."

Tom came out with Alice, all changed and ready for *Maman*. "Thanks, Tom." She and Alice cuddled on the sofa.

Tom called his parents. "Hi Dad, can you get Mom on the extension?" He told them the same thing about the move in.

His mother interrupted, "Are you safe now?"

"We are, Mom. I'll be able to tell you all tomorrow how and why we are safe. What we would like to do is have a potluck dinner over here like you were going to have last week before everything happened."

His dad said, "This is a new number. Are you telling me you got everything done so you are in the house, you have bought it, and the paperwork is all done? You must have had some good help."

"We did, our realtor, Jeanne, was amazing…"

"Hold on. Are you talking about Jeanne Hanley?"

Tom said, "The very one. Do you two know her?

"Yes, through various Catholic activities."

"We couldn't have done it without John Strahan who took care of all the financial details. The previous owners had moved to Florida so he had to do a lot of long-distance persuasion."

"Pretty high company you're in there, my boy."

"I know Dad, but it is just more we have to get used to. Well, what do you say, can you get together with Maria's parents and work up a potluck? We'll take care of the champagne for Kir Royales, the wine, beer and whatever else we can think of, say 5:30 p.m. Love you both."

32

____

Next morning, the family and their protection had breakfast at Cherokee. They were at Etterman's door when they opened. Tom and Maria filled two carts full with enough food and essentials so they wouldn't have to come back for a couple of weeks. The staff came around, greeted them all, especially Alice, as she was their favorite.

Maria set about arranging her cupboards and refrigerator to suit the way she wanted food and dishes. Alice was playing with her toys on the living room floor.

Tom called John Strahan. Tom told him what had happened with the three who were captured at the house. Tom filled him in on where things stood now. He said, "All is well now, John. And between you and Jeanne, everything is settled on the house."

John asked, "Could you all come by tomorrow morning to let me catch you up on where you stand with us and the Andersons, say 10 a.m.?"

"We'll be there. Thank you so much for all you have done."

"See you in the morning."

Tom then called the phone company to see how to get the new unlisted number set up and with a second line for Tom's office. They set it up for the next afternoon at 3:00 p.m.

Maria said, "Tom, I think I have the cupboards and the refrigerator arranged the way we can use it best. We'll see how it goes and change it if we need later."

Continuing, "I had an idea while I was doing the cupboards. I remembered that there is a top-notch French teacher at Muskegon Sr. High. I don't know her well but I want to call her to see if she can help in finding someone for us."

Tom said, "Go for it."

The phone rang. It was Maria's mom. She said, "We have the menu all set. Could you add some cheeses?"

Maria said, "I'll put an assortment of cheeses together and call it good. Will that be okay?"

"That will be fine. We'll see you at 5:30 with the rest of the potluck.. Bye sweetheart."

"Well that was easy. Mom said they have the rest covered if we take care of the cheeses.

"What would you think about inviting Jeanne and Bud? That would be a nice surprise for the folks. And Bud and Jeanne could take their camping gear home with them."

"Give them a call!"

Jeanne answered, "Hi Maria, how are things going over there?"

Maria said, "We are moved in with all our furniture from the old place. So you could pick up your camping items when you want. We're having a little celebration tonight. Could you and Bud come for dinner?"

"All the family went home this morning, so it is just Bud and I and our youngest Barb who is still here. Will that be okay?"

"That will be great. We have a big dining table. Dinner is at 5:30 p.m. So if you get here about 5:00 p.m., you can get you things loaded and be a surprise for some other guests."

"Okay, see you then. Thank you for including us."

By the time their parents arrived at 5:30 p.m., Alice had been awake from her nap for an hour or two. Jeanne, Bud, and Barb were fussing over her when all the parents arrived. When they walked in, they set their dishes of meat loaf, mashed potatoes, and green beans into a warming oven and turned around to see Bud, Jeanne, and Barb.

After handshakes, and hugs, they all got seated at the dining table, said grace *en français*, and Tom popped the champagne, got the Crème de Cassis open, and started fixing Kir Royales. Barb looked at her mother with a 'please' look. Mom gave in and Alice was the only one with juice in her special cup. She was seated as always between Tom and Maria. When everyone raised their glasses for a toast, Alice raised her special glass of juice. Tom said, "Thank you for family and friends to help us celebrate being in our new home." All clinked glasses and sipped their royales.

Maria walked behind her mother and said, "*Qui est ce?*"

Alice replied, "*Grand-maman.*" *Grand-maman* blew her a kiss and got one back.

Maria walked behind Tom's mother and said, "*Qui est ce?*"

Alice replied, "*Gran-mere.*" *Gran-mere* blew her a kiss and got one back.

Maria moved behind Tom's dad said, "*Qui est ce?*"

When Alice didn't answer, Maria said, "*Il est grand-père. Dire grand-père.*" Alice said, "*Grand-père.*" He blew her a kiss and got one back.

Maria moved behind her dad said, "*Qui est ce?*"

When Alice didn't answer, Maria said, "*Il est grand-papa. Dire grand-papa.*"Alice said, "*Grand-papa.*" He blew her a kiss and got one back.

Maria moved behind Jeanne and said, "*Qui est ce?*" Alice replied Jeanne. She moved behind Bud and said, "*Qui est ce?*" Alice replied Bud.

Finally she moved behind Barb and said "*Qui est ce?*"

When Alice didn't answer, Maria said, "*Il est Barb. Dire Barb.*" Alice said, "Barb." She blew her a kiss and got one back.

Everyone clapped for Alice and blew her kisses.

Maria said, "Thank you so much for being a part of what we do at every meal. Sometimes it is an English word, sometimes a French, and sometimes both. We'll soon, hopefully, have a teacher for all of us to help speed up the process."

"Let's have dinner." The two grandmothers got the food out of the warming oven and replaced the cheeses with dinner. Maria brought out clean plates and dinner was on. Doug took two plates to the protection team.

Tom poured each their wine of choice to all but Alice and Barb. They both got juice. The wine choices were a good Beaujolais or sauvignon blanc.

Tom had tea and coffee brewing during dinner. Tom's mother said, "we didn't do any special dessert." Maria said, "That's good since Jeanne brought two plates of her homemade scones. I can testify they are delicious."

Tom's dad said, "Tom, you promised you would let us in on why it is safe for you."

Tom said, "Doug said he would do that for us. He knows all the details better than we do and what can't be said."

Doug said, "We, being a team of FBI and the agency I represent, surprised the three-man team that blew two doors off their hinges. When they stepped in, FBI agents subdued them and they are now on the way back to the D.C. area for further questioning. I have a theory about it that I can't talk about now, but we are pretty certain of it. What it means is that Tom, Maria, and Alice are safe. None of our people were injured. A third man who drove the van was shot when he tried to shoot our outside team. The local police will now be the protection team as they were for the Group of Nine businessmen. Once we get confirmation of my thinking by the interrogators in D.C., we can drop that protection and just do drive-byes on a random basis. We think we won't need that after the end of this week. Do you have questions?"

"None. Good. I'm looking forward to those scones and coffee."

Tom said, "I can add a couple of things. Our focus right now is Alice, getting her more acquainted with her grandparents. She didn't have any in France. Celeste and Etienne were both orphans so grandparents are a new concept to Alice. We have been slow in having her meet other people than right here. We need to have her bond to us to be as strong as it can be. It's working so far."

Maria added, "We have some furniture to buy to fill up this big house. But even that will be a slow process. I keep hearing that children, even as young as she is, are very resilient and handle change well. We're just being careful. We have a special little girl as you will see next time you see her. She will know all your names, you'll see."

Tom said, "I'll be resuming my job as interim chief of detectives. We have someone coming through the ranks and getting his training right now. So that may take a month or two. In the meantime, Maria is now a full-time *Maman* who will be a busy lady here at home. When my last time with the police force is officially done, I will be on a consulting basis with them and be working at home building a more generalized consulting business. But that's a subject for another time."

Maria said, "I want all of you at our table to know how much we have come to love and appreciate Jeanne. We only discovered yesterday that both our parents knew you through the church. Jeanne, you went above and beyond to make this house become ours in such a short time. Thank you for that. We are here in our new home because you and John Strahan were there for us."

Tom held up his wine glass and said, "To you, Jeanne."

The others echoed the toast.

Jeanne said, "Thank you. This is a first for me. I'm overwhelmed."

Bud said, "We have a surprise for you. We know this is not an official housewarming party but we have brought you a gift."

Jeanne had gotten up and returned with the gift. She said, "Bud is too modest. He is a watercolor painter. This is a painting of one of your favorite spots, the ovals beach with the coast guard station and lighthouse in the background."

Maria said, "This is lovely. This is one of our special places and even plays a part in our courtship. Thank you."

Tom came around the table and asked, "Can I give your wife a hug?" Bud said, "Me too, Maria."

Alice was holding out her arms. She wanted to join in the hugging. She got hugs from all of them, then suddenly turned shy and said, "*Maman*" holding out her arms to Maria.

Alice then held out her arms to *oncle* Doug. She must have sensed he was leaving. Doug hugged her and said, "*Au revoir à vous tous*" and left.

33

Next morning they set out to the bank to meet with John Strahan. Mrs. Arnson met them and escorted them to John's office. John said, "I do believe this is a first, a collection of toys in the meeting room. I hope she takes to these."

John started with an explanation of how he had handled the mortgage. "Here are your copies of the documents. First the down payment of \$20,000 was taken from your joint savings account. This just about cleans out that account. We'll close it and put the money in your investment account. We paid the balance of \$95,000 from the investment account."

"We'll show, for the record, a mortgage payment out of the investment account. No money will move but your coupons will be a record of the transaction. So it is just a bookkeeping arrangement to show the payments for anyone who looks."

"We will also have to transfer money from your \$2 million to your checking account for your monthly needs. And finally as you buy your new furniture, we'll need to draw that directedly from the \$2 million account."

Tom asked, "Will we ever get used to having this much money

when all we've been used to instead of getting a check and making sure you stay on budget?"

Maria laughed, "It is a great problem to have. We just have to learn how."`

John smiled, "This lady will probably get a fix on the details before you do."

"You're likely to be right on that,"

"Eventually as your investments here and at Northern Trust make more and more, it may not be possible to keep your wealth private. You'll have enough income from that and everyone will know that you are well off."

"By the way, you'll get a record of all transactions with balances in all the accounts at the end of each month. You'll soon be pros at it. We have other clients who had to learn, you will too."

Maria said, "John, thank you for all this care and for getting the details covered so we could get moved in."

"Jeanne did the hard work. She found the house, got the Andersons to let you in that first night."

Maria said, "We had a great moving crew. Mark put together a big group of retired policemen. They were great! And in a couple of months we'll be having an open house. We would be pleased if you and your wife would come. It will likely be on a Saturday afternoon."

John replied, "Thank you for the invitation. We will be pleased to come."

They left, split up into two cars, Maria was off to her parents for lunch. Tom was doing the same with his parents.

34

———————

Maria parked in her parents' driveway and there on the front porch were *grand-papa* and *Grand-maman*. Almost in unison, they said, *"Bonjour* Alice."

Alice replied, *"Bonjour grand-maman et grand-papa."* They each got a hug and then Alice wanted down to walk between them, one each with a hand. Maria smiled and said, "There you are, she did learn and look at you walking with your granddaughter."

Lunch was ready, on the table and waiting for them. There was minestrone, Cole's garlic toast, and her lasagna, all made by *Grand-maman*. *Grand-papa* put Alice into her highchair with Maria next to her. They sat on the other side of the table. Grace was said, *Grand-maman* served the minestrone while *grand-papa* poured the wine. Maria took Alice's special cup out of her bag and it was filled with grape juice.

Alice asked, *"Mange?"* Maria took her spoon and started feeding her the minestrone. Alice wasn't having it. She reached for the spoon and was soon, blowing on it to cool it, and sipping the minestrone. She especially liked the noodles in it and the beans. They had a large coverlet under her plate since sure enough there was spillage. Maria cut up small pieces of garlic toast for Alice. When she saw Maria dip hers in the soup, she tried it. She said, "Mmm, *bon."*

Maria kept busy cutting up small bites of lasagna and garlic toast for Alice and then eating hers. She said, "This is a fine Chianti, where did you find this?"

"There is a new store in Grand Rapids called Thrifty Acres. They have a great wine collection. We're supposed to have one here in Norton Shores next year. It will be on Norton just kitty-corner across from the Comerica Bank on Norton and Henry."

Maria said, "I'll have to check into that."

They finished lunch. While Maria and her mom cleaned up the table, *grand-papa* took Alice with him to sit in his easy chair.

When Maria and her mom came in, her mom said, "Well would you look at this. She's made a friend already' Alice was sound asleep. She asked if he wanted his wine.

Grand-papa said, "Nope. I have all I want right here."

Grand-maman asked, "Shall we put her in her crib?"

"Nope, she's fine right here. Maria, can you tell us how things went this morning at the bank? Is everything okay with the house?"

"Everything is just fine with the house. It is ours fully paid for. John Strahan took care of all the details. The down payment came out of our savings account. Then John said he had a suggestion for a way to handle the rest."

Maria explained it just as John had done with the both of them. She said, "We only have to fill out a mortgage coupon for show in case anyone looks. And since the balance of $95,000 was paid out of our investment account, no payment was paid. It just looks like we did."

Maria's mom interrupted, "Are we allowed to know how much is in the investment account? It doesn't really matter if we know, but it would be nice to know you are okay."

"It's okay, Mom. Tom and I decided both sets of parents should know, but please keep it quiet. We are still trying to keep everything private for now. When we finally got almost all the money into the investment account, the total was nearly $2.5 million. Then when you add to that our accounts in Chicago in Northern Trust and Etienne's former partner, there is all told several million dollars more. It grows all the time faster than we'll ever spend it. We're still trying to adjust to that reality."

Maria's dad asked, "What about your plans about what you will do with your lives? I don't see either of you just sitting around. You both will want to be doing something."

"You're right, Dad. We were both brought up to believe that we have a purpose and to then carry it out. Tom, as it turns out, is a bit further along than I am. He will, as you know, spend the next one to two months getting his protégé ready for the job of chief of detectives. When Tom is done with that, he will be starting his consulting business. His first client will be the police department. His job will be to advise in investigations when needed or asked to help out. He'll then be working out of the house, looking for new clients. The first he hopes will be the city of Muskegon. He wants to help bring Fred's ideas to fruition, as he puts it. Then we'll see where it goes from there."

Her dad asked, "How about you?"

"Dad, you're holding my first job. We have found and I think you have seen that Alice is a pretty special little girl. We have our work cut out for us getting her ready to function in an English-speaking country, while preserving her French roots and language. Tom and I both believe that if you come to live in a new country, you need to learn the language and culture of that country. That means Alice needs to speak and read English. And at the same time we need to learn French to we can help her with French and keep that culture. We have a meeting with a crackerjack French teacher from Muskegon Senior High to see if she would be interested or if not, could help us find someone. We also need to find Alice a school where she can grow up at her own pace and is challenged to develop her potential. If there is nothing like that here, we may have to help get one started. We'll see. So, for the next three to four years I'll be home getting her on track to living here. How's that?"

Her dad said, "How is Tom with this approach?"

"He's right there with it. He is doing as much or more than me right now. He has already developed a new method to help her learn both languages. I think he would be content with doing what I'm doing but knows that he needs more. I'm fine with that."

Maria's mother said, 'It sounds as if you two have things pretty well in hand."

Alice began to stir. *Grand-papa* said, "*Réveille-toi, ma petite. Bonjour, Alice.*"

Alice looked around, spotted Maria, said, "*Maman,*" She gave *grand-papa* a kiss on the cheek, stopped to give *Grand-maman* a kiss on the cheek, then climbed into Maria's lap.

Maria said, 'I need to change her."

Her mom asked, "How is potty training coming?"

"She's coming along, but after a long nap, she sometimes forgets."

Grand-papa with a laugh said, "You're right, I can tell. I need to change too."

About 20 minutes later they were waving goodbye. Alice said, "*Au revoir.*"

Tom parked in his parents' driveway and they appeared on the front porch. "*Bonjour grand-mère and grand-père.*" Tom smiled, "Hi, Dad and Mom, you'll hear that from Alice many times. We'll bring her here next time. The two of them are at her parents' home as we speak. That's just right, I've been wanting some private catching-up time with you two."

His mother said, "Come on in. I have some hors d'oeuvres, cheeses, and crackers, and that sauvignon blanc you're so fond of."

"Thanks, Mom. You spoil me still. Here, let me pour." He did and had a toast, "Here's to good times ahead!"

Tom's dad said, "What can you tell us about the house arrangements?"

"Dad, John Strahan took care of everything. All our money is now in our investment account and our regular checking account. The regular account gets replenished on the first of every month, The house is paid for, in full. It's ours! We will fill out a mortgage payment coupon each month and then file them at the bank. Anyone who enquires about our finances will see us as buying a house and getting monies for everyday from Tom's consulting jobs, John thinks that one day down the line people will know better and it won't matter that they do."

Tom's dad asked, "Can we know how much you have?"

Tom smiled, "It's okay. Maria and I decided both parents should know, but please keep it quiet. We are still trying to keep everything private for now. When we finally got almost all the money into the investment account, the total was nearly $2.5 million. When you add to that our accounts in Chicago in Northern Trust and Etienne's former partner, there is all told several million dollars more. It grows all the time faster than we'll ever spend it. We're still trying to adjust to that reality."

"As my consulting business grows, it will provide the everyday expenses and eventually put any excess back into the investment account."

Tom's mom asked, "Did you or Maria know that this amount of money was to come to you?"

"We knew nothing, Mom, until the reading of the will. And even then, the total here and in the Chicago accounts is hard to reconcile. Just before Celeste passed, she told us there was money coming, we both said we didn't need that. We would raise Alice as ours regardless. She asked us to take it, take care of Alice, and do some good with the rest."

"We intend to hold to those promises. I suspect when I back away from police work and consulting focusses on other things, we'll see where it leads us."

Tom's mom said, "You have a big responsibility that you have taken on."

"We know and for the first few years, we are going to be so focused on Alice so the money will just grow. Maria will focus on how to do what we promised. Alice comes first in these early years. My consulting work will take some of my time. As you have seen, Alice is a special little girl, she is our first responsibility. The money will grow and it will be there when we are ready to do some good things as Celeste wanted."

Tom's dad asked, "How will you help her grow in both English and French speaking, learning a new culture, and preserving her French roots?"

"Good question, Dad. Maria remembered a top-notch French teacher at Muskegon Senior High. She is actually French who married an American soldier from Muskegon near the end of WWII. They moved back here. We're meeting with her later this afternoon. Maybe she will be the one who can help us with the language issues. We both have strong feelings about Alice learning English. We think it is the right thing to do that someone who comes to live in our country ought to learn English, no matter what their native tongue."

"There is one more thing we have come to understand. We believe that having this much money available to us brings a new responsibility, that a different kind of 'doing the right thing' has come to us. We don't know what this will lead to, but we'll get it figured out. We're counting on your counsel as we try to figure it out. Always have done that and that won't change."

By this time, they had finished an Irish stew with Guinness in it. Tom said, "I don't think I'll need much dinner tonight. This was all good, mom. I need to get going, the teacher is coming around four pm. I love you both."

35

———

When Tom got back home, he saw a different car in the driveway so he pulled off to the side grass. He was reminded of his thoughts a day or two ago. He wanted to put in a semi-circular drive so neither of them would have to back into a busy street. He reminded himself that he needed to talk to Maria about that.

He waved to their protection agent, went in the front door, and said, "I'm home, Maria."

Maria called out, "We're in the living room by the fire. Come in and I'll introduce you."

Tom hung his jacket up in the foyer closet and went in.

Maria said, "Amelie, this is my husband, Tom. Tom, this is Amelie McNeal, the French teacher from school."

Amelie said, "Hello Tom," and shook his hand.

He said, "Good to meet you. I don't believe we have met before." He turned to give Maria a kiss and hello.

She said with a twinkle in her eye, "You're right, we haven't met. You only had eyes for Maria and looks like that is still the case."

Maria asked, "Can I get you a cup of tea?"

"That would be good. Where's Alice?"

She handed him his tea and topped off hers and Amelie's. Tom sat facing them both,

Maria said, "She is still asleep but should be waking up soon. We've been talking for a half hour already so Amelie knows our story about how Alice came to us."

Amelie added, "I'm sorry for your loss of Celeste and Etienne."

"Thank you …" He was interrupted by Alice's "*Maman.*"

Maria said, "I'll go change her. We will be right back. Why don't you two get acquainted?"

Tom asked, "I understand that you are a native Parisian. What brought you to America and specifically to Muskegon?"

"That's an easy one. I studied nursing and English in college. At age 20 I went to work in a hospital that took care of soldiers from both France and America. Knowing both French and English as the war wound down helped at that job. One of my patients was an Irish American named Jerry McNeal. Our story is almost as sweet as yours with Maria. He swept me off my feet, so to speak, and asked me to wait for him while he finished his engineering degree back in the states. I wasn't sure I should believe him, but he sensed that I was concerned. He convinced me that he would be back. While he was back in the U.S. finishing his degree, I took an MA in English language and French literature. He came back several times during that period. He used to kid me saying I have to come back so you won't get taken with one of those Frenchmen."

"I went there when he graduated from Michigan. He took me home to meet his parents and show me where he had an engineering job waiting at Kaydon. Then he proposed to me again out at the Ovals. We were married the following spring after I received my MA."

"Do you have children?"

"We do, twins and both of them at the school where I now teach, a son and a daughter both seniors. We'll soon have two in college."

Maria came back in carrying Alice. She said, "Alice, this is *Madame* McNeal, Amelie this is Alice."

When Amelie answered with her native French, saying "*Bonjour, Alice.*"

Eyes twinkling over the French accent, Alice said, *"Bonjour, Madame* McNeal."

Amelie asked, *"Vous avez bien dormi?"*

"Oui, Madame McNeal."

Amelie smiled at Alice and said, "Someone has already been working with her. Didn't you say she was just almost three?"

"She is. She has had a lot of people helping her. Immersion on steroids. And then we have been working on a word or sometimes several at each meal. Trouble is, our French is so limited and my accent is terrible. Tom's is somewhat better and he devised a new technique that seems to work well. She is a quick learner."

"That shows. You have made remarkable progress."

"Alice has no concept of grandparents. Her mother and father were both orphans as I said earlier. But using Tom's technique, she knows that my parents are *grand-maman* and *grand-papa*. And she knows that Tom's parents are *grand-mère* and *grand-père*. This learning went on when there was a big group here, actually in the old house first and since here. She knows them by sight and has never missed calling the right one by the name each chose to be. Our thinking is that she doesn't have the concept of grandma and grandpa, but we think that will come as she grows and we get across the concept of they are our parents. We're not quite sure how to teach that yet."

Amelie smiled, "It seems you have it figured out already. Alice is further along than our children at that age. Oh, and you should know that we are a bi-lingual household. Both of our children speak French like natives. So what are you looking for in help?"

Tom answered, "We need to learn too. We need to learn more vocabulary, get stronger on our grammar and syntax, and develop a better accent. We are both at the level one high school year (two for me), and each one year in college. We need to grow as fast or faster than Alice so we can become a bi-lingual family and not slow Alice down. As you'll hear us say, Alice is a special little girl and we don't want to hold her back because of us. In Alice's case she needs to learn both languages so that she can be comfortable enough in them for school here."

Alice got down, picked up her special glass, and climbed up on

Tom's lap. She was rewarded with a hug and a kiss on the cheek which she returned to him. She said, *"Je t'aime, papa."*

Amelie said, "I think this young lady is a pretty lucky little girl. You've only had her three or four weeks and already there is a tight bond to both of you."

Maria said, 'We have worked hard, Tom will finish some work with the police department in a month or so, He'll then be starting his consulting business from home. He'll be setting up his office in that back bedroom overlooking the back yard. He'll be able to watch Alice while she plays out in the yard. We will both be here with her while she needs us the most. Eventually, Tom will be a consultant in several areas where he has skills but wants to grow his business slowly. I was all set to join him in the business but now I need to be right here."

Amelie said, "I'm going to be a little bold here. With what you've seen so far, are you looking at me to do this or to help you find someone else to do it?"

Tom and Maria looked at each other. Tom nodded to her and Maria said, "We would like to hire you to do this for us. One problem is that you are working full-time, and we want this to move as quickly as possible. An intermediate goal is to get us to a level where we can assume all the work within a year or so. Does that sound at all plausible to you?"

Amelie, a tear or two in her eyes, said, "It does sound plausible. And this could solve a problem I have been wrestling with. I applied for a grant to cover a one semester sabbatical from school for next winter/spring. The problem is that the grant fell through, so I'll have to give up the sabbatical. Would you be able to cover the money from the grant?"

Again Tom and Maria looked at each other, nodded and Tom said, "Amelie, we think you are the answer for us. We would like to hire you. We would like you to get us to the level of a bi-lingual home. Can you start in January and then continue on through much of the summer if you feel we need it? And since most grants don't come close to school salaries, we'll pay you your regular salary plus whatever it takes in books, supplies, whatever you need. Are you covered with insurance while on sabbatical?"

"I'm pretty sure that is true but I'll check it out."

Tom said, "When should we begin looking for books and other items? Can you make up a list of what you will need?"

"Why don't we put you on half-salary for November and December. Would you see if you can have the book people send the bill to us? We'll just pay them, as well as your salary, out of my consulting company. Oh, and will you want or need a small blackboard or some other furniture? Just let us know what you will need for Alice and for us. I think we can be counted on to do our homework. We would like to start as soon as we can on our studies. We think Alice will pass us quickly so we better get a head start."

"Will I have an agreement with you or your consulting company?"

"If it is okay with you we'll make it an agreement between you and both of us."

Maria said, "Amelie, will you be able to work with me here all the time and Tom as well? We'll have you set up somewhere in the living room with everything you need. I may be close if it would not make you nervous. But the main thing is that we're trying to build her trust in us. She hasn't even stayed overnight with grandparents yet. We simply want to get the bond as strong as we can before we share her with others. It's only been three weeks or so since she lost her parents."

"I understand. How do we get all this organized?"

"You'll want to talk with your husband. He may have questions too, so while you are doing that, we'll get an agreement drawn up. I don't think we need to call it a contract – I don't like that word. But an agreement is all we've talked about. This won't be a hire for a job but an agreement with you as an independent contractor. Then maybe the four of us could talk, review the agreement, and get things set so you can start putting your thoughts together. Please feel free to consult with an attorney if you want to. You might want to talk to some people at Muskegon Senior High, maybe except the principal. He and I didn't part company on the best of terms."

Amelie said, "I remember those times. I think you weren't treated very fairly. Here are our home phone and address. You can mail us the agreement or just call and drop it off. I can't wait to get home and tell Jerry the good news. There may be some questions at school about how we will be able to get along with the half salary the sabbatical pays."

"For what it is worth, I would just tell them that you found that you could get by on the half salary. They won't question you. And I wouldn't tell them about our relationship unless you feel strongly about it. I have one other question. Most teachers take a vacation during the summer. Will you want to do that? And how will that fit in with your schedule with us?"

"We usually do that too. This year, in fact, we were hoping to make a return trip to Paris. I have two siblings who still live in Paris and we try to go back to see them and renew our feelings for Paris. This year it is a little different with both children starting college somewhere. Actually we have been considering making the trip sometime in early June instead of our usual August time."

Maria jumped in, "We could make our first trip back to Sucy en Brie for a visit with all the people we met. That's where we first met Celeste and Etienne and where they are buried. This might be a good check of what you have done so far and what else you might want to do over the summer hours if it is needed."

Tom said, "Can you be ready by Friday to have a final talk with us and sign the agreement if it is to your liking? I can have a copy to you tomorrow, Wednesday that gives us Thursday to make any needed changes."

"We can do that. Do you mind if we do an informal check of you both. I know you wouldn't have made the offer but … "

"Of course, we will be doing something similar. Our bank is New Shores. We have been with them since we began teaching several years ago. Feel free to talk with them and our church parish. I'll give you the names of our priests as well."

They said their goodbyes. Alice said, "*Au revoir*, Madame McNeal."

Amelie smiled at her, saying, "This is going to be a time for all of us. *Au revoir*. Alice" They all shook hands. Maria and Amelie shared a hug.

36

When Amelie was gone, Maria asked, "Do you feel as content as I do about Amelie?"

"Maybe even more so. I could hardly contain myself. We can talk about it after dinner and Alice is in bed. I want to go see Mark tomorrow morning and will stop to talk with John at the bank. I want to share with him what we are doing with Amelie and just get his reaction. Then I'll come home, let you know what he said and write the agreement."

Alice got up from her toys and said to Maria, "*Maman, je dois faire pipi.*"

Tom looked at Maria in astonishment, "When did you teach her that?"

"I'll tell you later. Alice, *allons faire pipi.*" And away they went, leaving Tom shaking his head. While they were gone, Tom checked the refrigerator for ideas on dinner. He opened a bottle of wine to let it breathe and got their glasses on the coffee table with Alice's already filled with juice. He was sitting in his easy chair listening to some soft jazz when they came back.

Alice came marching back to jump up on his lap. Alice looked at him intently and said, *"Papa, j'ai fait pipi."* Both he and Maria had to stifle their laughter.

Maria said, "I'll have to teach her that she doesn't have to report back."

Tom poured their wine, they all toasted and joined in the cheese and crackers. Tom asked Maria, "How about some scrambled eggs, bacon, and pancakes for dinner?"

"That sounds great and a good lesson for Alice. She'll learn that eggs are anytime."'

"And I'll make us mimosas and pure OJ for Alice."

"Alice, *du crêpes*?

Alice squealed, *"Tres bien, Papa."*

Maria said, "Let's enjoy our wine and cheese. Alice and I will have some play time while you cook."

"Alice, say bacon, eggs, and pancakes." She did so, perfectly but with a slight accent. Tom said, "That was English."

"Alice, *dites lardon, œufs et crêpes.*" She did so, perfectly. "That was Français."

They casually returned to their wine and cheese as did Alice.

After their breakfast for dinner, Tom and Alice had some play time while Maria cleaned up the dishes. Alice soon tired and Tom said, "I'll put her to bed tonight. Now don't you go away, I won't be long."

Maria said, "Take your time, I want to get a shower."

Tom said, "I'll get a quick one after she goes to sleep. I'll read her a story but I won't be long."

Maria was finishing the last of her wine. She heard the shower turn off. While he was drying, she checked on Alice and slipped into their bedroom. While Tom was getting his PJs, she slipped out from behind the door, closed it and started swinging her robe tie and doing a little 'Ta dum, da dum' while she hummed a little tune. He turned around as she finished her dance. She said, "Why don't you join me in my boudoir, *Monsieur*?"

Tom caught her before she was in bed, kissing her with a deep intense kiss. She tumbled him into their bed without breaking their kiss. Sometime later they were cuddling in the afterglow. She whispered, "We need to meet here a little more often."

He kissed her and said, "*À tout moment ma Belle.*"
"*Maintenant, mon amour.*"
Later they slept.

The next morning Tom was sitting at the dining table making some notes on items to cover with John and Mark. The phone rang. "Hi, Doug. How are you and how are things out east?"

Doug said, "I'm doing just fine. And I have some good news. I'm preparing for a new assignment. I don't know any details yet, but I should know by the time I see you. The installers for your Level Three security are coming in with all the materials they will need. They are driving in and should be there by next Monday. I'll be on Sunday afternoon, flying into Lansing and driving up. I'll be able to observe what they do, learn more about it, and get a chance to see my two favorite, oops three favorite people."

"That's terrific, Doug. It'll be good to see you. How long will you be here?"

"I have some news about the people who came after you. My hunch was right, they are not OAS people. I'll tell you all about what we learned Sunday or Monday. And then I have to send all the teams home since they are no longer needed. I'll drive back to Lansing Wednesday morning, see my parents again, and fly back to more prep for the next assignment."

"Why don't you stay with us those two nights? We'll have the spare bedroom ready for you."

"Are you sure that will be okay?"

"Of course. It will give us more time to be together. We also have some good news as well. We'll tell you all about it."

"Okay then. I'll see you between three and four on Sunday. Looking forward to seeing you. Bye Doug."

Maria had been listening on the extension. She said, "I wonder where he is off to now. I am always concerned that we will lose our friend."

"To tell the truth, so am I. He hasn't said anything to me about how long he intends to keep doing it. Right now, he says he is needed so he does it. We'll have two good days with him. We have one more thing to get done, we need a bed and other furniture for the spare bedroom. Can we shop this afternoon?"

"I don't see why not. I'll put Alice down early for her afternoon nap. This morning I'll start looking for furniture stores. We'll need a bigger bed for Doug. I think there are bigger ones available for a few years now. I hope someone has one on hand. I'll make some calls while you are out and about. Don't forget we have to get the agreement to Amelie and Jerry."

"Thanks for the reminder. I'd better get moving."

Tom kissed both his girls and said, "*Je vous aime tous les deux.*"

37

---

om made it to the station just before nine am. The meeting was just breaking up. Everyone had been briefed on the day shift. All greeted Tom as if he were a long-lost brother. He promised to see them more often soon.

Mark asked him to step into his office. Gerri followed them in with coffees and Danish from the meeting. Tom said, "Spoiling me again, Gerri. I'll soon be here more often.'"

Gerri gave him a hug saying "You won't get that when you're back. When do I get to see Alice?"

"I'm sure that will happen in the next week or so. Doug's coming in. He is here to spread the good news about the bad guys, dismiss the protection groups, and check out the new security system. He says he has good news to share so we're waiting to see what that is."

Gerri left to attend to her duties, albeit with a little pout.

Mark smiled, "Beat me to the news again, Tom. He also told me he was headed overseas again soon. He likely can't tell me much about that."

"No, he can't. He won't have much time with us. He's staying with us while he is here. We are enjoying the larger house. We're about to start shopping for some furniture to get the house where we want it. The spare bedroom will be first."

Mark asked, "Do you have a time to start here again?"

"I'm thinking two weeks from the coming Monday. Will that work for you and my protégé? With all that he is learning, he may be far ahead of me."

Tom could see that Mark was thinking about something. He asked, "What are you thinking about so hard?"

"I'm going to make a suggestion. I was so impressed how you would come into the room, listen to what everyone was bringing to the table and you always had a new approach that no one had seen. What's the old saying, 'If I could bottle that, I'd make a fortune.' If you could take yourself back to the time we were after the Group of Nine and figure out what you did that was different, you might have a package that you could sell. One more thing for your consulting kitbag."

"Maybe if I could get some of it down before I work with my protégé, I could try it out on him. If it works for him, … This is a great idea, Mark. Thank you."

"Why don't we try to meet for lunch and talk more about it before you come back two weeks from Monday? Say maybe a week from this Monday?"

"I'll be there and have an outline at least by then and will be looking for another nudge from you. Thanks, Mark."

Tom stopped by Gerri's desk and told her that he would pass on to Maria about her getting together with Maria and Alice.

Tom left the station and in ten minutes he walked into the New Shores Bank. Mrs. Arnson spotted him and waved him over to her desk. 'Did you want to see Mr. Strahan?"

Tom replied, "I would like to. I don't have an appointment, but I don't remember how to do something I need to do today and I have something I would like his advice on. Will that work today?"

"He has nothing on his schedule until after lunch."

"I won't need him that long so how do we do this?"

"Can you tell me what you can't remember how to do? Wow, that's a little bad grammar, isn't it?"

Tom laughed, "I do that every now and then. We're about to do some furniture shopping this afternoon. I forgot how to transfer extra money from our investment account to regular checking."

She smiled, "I can fix you up on that. Why don't I take you in to get your advice? I'll round up the forms, bring them to you, and run through the procedure." She buzzed John and said, "Tom O'Banion is here for a little advice and my knowledge about a procedure. May I bring him in?"

"Please do." And he met them at the door. "Hello, Tom, do you want some coffee?"

"I've had enough. I'll pass, thank you."

"What's on your mind?"

Tom filled him in on the deal they had made with Amelie McNeal. Tom handed him the agreement draft. He read it.

John said, "I think they will be pleased with this and in my opinion, you have a great solution to what you need. Good job."

"Maria was the one who remembered her from school and brought her in. We both agreed we should do it."

"I know Jerry and Amelie. They are members of my parish, the best of the best in this town. Congratulations, Tom."

"Thank you, John."

"I have a question for you. Do you know yet when your open house will take place?"

"We don't have a firm day. There are things we want to get done with the house yet. We would like to make it a Christmas open house. We think that it would be a good atmosphere to get to know our friends better."

John said, "I would like to propose a dinner with the five of us at our home or yours if you prefer. I am interested in knowing what makes you tick, how you balance both sides of an issue. I would like to know you better, how you think, and to know something more about what you are about, what you want to do with your life. Can we set that up? The choice of where is yours."

"All my life I have listened to my elders. When the mayor died, I lost a good friend from whom I learned so much. I looked forward to our conversations. Fred was like an older brother that I never had. Plus, I have always talked with my dad a lot about my decisions and still do! I look forward to talking with you. What do you say we leave the details to the ladies? Maria may want it at our place so she can get Alice to bed and have some time with us."

John said, "Here is our home phone number and my wife Katherine's name. I'll call her and tell her to expect a call from Maria. Now, let me buzz Mrs. Arnson. She'll fix you up on the transfer process." He did so. "Can we make it before Thanksgiving?"

"I don't see why not. We'll be in touch."

Tom told Maria what John had said about the agreement and Amelie. She said, "Then maybe you should get the draft to them and if they approve we could have them stop by Friday after school and we'll have the formal signing with a notary present.

38

Maria was beside herself when Tom got back home. She had talked to several furniture stores and finally found one who had two queen size beds. She said, "I told them we could be there about three pm or so. I made some potato-leek soup for lunch."

Tom gave her a hug and a kiss. "You learned how to make that while watching me enjoy it at the school cafeteria. Now I get treated every now and then with a sample of your version."

Alice left her toys and came to Tom, "*Bonjour, Papa. Moi aussi?*"

Tom smiled, swept her up into his arms, gave her a hug, a kiss, and a little swing her around, "*Bonjour, Alice. Comment va ma petite fille?*"

She giggled, "*Très bon, Papa.*"

They sat down to a bowl of potato-leek soup, Irish soda bread, and lemonade for all. Then they were off on a shopping trip to Langlois Furniture. Maria had spoken with Bill Langlois who had founded the business in 1947 and was still active now, in 1963. During the phone call, he asked Maria if she would be sure to ask for him. He would like to take care of them personally.

When they arrived, Tom said, "We were told to ask for Bill Langlois. Please let him know we are here."

Bill walked up, "I thought that might be you. May I call you Maria?"

She said, "Please do. Here is my husband Tom O'Banion and our daughter, Alice."

He said, "Hello Tom, and this is little Alice."

Maria said, "Alice, Alice, Alice, *présentez-vous Monsieur Langlois.*"

Alice said, "*Bonjour Monsieur Langlois, je suis Alice O'Banion.*"

He said, "*Bonjour Alice.*"

Alice beamed, then turned shy and cuddled closer to *maman*.

Tom said, "We are looking to furnish our guest bedroom. Our most frequent guest is a 6 ft. 4 in. man so we are looking for a larger bed."

"Your wife mentioned you were talking about a queen size. I have two mattresses and box springs. Come this way please."

When they reached the beds, Bill asked, "Who wants to try it?"

"Let me," said Tom. "Oh, this is great," he added.

He turned to Maria and asked, "Would you like to try it?"

She blushed and Tom realized his mistake, "Here let me take Alice."

After Maria said, "This will be fine. Doug ought to be very comfortable in this. This will work just fine for Doug."

Tom said, "We need a bedstead for it, as well as a dresser, side table, and lamp. Anything else, Maria?"

Bill said, "We have some choices for you over in this next area."

Maria said, "I kind of like the walnut finish with the matching tables on either side. What do you think, Tom?"

"I think that will work just fine."

Bill said, "That's a great choice. Anything else that you can think of at this moment?"

Tom said, "I think that is good for now. What do you think, Maria?"

"Well Tom, I think we ought to make it two of them. We need a new spring, mattress, and bedstead for our bedroom."

"What are you thinking of?"

"How about another queen mattress, box spring, and a mahogany sleigh bed? Bill, do you have any of those to look at?"

They moved to the next section. Maria said, "Look sweetheart, there they are." She turned to Bill. "Could you set up a good price on all this at once?"

Bill smiled, "Tom, you have a tough negotiator here. You should be proud of her."

"I am proud of her. I just didn't know she had this skill."

Another half hour in Bill's office and they left with two beds, two bedsteads, one walnut standard, a mahogany sleigh bed, and a three-drawer dresser. Bill threw in the four bedside stands. They'll be there at 10 am and have you all set up by 11:30 or so."

Bill shook their hands, said an *'au revoir'* to Alice, and said, "There's nothing I like better that customers leaving here with big smiles. If we have done right by you, we look forward to seeing you again soon as the time is right for your living room. Thank you, all three. *Merci beaucoup* Alice!"

On the way home, Alice fell asleep. Maria said, "I bet she will sleep right through until dinnertime. We'll see."

Tom said, "That would be good. We need to talk about what happened this morning."

"Everything okay?"

"Of course. Mark already knew about Doug's visit. No, this is about a conversation John Strahan and I had. I'll tell you all about it when we get home."

Maria was right, Alice slept through the ride and then in her bed. When Maria returned to the living room, Tom had glasses of a fine chilled vin rosé. "Okay, what's the occasion?"

"I just want to toast a great job you did on the beds. To you, sweetheart, congratulations. You put together a great deal."

They touched glasses, sipped. Maria said, "You're not upset about the second bed."

"Not even a bit. I wouldn't have thought about it. But it was needed and you did it and saved us some money in the process. Congrats!" He sealed it with a long kiss.

She smiled, "Not now, I want to hear about the bank and your conversation with John."

Tom smiled back, "I now know how to get extra amounts from the investment account. Mostly it is a matter of documenting what the use is for our records, things we do already."

He continued, "As to John's reaction to the agreement with Amelie, he had only praise. To make it quick, he approved of the agreement. He said we were being very generous with them and understood the reasons why we did it. He said we have found just what we need for Alice and us. He knows Amelie and Jerry and says we have found the best solution to do what we need for Alice and us. He said congratulations and said to pass it on to you. I told him it was you doing it, not me."

"I told him you had found Amelie and had ironed out most of the details by the time I got involved. You know what he said?"

Tom went on, "I always knew you had a smart wife." He raised his glass for another toast to her!

"So what about your conversation with him?"

"To be brief and right to the heart of it, he proposed a dinner for all three of us with he and his wife, Katherine."

"I didn't see that coming. What does that mean, what do you think he wants?"

"I think there is nothing in it other than he is proposing that we get to know each other better. In particular, he wants to spend some time talking with me about my life, how I tick as he put it. He believes I have a lot going for me. He followed closely what happened last year during the Group of Nine, the trial I was put through, He wants to know how we found each other, about the arrangements regarding Alice and the money. He has great respect for Jean Paul and got some of his feelings about us from him."

"You don't think he has any other motives?"

"No, I don't. I think he genuinely wants to help us along the way to our becoming a major factor in this town. Plus, I think he likes us both."

"Do they have children?"

"They do. All grown up, building careers, married but no grand-children yet."

"And you don't see any possible downside to getting to know them better?"

"None. Remember that I had some dealings with him during the Group of nine affair. He was especially impressed about how I put together the strategy to get them to turn on each other. You'll remember how none of them trusted the others, and having spotted that, I was able to turn them on each other and split the group. Apparently he talked to Mark as well.

"Everyone I spoke with about him suggests a man who can be trusted. Here's what I'll do. I'll make discreet inquiries around town and we'll talk to Doug about it.'`

"So how do we set this up?"

Tom grinned, "Actually I suggested you and his wife Katherine work out the details. He said we could have it at either house, our house having the advantage that we could put Alice to bed at her usual time and we'd be able to talk. He also proposed that we keep the dinner casual and simple, nothing fancy but that we would leave it to you ladies. We could even cater it if you wanted, but then we would have the potential to be overheard. I would rather it be kept private myself."

"Will we be splitting the cost of the meal?"

"My thinking is that they will take care of the meal since it was John's invitation. And by the way, John asked if it could be during the week before Thanksgiving."

"Here is their phone number , her name, Katherine that John gave me. She is probably waiting for your call."

"Hello, is this Mrs. Strahan? This is Maria O'Banion."

"Hello Maria, I'm Katherine, please. My mother-in-law is Mrs. Stra-han. Is it okay if I call you Maria?"

"I would much prefer Maria for the same reason."

"Oh, we're going to get along just fine." They both had a little laugh. "I understand you and I have been assigned a task, figure out what to have for dinner. By the way, have you decided where to have the dinner?"

"If you don't mind, I'd rather have it here. That way I can get Alice to bed a little after dinner and we can talk more freely,"

"John thought you might say that. I'm looking forward to meeting Alice. By the way, how is that spelled? John seemed not to know."

"It is spelled like the American 'Alice' but pronounce by the French as 'Ahlese'."

"John says you will be engaging Amelie McNeal to teach all of you so that you can be a bi-lingual family."

"He knows them?"

"Yes, for years. They are members at St. Mary's downtown. You are going to love her."

"I already do. We are likely to become good friends while we work together."

"Now, about dinner. John and I would like to take care of that. He said that you might object but please allow us to do this. We invited you so we can get better acquainted. John said something simple. We have a cook who works directly for us on an as needed basis. She will make the dinner here, bring it in her van, along with us and come pick us up in case we drink too much. She does a quite tasty pot roast with all the veggies and that we'll have after a *salade capresse*."

"I was going to ask if you like wine with dinner. We have a wonderful Beaujolais for the roast and a lovely sauvignon blanc for the salad."

"Then we are all set. Thank you, Maria. When are we doing this?"

"Tom said that John had proposed a weekend in mid-November, a week and a half from Thanksgiving. Will that work?"

"I think it will. I'll check with John and cook, then give you a call back. Thank you, Maria. I'm looking forward to meeting you."

"And I you. Thank you, Katherine. We'll see you soon."

39

———

True to their word, the truck from Langlois backed up to the front door on time. Tom came out to greet them. "We have cleaned out the bed in our room. We can put it in the garage until the new ones are unloaded and set up. Bill said you would drop that one off to Goodwill as a donation."

The men followed Tom and Maria into their bedroom. Harold asked, "Will the new bed be in the same location?"

Tom said, "Yes, it will. I checked with the measurements Bill gave us. The mahogany headboard next to the walk-in closet helps a lot with room in our bedroom. So it's just take this one down and put the new sleigh bed in."

They walked into the spare bedroom with nothing in it. Maria showed them how she would like the walnut bed and chest of drawers arranged. "Thank you, Mrs. O'Banion. We'll have it all done in about an hour."

Alice wiggled to get down. She wanted to see what was going on. Harold said, 'Now who is this little lady? She is a pretty one!"

"This is our daughter Alice. She likes to be down where she can be a part of what's going on."

Harold said, "We have a three-year-old girl who is like that." After saying hello to Alice they got to work.

A little over an hour later, they were all done. Tom walked out with them, thanked them, and gave each a $20 tip.

When he got back in, Maria called him from their bedroom. He went in to see both his girls lying on their new, yet unmade, bed. So he joined them. Alice jumped up and sat on Tom's tummy. . "Oof," he said. "Now, *maman*," Alice jumped up and sat on Maria's tummy… "Oof, " she said. Alice giggled and got hugs from both of them. Maria took her from the bed and tried to put her into her chair to watch but she wanted down.

Maria said, "She wants to play, so we might as well do that. We'll finish the bed after lunch." After a play time, Alice said, "*Maman, j'ai faim.*"

Maria said, "This one gets hungry like I do. What do we have that we can do for lunch?"

Tom said, "I think we have enough for another lunch of your potato-leek soup. Let's do that along with a bacon-lettuce-tomato sandwich, a small one for her. Are you up for a glass of that sauvignon blanc from last night?"

"Sounds good. Alice seemed to like the potato soup too."

"I'll get it ready while you two play." Maria chose instead to read Alice a picture book with both French and English words. She made it like a game. Finally, *Papa* called them for lunch.

When they had finished, Tom took Alice off to her nap while Maria cleaned up the dishes. When he came back out, she was done. He said, "there's just enough of the wine for a half glass for each, are you game?"

Tom poured. They sat in the living room. Maria asked, "You have something on your mind?"

"I was just wondering how you were feeling about our progress with the house, with making it our own. Are we moving too fast or too slow? What do you think?"

"Doug's visit kind of got things going. I'm glad we did both at once, thank you Tom."

He said, "I was startled at first but it made good sense. Get the bedrooms done first. What's next and when do you want to do it?"

"I think we ought to make some changes in the living room and a larger dining room table and chairs next. The sofa is a good one, but it is a little small for this living room. And we need to start thinking about where a piano should go. And then I start thinking what might be changing too fast for Alice."

"You may be right about that. Why don't we think about another sofa about the size of this one? Then we could arrange them in a semi-circle facing the fireplace."

"Maybe we could get that done by the Christmas open house. Do you think Alice will be okay for that change by then?"

"I think she is ready for more than we know. She copes pretty well with changes."

40

———————

The phone rang. Tom grabbed it quickly so as not to wake Alice. "Hello."

Doug laughed, "Didn't know the number did you, Tom? I'm still at my parents. I got a late start from D.C."

"Maria just got on the extension."

"Hi Doug. I would guess you're going to be late. We're having my lasagna. I know you like it."

"Thanks for understanding. We have a lot to talk about. See you at 4:00 pm."

Doug rolled into the driveway at 3:50 pm. He knocked and entered to a handshake and two hugs, one from Maria, and one from Alice, who said," Bonjour, *oncle* Doug," as she was swept up into his arms.

Alice said, "*Oncle Doug, suis-moi dans ta chambre.*" She took his hand and led him in.

"*Merci beaucoup*, Alice. I feel special, thank you. This is the first I've seen one of these larger beds."

"We wanted it for you." Maria said. "It's your bedroom when you are back in town."

Tom put Doug's suitcase on one of those folding stands. He said, "Let's go celebrate. How about a Kir Royale?"

Tom made the drinks while the others found their spot on the sofa. Tom brought their three glasses and Alice's as well. He raised his glass and said, "Here's to you, Doug, a national treasure."

Doug said, "I have a toast as well. President Kennedy has set a date for your commendation presentation. He has a full schedule on a tour of Texas that takes up much of the first three weeks of November. Then Thanksgiving is on Thursday November 28th and he didn't want to take you away from home that week. He wonders if you could make it on Thursday December 5."

Tom and Maria looked at each other and said, "That will work for us."

"Good. I'll report back to the White House so that they can make all the arrangements. You'll be hearing from the office as they get things set up. Here's to you, Tom. A national hero."

Tom said, "I'm honored but that's enough on that. What is your schedule for tomorrow?"

"First, the installation. A four-man team will be here about 8:00 am. They figure to be done, instructional time and all by noon. They will leave for D.C. right away, have some lunch along the way and try to get in half the trip back. That will put them into northern Virginia where most of them live before the big traffic build-up on Tuesday afternoon. When they leave, we'll have to get ready for a meeting at the station. Mark is asking all team members to gather where I and you two, if you wish, can thank them for taking care of your safety. Will that work?"

Tom replied, "We'll make it work, won't we, Maria? Will we get lunch there too or after?"

"I'd like to take the three of you to lunch if that's okay."

Maria laughed, "You have it all figured out don't you? We may lose Alice to a nap at the restaurant. But she will be fine."

Tom said, "I'm ready for another Kir Royale. No one is going out tonight. I'll be right back and maybe you can tell us a little bit about your new assignment."

After refilling their glasses, Tom asked, "What can you tell us?"

"It will be brief and I'll swear you two to secrecy even for the little bit. I'm headed back to France to help track down the OAS group. We have some idea of where to start looking. Our prisoners finally opened up and talked when they realized they weren't going home until they talked."

"Will you have some help in France?"

"I do. The French have been trailing them as they work their way back to the south of France. The suspicion is that they will find a place to regroup? and plan their next attempt on President De Gaulle. You know, don't you, that attempts on De Gaulle are approaching 30 times? So the Sûreté is watching him while we try to put the OAS out of business. I'll know more about where they are in the search when I get with them."

"So now, what's going on with you?"

Maria asked him, "Do you remember Amelie McNeal the French teacher at Muskegon Senior High?"

"I do but not well enough to call her a friend."

"Well here goes. The short version of this story is that she is a French woman who married a soldier from Muskegon and moved here in 1949. Both had just finished their master's degrees. His was an MBA to follow up his engineering degree and hers was in English language and French literature. He has been at Kaydon for over twenty years and has moved up in the organization. She has taught French at the high school for the same time. The most important detail is that they have twins who, thanks to Amelie and Jerry, are bilingual, fluent in both French and English. Long story shortened – we just signed an agreement with them on Saturday. She is part-time until the first of the year and is on sabbatical from the high school for the second semester. She will be making us a bilingual family as well. She said with what we have done already teaching Alice English, we can be finished by next May or June."

"That is excellent. By the way, is Alice still napping?"

"She is and probably will be for another half hour or so."

"That's good. I sense that there's more to come."

"There is. We're having John and Katherine Strahan here for dinner in two weeks."

"Well, stepping up in the world, I see."

Tom said, "Not really, Doug. This was at his request. I went to see him regarding the agreement with Amelie. He not only approves of my agreement language but knows them both. He believes she is the answer to our goal of getting us competent in French and English for Alice as well as us fluent in French. So that problem is solved."

Maria said, "How about letting me finish this one, Tom?" He nodded, okay.

Continuing, Maria added, "John asked Tom where he thought his next direction might be. Tom told him that after the next two or three weeks, he would no longer be an active police detective but the department would be his first consulting contact. He doesn't think that will take a lot of time so Tom told him he was starting a broader consulting company. With me so far?" Doug nodded but puzzled where it was going.

Maria went on, "I can see you are curious about where this is leading. John set up this dinner so that he could learn more about Tom, saying to him that he thinks that Tom can be a mover and shaker for this town and that he could be what the town needs to move ahead in a good direction. In his words, he wants to know a lot more about Tom, how he developed the way he did, and just learn more about what makes Tom think the way he does. We'll find out more after dinner in a couple of weeks. Any thoughts, reactions so far…"

Doug asked, "Tom, any idea what brought this on?"

"The only clue I have is when he heard me say a little while back that I was very supportive of Fred and his plans for the city, he began to ask people he knows who know me. including the people in Chicago, Jean Paul, Jim, the former police chief and so on …"

Doug asked, "What about you, Maria? What do you think?"

"At first, I was a bit suspicious about his motives. But from thinking of all I knew about him, asking some questions of friends, and Tom's rational comments, I've lost my suspicions and can't wait to hear what he has in mind."

Tom exclaimed, "I didn't know you had changed your mind."

"I'm sorry, Tom. So much has happened the last few days, I haven't had a chance to tell you about it. Let's go for it and see what it brings.'

Tom said, "I still don't know what role I might play here, what problems there might be in being able to guide the city … and should I get into the politics of it or try to work in the background. Maybe the talk with John will help me resolve my thinking about it."

They were all interrupted by Alice's "*Maman.*" When Tom brought her out, she said "*Oncle* Doug" She jumped up on his lap, got a hug, and went around getting more hugs.

"Are you all ready for dinner? Good, I'll get the lasagna warming up, lay out the charcuterie, and *à la salle à manger.*"

Alice ran over and climbed into her chair. Doug asked, "When did she start doing that?"

"Since last week. She was pretty excited about it. She'll wait to be buckled in. See there!" Maria buckled her in while Tom brought out the board and opened a bottle of a fine chardonnay they had found at Etterman's. While they enjoyed the cheese on the charcuterie, Tom had opened that special Chianti to let it breathe before dinner.

They headed to the living room where Tom had stoked up the fireplace. It felt good in the late October chill. They spent some time sharing with Alice who had come to love watching the flames but had learned to keep a good distance.

When Alice was back in bed and fast asleep, they had some more time to share. Maria opened up more questions about his trip. "Will you be able to see Belle and Henri in Sucy en Brie? I'm sure they would love to have you."

Doug responded with a look that prompted another question from Maria, "Doug, you look a little pensive about Sucy?"

He hesitated and finally said. "I'd love to see them too, And there's another reason I'm trying to fit that in …"

Maria, impatient said, "Well, who is she?"

"What makes you think it is a she?"

"I just know, Doug. Come on now, spill it out."

"Well, it happened in Sucy … at the funeral. Do you remember the novitiate, Caroline, who helped me take care of Alice? While we baby sat, and while Alice slept, we talked a lot. She was questioning becoming a nun, didn't know if it was the right choice for her."

"I asked her how long she had been having these questions and wondering about it fitting for her."

She said, "It started when I was asked to help with the children in the nursery." Then she blushed, said, "Then you and Alice came along and we were together with a little sweetheart, Alice, and well ... Doug, I have feelings for you that are new for me. But they are real and I don't know what to do."

"I asked her if she had talked with the Reverend Mother about this. And whether some of the other nuns might suspect."

She looked at me, "No, I haven't. No one suspects. And then there comes you, and things are more complicated because of my feelings. I don't even know if you feel anything for me."

"I don't know if I should say until I know what you will be doing."

She added, "But I want to know now."

"But don't you think you should talk to the Reverend Mother and get her counsel before we talk more. You don't know much about me. You need to think about yourself first and what is right for you. Then she surprised me and asked me if I had ever been married before."

Doug now grinned a little and said, 'Yes, I was."

Tom and Maria in unison, "You were?"

"Yes, I was. And it was good until it wasn't anymore. It only lasted for two years and then it wasn't good. I didn't leave because I stopped loving her, I left because the longer I stayed, the less I liked myself."

He continued, "And I told Caroline the same thing."

She shook her head saying, "I don't understand."

"Let me try this. I was Tom's best man. When we had the champagne toast at the reception, I used some fancy quotes to try to get across what a good marriage was made of. But in a nutshell, it is that you need to be best pals, best person to talk to, agree and disagree with so you can both learn from each other, and each dedicated to what he/she or she/he wanted to be/do. I ended it with a quote from Antoine de Saint Exupery, 'Love does not consist in gazing at each other but in looking outward together in the same changing direction."

And you know what, they are living that. I see in them something that is going to last. That is the kind of marriage I want if it comes again for me." The conversation continued.

"She asked if I would do something for her. I said 'Of course, what is it?'"

"She said that she wanted to set up a meeting with Reverend

Mother after Mass on Sunday and asked if I would stick around to talk to the Reverend Mother afterwards or even both of us with her if she wants. Of course, I said, 'Yes, I will.'"

Doug said, "That's the end of the conversation we had. Caroline talked to the Reverend Mother. When she came out, she told me that the Reverend Mother had advised her to think and pray on it for a little while yet. And then to tell Doug that she, Caroline, is to contact him after some more weeks and another talk with Reverend Mother. Well, I heard last week, she is leaving the church and wants me to come see her as soon as I can. I called her right away before I left to come here and told her I would see her before I started my next assignment."

Maria interrupted, "Doug, I think that is wonderful. Did you tell her you love her? It must have been love at first sight or en Français, *le coup de foudre*. Do you think it will work? Do you think you will stay in the work you do and if not, what might you do?"

"All good questions, Maria. And yes I did tell her of my feelings for her. I can't think of anything but her right now. I don't know the answer to your other questions but I want to find out. I can't wait to talk with her. I don't know what she will do when she leaves the novitiate. But I owe the agency a good job on this next assignment too, so ..."

Tom said, "What will you do if you leave the agency?"

"Right now, I haven't a clue. Now that you know this much. Maybe we can talk about this more tomorrow night. I need your thinking, your wisdom.."

Maria added, "I hope it all works out. I haven't seen you this way ever before. You're in love my friend. It will work out."

Tom said, "Maybe we should all get some sleep. We have a full day tomorrow."

41

———————

The next morning, all were up early, having bacon and eggs for breakfast. They had just finished when the installation crew arrived promptly at 8:00 am.

Tom and Doug took them on a walk through the house and grounds. The lead installer, Jimmie, said, "This is just as we pictured it from the plans and notes you sent us, Doug. We have everything we need to finish it up. I have just one question. Do you want something added for the replacement fence that you'll be installing to close in the back yard? We brought materials along in case you did."

Tom asked, "Why would we need that?"

"It only takes a minute or two for someone to come in through a gate and grab Alice. We can guard against that. But you don't have the right kind of fence yet for that."

Tom said, "If you give me the specs on it, we can have the fence set up next spring."

Jimmie said, "We will go ahead and add that component to the system now. Then when the fence is done, it will just be a matter of connecting it to the system. Let's get to work guys.

They were done at 11:30 am. They gave Tom and Maria the walkaround and instructions while Doug took care of Alice. The crew were on their way at noon for the East Coast.

Tom, Maria, and Alice left in their car. Doug drove his as he wanted to talk to Mark after their luncheon for the protection squads. The luncheon was about over when they arrived at the station. Maria stopped at Gerri's desk to introduce her to Alice and set up a date for Gerri to stop in on her way home to have a visit at the house. Gerri, as planned, brought them all into the meeting room. Lunch was done. Mark introduced them all and said, "These are the folks you have been keeping safe for the last few weeks. They have something to say to all of you."

Tom went first, "I'll keep it short and simple. I suspect you are ready to be home. We are so grateful for your care as you kept us safe and forever in your debt. Maria and I have been through some things but change when you have a little one around. You did your job so well. Alice never knew there was anything going on but a new adventure. And she loves those. Here's Maria and Alice."

Maria stood Alice on the corner of the head table. She said, 'This is our daughter. She is our *raison d'être*, our reason for being now. You, like those of you, most of you who have children know that things kept her safe, words can't tell how grateful we are that you did. She doesn't speak much English yet, but Alice, say thank you."

Alice said, "*Merci beaucoup, messieurs.*" The whistles and applause came rolling out. Alice waved to them and then cuddled close to *maman*.

Mark said, "Doug, are you sure you want to follow that?"

"I'll try. Gentlemen, you came here not knowing what you would be up against. You rose to the occasion as you always do. These three are special friends of mine, I am so proud of what you did. They are safe! Thank you. Have a safe trip home."

As they left to get their lunch, there was more applause and whistles. Doug said, "Follow me into U.S. 31 Barbeque. We need to see how Alice likes this."

Doug said, "How about this booth?"

The waitress came over to wait on them. There was a 12-year-old girl who trailed along behind her, attracted to Alice. "Who is this little charmer?"

Maria said, "I'd like you to meet our new daughter Alice. She is French and doesn't speak much English yet."

"Hello, Alice. I'm Kristi."

"Bonjour, Mademoiselle"

As Kristi reached out for Alice, she said, *"Ooh la la, a mademoiselle,* Thank you,"

Their waitress brought their orders. Three pork barbeques, with French fries, and lemonade for all.

Maria had asked for forks for herself and Alice. She started cutting the French fries into bite size bits. No doubt about this, Alice loved them. Maria then cut off some bites of the barbeque. She took a bite of it and then put one on Alice's plate. Alice forked a bite into her mouth and stopped chewing. She shook her head, spitting it out. She looked at *maman* who frowned and put out another bite for Alice. Alice was having another fry, better! Kristi said, "Alice, try it again.?

Maman pushed the barbeque closer. Alice shook her head. *Maman* pushed it closer to her. Alice took a small bite with less sauce. She frowned, but a look from *maman* meant don't spit it out. She took her glass that Maria had filled with lemonade and had a quick drink. Slowly, gradually, she began to work it in between French fry bites and lemonade.

Kristi asked, "Shall I get her a sweet treat? We have great sugar cookies here."

Alice finished her part of the barbeque and fries. Four cookies were served and maman broke hers up, so did Alice. Alice had a smile for *maman*. Alice held out a piece of cookie to Kristi who enjoyed it and smiled at Alice.

Kristi said, "Come again, Alice."

Maman said, "Kristi said, '*Revenez,* Alice.'"

Alice said, *"Merci beaucoup."*

Alice fell asleep in Maria's lap as they drove home.

~

After Maria put Alice down for her nap, she joined Tom and Doug who were already talking about his new romance. Tom said to Maria, "I've never seen our friend as shook up as he is now."

"A new lady in his life can do that. I'm hoping it works out the way they both want. And, Doug, I want to thank you for what you said about our marriage. We agree, we have a good thing going, but it is great to have someone else see it and comment on it."

Tom asked, "Assuming you can see her in Sucy, what do you see happening there?"

Doug grinned and said, "Well, I will ask her to marry me. I will buy an engagement ring, I'm remembering le coup de foudre, before I leave for Sucy and find a romantic way to pop the question. I need to figure that out yet. And then I'll have to get busy and take care of the OAS and get back to her."

Maria laughed, "Oh, you are taken with her. Do you think she knows?"

"I think she does and that's why she set up the talk with Reverend Mother."

"Where will she stay after she leaves the church?"

"I don't know yet, but we'll figure it out."

Tom said, "Do you think she would be comfortable at our house in Sucy? I'm sure Henri and Belle would love having her there, you as well. Will you let us set that up for you?"

"That would be perfect."

"Consider it done."

"Can you hold off on the wedding date until June? We are planning a trip to Sucy for our first trip back."

"Then will you be my best man? And Maria, I'll bet Caroline will ask if you will be her matron of honor. Listen to us. She hasn't even said yes."

Again Maria laughed, "The way you are right now, it would be a good bet she is more ready to say yes if you ask. But Doug, are you sure about all this?"

"If she says yes, I'm ready. I don't know whether she will be willing to move to Michigan. That's what I would like to do."

"That would be great, Doug. Let her bring it up."

"See, I knew you would have some words of wisdom."

Tom asked, "How old is she? Do you know?"

"No, I don't. I think in her early twenties. But I'm only 32 years old so we should be okay. Say, I just happened to think, I will need to learn some French."

Maria said, "Caroline is bi-lingual. I'm sure she could help you with that. By the way, does she have a vocation?"

"I have no idea. But I can pretty well guarantee she wants children. She is really good with the kids in the nursery. So much to learn and decide on."

"Don't be discouraged, Doug. The two of you will figure it out. Remember what you told us in your toast and follow your advice to us."

After breakfast the next morning, there was a tearful goodbye. Tom and Maria didn't know when they would see him again. Tom held Maria. She had teared up as Doug drove away. He said, "He'll be okay."

42

———————

The next two weeks were filled with Tom full-time at the police station. Most of that time was working with his protégé, Gene, soon-to-be chief of detectives. A lot of it was Tom answering questions Gene had from his studies with the state police detective training. Gene had taken good notes and kept a record of what he was unsure of. Their sessions mainly consisted in getting Gene ready for his examination coming up just before Thanksgiving.

Tom got a good start to these sessions keeping his own notes for the book he would write as Mark had suggested. He was teaching Gene those techniques that he, Tom, had become aware of doing when he was working on the Group of Nine case. The two weeks flew by. Tom asked him, "Gene, do you think you are ready?"

Gene replied, "I do, but I'm going to spend the weekend prepping for my Monday test at the State Police school in Lansing."

Tom said, "I think you will do fine. If I may offer a suggestion, don't study all weekend. Just do a quick review of all that we did these two weeks. Then take Sunday off. Maybe do something special with your family but don't try to cram any more. It worked for me a lot when I was studying for finals."

"Thanks for all the time and help, Tom."

While Tom was finishing up at the station, Maria and Alice were spending some good time with the grandparents as well as another visit with Sara and their Ariana. By this time Alice and Arianna were great playmates. While they were occupied with toys and such, Sara and Maria had a chance for a good talk.

On the Monday that Gene was taking his test, Tom spent his last afternoon with Mark. Mark asked Tom some questions about his plans.

Tom said, "After finishing up with Gene and signing our agreement this morning, I have my first consulting contract. My next client, I hope, will be the city of Muskegon but I'm not going to do that right away."

Mark asked, "Are you concerned you will be rejected?"

Tom answered, "It's not that. I'll take my time working up to it. But I'm going to share something with you." He told Mark about the conversation with John Strahan and the dinner to come next week.

Mark smiled, "I didn't know about dinner until now. But I had a great conversation with Mr. Strahan last week. When I asked him why he was enquiring about you, he told me the same thing he told you. He said he believes this town has a lot of potential and that he believes you are the one to make it happen."

Tom laughed, "I didn't know he was coming to you. I wonder who else he has talked to."

"He didn't say anything about others except for Jim, our former boss."

Tom was thoughtful, "Knowing he is gathering info about me puts a little different spin on our dinner next week. I have no idea what he is going to say to me, but he said he will have a lot of questions. He wants to know what 'makes me "tick.' I never have thought about being as he puts it, 'a mover and a shaker.' Maria was a little concerned about his motives at first but now can't wait to hear what he has to say."

Tom stood up to leave.

"I'd better get home. Maria will wonder where I am and where Gerri is. Thanks for giving her an early out today. Gerri can't wait to get to know Alice. Oh, one more thing. We're having a Christmas open house on December 7th from 1-5 pm. We'll be sending some individual invitations. You and your family are invited. I'll also send you one to notify the department. We'll have lots of finger food, some music, and a lot of conversation. I hope you can come."

"We'll be there. Here comes Gerri. She's ready to roll.

Mark went on, "Tom, just take it as it comes. I happen to agree with him. I didn't say anything to you when you said you were thinking of working to expand on Fred's ideas for the city. That's why I didn't push to keep you on the force."

"Thank you for the vote of confidence, Mark. I hope I am worthy of all this."

Mark smiled, "I can't wait to see what you come up with. Go into it with your open mind. You'll do fine, my friend."

Tom led the way to their home. Gerri hadn't been there yet so she had to follow Tom. When Tom walked in, he called out, "We're here."

Maria and Alice came running for hugs from both Tom and Gerri. Alice found *Papa* first, then Maria said, "Alice, *voici Madame Gerri*"

Alice said, "*Bonjour, Madame Gerri.*"

Gerri said, "Will she someday call me Gerri?"

"In time she will, you will become good friends." She handed Alice to Gerri, pointing to her cheek. Alice remembered and kissed Gerri on the cheek. She teared up and said, "Aww."

Tom said, "Gerri, would you like a glass of wine before you drive home?"

Gerri said, "I thought you would never ask!"

The ladies made their way to the living room with the fireplace blazing. Tom was right back with three wine glasses of sauvignon blanc and Alice's glass with her juice. They all had a toast and welcome to Gerri.

Gerri, seeing Alice clinking all the glasses, asked, "Does she have some wine like I have heard children do in France?"

Maria laughed, "Not yet. It's just grape juice. Have a *profiterole* if you would like, please."

"What's in them?"

"Try it and I'll tell you."

43

"Here they come, right on time as I would have expected," Tom said.

Tom and Maria with Alice in her arms greeted John and Katherine in the foyer. John and Tom shook hands, Maria and Katherine had a hug and Alice said, "*Bonsoir, Madame et Monsieur* Strahan."

To Alice's joy, they replied, "*Bonsoir*, Alice."

Katherine said, "*Alice, nous serons de si bons amis.*"

Alice held out her arms to get her hug and then wanted down.

Katherine said, "Here comes Marlene, our cook. She has everything on one cart. Maria, would you show her where to put things in the kitchen? She will need two plugs to keep things hot."

While Maria was getting Marlene set in the kitchen, Tom took Alice, Katherine, and John into the living room. They found their seats near the fireplace and were chatting. Tom said, "I hope you don't mind that we have a small charcuterie board with some cheeses and crackers. Have you ever had a *Kir Royale*?"

Neither had Tom explained what they were. He had champagne in an ice bucket, the cream de cassis next to it, and the champagne glasses. He said, "May I make you one?"

Maria and Marlene had settled the beef stew on a burner, the Irish bread in a warming *oven*, and *salade capresse* chilling in the refrigerator. Marlene said, "Katherine, I will be back at 10:00 pm to pick you up. Is that right?"

Katherine looked at Tom and Maria who nodded, saying, "That's perfect, Marlene. Thank you, see you at 10:00 pm."

Tom had four champagne glasses with *Kir Royales* in each. They were all seated around the coffee table with the charcuterie board. Tom said, "May I make a toast? Here's to new friends, to become special friends." Alice, seated on the floor with her back to the fire and her glass on the coffee table, lifted her glass.

John asked, "May I also add a toast?" Tom nodded.

John said, "To Tom, a future leader of this community, who will bring many changes to a reality. Here, here." Glasses clinked once more including Alice.

Katherine exclaimed, "Alice has done this before, hasn't she. Does she have a *Kir Royale* in there?"

Maria laughed, "We were asked that question a few days ago. The answer is not yet. It's just grape juice. But she knows the routine."

They all sampled the board, had their *Kir Royales*, and chatted.

Tom finally said, "I have the Beaujolais open and breathing. Everyone ready for dinner?"

They were soon seated at the dining room table, Tom and Maria with Alice between them, Katherine and John across the table from them. Tom had set the big bowl of pot roast with veggies on the table and poured the dinner wine, Maria sliced the French bread to have with an olive oil, parmesan cheese and spices for dipping the bread. The salad was yet to come.

As was their custom, they said grace *en Français* to the delight of John and Katherine. Katherine said, "You have some routines already established with Alice. I'll bet she is a fast learner."

"She is. Tom's French is better than mine so he is the one who has brought her along so far. We're both working on it and can't wait until we start with Amelie."

Maria continued, "This is a wonderful beef stew. I'll have to remember to let Marlene know that. The beef is so tender, Alice is just going right after it, bite by bite. We'll see how it goes with the *salade capresse,* That will be a new experience for her."

Tom said, "I give you a choice to go with the salad, another Kir Royale or a sauvignon blanc that is one of our favorites."

John said, "I like the Kir Royale, but I want to try the sauvignon blanc please." Katherine echoed him. Tom poured four glasses as Maria brought out the *salade capresse* and salad plates. Maria cut up some pieces of tomato from the salad. All got a good look at Alice's way of tasting something new, put a little bite in her mouth, swirl it around, and express an opinion with her face. She liked the tomatoes! Maria told them about the experience when Doug took them to U.S. 31 Barbeques, and Alice not liking the sauce right away.

John asked, "Is Doug still here?"

Tom said, "No, he went to see his parents in Lansing and is now back in France on assignment. He hopes to be back in time for the presentation."

Katherine said, "I hadn't heard anything about a presentation. What is that all about?"

Maria interrupted, "Let me share that with you. Tom and I were part of a team led by Doug when there was another attempt on the life of President Charles de Gaulle. Tom's actions saved the day when he broke up the attack by the OAS. Tom shot and killed one of the members. Some members of the OAS followed us to Muskegon. The task force of FBI and Doug's agency stopped them cold. That's what the big fuss was about with the quick move into this house. Fortunately, Doug's team and the FBI stopped it, and captured the people at the old house. So now it is all over. No danger. Tom has received a commendation for what he did in France and JFK wants to formalize it when he returns from his tour of Texas. Doug is hoping to be back for that. We'll see."

"Very good, sweetheart. You didn't miss anything except the role you played. The commendation is for both of us no matter what JFK says.""

Katherine said, "May we have a dessert while we talk by the fireplace?"

"I have some scones, courtesy of Jeanne's recipe. They go well with coffee."

John said, "I don't want coffee with mine. I'm taking Tom up on his offer of another Kir Royalle to go with my scones. Then Tom and I will be ready to talk."

Alice had a little milk in her special cup. She sampled *Maman*'s scone and loved it. But she soon climbed up on *Maman*'s lap. Maria said, "I think it is time to put someone to bed."

Katherine asked, "May I join you as you do that? We'll let the men get their talk started."

Maria said to Alice, "Say goodnight to *Papa*." She climbed up on Tom's lap, gave him a hug and kiss on the cheek. She shyly waved to John and then Maria and Katherine went to put her to bed.

John said, "Well Tom. It's time. Tell me something about how you became the man you are today."

"I'm going to do the early part as though I were someone else telling you about a man named Tom O'Banion. When your questions start, we'll begin a conversation."

Tom started out talking about his loving parents. He had a younger sister who was an Rh factor baby. There was no treatment or cure in those days. She died when she was a year old and Tom was three. They couldn't have more children after that, so Tom became an only child. His parents focused all their attention on him. His mother was a pianist and noticed Tom starting to play with it when he was four years old. She made sure he had the piano lessons he needed. He had been taking lessons from age six, just took to it. The sister's death was a blow to the family and Tom in particular. He turned inward, spending a lot of time on the piano, and reading a wide variety of books, the children's classics, and in his teens moving up to biographies particularly about the country's founders. He read newspaper articles about political leaders of the day. He remembered being impressed with the new United Nations and what they did in the early days. He even took a course in college dedicated to the United Nations, its promises, and real achievements. His teachers also found he had strong mathematics skills where he learned to look for patterns as he studied more advanced math. Learning classical and jazz music came as his piano skills grew. Then when he was in 11th grade, he developed mumps orchitis and had to spend the rest of his junior year recuperating. During that time, he followed his dad's lead and read mysteries. They fascinated him, he studied the stories of Sherlock Holmes and learned how Holmes put observations and clues together. In short he learned how to be an investigator. His parents had hoped he would pursue the classics, but he fell in love with jazz music. The patterns in mathematics, he felt contributed to his ability to solve mysteries.

John interrupted, "The obvious effect of mumps orchitis prevented you from fathering children (I remember that from your trial), but what other effects did you experience? The question becomes, how much did that affect what you wanted to do with your life?"

"I didn't realize how all the reading I had done, and was still doing, was affecting my choices. I wanted to be a choir conductor but didn't want to let go of mathematics, history, and politics. And since I had a double major in music and mathematics, I also got exposed to physics at the university level. What I learned studying physics during that period was that what was true today might not be with new data. You had to be open minded when you read and researched physics to know that what is true today might not be tomorrow. More inputs from other researchers could change your thinking about a phenomenon."

Tom stopped for a moment and then went on, "That's when it dawned on me that if you don't read both sides of a question in math, physics, even politics, life – again, if you don't read all sides of an issue, you don't know or understand the issue. You are not the only one who has an idea and someone else with a similar idea may interpret it differently. If you don't listen to both sides you won't have anything close to reality or, the 'truth.'"

He continued, "Fred used to have a saying. 'If you don't listen to the other guy's input, you may miss something that will lead you to the truth. He was right."

"And one last point. You must always remember that your answer just might be the right one. If you give in too soon to adopt the other person's way, you and the truth might suffer. You should make that other person convince you."

John asked, "I'm beginning to see where your ideas about the city came from. The question, however, is not only how you convince the people of the city that your ideas are good ones, but how you encourage them to get on board and help you make them reality. People like to hear about new ideas but often won't change their old ways."

Tom said, "One of the things I have to be careful about is that I don't want to become another 'Group of Nine.' They, at least the leaders, had the notion that if they tied up all the property along the lakeshore, they could control what was built, and make a lot of money. I need input on how to find the kind of people who will generate ideas that will help us build this city as an intellectual center. I think the city missed a good bet to do that when it lost the opportunity to have the new Grand Valley College be located here."

"Then as we look around us, we have a city with an amazing potential to become a destination point. If we do this right, we can make that happen as well …" Tom hesitated, but John didn't interrupt him.. He waited for Tom to organize his thoughts.

Tom went on, "The city has grown from a lumber town to a town known for its industrial base. I'm not saying that I was wrong, but it is time to move on. The electronic company that Fred was trying to bring here could be just the beginning of a shift to a lighter cleaner industrial base out away from the lake. I think we can still get them to come here and that would be a good start."

John said, "You've given me a lot to think about. I haven't changed my mind, you're the man to do it but you need some people who will come on board with some of those ideas both for new industries and for what we need to make this a destination center, no longer skipped over when Chicago people come up the coastline. I know of some people who could help …"

Tom began again, "If you're not too tired, I have one more thing to touch on."

By this time, the ladies had rejoined them. John said, "Are you ready ladies?"

They nodded so he said, "Go for it."

Tom said, "Let me begin by telling you of my voting history. I came from a working-class family who were strictly Democrats, or as they want to be called today, liberals. My first year thinking about voting was in 1952 when I was in my first year at Muskegon Jr. College. That year it was Dwight Eisenhour vs Adlai Stevenson. I read about both men and chose Ike but couldn't vote for him. I was two months away from my 21st birthday and the 26th amendment wasn't ratified or signed into law until July 5, 1971. Still Ike was who I would have chosen and voted for. I went to hear Harry Truman try to sell Adlai Stevenson at the Muskegon Train Depot. I liked how President Truman talked but after reading about Ike said to myself, 'I can't vote for Stevenson.' From that day on, I believed myself to be an independent. There wasn't a big difference between their respective platforms in those days. If you read enough you could figure out who you thought was the best person to vote for. That's what I set out to do."

"I still read the platforms, listen to what they tell me in this year of 1963. One of the reasons I keep reading the way I do is because I believe that patterns make themselves known if you look. Since I am now 31 and have been studying the issues and voting, local and federal, for 10 years, the habit I built has paid off revealing patterns that help me know who to vote for. Now as I look at today's patterns, it seems to me in 1963 that there is a dissension between Democrats and Republicans that seems to be growing deeper every year. Every year it gets harder and harder to get a compromise solution. Now the question becomes, how will this affect what will happen to any plans we have for the city of Muskegon? The deepening dissension may become so bad, it will be more and more difficult to make any progress. If, and I admit that it is a big if, ... if that is the case it may be many years before we can bring about a change here. Now I'm done. If any of you have more questions, now is the time. But you may want to think about all this a little more. It is my pledge that if we undertake these changes, I will work hard to make them happen. There is an old saying, 'Keep your doubts to yourself, I have enough of my own.' I hope I didn't plant some in your minds."

John said, "I'm okay with you bringing this into the discussion. I, for one, needed to hear it. We'll see, indeed."

Katherine said, "I just saw Marlene drive in. We want to thank you for a lovely evening."

Maria said, "Thank you so much for a great dinner. It was good getting to know you. You'll get an invitation about the open house soon."

44

Cuddling in their new queen bed, Tom and Maria listened. No Alice awake yet. Tom started singing *Sunday, Sweet Sunday*.

Maria snuggled to him, "Wasn't it a lovely night?"

After a long passionate kiss, Maria asked, "Again?"

There was a knock on their door. Tom said," Uh oh, I think not."

Alice was getting out of her bed on her own now. They had taught her to knock first. Both got their nightclothes on and asked her in. After Tom lifted her up on the new big bed, it was all three laughing, giggling, and snuggling,

Maria said, "You know what I would like to do?"

Tom said, "I do know, sorry we can't."

"No, silly. I would like to spend a day with just the three of us. We have had a lot of company lately. I know it's Sunday but let's not get dressed up. We haven't missed a mass in some time, let's skip it today and just veg out."

Tom said, "You ladies just keep snuggling in this big bed. I'll build a fire in the fireplace and then make us some Sunday waffles and bacon. I'll spread out a blanket and we'll dine in style on Sunday waffles. I'll serve you a black coffee, Alice a milk with a taste of coffee in it.."

Tom kissed them both and said, "Now don't you move a muscle until I call you."

Tom got the waffles and bacon done and in the oven keeping warm. The coffees and milk coffee were ready. He spread the blanket in front of the fire and put some plastic over the blanket. Tom went to the foyer closet, put on his tuxedo jacket, a crooked bowtie, and top hat. Going to their bedroom, he knocked, opened the door, then said, "*Bonjour, mesdames suivez-moi.*"

They followed him into the living room to their places near the fireplace. He bowed to each one, held his tray with coffees high, served them each. Then he said, "*Disons la* grâce."

He waggled his finger at them and said, "Now, now, *en français, s'il vous plaît.*" They did so and toasted the brunch with their coffees.

Tom said, "*Excusez-moi mesdames.*" And went to the kitchen. He returned with a tray and three plates of waffles and bacon. As he bent over to put Alice's plate down, his top hat fell off. Maria caught it in the air and put it on Alice where it swallowed her head. Taking it right back off, she put it on herself, took Tom's plate, and put it where he would sit. When he was seated, there was laughter and giggles. Tom got caught up in the spirit.

Maria turned to Alice, and said, "Papa is silly, and he is funny. *En français,* she said, "*Papa est rigolo, et il est drôle.*"

They all burst into laughter again.

Maria cleaned up the blanket while Tom and Alice drank their coffee and milk coffee. Then they cuddled with Alice between and watched the fire. It didn't take long for all three to fall asleep.

About 15 minutes into their snooze, the phone rang. Tom grabbed it quickly so as not to wake Alice until she got her nap in. It was Doug.

Tom said, "Hi Doug. How is it going in Sucy?" Doug started out in a rush. Tom said, "Can you hold the good news for a couple of minutes? Maria will want to hear this too. So, how are things in Sucy?"

"Belle and Henri have been great. They are here and will be listening. They haven't heard the details yet. They are making some good progress on where things are going to go with your home here. They are almost ready to start slowly adding staff and booking events."

Maria got on the extension, "Hi Doug, what's happening with you and Caroline?"

Doug said, "Henri and Belle brought Caroline to Orly to pick me up. We sat together in the back seat. We were very careful, me because I didn't want to assume anything and Caroline because she didn't want to upset the Reverend Mother. Belle smiled when she caught us holding hands when she turned to talk with us." When they got back to the house in Sucy, Doug took the car and drove them both to the church for Caroline's meeting with the Reverend Mother. She came to her door, smiled, said hello to Doug, and beckoned Caroline to come with her.

"I'll let her tell you as much as she wants to when you see her again. I'll play all the roles and give you the story. Here's what Caroline did. She confessed to the Reverend Mother that she and I had been talking while Alice slept. She also saw how happy Tom and Maria are and began to see herself in that light. She remembered what I had told her about the way I think about marriage and how you two, Tom and Maria, were like that. I guess you could say 'she sold' the Reverend Mother. The Reverend Mother told Caroline to ask me to come in and she asked Father Lemire in. The conversation starts now."

Father Lemire didn't waste any time. He asked, "Caroline, do you love this man … enough to spend the rest of your life with him?"

She said, "Yes, and I have finally told him that. I can make that commitment. I know it is what I'm supposed to do, love him, and hopefully, have a house full of children."

"Has he said the same to you?"

"He has now. Doug wouldn't even tell me of his feelings for me or touch me. He wanted me to talk to Reverend Mother again about where to put my love."

Father Lemire turned to Doug, "Do you love her?"

"Father, I love her so much and believe we can build the kind of marriage that I have described to her, a marriage such as Tom and Maria have." Doug spent the next five minutes describing the kind of marriage he was talking about.

Then Doug smiled, "How soon can it happen?"

"Hold on a minute. I have some more questions for you. What happened in your first marriage?"

"I was still in the military at that time, a member of the CIA. I was gone a lot and began to not like myself. So though I still cared for her, I wasn't leaving the military, she didn't like being alone, and I was no longer happy. We parted amicably. I haven't seen her in over 10 years. I'm ready to work to do it right."

"Are you Catholic and if not, are you willing to take on the Catholic faith?"

Doug looked at each in turn, finally to Caroline, and said, "I'm ready to do whatever I need to, to make a good marriage with this woman." He took her hand.

Father Lemire and Reverend Mother laughed, and she said, "I believe she has a good one waiting for her to share her love."

Doug said, "Good. When can we do it? We want Tom and Maria to be our best man and matron of honor. They are planning a trip to Sucy sometime in late spring. I/we were hoping we could do a quick wedding soon and have a full ceremony with a full mass when they come back."

"I don't know if it can move that fast. When do you leave for this last mission?"

"I've talked with the French authorities that I work with and they want to start next week. They have already begun surveillance and think it won't take long."

Father Lemire said, "Let me talk to the Bishop. Because of the divorce, we may have to get a dispensation from the Pope, we'll see. Where will you be staying?"

"Henri and Belle have agreed to put me up before I leave and put us both up after. I think Maria and Tom had something to do with that."

"That's the gist of the conversation. But there's one more thing. We shared our first kiss before driving back here."

The next afternoon, Doug and Caroline were sitting in the big main room with Belle and Henri having a glass of wine and some cheese and crackers. Belle was teasing them about sitting so close and holding hands. Belle said, "We thank you for asking Henri and I to be your witnesses er… stand-ins for Tom and Maria. We are honored."

`Caroline said, "We thank you for doing it. And as to holding hands, that is all that can happen until we get the word from Father Lemire and the Bishop, maybe even the Pope."

Doug started to answer as well when the phone rang. Belle took the call and said, "It's Father Lemire. He wants you, Caroline, and Doug on the extension."

Father Lemire, "Someone is looking after you two, When I was called back in a conference call with the Bishop and the Pope, I was holding my breath until the Pope said to get you married. Someone as devoted as you two need to be together. How would you like to get married Saturday afternoon?"

They replied together, "We would love it. Will you handle the wedding?"

"I will. May l speak with Belle please?"

He asked Belle, "Do you think it would be possible to have the wedding at the house there on Saturday afternoon?"

Belle said, "I figured it went well. They are hugging, oops."

"But please tell them it's only a day and a half away. Patience, patience. And Belle, could you have your cooking staff do a small dinner? It will be the Reverend Mother and I, the four of you, and Jean Paul and his wife."

"How about your nuns? Will any of them be coming?"

"No, that would be too many for here. They know they will be a big part of the more formal ceremony next June in the chapel."

"I'll get that all set when we hang up. Do you need to talk to Doug or Caroline?"

He said, "Yes to both if you have an extension."

Henri took Tom to the kitchen so he could get on the extension. So they were both on now with Father Lemire. He said, "Could you both come over about nine tomorrow morning? I need to go over a shortened version of the Pre-Marriage that you are both supposed to go through. It should take until 11:30 or so. Then I'll have some reading material for you to read together."

Caroline answered, "We can do that, Father.

45

———

When they arrived the next morning, Caroline was taken in hand by the Reverend Mother. Doug asked Father Lemire, "I thought we would both be with you for the instructions."

"You will be. Reverend Mother just has some final instruction for her and will give her some new civilian clothes and she will change into those before she comes to us. There are some things she might need to know about before Saturday. Belle has agreed to quiz her as to the extent of her knowledge about sex and answer any questions she might have. Then because you are more knowledgeable than Caroline, Belle may find that she wants to get her questions answered from you. Do you have any thoughts about this?"

Doug said, "I have no problem with Belle talking to her. But I'll bet she will prefer to get her questions answered by me. She is pretty independent. I trust Belle and have no problem either way it goes."

"We have seen that in her. You may be right." There was a knock on the door. "Come in."

Reverend Mother said to Doug, "Here is your bride-to-be. She is all dressed in blue to match those beautiful blue eyes she has."

Doug's mouth dropped, he stuttered, … Then finally said, "You are lovely, Caroline.' He reached out to her. She smiled, took his hand, and said, "Thank you, kind sir. I'm in love with you, you know."

Doug, with tears trying to escape, said, "And I with you. I love you so much."

Both Reverend Mother and Father Lemire smiled, and said, "We think these two are going to be just right together. Come in, ladies."

The nuns of the chapel came in with a coffee pot, plates of cookies, and big smiles for them both. One of them said, "I've been selected to congratulate you both from all of us. We have never seen a more beautiful bride and handsome man. We will be with you in spirit tomorrow afternoon and pleased to be a part of the more formal full service in June."

Caroline and Doug both teared up. Then she was getting hugs from each nun and Doug shook a lot of the ladies' hands. He shook hands with Father Lemire and got a sort of hug from Reverend Mother. The nuns all sat around talking with each other and Caroline. Doug could see how much Caroline was loved by this group. He said, "Thank you all for being a part of the start of our marriage. I could tell from the looks on your faces that you love her a lot. I'll take good care of her."

Caroline said, "That was a touching time. I will miss you all. You have been my family for a long time now. I will cherish my memories of each of you."

When all the other ladies had left, there was a hush for a moment. Father Lemire said, "I don't have much more to talk to you about. With your idea or concept of what makes a marriage work, I think you are both ready right now. Do either of you have questions?"

They looked at each other and said together that they had none.

Father Lemire asked Doug, "Would you do something for me? I wonder if you would be willing to write down what you said as you described your picture of a good marriage. I would like, with your permission, to use parts of it at your formal wedding in June and maybe beyond if you allow me?"

Doug said, "Father, I am flattered. And yes, for our wedding in June and then beyond. I'll get it written up before I leave on my trip."

"Good. Thank you. We'll see you tomorrow afternoon,"

When they got into the car, they looked at each other, smiled, held hands tightly, and each said, 'I love you.'

Doug said, "I'm going to call the house on my agency phone, ask them if Jean Paul and his wife are coming and tell them we will be back to the house in a couple of hours. We'll stop and have lunch somewhere and then I want to go to the park by the lake and talk. How does that sound to you?"

Caroline said, "I like that. I'm so overwhelmed by how fast it is all happening that I'm not sure how much I can eat,"

"Maybe we could just get some snacks and something to drink and go right out to the park." She nodded yes.

Doug called Belle, "Hello, Belle, Doug here. We are so happy. It has gone well and we are having a wedding tomorrow."

"Congratulations to you both. When will you be home?"

"We are going to get some takeout and have a little picnic in the park by the lake. We should be home between three and 4 p.m. Is that okay?"

"That's fine. I just got off the phone with Reverend Mother so we are already putting things together. I will be calling Jean Paul and letting him know when to be here tomorrow. I'll have all the details done by the time you get here. See you then."

"Thank you Belle, for all you are doing. Goodbye for now."

Doug headed for a small restaurant he knew about. They asked if takeout was available. They soon had their sandwiches and lemonade and were on the way to the park. Doug said, "I have a jacket for you to wear when we are at the picnic table. I don't like covering up your new dress but it is somewhat chilly."

Before they left the car, Doug reached for Caroline, They kissed, a long kiss, gentle but deep. They held on to each other for a few more minutes. Caroline said, "Now we can get out and have a good long talk." Doug put the jacket on her. They found a clean table close to the water's edge.

He said, "Now, may I serve you, *chèrie.?*"

She said, "But, of course."

They ate as they talked. They covered what would be happening on the morrow and later that night. Caroline smiled, saying "I want you and I am ready for you. But tomorrow night after the wedding. Do you mind the wait?"

"Not at all. There is right and proper, that is the way it will be."

She leaned over for a quick kiss and then laughed. He looked puzzled. She said, "You have some of my mayonnaise on your lips."

He licked his lips, and said, "That's okay, you can feed me that way anytime." They both laughed, she kissed him again.

The conversation continued on many lines, their future together, where they would live, how many children they wanted, and how they would grow together.

Doug soon said, "We had better get moving. We have about 30 minutes from here to home." They cleaned up, took off their jackets, and were soon on their way.

Doug and Caroline were about to knock on the door when it flew open. Caroline and Belle hugged, Henri and Doug shook hands. All of a sudden they all started talking. Belle finally got the floor and said, "I have a bottle of champagne chilling and some cheese and crackers ready. We need to celebrate the way things turned out. Maybe while we are doing that you can tell Henri and I what happened."

Doug said, "That sounds great but I need to get a couple of phone calls done first. I need to talk with Jean Paul, just one question for him. And then we need to talk with Maria and Tom." Can we get those calls in first?"

"Sure, that will work. Caroline, you and I can get the goodies together while Doug is talking with Jean Paul." Doug, smiling, watched as Caroline followed Belle into the kitchen. As he turned to get his satellite phone, he noticed Henri smiling and shaking his head.

"Hello, Jean Paul."

"I hear things are moving right along for you and Caroline. Did it surprise you that it fell into place that quickly?"

"It did. But then Father Lemire can be very persuasive as can the Bishop. We're so happy it worked out quickly."

"My wife and I will be there for both ceremonies. Is there something else you need before tomorrow?"

"Just one quick question. Have you gotten one of those Ericsson speaker phones yet?"

"I have, but I haven't even tried to use it yet."

"Would you be interested in using it to try and connect Tom and Maria into the ceremony?"

"Have you used one yet?"

"I have but a tech at the agency set it up for me. I'm changing my mind. I'm not so sure I want to try this. We'll just pick them up on the satellite phone."

"I wouldn't mind using it, but it occurs to me you'll have other things on your mind."

"I think you are right. See you tomorrow, Jean Paul."

Doug immediately dialed Tom and Maria. "Hello Tom."

"Hi, Doug. We have been looking forward to hearing from you. How are you and Caroline doing?"

"Tom, it is like all our dreams come true. The Bishop and the Pope were persuaded by Father Lemire that it was the right thing to do." After Maria and Alice had joined the party, Doug did a quick rundown of how everything was going to be, the simple ceremony tomorrow and the full ceremony at the church with a high mass. "With your permission, Belle and Henri will be witnesses. So it is almost like a civil ceremony and the real thing next summer with you as my best man and Maria, you as her matron of honor."

Maria asks, "Caroline is okay with this arrangement?"

Watching for Caroline, Doug said, "Yes, actually proposed it, and the church folks approved it."

"I'll have my sat-phone going tomorrow so you can hear us. I think it will work out so you can,"

"And here's one more piece of news. We're coming to Muskegon in about two weeks. What do you think about that?'

Tom asked, "Does that mean you'll be moving back here?"

"That's what we are thinking. We've had long talks about that. We'll have much to talk about when we get there."

"The ceremony is at three pm here so that will be 9:00PM Michigan time. We'll talk to you then. Love you both."

46

———————

Doug woke early in the small bedroom downstairs. He could smell the coffee so he dressed and headed for the kitchen, bringing his paper and pen. He had to get the words down for Father Lemire.

Belle said, "I'll have breakfast ready in a few minutes."

She heard a voice from upstairs, "Good morning, Belle. That coffee sure smells good."

Belle said, "*Non, non, non.* You can't be down here right now."

"Why not?"

"Doug is here at the kitchen table writing his words for Father Lemire. I'll get him moved somewhere and call you down in a few minutes."

Doug asked, "What's this all about?"

"Tradition says that a husband-to-be can't see his future bride on their wedding day before he sees her walking down the aisle."

Caroline said, "That's a silly rule!"

"Just the same. I've been asked to see to this wedding ceremony and we are going to follow the rules."

Henri, on cue, came to take Doug into the library. He said, "Belle says she will bring you bacon and eggs shortly. When you're ready.

we'll sneak out, have a draft and a light lunch. I'll get you back in time to get dressed for the wedding."

Belle called upstairs, "You can come down now, Caroline."

She came down to the kitchen and said, "I still think it is a silly rule."

Belle said, "You have some spunk, Caroline. Don't lose it!" The three of them, Belle, Henri, and Caroline had a bacon and eggs breakfast with some fruit on the side. And lots of Belle's good coffee.

When Henri had finished his breakfast, Belle said, "Henri, could I get you to find another place to be? Caroline and I have a conversation to finish."

Henri said, "Okay, but when he finishes his words for the good Father, we'll be leaving for a little ride around town. Don't worry, we'll be back in plenty of time for Doug to get dressed and ready."

Cariline asked, "Will he really get Doug back here?"

"He will. He is just being Henri for Doug's benefit."

Belle smiled, "Now do you have any questions for me? Your mother is not around and a nunnery has no one there who can answer them. So, ..."

Caroline blushed and said, "I do know a little bit, but only a little. I was only 14 when we lost Mom. Dad did the best he could but he fumbled it a bit. And before I left high school, I heard a lot from the other girls. But they mostly ignored me because I was so shy. Same for the boys. I was too shy for most of them."

"Then when I went to college, my roommate tried to tell me some things. So my knowledge is pretty sparse. not very complete. My feeling is that Doug will be gentle, ... but still."

Belle gave her a quick talk about the parts of both bodies, male and female. She drew some pictures and gave names to parts. Then she pointed out what Doug would do. She said, "I'm pretty sure you are a virgin, so the first time may hurt. It won't happen again." She went on to explain things. She said that if sex is done right, it can be a great sharing of your love for each other. "Do you know what a condom is?"

"I do. I've seen pictures. Doug plans to use them for now."

"I hope he will for a while, unless you both want children right away."

"Doug and I talked about that yesterday. He thinks we should use them for the first few months. He said that it wouldn't do to have a baby on the way that people would see in the church."

"What do you think? Are you okay? Any other questions?"

Caroline said, "It seems to me that in the beginning we will be learning each other's body and what works best for us. Thank you. We'll figure it out."

Belle said, "I just heard them drive away. Now we can talk about the wedding proper. Father Lemire will keep things moving. He, Doug, and Henri will be standing with their backs to the fireplace."

"Once we know that everyone is seated, the men are in place, one of my servers will signal me. I'll come walking down our makeshift aisle. She'll stop my music and put Mendelssohn's Wedding Song on the record player. She will help you down the last few steps and Henri will come, take your arm, then walk you down to Doug. Do you want to go through a non-musical walk through?"

"I don't think I need it. I remember directions pretty well."

"Do you have Doug's ring for me?"

"I brought it down," she said, and gave it to Belle.

Belle said, "It's going to be a lovely wedding. Give me a hug."

They heard a loud knock on the front door. Belle said, "The men are back. You had better get upstairs. Want a little glass of wine to relax you?"

Caroline said, "No thank you. I have something else. My prayers will keep me calm and relaxed.

Guests started arriving, Jean Paul and his wife Joline, Reverend Mother and Father Lemire. Father Lemire and the men got in position facing where Caroline would come from. Doug was wearing a pair of light grey pants, a white shirt, tie, and linen sport jacket with a bouton-niere. Father Lemire had brought his materials and laid them out on a high table. He nodded to the lady running the music and Belle walked down to the men in her pale blue gown and corsage on her left shoul-der. When she moved left, Mendelssohn's Wedding Song started. Caro-line walked in on Henri's arm and in her new white knee length skirt, white silk blouse, and French Style Lace Eyelet top. She was carrying a bouquet featuring perfect yellow roses, picked by Caroline for their meaning which is: the wearing of yellow roses includes optimism, hope, and happiness.

Doug saw her coming down the aisle, his knees started to buckle. Father Lemire put Doug's hand on the high table until he steadied. Father Lemire completed the service, the rings were on fingers, he told them to kiss, and said, "Ladies and gentlemen, please say hello to Douglas and Caroline McDermott." Then for this small group everyone just converged on the happy couple. All formality was gone and people who cared for each other wished all well and just hugged.

Belle raised her voice, saying *"Allons à de la salle à manger.* Champagne awaits. Doug and Caroline are going to take a few minutes to talk to Tom, Maria, and Alice. They have been listening on the satphone."

Doug said, "Tom, Maria, and Alice, I would like to introduce you to Caroline McDermott. I wish you could see how lovely she is. You'll see her soon."

They talked for another few minutes with a promise to call back tomorrow and let Tom and Maria know where they were honeymooning.

They kissed again. A kiss of promise. Caroline said, "Let's go be with our guests."

47

Caroline and Doug hummed the Mendelsohn wedding song as they walked in. Everyone stood and clapped for their entry. As they all sat, the champagne was poured for the toasts to them. Jean Paul's toast was short and to the point of what he had learned about them, saying, "Welcome to your new world. May it be filled with joy and that big family you told me you wanted!"

Belle's, equally short, saying, "I've seen how deep your love is. Make it count for a good life filled with joy."

Father Lemire said, "I've shared my thoughts with both of you. I am never so pleased as I am today to have lost a potential nun, a loving one, to her friend and loved one, Doug. I'm now deferring to the Reverend Mother."

She said, "Caroline, when you came to tell me of what you wanted, I was filled with misgivings. I wasn't sure you had found your way to share your love. But the more I got to know Doug and saw you together with him, the more certain I was that you both had found your way. Many years of happiness to you."

The charcuterie boards and more champagne were there for them after the toasts. Caroline and Doug shared what they had talked about with Tom and Maria. Doug said, "They were pleased to be able to hear the ceremony and thanked everyone for speaking up so they could. When Alice heard our voices, she knew both of them, saying Oncle Doug and Caroline They can't wait to see us in about two weeks."

Belle said, "What is this? We hadn't heard about this yet."

Caroline said, "We decided it yesterday. I forgot to tell you, I'm sorry."

Doug added, "We need to see them. They brought us together at the church."

Father Lemire asked, "Are you considering moving back there?"

"That is one of the things we're looking at. We need to find what is the right path for us for the long run. I need to get 'mustered out' as they still call it. Though I have officially been a member of the CIA SO team, I was still in the Army and at the rank now of Major. At my request and Caroline's agreement, breaking that bond will free us up to make a permanent choice for our best future."

Caroline added, "There is another reason for going. I know very little about the United States. I need to spend a little time there seeing if my impressions are accurate. Also if I feel comfortable there. So much to learn. I'm anxious to meet Doug's parents. They are so proud of him, his career. How will they feel about him leaving it behind? So many questions."

Doug continued, "We'll be coming back after Thanksgiving to see you all again, to see Caroline's dad in his nursing home, and to finish our honeymoon in the Swiss Alps. We haven't made plans beyond that."

Belle signaled to the servers. They brought wine glasses and offered the same Sauvignon blanc Tom and Maria had taken back to the states with them, a lovely vin rosé, and a full-bodied Beaujolais. They were told dinner was a special Belle recipe chicken Cordon bleu.

Wines were poured; Father Lemire led grace *en français*.

The dinner was up to Belle's standards and many said so. It finished with a tasty *salade capresse*.

Belle said, "We'll let our dinner settle a little and have dessert later in the living room.

Doug said, "Belle, I will report to Tom and Maria that you have taken dining to the level of a top-notch restaurant in France. Well done, milady!" All toasted and gave Belle a round of applause.

Belle noticed and asked Caroline, "Did you not like any of the wines tonight? I noticed you just sipping a little of each offering. And for that matter, you too Doug, you have been barely sipping the wines. What's going on with you two?"

Caroline blushed, smiled and said, "We made a pact yesterday out at the lake that we would not overdo on the wine." She blushed again and said, "This is a special night for us and we don't want to have drunk too much."

Reverend Mother, "What a pair you both make. So much wisdom in two so young."

Caroline started tearing up. Doug held her. She said, "I am going to miss you all at the church. I know we said our goodbyes yesterday, but .. well it is a sweet parting. Leaving behind people you have loved and been with so long." Doug held her tight.

Reverend Mother said, "But look ahead at the new life you will be building. That is what will carry you on."

Doug kissed her, she brightened up, Belle beckoned the servers for the dessert and digestif.

Dessert was one of Belle's inventions, a profiterole body in the shape of a small wedding cake and her coffee. They adjourned to the living room. The happy couple cuddled across from all of the rest. They were to have a *digestif* of *Armagnac* from the *région de Gascogne*. Doug and Caroline barely tasted theirs.

The happy couple slipped away upstairs amid promises to see them before they left for the States. When they all had left, Henri and Belle sat at their kitchen table sipping their wine talking with the ladies. When the crew left, Henri said, "Let's go upstairs and celebrate with them!!"

Belle said, "Henri! ...

He said, "Come on. We're on the other side of the building from the new bridal suite." He took Belle's hand and away they went!

Next morning, the four of them enjoyed Belle's breakfast of waffles and crisp bacon. Doug and Caroline thanked them for everything over and over. Doug said, "I want to pay for this, may I?"

Belle said, "We have strict instructions about that. Tom and Maria said 'No charge to these two, not a penny. Not these two.'"

"We will be in Paris. We will be staying at the *Hotel Des Deux-Iles* on *Ile Saint-Louis* across a short bridge to the *Île de la Cité* and *Notre Dame*. We'll be there three days and two nights, so much to see, then we'll be right back here on Wednesday. Can Caroline stay until I get back from my short job? Then we fly back to the United States next Saturday, the 23rd?" Doug asked.

Belle said, "We look forward to you coming back, I know you have an appointment with Jean Paul. We'll plan on dinner here Wednesday night. We will enjoy you while you are here. And wish you back soon."

Caroline said, "You are the best, Belle. I've known you for a while through the church, but now our relationship has changed, for the better. I feel close to you."

Belle grabbed her for a prolonged hug. Since the men were loading luggage, she asked, "Were you okay with last night?"Caroline blushed one more time and said, "It was as special as you said."

Henri and Doug came back in. Doug said, "We're off! You have my sat-phone number if anything comes up." Doug hugged Belle and Henri hugged Caroline. Belle and Henri stood with arms entwined, Belle sniffling a little. She told Henri about Caroline's feeling close to her.

"Almost like having a daughter."

Belle said, "How did you know I was thinking that?" Henri just smiled.

48

Caroline and Doug found so much to do in and around their honeymoon hotel. So many new experiences for Caroline. She had never been to Paris. They toured Notre Dame cathedral, Sainte Chapple, some of the bridges across the Seine, They found a bookstore on the Seine's left bank with an interesting history. When talking with the shop owner, he spoke of the history and sold them a small booklet that laid out the story. On the way back to Sucy Caroline read while Doug drove. She was ready to tell the story to Belle and Henri. Belle saw how excited she was about the story and said, "Take your luggage up to your room. I'll set out some gougère, a new treat, for me, a choux pastry dessert with Emmentaler cheese. While we enjoy the gougère and some wine, you can tell us your story.

Once they were settled in with everything, Caroline started in. "It seems that back in 1919, a woman named Sylvia Beach started a bookstore on the Left Bank right where the store is today. She chose the name Shakespeare and Company. Her store closed in 1941 just as World War II was starting. Then in 1951, George Whitman, an ex-soldier in World War II started an English language bookstore in the same spot with the name 'Le Mistral'. He modeled his store after Sylvia Beach's. Ms. Beach gave him her store name in 1958. But even with his name Whitman's store, Le Mistral, quickly became the focal point of literary culture in Paris. Henri and especially Belle had so many questions.

When Caroline finished her story, Belle said, "I see some new clothes for you, Caroline."

"Yes, it was so much fun shopping in Paris. I still need some things. There must be a women's shop here in town. Would you take me shopping?"

"I would love to. Will Doug be going too?"

Doug said, "Why don't you two have a ladies' day out tomorrow and surprise me with a fashion show when you return? Henri and I will be leaving early in the morning to talk with the Sûreté. They have the OAS routed already. They are in custody and will be deported to their homeland. No more active missions for me! Henri is making first overtures to them concerning the home here being cleared as a place for foreign dignitaries. When we get back, I'll take you all to dinner tonight. Henri said he would find a good restaurant close by and make reservations."

"That sounds great. We'll leave at ten a.m. and be back home by three or so."

Doug said, "The only meeting we have left is with Jean Paul. That's tomorrow, Thursday the 21st. Then we're yours until Saturday the 23rd when we fly to Washington and then on to Muskegon after a brief stop."

Belle said, "Now that the rest of your time here is all laid out. How about telling us of some of the other highlights of your Parisien play time?"

Caroline said, "Do you mind if we postpone that? I think I'll get me a nap, How about you, Doug, join me?"

"I think I will. Do you two mind? We'll be all ready for dinner later." She grabbed Doug's hand and headed up the stairs.

When they heard the honeymoon door close, Belle and Henri looked at each other and smiled. Belle said, "They'll sleep eventually. Right now they can't get enough of each other."

"You're right. I'm going to make the reservation for tomorrow night at our favorite little bistro downtown. What do you think, 6:00 p.m.?

"That's a good time. I guess we'll find out about their sightseeing tonight at dinner. I'm going to make something simple, just a light dinner for tonight."

In the meantime, Caroline came out of the bathroom in one of her delicate nighties. Doug was already in bed, watching her, he said. "you are beautiful, *Cherie*."

He sang to her, "Come to me, come to me, kiss me goodnight."

She slipped her nightie off. He took her into his arms, kissed her, a long deep kiss. She said, "Now, Doug, now."

He held her close and whispered in her ear, "I love you. I thought this would never happen to me."

"But we found it, didn't we? Or it found us. And we have so much ahead of us."

Doug pulled the covers up around them. They slept.

Next morning, they awoke, smelled coffee, and Doug said, "I think we ought to get pajamas and robes on."

"Do you think they heard us last night?"

"I don't know if they heard us. But if they did, they wouldn't say a word. They are a class act."

They started downstairs, Caroline asking, "Can we come down?"

"Come on down, the coffee's ready and Belle is making scrambled eggs and tomatoes."

They came down the stairs holding hands. Belle took pictures. "I'll make sure I get the wedding and these printed before you go." She gave each of them a cup of coffee.

"Ah, your coffee is so good, Belle, award winning.

They gathered at the table and enjoyed Belle's eggs and tomatoes. Caroline liked the taste of tomatoes with the eggs and told Belle so. She said, "I'll have to share this combination with the nuns. I bet they would like it too."

Doug said, "You may need to pick up another suitcase for your new clothes. Here is money that should be enough for clothing and the suitcase. I'm sure Belle can help with styles and colors. I'm looking forward to your style show tonight."

Henri and Doug left first, headed for the Sûreté offices near Orly. Director Garnier has business there so he asked if they could meet there.

When Henri drove into the parking area for headquarters, he saw not only the Sûreté dark sedans, but a big limousine with official French markings on it. Henri said, "I wonder what else is happening here."

Doug said "The director said nothing to me. I'm in the dark. Well, let's get this done."

Director Garnier was waiting for them just outside a door to another room in the back. "Come along Doug and Henri. You both need to be here but for different reasons."

The room was a large meeting area to the right. On the left, there was a room for more formal meetings, a fireplace at the far end, and a coffee table in the center of the seatings. The man with a glass of champagne was standing at the fireplace. When he heard them come in, he turned and said, "Douglas McDermott, it's so good to see you again. I appreciate you coming today."

"President De Gaulle, good to see you again as well. But I don't understand why we both are here together. My meeting was with Director Garnier."

"The steward is behind you and the others with a glass of champagne for each, including you Henri. I'm so glad you came. Doug, the reason I am here today is to present you with our *Légion d'honneur*."

"We have a commendation for the years you have been of service to France along with the *Légion d'honneur* which I would like to pin to your lapel. It is my great pleasure and honor to present them both to you." They all raised their glasses to toast Doug as it was being pinned on. Then there was a round of applause and more champagne.

"Mr. President, I deeply appreciate the commendation and the *Légion d'honneur*. France has become my second country. I love her sense of honor and citizenship. It has been an important alliance for me. Thank you so very much."

Another toast and round of applause. Doug caught the twinkle in Henri's eyes and waggled his finger at him. He had known what was coming.

The President said, "When I mention this next good achievement, I will call you Doug. Would you please call me 'Charles'?"

Doug said, "That I cannot do, Mr. President. In our country, the President is always called President Kennedy and not Jack, or just Kennedy. It is our symbol of respect. Mr. President, what is this next 'good' achievement?"

"Doug, thank you for your honoring your tradition with me in our country. The other achievement is your recent marriage with Caroline, one of our French ladies. From what I hear, it is a good choice for both of you. Congratulations!" There was one more toast and applause.

He continued, "Now I must move on. We have business back at the palace and you have business here. Thank you again, so much, Doug." He shook hands with each person in the group and was soon on his way.

For the next 15 minutes, Doug and the Director were in one room discussing the elimination of the OAS and the likelihood that it would be permanent. He ended with "Now that you are no longer active in the business of helping us solve problems, I would be pleased if you would call me Jules. The 's' is not pronounced."

Doug said, "I am pleased to meet you as Jules."

Director Garnier thanked Henri and said that a contact person would be in touch soon to take the next steps to see if the home could be designated a government refuge for visiting dignitaries. He thanked Henri Picard for getting Doug here.

When the ladies arrived back home in the afternoon, Henri and Doug were already there chatting like the two best friends they had become.

After kissing the appropriate spouse, the two ladies were offered a glass of the Sauvignon blanc the men were enjoying. When Henri returned with their glasses and topped off the men's, Caroline came in from the kitchen. She had on a light coat, she turned to show it off, and when she did, Doug saw her in one of the new fashions, a pair of navy-blue slacks with a pale blue top dressy enough to make the combo fashionable. Doug clapped. "I love the combination. You look *sophistiqué et charmant*. I applaud you."

She said, "But no kiss this time?"

He grabbed her, kissed her, and swung her around the room in a waltz step. Henri was prompted to do the same with Belle, to her great pleasure.

Caroline asked, "Do you think I should wear it tonight? Is it too much of a change if we see someone we know?"

Doug said, *"Oui absolu*, you are your own woman now. You may set your own ideas now!"

With a smile, Caroline hugged him saying, "I love you."

Belle opened her new light coat to show off her new dress. Henri said, "Oh la la. Look at you, lady."

Belle said, "Caroline bought it for me. Isn't it lovely?"

Doug looked at Caroline, applauded her with small claps.

Henri said "We need to leave soon. Shall we take these two grand ladies to dinner?"

49

They walked into the lovely bistro and were greeted by the owner, "Good evening, *Monsieur* Picard, we are all ready for your special occasion. We have you seated in the little bay window overlooking the pond out back." The candles were already lit, water glasses full, and a bottle of champagne chilled. All eyes were following them and when the ladies' coats were removed, there was a stir of conversation.

Doug held a chair for Caroline, as did Henri for Belle. The owner introduced Andre, their waiter for the evening. The waiter said, "I am told to ask who is Doug?"

Doug said, "Here I am. And please call me Doug while you serve us."

Andre asked, "May I serve your champagne?"

"Please do. And may we have your appetizer of *gougère* with *Provençale* Sauce."

"Certainly, Doug," as he filled their glasses. He left them with their toasts while getting the *gougère*.

Caroline asked Doug, "Will you tell us something about *gougère* with *Provençale* Sauce?"

Doug replied, "*Gougère* is a *pâte à choux*, or a *Choux* pastry, very delicate and served tonight with a tomato-based herbed sauce and drizzled with a little olive oil to give a Mediterranean twist. I hope you like it."

Doug said, "Here's to Belle and Henri for being superb hosts since we have been here. And Belle, as a gourmet cook, may we ask what is good here" Everyone began thinking about their entrée.

Andre arrived with the *gougère* with *Provençale* Sauce. He served it and asked, "Do you have any questions about entrees, or do you need more time?"

Doug asked, "Henri or Belle, would you like to recommend a dish for us all?"

Henri said, "I defer to Belle, she never misses.

She said, "Andre how is the *boeuf bourguignon tonight?"*

"Madame Belle, tonight the chef has excelled. It is at its best ever. A good choice."

"Fine, we will have that and one of your crusted breads, warm and with a dipping sauce of olive oil with your herbs."

"*Oui*, Madame, excellent *choices*."

Doug asked, "And a wine to fit such excellence?"

"I normally recommend the *Beaujolais* that compliments the *Bourguignon* very well. But if you would like to be a little more adventurous, I would suggest a tempranillo from Spain."

Doug looked around and with the nods, he chose the tempranillo. Doug asked, "How about we skip the salad and end on some *profiteroles* with coffees or tea?"

Everyone enjoyed the rest of the evening with Henri and Belle finally hearing more about their sightseeing in Paris.

50

Next morning, Doug and Caroline met Jean Paul. Caroline saw his door, Jean Paul Lament, Atty at Law. Caroline whispered, "This is the first time I have ever been at an attorney's office."

Doug said, "It's Jean Paul. You'll remember him from the wedding."

Jean Paul was waiting for them at his inner door. "Ah, here are the newlyweds, Doug and Caroline, so glad to see you. This is my assistant, Aileen."

Doug shook hands with both, saying, "Good morning Jean Paul."

Caroline, with her permission, had quick cheek kisses from them both, and said, "Hello Monsieur Lament and Aileen."

Jean Paul said, "I would prefer Jean Paul, if it is okay with you."

Cariline said, "Jean Paul, good to see you, too. And good to meet you, Aileen. This is all so new to me."

Jean Paul said, "Come on in. Let's chit-chat for a few minutes. Aileen will be joining us shortly. Caroline, what did you see in Paris that you would like to tell me about?"

Caroline smiled, "There is so much for me to see, new things that I've known about but never seen. My mother passed when I was quite young, and Dad had health issues that shortly confined him to a nursing home. Doug is trying to make up for some of those things I hadn't seen. We toured the Notre Dame Cathedral. You could see it from our hotel room on Ile Saint Louis. Then we toured Sainte Chapple on Ile de la Cite. Such magnificent stained-glass displays. And then the shops on both Iles, they were wonderful. So many new clothes!"

"Is what you are wearing a part of your new wardrobe? I must compliment you on it."

"It is. I especially like it. It's supposed to be the latest fashion for women. Doug says I look best with white and a light blue top that works well for me. He kept insisting on one more ensemble," as she smiled at him.

Aileen walked in with coffee and cookies. She said, "I like it too. You are lovely."

"Thank you, Aileen."

Jean Paul said, "I understand also that congratulations are in order. Monsieur Garnier called with the news yesterday afternoon of your award from President De Gaulle. Well done, Doug, this is special and well deserved.

Doug said, "Thank you, Jean Paul. It was a complete surprise. It sort of changed our flights on Saturday morning early. The agency from which I just retired is sending their plane to pick us up and fly us to Muskegon after a stopover in the D.C. area. I'm told that President Kennedy has been informed of the award and wants to combine it with Tom's presentation. I'm to be met at Andrews Air Force Base by Vice President Johnson."

He continued, "When we leave here, we'll be stopping by to see Father Lemire and the Reverend Mother for one last short visit. Then Friday we'll be going to see Caroline's dad. The nursing home is to the north of Paris. We want Caroline to see him and introduce me. When we return, we'll spend the rest of the day packing for our trip."

Jean Paul said, "We better get things going here. Aileen will stay to take notes and to notarize all documents. The documents are all ready and need only signatures."

"What documents are those? Please, I don't understand."

Doug said, "Jean Paul, let me try. Caroline, I need to tell you some things that I should have done before. You'll remember that when we found how much we loved each other and that we wanted to marry and have a bundle of children, I said then, I've been looking for this for a long time. Now there is you. What I want and what you want are a perfect match. I long for that family and this is the right time and you are the right person to do it with. I have a Master's in orchestral conducting and play several stringed instruments. I've always dreamed of playing with the local symphony and have been told I'm good enough for that. No matter which one works out, we'll have a good living. Are you with me so far?"

"I didn't know about any of this. I just assumed you could make a living for us and didn't think about it further. So what are all the documents for?"

With a twinkle in his eye, he said, "Well we didn't have that kind of thing on our mind since we met, did we?"

Caroline blushed, "Douglas! … I think you are right. So what are the documents?"

"You know that as of last week, I am no longer associated with the government agency. Jean Paul drew up the paper, it is ironclad. But what I haven't had a chance to tell you yet is that if I don't do any of what I outlined a bit ago, we have enough money that I will never have to work for a living. I can stay at home and be the best 'daddy' to all of our children. We have all the money we'll need. The documents are to protect you if something happens to me."

Caroline teared up, "But nothing is going to happen to you, is it?"

"Don't cry, darling. Nothing's going to happen to me."

"Better not."

"I'm here to stay and there's one more thing I'd like to tell you."

Doug said, "You are my lovely wife but I sense that you have more going for you that you know. I feel that you will figure that out in time. I can't wait to hear what they are. But if you decide that you want to be a mother and that only, that is great. I'll be there with you raising the little ones. I love you very much.

Caroline got up and said, "Excuse us a second." They were kissing until Jean Paul said, "Shall we give them some privacy?"

"No need, Jean Paul, I'm ready to sign now."

Aileen said, "Where did you find this one? I want one like him."

They all laughed. The papers got signed. After Caroline said goodbye to Jean Paul, she and Aileen walked out to her office like they had been buddies forever.

Jean Paul stopped Doug for another word. "Excellent job of explaining to Caroline and bringing out her possible skills. I think you may be right about her discovering there is more for her. Oh, and by the way, do you have her dad's address at the nursing home? I'd kind of like to check it out and see for myself how he is doing."

"It's at the house. I'll call you with it tomorrow and mail a follow-up note."

"If you need anything, please let me know. We'll see you in June."

51

Doug and Caroline walked into Father Lemire's office, and he invited Reverend Mother over. He had coffee, tea, and cookies ready.

Reverend Mother said, "Caroline, I have never seen you with such a joyous look on your face. I couldn't be happier for you."

"Thank you. You kept me on the good path, the right path, until I figured out that God has a different plan for me. I still don't know all the answers to what will happen, but I know I'm with the right man to make it work."

Father Lemire said, "I echo what the Reverend Mother said. I'm looking forward to marrying you the second time, full program."

"Will you get someone in to replace me?" Caroline asked.

"We'll find someone before you get back, but she won't be you, child."

Father Lemire asked, "Are there any special requirements that you might want for the church ceremony?"

Caroline replied, "We'll just leave it in your hands and with God's wisdom. We know it will be done right."

Doug said, "Please make sure that you have the budget set so we can get you the money for everything plus something extra for the church. I spoke with Jean Paul this morning about it. He said he would await your figures and get you what you need."

"What are your plans for the rest of your stay?"

"We will spend a part of this afternoon packing and readying for a trip to see Caroline's papa the next day. We will ask Henri and Belle to go with us and enjoy lunch somewhere along the way. We haven't had much time alone with them and they've been so good to us. We fly out early Saturday morning in the agency's jet. It is the last special favor they will do for us..."

Caroline interrupted, "I can see that Doug is as modest about his achievements as his friend Tom is. So I'm going to tell you what happened yesterday morning."

"Belle and I went shopping. Henri drove him and Doug to the Orly private terminal supposedly to talk with the director, Jules Garnier. But who else should be there but President Charle de Gaulle. He was there to present Doug with a commendation and the *Légion d'honneur* for his years of service to France."

Doug said, "I just knew you were going to do that!"

Father Lemire said, "I am so pleased you did, Caroline. You are supporting your husband. Brava! Congratulations to you, Doug. From what I hear, it is well deserved. Thank you for your service."

Caroline said, "The official announcement from the President's office will be on Saturday. You could mention it Sunday if you would like."

Doug just grinned, "Isn't she wonderful, lovely, and supportive too?"

They parted with laughter on his comment.

The next morning they had their last leisurely breakfast out in the kitchen. It was Belle's scrambled eggs, tomatoes, special pancakes, and lots of coffee. Doug said, "I'm so glad you will drive us all to see Caroline's papa. We'll have a leisurely lunch afterward on the way home. Our flight tomorrow is early. We leave Orly at 8:30 a.m."

Belle said, "I've been waiting to say this. We, Henri and I, want to thank you so much for making this your headquarters so to speak. We enjoyed everything about your visit, including that you were married here. It's almost like having a bird's eye view to all the proceedings. Except, er, uh … oops!"

Caroline blushed, "Will I ever get over blushing when someone mentions … ?"

"You will. We've watched the two of you fall more deeply in love as everything fell into place. It has been a joy for us."

Doug asked, "Henri, you're all set on your route?"

"I am. I can take you right to the front door. Be there in about 45 minutes. We'd better get moving."

He had them there in front of the nursing home at 10:00 a.m.

Caroline went right to the desk. She asked if she could see her papa. He is *Monsieur* Laine. "This is my husband Doug McDermott and these are our friends Belle and Henri."

The desk attendant said, "Oh, yes. Mr. McDermott called yesterday. Your father is not having one of his best days, but he is looking forward to seeing you all. I'll ask someone to take you down."

His nurse took them to his room, knocked on the door, and said, "*Monsieur* Laine. You have company."

A weak voice said, "Come in, please." When he saw Caroline, he teared up, and said, "I didn't know when I would see you. Come here, daughter, give your *papa* a little hug."

Then he asked, "Where are your nun clothes?"

"I had my doubts for a long time that it wasn't what God wanted for me. And then this man, Doug, came along and here we are. Doug, here is my papa."

"Monsieur Laine, I am so pleased to meet you."

"What makes you think you are good enough for my Caroline?"

"*Papa*, please wait until you get to know him before you make judgements."

"Leave, leave, all of you except Caroline, my nurse, and this other woman who must have a reason for being here."

When they had left, he said, "Now, tell me again who that man is."

"*Papa*, he is my husband, blessed by the church, from Father Lemire who is the head of the church where I was a novitiate, to the Bishop of the district, and then on to the Pope. Our marriage is truly blessed. They all agree that my decision to leave the novitiate and marry is the right one. There was a papal encyclical. I have all the papers here if you insist on seeing them."

"It just doesn't seem right. You were going to be a nun."

At this, Doug came back in and said, "*Monsieur* Laine, you have a beautiful daughter, a smart daughter, who was able to decide for herself that being a nun wasn't what God wanted her to do. She kept at it inside the church until she convinced the reverend Mother and Father Lemire that it was the right life for her. Then they called me into the room asked me lots of questions, looked at me, looked at her, and said together, "Seems to me and to God that this couple belong together. I asked her that minute if she would marry me. And thank the Lord, she said yes. Now, sir, we would like your blessing on this marriage. If you don't bless it, it will be your loss and ours because that is what we want. We want to give you grandchildren. I hope you want some too."

"*C'est un homme bien*. I was afraid you would wait too long to come back in, but here you are." He held out his hand. Doug took the hand gently, squeezed it. He said, "Welcome to the family, son."

"Papa, you were just checking him out."

Doug said with a grin, "Did a great job of it, too.

Papa said, "Well, let me see you kiss that lovely bride of yours. A good kiss now!"

And they did. All's well.

They spent another 45 minutes. Papa had lots more questions including where they were going to live. Caroline said, "We don't know for sure but we're leaning toward the States. Doug has job opportunities there. You just remember we'll be back here in June for the big repeat wedding with everything the church has. And, *Papa*, we want you there. You just keep on getting better."

His nurse brought his lunch. They said their goodbyes and Caroline told him, "I'll start writing regularly. See you in June *Papa*."

They stopped for some time with his nurse and asked her about his general condition. She said, "Today, seeing you and seeing how happy you are did him a world of good. I would lay you odds he'll be at that wedding in June."

"Will he be able to travel to *Sucy-en-Brie*?"

"Like I said, I would take that bet. Any further, we'll see. Here's my card. This number is for the facility and mine is there as well. Please feel free to call as often as you can afford."

"Thank you."

It was a lighthearted trip going back. Doug found his restaurant where they were seated at his favorite table. It was in a little cove overlooking the water wheel and the pond beyond. The golf course could be seen a little further away from the other side of the pond. They enjoyed what Doug promised, the best French onion soup in France and each a sandwich of their choosing. They shared a bottle of Sauvignon Blanc wine.

The conversation ranged from Caroline's joy at seeing her *Papa* in such good spirits and so willing to fight for his little girl. On the other hand, they were realizing that their time together was coming down to its final hours. This parting would be hard since they had become a tightly knit family and they would soon be separated.

Belle and Caroline fell asleep in the back seat. Doug and Henri were chatting as Henri drove. He was asking Doug questions so he would have all the answers about their plans to pass on to Belle. He finally told Doug, "We want to take you to the Orly private building tomorrow."

Doug started to protest, but Henri said, "Please, you are like our children and we won't see you until next June. We are looking forward to seeing and holding all those children you want as if they were our grandchildren. Tomorrow morning is something we need to do."

Doug asked, "What about my rental car?"

"I've already talked to Jean Paul about it. We'll take care of it."

52

Next morning, they were at Orly Private terminal by 7:30 A.M. The manager knew them all except Caroline and Belle. Doug and Henri each introduced his wife.

The manager said, "The pilots are due in about ten minutes. We'll get your luggage on board so you can leave at your pleasure. The waiting room has coffee and breakfast buns."

He continued, "And Doug, I didn't get a chance before so let me add my congratulations on your commendation and the award of the *Légion d'honneur*. He extended his hand to shake Doug's and went on to give him a hug as well."

They were enjoying coffee and conversation when the crew walked in and were introduced to the wives. The chief pilot said, "We'll do our plane check and let you know when we are ready for you."

The manager left to keep up with business and to give the two couples some privacy for their goodbyes. He had known from conversation with Henri of their closeness.

The four of them gathered around a table, the women engaged in their private goodbyes, the men their own. Doug said, "I'll get on the company line while we wait for our takeoff and let them know we are on our way. I think Caroline will enjoy her first flight. We'll see. Then we'll call you again tomorrow when we settle in Muskegon."

The manager came in, said. "They are ready for you. Your host will greet you inside."

Their host, Anne, introduced herself saying, "Welcome aboard *Monsieur et Madame* McDermott. Here are your seats. I'll get you buckled in. Your chief pilot, Ted, is ready to get on the way. When we are at altitude, I'll come back and explain some of the features of this amazing aircraft, even though Mr. McDermott knows it well. I'll be just up near the front. If you need me, just press your button up here."

Doug said, "Anne. could I ask you one favor?" At her nod, he continued, "We would be pleased if you could call us Caroline and Doug."

Anne said, "Good morning, Caroline, and Doug. See you for a chat in a few."

Anne called to Ted, "Our guests are ready and so am I.'

When they reached cruising altitude, Anne came back, sat down across from them, and said, "Caroline, how are you doing with your first takeoff?"

Caroline smiled, "Please tell your chief pilot he made it the smoothest ever. But Doug had one arm around me and the other hand holding both of mine. He is my rock." She held out her hand, "See, no shaking" smiling at Anne.

Anne said, "Will my hand do for a few minutes? We can get acquainted while Doug takes a call from the White House. He'll be back in a few minutes and he can fill you in on the details. Okay?"

Caroline looked at Doug, he squeezed her hand and nodded. She said, "I'm ready. I have some questions for you as well. We'll have a good talk."

"Good, Caroline." Doug got up and Anne sat in his seat, buckled in. Anne said to Doug, "They are holding for you."

As Doug walked away, he heard Anne ask, 'Caroline, I understand you are a new bride."

As he reached the cockpit, he heard Caroline say, "I didn't know the news had gotten this far yet," and laughed.

Doug knocked on the door, got a "Come in, Doug, and buckle in the jump seat," from Ted, plus "LBJ's aide-de-camp, Captain Jim Hansen, is holding for you. We will hear all the conversation, Doug."

Doug said, "Good morning, Captain Hansen."

"Doug, please call me Jim, I am with the Vice President in Dallas. Yesterday, Friday, at 12:30 p.m. President John F. Kennedy was assassinated, shot twice while traveling in a motorcade. One bullet hit him in his back, the second in the back of his head. He was pronounced dead at Parkland Memorial Hospital at 1:00 p.m. CT. His body was loaded on Air Force One and at 2:38 p.m. Lyndon B. Johnson was sworn in as President of the United States."

He continued, "We have other details about who was the assassin and other persons names but are withholding those for the moment. I will have a summary for you when you get to Andrews, I'm so sorry we don't have more details at this point except that my boss, President Johnson, is now back in the White House and working hard to reassure the nation."

"Doug, we are asking you not to say anything to anyone except to your wife, then when you get to Muskegon, your friends, Tom and Maria. The official word for you is that you are awaiting further details. We will be releasing data as it develops. When you settle in Muskegon, please call me and give me at least one phone number where we can reach you. Do you have any questions?"

Doug said, "Only one at the moment. How is Mrs. Kennedy holding up?"

"She is doing as well as one would expect from her. She is surrounded by family and friends. Mostly just working her way through this time. I will try to meet you at Andrews later, but if I can't, I'll send word and I will be in touch, Doug. Say hello to your bride for me please."

He said to Ted, "If any questions come up that won't wait, call me. Goodbye."

Ted asked, "Doug, how are you doing with this news? I know that you were on several teams protecting him."

Doug said, "I'm okay. I'm wondering how I break this news to Caroline. Does Anne know any of this?"

"She does. I'll be directing her to stay close to you two as the flight progresses. We're making good time. She'll be a big help if you need it."

As Doug stepped out, Ted said into Anne's private earphone, "Keep a good eye on them, Anne. Doug is strong but he was impacted."'

Doug walked back to his seat and said, "Hi sweetheart, looks like you and Anne are having a great chat."

"We are but you look upset. What was your news?"

Anne had gotten up so Doug could get into his seat and take Caroline's hand. Anne said, "If you don't mind, I would like to stay close while you two talk about your news, Doug."

He said, "Thank you, that would be great. Is there a chance we could get a small glass of wine before we get started?"

"Of course, let me get you something. Any preference?"

"No. Is it okay for us to stand up so we can hug? I need a hug."

"Go right ahead. I'll be back in a few minutes."

Anne double checked with Ted that the wine would be okay. It was. When she returned with the wine, they were already seated and holding hands. Caroline said, "Sweetheart, our hostess is an Air Force Captain and her husband Sam McConnell is a Colonel assigned as liaison to the army in the Pentagon. I'm sure anything you have to say can be said in front of Anne. So, now I need to know what's going on, please."

He set her wine and his down and said, "Yesterday at 12:30 p.m., Dallas time, President John F. Kennedy was assassinated." Saying that aloud for the first time put an expression on his face that made Caroline reach out and hold him. "Were you close to him?"

"We were friends, not close but friends. We have lost a man who could have been one of our best. We will miss him. I was just talking with Vice President – I mean – President Johnson's aide-de-camp, Captain Jim Hansen. He'll likely have a new title after the new administration comes together. From what he told me, we will be sent right on to Muskegon and they will be in touch later."

Anne said, "That means they will have another crew there for the next leg. We will have too many hours."

Caroline asked, "Does that mean we won't see you again?"

Amne answered, "At least right now, that's what it means. I hope down the line we get to spend a little time together. Would you like a light lunch now? You may not have a lot of time to get anything at Andrews."

Doug looked at Caroline, she nodded, and he said to Anne, "We would. Will you be joining us?"

"I'll check with Ted, but I'm sure he will say okay. I'll have to get them something as well first then I'll join you."

Caroline said, "I hope we don't lose contact with Anne and her husband. They are both career military. I like her."

Doug said, "I like her too. Maybe on a trip back to the D.C. area we can get together for a dinner. We'll be sure to get contact info. How are you holding up with all this change?"

"I'm better than I thought I would be. Are you okay with the news settling in? And how do you think the nation is right now?"

"My guess is that people are going to be somewhat in a shock. Our country is one that comes together for each other in times like these. That's what they'll do this time."

He continued, "Here she comes with lunches."

They settled in to enjoy 'Croque Monsieur' sandwiches and a little more wine.

Doug asked, "Caroline and I would like to see you and your husband when we come back this way. We both like you a lot and hope to meet your husband. Is it possible?"

"Of course. Caroline and I have shared some of our life stories and I'm looking forward to hearing more. I know Hal will want to meet you both. He knows of your work, Doug."

Doug said, "Here are our names and a phone number in Muskegon where you can reach us. It is Tom and Maria's home. When that changes we'll let you know. I have no idea at this time when that will be."

"That's okay. It may take some time for us to call back. Here is our info with our home phone and my work contact number."

She continued, "I'd better do some clean up. We're only about 45 minutes out. Please buckle up. I'll keep you posted from my seat near the front."

Fifty-five minutes later they were walking into the Andrews terminal.

The terminal manager, Jonathan, escorted them to meet Jim, Captain Hansen.

Jim said, "Things have settled down as far as the new President and his contacts in other countries, who's coming and who is not. We talked about having you there, but with about 1200 guests from 90 different countries, it was decided that they want you, Tom, and your families to be the focus when we finally honor the two of you. It will likely be sometime in the new year. We'll give you plenty of notice. I've brought our latest summary on what happened and when it happened last Friday and since. We'll let you know when and bring the five of you here."

Caroline said, "Thank you, Jim. Whatever you need us to do, any way we can help, please let us know."

Doug added, "Thank you for this update. I'll keep you posted with the best phone number as we get settled and it changes. We'll be watching."

Jim said, "Thank you both for understanding. Goodbye for now."

Doug reported into his agency contact and said, "We are headed for Muskegon as soon as they have the plane refueled. Thanks for sending it for us."

Doug then called Tom to let them know they would be in sometime near four p.m. He told Tom he had to go; the plane had been readied and the new flight crew were there. "We'll see you soon."

Ted, Anne, and the copilot stepped into the meeting room as soon as Doug and his bride were free. Tim said, "We wanted to say goodbye until next time. We hope we can get you for a future trip."

Doug said, "That could happen soon. We were told we would be brought back early in the new year. When Jim Hansen lets us know when, I will put in a request for you as a crew. And then maybe we can arrange a dinner or something." Anne and Caroline hugged, the men shook hands.

They were soon on their way with memories and some new friends.

53

———————

I n Muskegon they landed on the main runway and were slowing down already as they went by the private terminal. Doug saw Alice on Tom's shoulder waving and told Caroline.

She asked, "How did you see them in that flash by?"

"There's a secret to it. I'll teach you how when we can practice."

As they passed the main terminal, there they all were waiting and waving. Now Alice was bouncing up and down at the big window. Doug was barely in the door when Alice cried out, *"Bonjour, Oncle* Doug.

She practically jumped into his arms. He twirled her around and then asked Alice, 'Do you know who this is?" while pointing to Caroline.

Alice said, *"Elle est* Caroline." and held out her arms for a hug.

Oncle Doug said, *"Elle est maintenant mariée à moi, alors vous pouvez l'appeler 'tante* Caroline.'"

Papa said to her, "She is married to *Oncle* Doug, so you may call her *'Tante* Caroline.'"

Alice said, *"Bonjour, Tante* Caroline. *Je t'aime."* She jumped into Caroline's arms for another hug.

The crew took this in with wonderment. The chief pilot said. "She is a bright young child. We'll be sure to tell the other crew about this. It has been our pleasure to know you all. Your luggage is in your car and our plane is ready to go so it's farewell for now."

Tom and Doug were riding in the front seat. Doug said, "Listen to those three back there. You'd think that you hadn't seen each other in years. And that mixture of French and English from all three. We'll have our time. Do you mind if I call Belle and Henri? The agency hasn't reclaimed my sat-phone so I guess it's ok to use it."

"Go ahead. Say hello for us and tell her we'll talk later."

Henri answered, *"Bonjour* Doug, you have landed in Muskegon, yes, no?"

Doug answered, "We are on the way to Tom, Maria, and Alice's home. Caroline did very well for her first flight ever, a real champ. The crews took good care of us. We have made new friends in the crew from Orly. We'll be staying at Tom and Maria's until we can find a rental. And then we'll see what happens and will keep you posted. Thanks for everything, Henri. Would you put Belle on? I'll say 'hello' and get the phone to the three ladies. The back seat crew is ready to talk, Ladies, you have about ten minutes and we'll be home."

Doug continues, "Belle, you are in for a treat. This trio of ladies will impress. When I motion for the phone, please put Henri on for Tom and I for a quick hello. Thanks Belle for everything."

Doug continued, "We'll get a chance with Belle first and then Henri."

The back seat exploded with 'hellos, bonjours, I love you…'

Finally Doug turned around, nodded to Belle. She got the phone, all shouted 'goodbye' and then Doug said, "Thank you so much for all you have done for us. We think of you as our adopted parents, we love you. I'm going to hold the phone for Tom for a quick hello, he's driving. Bye."

Belle said, "Hello Tom. You are all our family, always will be. Everything is going fine here. Next time we'll talk about the business. All is on schedule. Love you all. Give Maria a hug for me. Bye for now."

Doug put the phone away and said, "Tom, are you sure about us staying with you?"

"We are not only sure. We wouldn't have it any other way. You remember the bedroom with a queen-size bed on the other side of the house. There is, you'll remember, another full bath over there. You'll have complete privacy back there. After all you are still newlyweds."

Smiling as he took that in, Doug said, "Looking out after your old buddy."

Tom said, "We have so much to talk about. The people in Muskegon are in shock over John Kennedy. I can't wait to hear what you can share with us about the who's, and why's, and how did it ever happen."

Doug said, "We'll get to it and lots of other things, too. We will spend some time showing Caroline the town, the lake, all the things that make Muskegon a great place to live. Hey! Here we are sweetheart. What do you think of this?"

Tom wheeled into the new circular driveway. Doug said, "Say, this is new. Whose idea was this?"

"It was mine. But it didn't take long for Maria to come to think about how much safer it would be to be able to get onto Beech Street without backing into it. It has only been drivable for about a week." He stopped at the front door. "Maria has shown a new creativity in redoing the living room. It's only partly done, but it's already showing the effect she wanted."

Tom opened his rear door and gave Caroline his arm, "*Madame.*"

Doug did the same on the passenger side, gave Maria his arm, "*Madame et Mademoiselle.*"`

Tom opened the front door and let them all go in, Maria first with Alice had both her hands with *mannan* and *tante* Caroline.

Doug stopped open mouthed, "What a change. This is lovely, Maria."

She said, "Why thank you sir. It's not quite finished but it is taking on the character I wanted. I can't wait to start on Tom's piano room as I call it. He calls it his music room. The other pieces for the living room will come as I see something that I think fits."

Caroline said, "Tom, I didn't know you played the piano."

Doug said, "He doesn't just play. He's like a genius, mostly jazz, with a good feel for the classics. He doesn't like to toot his own horn."

Caroline smiled and said, "Sounds like someone else I know."

Caroline, turned to Maria, "Will you help me when we start furnishing a house?"

"I will if you'll create what you want and just let me help you find it. It has to be yours and Doug's decisions."

"Doug, shall we get your luggage into your room? Maria and Alice will bring Caroline by shortly."

While the newlyweds arranged their luggage, put some away and settled in, he went partway down the hall toward their room and said, "We have a charcuterie board and some wine for you love-birds. Are you ready?"

Doug said, "We'll be right out."

Five minutes later they came out. Maria said, "Have a seat on the long sofa. We'll pull up the single chairs and Alice is in one of her small chairs."

Maria took another look at Caroline and said, "You look like you have had an emotional event. Are you okay?"

Caroline teared up again, and said, "It was, or should I say is the reality of all this love I have been shown by everyone I come to. I know both of you already, but you have made me feel right at home here in Muskegon. Already and I've only been here an hour or so."

Maria walked over and gave her a hug. She said, "Tom and I are so happy. We never thought things would happen the way they did. We have had some travails, but they don't compare to the joy that has come our way. We want everyone to have that."

Doug and his bride sat down. Tom said, "We like to celebrate the beginnings, and things along the way. Tonight is part of both. I have a chilled bottle of champagne. Are you ready for a glass?"

Four glasses of champagne, one special glass for Alice, and Tom said, "Here's to new and longtime friends. May we keep those feelings a lifetime."

They raised their glasses, clinked them, and Doug said, "Here, here!"

Caroline, teared up again, "May I say something?"

They all nodded. She continued, "This night, this time, it is for me a sign from God that I made the right decision. This is a new loving path for me. Here's to all of you who have brought it."

Alice said, 'To *tante* Caroline." They clinked and sipped.

Tom said, "Caroline, would you lead grace, *en français*?"

She did so.

Then Tom said, "Let's eat. *Allons manger*."

Caroline asked, "Who builds the charcuterie board?"

Maria said, "We have done it together enough that we call it our board. We hope you like it, too."

Tom said, "But save some room for dinner. We have a special pot roast with all the veggies, French seasonings, and finish with a *salade capresse*. We'll tell you where the recipe for the pot roast came from later."

An hour or so later, everyone pronounced that they had enough. A little girl's eyes were drooping. Both ladies went to put her to bed. Caroline asked and was allowed to read to Alice. It didn't take long and Alice was sound asleep..

Tom had cleaned off the table and built a fire in the fireplace. He and Doug had a chair for each near the fireplace and a smaller table for a digestif .Tom poured a little for each and said, "You can have more."

Tom asked, 'Doug, can you share some of what you know and what has happened since Friday?"

"I was told by President Johnson's attaché, Captain Jim Hansen, that I could tell you three anything that came up. He said to be sure to keep it to ourselves. Caroline hasn't heard all of this. Some of it came from a dossier from Jim Hansen. So whatever you want to ask. I'll start this off."

He told them about Lee Harvey Oswald and that he had been shot by a man named Jack Ruby. "The public will know those names and some others before the day is over. No one knows yet about their motivation. The dossier they gave me doesn't have much more. They will keep me updated and then I will do the same for you. And the dossier will be here for you to read anytime you want."

"What I want to hear is how you're all doing? I see progress in Alice. How did that happen?"

Caroline said, "I can see that too. How did her skills grow so fast?"

Tom and Maria both started to talk. Tom deferred to her. Maria said, "It was a joint effort on our part but to be truthful. Tom figured out a new approach, you heard him say something in English and then the same in French. It has worked."

She continued, "Last week, we signed an agreement with Amelie McNeal. She is French, a nurse, and now is the local high school French teacher. She married a local man who was wounded in WWII, she took care of him and they fell in love. I'll tell you the whole story sometime. Anyway, she is on sabbatical next semester and will be teaching Alice, and us, what we need to become a bilingual family."

Caroline asked, "And what will you be doing while the teaching is going on and Amelie is working with Alice?"

"I made up my mind soon after we got back home. My focus is on our family, especially Alice, at least until she is bonded with us and we have found a school for her. So I am content to make Alice and Tom my life for now. There will be time later to find what I want to do with the rest of my life."

Doug said, "Say Tom, how did your meeting with Mr. Strahan turn out?"

Tom said, "He has really challenged me. It fits to some degree my own idea of a consulting business which I can base here at home. Then I can be close to Maria and Alice and build my business. Can we talk about this later? I want to hear about your wedding and how you got it done."

Maria said, "Me too. I couldn't imagine how everything happened so quickly."

Caroline said, "I couldn't either. But Doug is so persuasive. When he laid out his notion of what a marriage is to Father Lemire and the Reverend Mother, they started laying out a plan. And Doug proposed to me right there in front of them, had the ring right there, he did. This is the first time we have told anyone about Doug's 'right now' proposal. Father Lemire, the Bishop, and ultimately the Pope got it done."

She continued, "May I say something else?" They all nodded. She turned to Doug, took his hand, and said, "Doug, darling, you have kept your own plans to yourself. I've heard snatches of conversation with Henri and Belle after they asked what our plans are. So I want to share with you all what I want. I want to stay right here in Muskegon to raise a big family. How many? I'm an only child; I don't want just one child. Again, how many? We'll decide together. And I only have one parent left, but we could bring Dad here and find a home for him like the one he's in now. I bet he would love it here."

Doug took her in his arms and kissed her. Maria looked at Tom and asked, "Should we leave and give them some privacy?"

At that, Caroline and Doug broke the hug and started laughing. Caroline said, "Well, it has been three days since …"

Maria said, "My kind of girl!"

They all started laughing. Caroline said, "I think I finally referred to sex without blushing."

Caroline went on, "I think I had made this decision about living in Muskegon when we talked to Jean Paul. When I heard you talking with him about music, playing in the local symphony, and then what you said about money and you didn't need to make a big salary, that you had all the money we would ever need."

Tom said, "Doug, you have the magic. I'm going to be so proud to be your best man in June when we all get back to Sucy. Maria and I have decided to stay home tomorrow, no church. It will be all about President Kennedy. Then Monday will be the funeral so we will watch it on television. If you and Caroline feel the same, we'll just stay in. Get reacquainted. You know the town quite well, but Caroline will want to see what her decision is going to mean to her as a place to settle. So we will want to take a ride or two around town."

Doug looked to Caroline and said, "That will be good. Then I want to call Dad and Mom tomorrow and arrange a time for them to meet my bride. And then I have to get my car up here."

Maria asked, "Would they be willing to drive two cars up, yours and theirs? We could have a big get together dinner here."

"I suspect Dad will want to watch every minute of what happens with the funeral and all. Could that be put off until Tuesday?"

Maria and Tom nodded and she said, "I think that could be arranged. How about we have our four parents over for lunch after mass tomorrow? That way Caroline can meet all the parents. Sound good?"

Caroline said, "Can we finalize things tomorrow? I'm beginning to fade."

After hugging around, Doug and Caroline said goodnight. Tom cleaned up and wasn't far behind.

$$54$$

Next morning, Alice made the rounds and woke them all up. Tom got the coffee going and started breakfast. Soon all were seated in the informal dining alcove with scrambled eggs, crispy bacon, sliced tomatoes, and pancakes with superb maple syrup. Maria nodded to Alice who said *"Disons la grâce."* She started, all joined *en français.*

As the conversation went on, Tom as usual asked Alice to repeat the French phrase in English. *Tante* Caroline soon picked up on their routine and contributed as well. *Oncle* Doug and *Maman* enjoyed watching the learning going on. *Oncle* Doug said, "I can see why Alice's vocabulary has improved."

Maria said, "We ladies are going to take a ride around Muskegon. Caroline wants to get acquainted with her new hometown. And that will leave the two of you to catch up with each other."

By the time Tom had things cleaned up and put on a fresh pot of coffee, the ladies were ready to go on an adventure. Tom and Doug saw them off with hugs and kisses. Then they settled down with their coffee in front of the fireplace. Tom asked, "Doug, would you start off by telling me about this first marriage of yours? You never let it slip while we were teaching together at Muskegon Sr. High School."

"Okay, here goes. I'll have to trace back through how I came to the army before we met. I was at Western Michigan University doing my undergraduate work. I got my BA in music with majors in conducting and performance on the cello."

"I didn't know you had the performance major either."

"Caroline tells me I don't 'toot my own horn' enough. Anyway, to move on. While I was doing my BA, I was persuaded to join the ROTC which meant a two-year commitment to a reserve unit. But I found I liked military life so much that I converted that obligation to a two-year enlistment. I also did officers training and speeded up my music studies so I was done a year early, graduating with a BA in music and second lieutenant stripes at the same time. That was in 1946. During my early years in the Army, someone noticed some skills I had that made me a candidate for SO (Special Operator) in what became the CIA when President Truman signed a bill forming it in 1947. Two years later it was strengthened when he signed the Central Intelligence Agency Act. So here I was, a Captain in the army assigned to the CIA. After a year of training at the CIA facility, they gave me ten months off to do my MA in orchestral conducting at WMU."

Tom asked, "Where does the first wife come in?"

"If you'll stop interrupting my story, I'll tell you. While doing my MA, I met her. She was in the vocal music program, working on a teaching certificate at Western and was graduating the same time I was, in May 1946. Our relationship grew as we learned about each other. I told her about my army career and the need for me to travel on assignment as needed. She insisted that it would not be a problem. We were married two months after we met. My parents tried to tell me it was too fast, but I ignored them to my later regret. She moved with me to a small home close to McLean, VA near CIA headquarters. My first assignment overseas, in France, by the way, wasn't until I had more advanced training for another six months. Everything seemed hunky-dory. Except it wasn't. The mission was only three months long but getting home and debriefed added another week before we could have much of a life together. I finally got home. She was cool to me. When I asked what was going on, she told me she was lonely when I was gone. She didn't think this was going to work. I told her I would be home for quite a while, maybe four or five months. We'll be just fine with some time together."

He continued, "It didn't work out. Things didn't get better."

She told me, "I've been talking to your boss about it, He said they would see if they could work out a desk job for you."

"Why would you think you could change my career path without talking with me? You can't. You and I should talk about it, just the two of us first."

She said, "Well Doug, if a job on a desk comes along and you don't take it, I'm getting a divorce."

"There was nothing you could do to save it?"

"Nope, we tried counseling, alone and as a pair. Nothing worked. Her mind was made up."

"Long story short, I got my orders for the next assignment, I told her I was going. She filed for divorce as soon as I left. It was granted three months or so later, shortly after I returned from the assignment. My attorney had no way to prevent it. At that time in our society, it was hard for a man to get a fair shake in a divorce. The papers were ready for me to sign and start paying a hefty alimony. That was okay, it was the right thing to do. My attorney told me it would be that way as long as she was single. The only way it would stop would be if she remarried."

"What happened?"

"Nine months later, she married a man she had been dating while I was gone from the first time on. End of marriage. End of story."

Tom asked, "We always wondered why you didn't marry after we were all together here. Lots of the ladies expressed an interest in you."

"I didn't even think about it again until I saw what you and Maria have. I had to firm up my thinking about marriage in a hurry when you pushed up your wedding date. But you listened to what I had to say and put it and your own ideas into play and it worked!"

"When I was courting Caroline, I remembered all this, what a special thing you have, it just came out like it was right for Caroline and me. So did all of them. And here we are. I'm a happy man; Caroline is even happier. And she surprises me more and more every day."

"Just one more thing. I think we'll rent for a few months. That way

Caroline will know the town better and can make the choice better when we start looking to buy. By the way, like you, money is not a problem. Being an independent agent for the CIA and a President or two pays well. We are worth a little over $1 million. Jean Paul and I talked about it and he said I should get us into an investment that will make that grow and that you could lead me to it."

"I agree with him. We'll start that when you are settled and ready. Uh. Oh. I hear the ladies. We'll talk about what Mr. Strahan brought to me later."

The front door popped open and the three burst in. Alice said, "*Papa* and *Oncle* Doug, we have Doo Drop lunches."

"All in English, Alice, brava."

"We've been practicing her announcement since we left Doo Drop. I thought it was time Caroline had a chance to see if she liked the perch and trimmings."

The ladies and Alice got all the food on the table. Tom and Doug put the dishes out along with wine glasses. He asked if anyone wanted beer instead. They all wanted the Sauvignon blanc. Maria tapped Alice on the cheek and pointed to *Papa*. Tom pointed to himself and said, "Grace here."

Alice smiled and waited for Papa. He did so *en français*. Alice said, "Bravo, *Papa*. Amen, *allons manger.*" It brought smiles and a little giggle from Alice.

While Tom was pouring the wine, *Maman* tapped Alice on the cheek, pointing at T*ante* Caroline and *Oncle* Doug, Alice unbuckled her belt, got down and rounded the table. She kissed *Tante* and *Oncle*, then jumped into *Tante*'s lap saying, "*Bienvenue dans notre maison.*" And "Welcome to our home." She cuddled a little with each of them. *Papa* put her back in her chair, saying *mange, mange.*

Caroline took her first bite of Lake Michigan perch. "Ooh, this is wonderful." She smiled at the way Alice was going after hers.

They finished their lunch. Alice was nodding so the ladies put her down for her nap. Tom finished the clean-up and joined the rest at the fireplace. As he sat, he asked, "Caroline, tell me what you saw and what you think."

"I had a very good guide. Maria took us north I think she said. We came around a curve and there was Lake Michigan on your left and a beautiful high sand dune on your right. We followed that to the channel connecting Muskegon Lake to Lake Michigan. When we started back from the channel, we followed the road closer to the lake and had a good view of the two lighthouses, one at the Coast Guard Station and the other at the end of a long pier. What a big lake! The only lakes I've seen you can see across, not this one. As we came back away from the lake down Lakeshore Drive past where there were a number of stores of various kinds, we took a road that ran along Muskegon Lake. Then we met up with some smelly old factories and finally went onto Western Avenue and more factories until we were downtown. The old Occidental Hotel is a lovely piece of architecture. It still looks great, but I'll bet it was gorgeous in its heyday."

"We saw Hackley Park named for a man responsible for making Muskegon what it was in its early days. Then finally on Western Ave and the downtown. I was surprised to see how many businesses were closed up. Sad. Then leaving town and going down Sanford Street we saw the high school where you taught and a lovely residential area further on. The next place I remember is Doo Drop Inn. I may have missed some things."

"I think you did a marvelous job remembering all you did."

Maria said, "I promised her that next time we would find a lot more residential areas. Maybe we should make a five-person ride or you two may just want to go alone. We're open to whatever you need."

"You're so good to us."

"That's what friends do."

Maria asked, "What did the two of you talk about?"

Doug said, "Tom wanted to know about this earlier marriage from a long time ago. Tom can tell you all about it. We need another session to get to what Mr. Strahan said to Tom."

Doug continued, "Is there anyone coming tonight?"

Tom looked at Maria and said, "Not tonight. You said something about your parents coming tomorrow or Wednesday. Is that still on?"

"It is as far as we're concerned?"

Doug smiled and said, "They would like to come over the lunch hour on Wednesday. They want to get back before dark. That means leaving Muskegon by 4:00 p.m. It didn't surprise me that they asked me to change it to that. I'll take us out to lunch that day at Bill Knapps. I was told by some of my guys who were here that it's good food and some of the best au gratin potatoes in town. No wine, they don't drink. They'll be happy with that. Will it work for you?"

"Good. That's settled then. And I'd like to take us all out tonight at The Holiday Inn on Seaway Dr. What do you think?"

Maria looked at Tom and said, "That will be great. We've heard of it but have not tried it yet."

<h1 style="text-align:center">55</h1>

Next morning after breakfast, Doug and Caroline borrowed the car and left for a tour of residential areas. They said they would be back by lunchtime and bring pizzas from Mr. Scribs. We would watch the rest of the President Kennedy funeral service.

The service was supposed to be over by around 3:30 pm. They would finish their catch-up talks and then get ready for a potluck dinner with the two sets of parents. When all arrived, Alice made the rounds, getting hugs and kisses from each, *grand-mère et grand-père*, then *grand-maman et grand-papa*. Doug was astonished that she knew all four. Doug introduced his bride, Caroline, to all four grandparents.

Maria made her lasagna, her mother made a big salad with Cole's garlic toast, and Tom's mother brought two pies, coconut cream and apple. Tom had a smooth chianti for the lasagna and a delicate dry Reisling for the salad. Some switched those around and it worked for them. They were soon seated around the big table. Alice looked at *Papa* who nodded and pointed to Alice who then said, "Let's say grace. Or *Disons la grâce*." She then led it off en français.

Maria served the lasagna for those who wanted to start with it. The salad bowl was passed to those who wanted to start with that. Caroline said, "You give people their choice for a starter, that's good. This is wonderful. We never had lasagna at church. It's a real treat for me."

All were full of questions for Caroline and Doug. They wanted the details of the informal ceremony and then to know how they got the permission from the Bishop and then the Pope to have a second more formal one. Caroline said, "Father Lemire and then the Bishop were very persuasive to get the Pope's blessing on it."

They took their desserts and either coffee or tea out into the living room. Everyone was suddenly aware of the changes Maria had made. "This looks good already." Her mother asked, "What more do you want to change?"

Maria responded, "We need another sofa to go across from the first one. Then the two chairs will come down to this end And I still have to find something to do with the far wall with the fireplace. It needs something else. I'll know it when I see it."

Maria continued, "We probably won't make many changes for the next few months. I promised some people an open house. We're going to make it a Christmas Open House Sunday afternoon, December 7th. Marlene is a caterer who Katherine Strahan uses. They brought her here for a dinner and she did a marvelous job. I spoke to her the next day, and she agreed to do it. We'll have finger foods, a punch bowl, and in honor of the season we'll have a Wassail bowl. The invitations go out tomorrow. I hope you all can come."

Tom said, "And then our first Christmas with Alice. Later we'll work out the details on when we get together."

Maria added, "Now we're into January with two things happening. We don't know the date yet. The White House will let us know when the presentations will be made. The other thing starting in January is our intensive learning of French for us and for Alice, learning both new French words as well as English. Our goal is to become a bilingual family, fluent in both French and English. Our teacher will be Amalie McNeal. You'll all meet her in time. She has a story, something like yours, Caroline. She was a Parisien who married Jerry, a GI from Muskegon and moved here right after the war. She has been teaching French at Muskegon Senior High ever since. Their twins, who start college next fall, grew up in a bilingual family. We were lucky to find her."

Caroline beamed, "I can't wait to meet her."

"You will soon. We'll have she and Jerry here for lunch sometime soon to talk about our schedule for the four months starting in January. During that time, in addition to our French studies, Tom will be working on his consulting company. But our main focus for that time will be our studies of French and how to continue the learning after Amalie is done."

Her dad asked, "That's going to be a pretty fast pace. Do you think Alice is ready for that? She is pretty young."

"Good question Dad. Tom and I talked about that with Amalie. She started with her twins soon after they began to form words. She thinks Alice is ready. I hope I can keep up. I know Tom can but he's further along than I am."

Tom's dad asked Caroline and Doug, "When is your next travel, for this second full Catholic wedding for you two?"

Caroline answered, "That will be an early June wedding at the church I just left in Sucy en Brie. Doug and I worked it out with Father Lemire and the Reverend Mother before we left. We'll have the full traditional Catholic wedding on Saturday June 13, 1964. You're all invited. And my papa will be there. Doug's dad and mom too."

Tom added, "We hope you all can come. We're covering the expenses. I may charter a plane."

Tom's dad said, "That's a lot of money, Tom."

"I know that, but we can afford it. And remember what you always taught me 'One of the best things about having money is that it lets you do things for the people you love.' We love you all."

Doug said, "That warrants a toast. It just so happens that I have a chilled bottle of champagne and Caroline is coming with the glasses.

56

On Tuesday after breakfast all were sitting around the breakfast nook. Doug said, "Caroline and I have an announcement."

Maria said, "You're pregnant."

They all laughed. Caroline said, "Remember, no baby bumps at the wedding in Sucy."

Doug smiled, "We've found where we want to rent. It will take a week or so to get it ready for us. Do you think you can put up with us for another week?"

Maria smiled back, "Don't you remember what we said? You can stay as long as you need to. Where is it?"

Doug told them the address. Both burst out laughing. It was the place where Tom had lived and later, Tom and Maria lived later.

Tom said, "Many good memories there. How did this come about?"

"I took Caroline by there to let her see it. She fell in love with it and wanted to see it all right away. We called the owner, Al, who came right over. The rest is history. There's just one hitch, the one bedroom wasn't big enough. We persuaded him to let us enlarge it so it would accommodate a queen size bed. You have spoiled me with the bed in the guest room. We called Bill Langlois, explained who we were, and asked if he had another queen size bed. He did, so we bought it. I figure it will take about a week to move two walls a foot or so. Anyway, we will move sometime in the next week. And, oh, by the way, after the remodel and when we move out, he is going to start advertising it as a first night honeymoon getaway."

Maria said, "That is terrific. Can we help?"

Doug answered, "I hoped you would ask."

~

Later that afternoon, Tom and Doug stood looking at the bedroom door, studying and thinking about how to expand the area.

Tom said, "Funny I never noticed how much room there is on the sides of the bed. I wonder how it would fit if it turned 90 degrees and back the head up against the bathroom wall. Then the only place it would be a little tight is going around the foot of the bed."

Doug was excited, "Let's try it with this bed." They turned it and put the head of the bed against the windowless east wall. "Look at the room down at the foot of the bed, a little over three feet to that west wall.'

"But how much of that is taken of that with the bigger bed?"

Doug grinned, took out his measurements on a three by five card.

"Only five inches longer, 80 inches instead of 75 inches." They slid the old regular bed out five inches.

Doug shouted, "Look at the room down there. The bigger difference is in the width. The queen is 22 inches wider than this one. It's going to work without moving any walls. Tom, you're a genius."

"Not so much. Why didn't I figure that out a long time ago when we were living here? There's a good lesson in this, Doug. Sometimes the need to solve a problem makes you take a different look at the problem. I'm going to have to remember that."

"I'll have to call Bill Langlois and ask him to deliver it right away. And best part is we can move in tomorrow."

"Let's go tell the ladies and celebrate." Twenty minutes later, they walked through the door. Tom shouted, "Ladies we don't have to do any carpentry, no walls to get moved."

Then he saw there were three ladies sitting there. "Oops, I'm sorry. I didn't realize we have a guest, Hello, Amalie."

Maria said, "Doug, this is Amalie McNeal. our teacher to be in January, She called and asked if she could drop off a list of books and materials for us to get before January. She and Caroline have been getting acquainted. Why don't the two of you join us with our tea and Rykes butter cookies?"

"Gladly after I kiss my bride." Doug sat beside Caroline and kissed her. As Maria walked by to get two more cups and saucers, Tom stopped her for a kiss.

"Where's my little girl?"

"She's still napping. She should wake up soon."

The men soon had their tea and cookies and joined the conversation. Amalie said to Doug, "I love how you and Caroline persuaded everyone to allow two ceremonies."

Caroline asked, "What were the two of you so excited about when you burst in here?"

Doug, still excited about it, burst in with, "Our local genius here figured it out. We just turned the bed 90 degrees and put the head against the east wall. When you add on the extra five inches of length that our new queen bed will take, there is still a little over two feet of room from the west wall. Genius!"

Maria asked, "Tom, why didn't we think of that?"

"Turns out, it's need that made me think of it. We didn't have a queen-size bed, so there was no need. The need to get a longer bed didn't come up. Good principle there that I may be able to use in other settings. A need can prompt you to think about something in a different way. Then a solution just pops up. Not really much genius just a new perspective."

Amalie said, "But that new way of thinking could be promoted in many areas. You might want to write that up as a paper on the idea."

"Where would one publish such a paper?"

"I don't know right off hand, but I bet we could find out. Genius, indeed, Tom."

The phone rang. When Tom answered and said to Amalie, "There's a man named Jerry looking for you."

"Hi, Jerry. I brought some materials over, and time got away from me. Jerry, can you hold on a minute? Maria is signaling me for something."

Maria said, "We've been wanting to get acquainted with you and Jerry. Could you stay and have Jerry and the twins, if they want, join you for dinner here?"

"Jerry, we have an invitation for dinner. I don't think there were any plans. Could you just come on over here or do you want me to come pick you up?"

Jerry said, "That sounds like a great idea. I'll clean up a little and be right there. What is the address?"

She said, "Good! And Jerry, bring that box of baked goods I did this afternoon. They are in the refrigerator. I'll give you Tom now and he'll give you the address. Love you, Jerry."

Tom said, "Hello again, Jerry. Here's the address and you can come either past the water works coming from the ovals south or if you come Sherman past the country club, you'll come around the curve and be on Beech St. We're the only house with a semi-circular drive. See you soon, Bye."

Amalie exclaimed, "I'm glad Jerry's coming. There's so much that this group has in common, it will be like a little reunion to get acquainted all over again. The twins may not come, Jerry will try to persuade them, but they are both independent thinkers. They may stay home with pizza or hot dogs or who knows what they will find to fix. We'll see what they say. Maybe they'll be here or maybe not."

Maria said, "Whatever they decide, we'll be okay."

Tom asked, "Does everyone like fish, haddock in particular?

Doug asked, "Is the Pope Catholic? I'm sure we all do." Everyone nodded.

Tom said, "I have a special recipe for haddock. We'll have the haddock, red potatoes, and *haricots verts*. The *salade capresse and haricots verts* are the only French names I have for the menu. You have your work cut out for you with me, Amalie."

Amalie said, "*aiglefin, pommes de terre rouges, haricots verts, and salade capresse*. Your first lesson, Tom. Repeat it after me please,"

Tom did so with an accent that was lacking but he smiled. "I have a way to go."

Maria walked in with Alice. Alice ran to Tom, jumped up on him, and said, *"Je t'aime papa."* She darted off to find some others to talk with.

Tom said, "I have the haddock thawing. We'll get the charcuterie board ready, the wine's chilling. So relax and enjoy. We'll be right with you."

Fifteen minutes later there was a knock on the door. Tom let Jerry in, the twins sent a note "Thank you for the invitation. We'll be at your open house. Looking forward to meeting you all."

Amalie took the box he was carrying and put it in the refrigerator.

57

Soon they were all seated enjoying their Kir Royales, the various cheese, meats, and crackers. Tom got his dinner going and joined them. Jerry McNeal soon bonded with Doug as fellow servicemen. Caroline and Amalie found much to talk about as women who had come to Muskegon with their servicemen husbands.

Tom called them to dinner. He turned to Alice and pointed to himself. He started and all joined in grace *en Français*. Tom then refilled their glasses with chilled champagne. "I have a toast. Here's to friends, old and new. May we grow closer over the years." All clinked their glasses.

All the food was in bowls served family style except for the haddock. Tom served that as he walked around the table, ladies first including Alice, then the gentlemen. Amalie asked, "May I know what is the little puffy stuff browned on top of the haddock?"

Tom said, "I'll share that with you later. Try it." The bowls started moving around. "I have some beer, two wines, a good Italian rioja and our favorite sauvignon blanc. I'll pour your choices and then join you."

All were quiet except for the noises of appreciation for the flavors. Amalie again, "Okay Tom, what is it? It has a cheese base with herbs."

"You are close. It's a cheese spread that the French like to use on their fish. Each is different depending on what a family's tastes may be. I don't believe any company has developed a commercial package yet. I got started with it the way Belle did it."

"Now I can ask, who is Belle?

"Belle is our friend in Sucy en Brie, France. We met her through Maria's pen pal Celeste, from early years. Maria should be telling this story."

"You are doing just fine. I'm keeping busy taking bones out of the haddock for Alice. She loves it."

"Belle and her first husband had a dairy farm outside Sucy and must have experimented with soft cheeses but only for themselves. When her husband died, she sold the farm and moved into town. Eventually she became Celeste and Etienne's cook, almost a chef. She is a wonderful cook."

Tom continued, "We have Alice as an adopted daughter when Celeste and Etienne were killed in a car accident just a few months ago now."

Jerry said, "I followed what happened with the Group of Nine. You were an integral part of the task force who broke it up. You ended up being made chief of detectives when Jim retired, didn't you? Are you still in that role?"

"No, I'm not. After our adoption of Alice, we decided we wanted to become full-time parents. We were going to have the first in the state husband and wife detective business. It is on the books, but for now is inactive. Maria decided that she would be a full-time mother and not work at all until Alice has a good start in a school we haven't decided on yet. So, I decided to start a consulting business. I can and will do that from a home office. Chief Mark and I have agreed on a consulting role with the police department, my first client. Our most important job over the next two or three years is Alice. That's where Amalie comes in. We want to become a bilingual family like yours. We have a busy few months ahead of us. We were lucky to find her."

Maria added, "Tom might not share this with you, but I will. Tom was given a commendation for his work with Doug when we were in France on our honeymoon. We have already seen it but the formal ceremony at the White House will be made in early January. We don't know exactly but likely sometime the latter part of the first week. That may mean a slower start to our lessons with Amalie. Your contract doesn't change but we'll miss about a week while we're in D.C."

Tom asked, "Everyone ready for dessert? I have coffee ready and hot water if anyone prefers tea. Amalie has brought a special dessert treat. We don't know what it is yet. It's a surprise."

Maria said. "Why don't we gather around the table again? I'm sorry we don't have more seating in the living room, next time you are here, we will. Amalie is ready to serve us."

Tom poured the coffee. Amalie was stationed at one end of the table with a big platter of *profiteroles*, a bowl of warmed chocolate and a bowl of warmed caramel. From around the table one heard sighs of 'oh boy, hmm, looking good.' Amalie said, "Each get two. The caramel is a variation I have added. You may have the traditional all chocolate, one chocolate and one caramel, and either one or both dusted with a secret element of my making. Who's first?" Every hand went up.

As each made their preference, Amalie fixed each choice and dusted with the secret element. Soon all were ready. Amalie sat down and said, 'Enjoy!"

"Where did you learn to make these?"

"At my *grand-maman's* knee when I was very small, gradually being allowed to do a little batch to see if her teaching was hitting home. It took a few failures but finally by the time I was out of high school, I sort of had it down. Her last words of advice, besides 'Be good' was 'don't be experimenting until you made the standard recipe and it works every time.' There wasn't much time the first year in college, but the word got out. In sophomore year one of my friends came home with me for Thanksgiving. She caught me making them. Somehow the word spread around the campus, and I had a little business going. That was okay, I enjoyed watching them have a feast on them occasionally. There that's a quick synopsis of how it happened."

Someone said, "I'll bet you could make good money doing it here."

Amalie said, "Not interested. This is just for my family and friends." Noticing Alice's face with chocolate from ear to ear, she smiled, "Alice, you didn't like them, did you?" She repeated it in

French, "*Alice, tu ne les aimais pas, n'est-ce pas?*" She just smiled and had another bite.

Amalie said, "It's getting late. Can we help with the cleanup?

Maria said, "Thank you, but no. Most of the dishes are already in the dishwasher and the rest won't take long. This has been a wonderful get-acquainted with everyone this evening. I'm so glad you came."

"Thank you for having us."

There were hugs around for the ladies and handshakes for the men.

Since Tom had done the cooking, Maria and Caroline took charge of the cleanup. It didn't take long and soon they were all relaxing in the living room. Tom had put Alice to bed, read her a story and she was out.

Maria said, "They are a fun couple. We're going to enjoy working with Amalie."

Caroline added, "She will do a great job for you. I look forward to seeing the progress that you will all make. Everyone back in Sucy will be surprised at how fast you have come along when we go in June."

58

The next day, Wednesday, they all met at Bill Knapps. They had set their meeting for 11:30 a.m. Doug's parents, Harry and Ann, were already seated even earlier at the big roundtable with Alice's highchair already in place. They rose when they saw Doug and the others coming. Introductions were made, hugs and handshakes.

When they were seated, Ann said, "Caroline, welcome to the family. We weren't sure Doug would ever marry, now here you are."

Caroline replied, "I'm so happy to meet both of you. Doug has told me so much about you both."

Their waitress came with their water and silver, and took their drink orders, coffee, and iced tea for the adults. She came to Alice and said, "Look at this beautiful little girl. I am Christine, what is your name?"

Alice said, "*Bonjour* Christine. *Je m'appelle Alice. J'aime la limonade.*"

Christine said, "What beautiful French she speaks. How did she learn that so young?"

Maria smiled, "She is French. She is learning English."

Alice replied, "Hello, Christine. I am Alice. I like lemonade."

Christine exclaimed, "And she is doing so well already."

Tom said, "She likes to show off."

"I'll get your drinks, Be right back."

They started studying the menu so they would be ready when Christine returned. Doug reminded them that the perch was ocean perch. "Next time you are up, we'll bring in some Lake Michigan perch at the house."

Harry asked Doug, "You told us you had made a decision about where to live. So what's up?"

Doug said, "Caroline decided early that she likes Muskegon and so we'll be settling here. We found a small house to rent until we find a house we want to buy. Our house to buy will have to be bigger, we both want a large family."

Ann clapped her hands and said, "Grandchildren. I'm looking forward to that."

Doug said, "We don't want to have the first one too soon. Two reasons, we don't want to be pregnant when the formal Catholic ceremony happens next June and second, we want some time with just us around. By that time, we will have bought a house, furnished it, and settled into it."

"What will you do for a living?"

"Dad, I have a great retirement from the government and the CIA, as well as some money I've saved. Then I want to get back to my music, try to get a position in the local symphony or maybe teach at the junior college level. Before I audition for the symphony, I have to bring my skills on the cello back to the level I had after my M.A. degree and lessons with a master."

Their food arrived, some small plate dinners, some sandwiches, but all with a dish of Bill Knapps famous au gratin potatoes.

Maria had ordered au gratin potatoes for Alice, suspecting she might like them. She did and it went well with her hamburger patty.

When they left, Doug drove his car with his Dad, Ann drove his parent's car with Caroline to see the rental. The O'Banions headed home for Alice's nap and to get the dessert ready when they all came to their house.

About a half hour later, near 1:30 pm , the four of them, Doug, Caroline, and his parents arrived at Tom and Maria's. Alice was napping, so it was just the six of them settled at the dining room table.

Maria had the leftover *profiteroles* and warm chocolate to be drizzled on them. She was playing it safe, having them with only chocolate and coffee.

Doug and Caroline told how they had met and fallen in love. Doug said, "It took some persuasion to get it all arranged for next June."

Doug said, "We would like for you to be there in Sucy with us. Will you come to the wedding there?"

Harry said, "We would love to be there, son. But we know nothing about overseas travel and with my pension and social security I'm not sure we can do it."

Tom jumped in, "Doug can help you get your passports and I will be chartering a plane so there is no travel expense for you. My parents and Maria's are coming. And our French teacher and her husband are coming. And you will be staying at our home, a chateau in Sucy en Brie where the food is great and free."

Doug added, "And you'll see me as a person of faith, not yours, but one I am comfortable with. Please come."

Harry looked at Ann, she mouthed 'please,' and he said "Okay, son." All clapped, smiled or laughed.

Doug and Caroline walked out with his parents to see them off. Doug said to them, "You've made us very happy. I love you Mom and Dad. We'll be in touch. You have our phone numbers."

59

Next day, Wednesday, Doug and Caroline went to see Mr. Strahan at the New Shores Bank. Mrs. Arnson, Mr. Strahan's executive assistant,, spotted them when they came in and greeted them. She said, "Good morning Doug, and who is this lovely lady?"

"Mrs. Arnson, this is Caroline, my wife."

"Your wife! You weren't married when you left here a few weeks ago. I'm so happy to meet you. You've married a good man here."

Caroline said, "So I keep hearing. I think so as well. I'm pleased to meet you."

"You have a lovely accent. Are you French?" Caroline smiled.

Doug said, "Please take us in to see Mr. Strahan and we'll tell you the short version of how this happened."

'Mr. Strahan, here are Doug and his new bride Caroline."

"I've been looking forward to meeting you. When Doug called for the appointment, he told me about you and said he would tell us how this happened so quickly. Let's sit over in the easy chairs."

Doug said, "Mr. Strahan, may Mrs. Arnson stay? She is bursting with curiosity so I promised her I would tell her."

"Mrs. Arnson, please join us but order us coffee and some of those Rykes butter cookies before you sit."

She said, "Thank you, sir. The coffee will be right in."

"Caroline, what do you think of Muskegon so far?

"I like your city enough that we've made the decision to stay. Tom and Maria have been showing me around but there is so much more for me to learn about it."

"I love your accent. You are native French, right?" A knock sounded. Mrs. Arnson went to the door and brought in the coffee and cookies and set them on the table. She served them all and sat down to wait for the story.

"I am a native French woman and as well, a former novitiate at the parish church in Sucy en Brie. Sucy en Brie is a small town a half hour southeast of Paris."

"So how did you and Doug meet?

Caroline said, "Why don't you take the lead in the telling, Doug?"

He said, "You'll remember that Tom and Maria lost their friends, Celeste and Etienne, in a bad automobile accident. Celeste and Maria have known each other since their early teens as pen pals. They had made a pact that Maria would adopt their child, Alice, if this kind of thing happened. You know the rest of the story of the adoption and the inheritance that came with it."

Mr. Strahan interrupted saying to Mrs. Arnson, "Just a reminder that the O'Banions or Doug and Caroline want their financial situation to stay private as long as they can."

"Yes, of course, sir. Thank you for the reminder."

Doug continued, "I was there with them when they heard about the accident. To be quick about it, I wasn't Catholic then so I asked to be excused from the services and the funerals. I asked what I could do and the answer changed my life."

Caroline put her hand on Doug's arm and said, "I was still a novitiate at that time. My duties were to learn and do some cooking and to work in the nursery during services. The Reverend Mother brought Maria and Alice to the nursery. I knew Alice since this was their church. Doug was brought in, introduced, and said he would help in the nursery since he was already bonding with Alice. By the time the service was over, Doug and I talked a lot. I sensed something with him but didn't say anything. Doug felt it too but also didn't say anything either. Over the course of the next few days with the funeral services and conferences with Father Lemire, we were together a lot more, always talking and learning about each other. When it came to our last time to see each other, I worked up my courage and told Doug that I wanted to see him again. He left. I spent a lot of time praying about my feelings as well as talking with the Reverend Mother about it. When he had another trip to France, he came back to Sucy to see me. We had two meetings with Father Lemire and the Reverend Mother. They finally were convinced that it was what God wanted for me. Doug wouldn't touch me throughout this process or confess his feelings. But when both of them agreed with me, he brought out an engagement ring and proposed to me right there with them as witnesses to the event. Father Lemire, and the Bishop of the parish worked hard to get a dispensation from the Pope. We've been married in a civil ceremony and as they insisted, there will be a full service with a mass when we go back in early June of next year. All married and blessed by the Pope. How did I do, Doug?"

"Beautiful, sweetheart!" Everyone laughed and congratulated them.

Mr. Strahan said, "Shall we get to your business?" He asked Mrs. Arnson to get her note pad and take some notes about accounts.

He continued, "Will you tell me now of your financial situation?"

Doug said, "I have discussed all this with Jean Paul. He is our attorney of record in France, and it was he who suggested I lean to your knowledge in getting all this done. I still have a checking account with you from when I was teaching here. I would like to make that a joint account so that Caroline can draw on it. We are renting a small house that we'll likely stay in while we look for a house to buy. I have enough cash to get by until our new accounts are set up. I have here a certified check in the amount of $25,000 that we would like to deposit right away. We would like an investment account set up like Tom and Maria's so that we can draw from that into the checking account. As soon as that is done, I will be arranging for my retirement checks, one from the Army and one from the CIA deposited in the investment account here."

"We also have an account in a Sucy en Brie bank. It has several thousand francs in it. The exact amount varies because it is an interest-bearing account but it is worth somewhere near $10,000. I kept it there because my assignments for the most part were in France. I also have a Swiss bank account currently with a balance of a little over $100,000. At Jean Paul's suggestion, we will keep the account in Sucy open so that when we go back on occasion, we have a money source there. I don't know what to do about the Swiss account. Jean Paul suggested that you and I talk about it and figure it out. I will be looking forward to your thinking on that."

"Then in the states, there are two accounts in the D.C. area. One is a checking account where my regular paycheck has been deposited for years. It is also linked with an account like Northern Trust in Chicago where as it grows over a certain level some of it is forwarded to the D.C. area trust company. Those two accounts come to something over $1,000,000 and growing quite well. So there you have it. I think I would like to get the trust account closed and put some in your bank and some into Northern Trust. Jean Paul suggested that we see about getting us set up something like Tom and Maria are. But again, I will lean on your thinking. We'll likely have to meet again soon to see what should be done."

"I think that in a few days I can be ready to talk again. I may want to talk with Jean Paul again. If we make some changes, I'm sure he would have some input. And now I have a question I have to ask, please don't be offended. Is all of this money all legitimate, that is to say, earnings or bonuses?"

"No offense taken. I have a safe deposit box at my bank in Virginia full of records covering all my earnings for work, interest, and bonuses. I have a tax man out there who insisted I save them all for a while."

Mr. Strahan said, "Mrs. Arnson, would you get things started, please? It will take a little time to get the new checks printed but Mrs. Arnson will have your receipts for this deposit in a few minutes."

When she left to take care of business, Mr. Strahan asked, "Caroline, what do you think of all this? Doug has done very well for himself. And, by the way, when it is just us in this kind of meeting, would you be so kind as to call me John?"

She smiled, "I'd love to call you John. As to the money situation, I'm still trying to absorb that news. Doug had not said a word about money, just about what he would like to do to earn a living besides his retirement. So when Jean Paul explained it, I was taken aback. It still hasn't sunk in."

"Maybe I shouldn't ask, do the two of you want children?"

Doug answered, "When we started talking with the Reverend Mother about everything, Caroline said that she wanted children, a lot of children. So do I. I am an only child and always wanted brothers and sisters. We don't want a child for a year or so. We think it is important for us to have some time alone together before we take on the responsibility."

"Finally, one more question for you if you don't mind. How do your parents feel about your marriage? Who is going to take this one?"

Caroline answered first, "I lost my mother some years ago when I was quite young. My papa is not in good shape physically. He is in a nursing home now and seems to be better that he was when he went in. We are hopeful he will agree to come here where we will find him a nursing home for as long as he needs it."

Doug said, "We just had lunch yesterday with my parents. They are excited about our marriage. They never thought I would do it. And my Mom is all excited about grandchildren."

Mrs. Arnson knocked and came in with their receipt and documents to sign. When they had done so, John said, "I'll talk with Jean Paul, with your permission, about what he thinks. I'll be in touch soon, maybe even before Tom and Maria's Christmas open house. You'll be there, I would guess. You'll meet my wife, Katherine."

"Thank you for your business and your trust."

60

All five went to a tree farm where you could cut down your own Christmas tree. They both bought one each, stopped at Sears downtown and bought two stands. By noon, both trees were standing in their places. Doug and Caroline had to pick out trimmings and they would decorate theirs later. They came back to Maria and Caroline's lunch, and when Alice was napping, they got the garlands wrapped, lights strung and connected. They would put the ornaments on later when Alice could be part of the process. They would be ready for the open house tomorrow. Doug and Caroline left to buy their decorations but didn't plan to put theirs up until later.

The next day December 7th, Marlene was there with the finger foods, and the wassail bowl. The chairs that Father Flannery had loaned them from the church were scattered throughout the living and dining rooms. Tom had found an FM radio station that was an early player of Christmas music. Tom had it set to be in the background. At two p.m. the first guests began to arrive, few in number at first, but soon there was a big crowd. The room was filled with the Strahan family,

Katherine and John, Bob and Sara with their three-year-old girl, Bud and Jean Hanley and daughter Barb, Jerry and Amalie McNeal, and so many from the protection teams from earlier in the year. Mark, the chief and his wife were there, and former chief Jim Johnson and his wife as well.

There was a buzz of conversations, people introducing themselves, just as Tom and Maria had hoped. Father Flanery was there finding many to talk with. Doug was renewing his relations with their protection people.

With Marlene and her helpers there keeping the finger food platters full and keeping the coffee, tea, and drinks topped off, Tom and Maria were able to float and talk to everyone as they went through the crowd.

When some people started to approach Tom and Maria to thank them, Tom asked if they would stay for him to say something to the group. He stood on a small platform with Alice on his shoulder, Maria by his side, all near the front door and rang Christmas bells until he had the attention of the crowd. They quieted down,

Tom moved Alice to his left arm and said, "Thank you for letting us say a few words to you all. There is a message that Maria, Alice, and I want you to hear. By now you all know there has been a big change in our lives. We have adopted our Alice who is French and doesn't speak much English yet. She will soon, thanks to Amalie McNeal. She has a message for you first."

He touched Alice's cheek and she said, *"Bonjour mes amis, merci d'être venus.* In English, that means, hello our friends, thank you for coming." She smiled at the applause but got suddenly shy and reached for *maman* who took her.

"She is a bit shy with all the people here. Now to the rest of our message. We are so pleased you are here. You have blessed our Christmas season with your presence and willingness to share this time with us. Maria and I have spent most of our lives here and intend to stay. You have made us very happy by being here. Merry Christmas early to all of you. One more thing. If you have not yet met Caroline, Doug's new bride of two weeks, please welcome her. She is French also. They are standing over there near the Christmas tree. Caroline, please raise your hand. Thank you. Maria, do you have something to add?"

"Only that I can feel the love and support of your being here. Thank you so much and again, Merry Christmas to you all. Don't feel you have to leave yet. We want to be sure to meet all of you."

By five p.m. the last ones had left. Marlene and her ladies loaded up. As they left, Maria handed each an envelope, saying, "This is something extra for each of you. Thank you for your wonderful work. Merry Christmas!"

61

Tom and Maria decided to have an old-fashioned American Christmas with French touches for their first year with Alice. They were talking about it after the open house. It had been such a good time.

Maria said, "I'm thinking Christmas Eve with our parents and the newlyweds. That will give Doug and Caroline the option to do their own thing on Christmas Day. How does that sound to you?"

"I think that will work. Do you have a menu yet?"

"No. I thought I'd talk with both moms and we'll make it a Christmas potluck."

Tom asked, "What do you want to bet all the grandparents will want to come over again Christmas day?"

"I wouldn't bet against that. We'll figure something out if they want to. I'll call them in the morning and the three of us gals will make the plans."

"That will give Alice and I some time together. We'll have a good time, games, reading, working on words... Are you still comfortable with an American style this first year?"

"I think so. We can still use some French influence like calling

Santa, *Père Noël.* Does he still come down the chimney and travel to all the houses like here?"

"We could ask Caroline. She might have some ideas about French things we could bring in. Say, maybe she should be at the meeting with the ladies?"

Maria said, "I'm so glad you thought of that. I'm not used to having another French woman here, or, for that matter she and Doug being married. I'll pick her up."

The next day, the ladies all met at Tom's parents' house to plan the menu. Doug called Tom and said," Langlois is delivering our new bed this morning. Can I join you and Alice after they have it set up?"

After Tom said yes, Doug told him, "Okay if I bring our favorite Scribs pizza along, likely about lunch time?"

"That will be great. I'll fix something for Alice just in case that doesn't work for her."

When Doug knocked, Tom left Alice with a puzzle of big pieces. She heard Doug's voice and cried, *"Oncle* Doug!" and came running. Tom took the pizza before she jumped into his arms.

They were in the breakfast nook, the pizza sliced, and Alice with a small bowl of her favorite potato leek soup. There were beers for the men and Alice had her juice.

Alice was enjoying her soup but eyeing the pizza. She said, *"Avoir un peu?"*

Tom pointed to it, cut her a small piece with sausage, sauce, and cheese on it. At first, she shook her head, but the flavors set in and she pushed her soup away and said, *"plus s'il vous plait."*

Tom said, "In English, more please."

Alice said, "More please." Tom smiled and gave her another small bite, this time with a tiny piece of salami. Alice said, "Mmm, *bon"*

Alice was soon ready for her nap. Tom read her a story, one of her favorites that she liked from him. She was out before it was finished.

Doug had cleaned up their pizza leavings and was ready to talk.

He asked, "May I make a call to your parents and arrange for Caroline to come back here with Maria? Then we can head home and get our bed put together." He did so while learning it would be another hour or so.

Tom asked, "How is the old place working out for you and Caroline?"

"It will work until we can find a house. Having the new queen bed will help. I won't be hanging off the bed. We got one just like you have in your guest room. We want to leave it when we move. I promised our landlord, Al, I would do that. The winter is not the best time to buy but who knows? That likely means at least next spring before we can find something that works for us."

"Mind a suggestion?"

"Let me have it."

"We had a terrific realtor who found this house. You've met her, Jeanne Hanley. She will help you and Caroline figure out what you want and then she'll start looking. You may still not find one until the weather breaks but you never know."

"That sounds great. Please have her give me a call."

Doug continued, "Now how about a quick run-down on your conversation with John Strahan."

Tom shook his head and said, "He believes that I am the man who can make a difference in this town. He believes that, in his words, I have the strength of character and skills of persuasion to make a difference in this town. He said that I could make Fred's dreams come true."

"How do you feel about that?"

"A bit overwhelmed for one, flattered for another, and a bit of 'am I the one to do it.' Doug, I don't want to start something that I might not be able to do."

"That won't happen with you, old buddy. If you decide to make a run at it, you'll do it. That's the way you are made."

"That's what Maria keeps telling me. She said that Fred's dreams became mine but got put on the back burner with the Group of Nine business. She thinks I'll regret it if I don't do it."

"I think she is right on that score. Do you have any ideas yet about how to proceed?"

"You know I have started a consulting company offering services that are not completely firmed up yet. I have my first contract already with the police department. Mark and I haven't set any goals for them yet, but we'll start talking soon."

He continued, "Maria and I have a full schedule of learning French and helping Alice learn both more French vocabulary and grammar and the same for English. That will be over the next five months. But that won't take all my time. I want to start talking with the city officials, on a casual basis, to see if I can work my way into a contract with them. I need to earn their trust before that will happen."

"Did you give any thought toward running for office?"

"I did but discarded it. I made that decision and let it noodle. It seems after a couple of weeks that I can do more from the outside."

"I think that's a good decision. You have a way to put things to people that make them think like you. That's the skill that will get them listening to you."

"Are you that sure of my ability to do that?"

"I've seen you do it over the whole time of getting the Group of Nine. Getting things done in the city won't be easy, but you can do it."

"I want to start reading about city and county government, how things run, that is, how they are supposed to run. I have a lot to learn."

Doug smiled and asked, "Another suggestion for you?"

"Sure, fire away."

"I wouldn't get too steeped in city and county government. You didn't know much about the police department but look what you brought to it from your own skill set. That's what will convince them that you have something to offer them that their people can't see."

"That's a great suggestion. That takes some thinking of how I might do it and how I might convince them to think in different ways. Thanks, Doug."

The front door opened, Caroline and Maria came in and Alice walked out of her room saying, *"Papa."* Tom picked her up for a hug but it didn't last. She saw *maman, tante* Caroline, and *Oncle* Doug and each needed a hug from her.'

Tom asked, "Well do you ladies have the French Christmas menu figured out and what I should be doing?"

Maria said, "You only need to assemble the wines to match the food and appetizers that I'll tell you about later. Then you need to find where you can get brie and camembert cheeses. The French Christmas cheese course is *Brie* and *Camembert* on thin slice *baguette* toast.. Then make enough French Onion soup for eight plus people. The celebration will start at 5:00 p.m. on Christmas Eve. How's that?"

"I think I can handle that. I wonder where I can find the right cheeses. Etterman's is a great market but doesn't have many varieties in cheeses."

Maria suggested, "Remember our trip to Grand Haven and that store we found downtown. I think it was called Fortinos. I remember they had quite a variety of wines and cheeses."

Tom said, "Good call. I'll check that out."

Doug asked, "What can I do?"

Caroline responded, "Just be my sous-chef while I make my dessert treat. One of the nuns taught me how at the church in Sucy."

"I don't know what a sous-chef does but I'll try."

Caroline looked at him, fluttered her eyes and said, "You have other skills that count," and fluttered her eyes again.

Maria said, "That works, doesn't it!"

Doug said, "Hush now, the little one is here."

He continued, "We need to get home and put the bedroom in order with the new bed in it. We'll see you on Christmas Eve."

62

"The Christmas menu is a combination of American and French specialties." Maria said, "Let me tell you about the rest of the menu and what we will do during it."

She continued, "I'm sure the grandparents will bring lots of presents. We'll put them under the tree and while we're sitting around the Christmas tree, we will all have Kir Royales and we'll read Alice the story of *Père Noël* and how he travels around the world, down the chimneys, and leaves presents for all the good little boys and girls. We need to convince her that *Père Noël* will leave her gifts that she will get on Christmas Day."

"Do you think she'll be okay with the story?"

"She might question some parts of it. We'll make sure that she buys it at this age. She'll be three in January, but I think it will work."

Maria continued, "When we're finished with that, we'll move to the table, say grace *en Français* and you'll serve the French Onion soup you are making. I'm making *jambon avec sauce de raison*, ham with raison sauce. Caroline gave me the recipe for the *sauce de raison*. Your mom is bringing *Gratin Dauphinois*, which is potatoes combined with cheese, bacon, and fresh spinach. Another Caroline recipe, by the way."

"We will finish the main courses with *salade capresse* which my mom is bringing. Then here's where you come in again. The cheese course will consist of the *brie and camembert* cheeses and *mince* toast *d'une bague* which you are making. For dessert, the *piece de resistance, Bûche de Noël,* which is a traditional log cake. Guess who is making that?"

Tom said, "Caroline."

"You're right. She learned how to make it at the church where she was a novitiate."

"Alice is awake and they'll be here in about 15 minutes." Maria dressed her in a special Christmas dress for their first Christmas with the whole family, *grand-mère and grand-père, Grand-maman and grand-papa,* and now *oncle* Doug and *tante* Caroline. So many names for Alice to remember but she seemed to have them right.

When all arrived at 5:00 p.m. promptly, the three greeted them all at the door and after hugs, Alice led them to chairs around the Christmas tree which was now filled with Christmas gifts. Tom brought a tray with eight Kir Royales plus Alice's juice cup. They toasted the Christmas season and the Baby Jesus.

Alice wanted to open her gifts. Maman said, "After dinner." Alice pouted a little but said, "*Oui, maman.*" They adjourned to the dining table where Alice was asked to start grace *en français.*

Tom then served the French Onion soup. The rest of the dinner was on the table family style but all followed the French tradition of the baked ham with raison sauce and potatoes, then the *salade capresse.* Tom offered a choice of a dry Zinfandel and a dry Reisling. The choices were evenly split. He switched to their favorite sauvignon blanc for the salade caprese. The cheese course was enhanced with a delicate chenin blanc.

When all seemed done, Tom said, "We have one more very special treat. Caroline, as you all know, was a novitiate in a church in Sucy en Brie when she fell in love with Doug and here they are, newlyweds. Caroline learned to make a special Christmas dessert while she was there and she made one for us. It is called *Bûche de Noël.*" With a flourish, he uncovered a log shaped *génoise* cake. "This is a French sponge cake rolled into a log as you see and covered with *ganache au chocolat.*

The coffee is ready so if you, Caroline would slice it, I'll get the coffee to go with it."

As everyone enjoyed it, Tom said, "You all have some chenin blanc and if we could use that for a toast. Thank you all for being here. Good food. Good people. Good conversations. What a lovely first Christmas with Alice in our home. Merry Christmas one and all."

They all gathered around the Christmas tree, exchanged gifts, and had the most pleasure out of watching Alice open her gifts. Tom's dad said, "If you have another Kir Royale left, I have one more thought as a toast."

Tom's dad said "I think I can speak for at least four people at this table tonight. We as we are now, new grandparents, are happy people. As busy as your lives are we were not sure it was going to happen. But you have taken this little girl to your hearts and are devoted to her and her life to come. You have made us all very happy. And Caroline and Doug, we understand you want many children. We look forward to that and will likely start thinking your children are like our grandchildren also if you don't mind. Thank you all four for making our lives fuller. We love you all."

And all the grandparents said, " Here, here, to all you have said."

They touched glasses and sipped the Kir Royales.

A short time later, someone noticed that Alice was nodding. Maria's dad said, "This little darling needs to get to bed so that *Père Noël* can start making his rounds."

Doug said, "We should all head home. Is everyone okay to drive?"

Of course all said yes. Hugs, goodbyes, *au revoir* was said. All became quiet as Alice fell asleep, *Père Noël* came and went.

63

———

On Monday December 30th, Tom answered the phone. It was President Johnson's aide-de-camp, Captain Jim Hansen. Tom said, "Hello Jim, it is good to hear from you."

"Same here, Tom. I'm calling to ask you if you can come to the White House on Wednesday, January 8th for a presentation by President Johnson. We know that you and Doug McDermott are quite close friends and if you have no objections, we would like to do a presentation of a special award to Doug that day, too."

"Of course."

"Good. We'll have a plane pick you up at Muskegon at 8:00 am. If you can get all the parents to come with you that would be great. There is enough room. Oh, and by the way, President Johnson said to be sure and bring that little girl of yours. We'll helicopter you from Andrews to the Whitehouse. We'll have the ceremony at 11:30 am, have a lunch at the White House and have you home by 5:00 pm latest."

"That sounds wonderful. We'll be there. Thank you Jim and thank the President please."

"Done. See you soon. Please let us know how many are coming."

Jim Hansen also made a call to Doug and received the same confirmation that they would be ready to leave at 8:00 am, January 8th.

Everyone boarded just before 8:00 a.m. Doug and Caroline were happy to see the flight crew. Chief pilot Ted and host Anne were on their flight crew again. Anne said that they would chat later.

Takeoff was promptly at 8:00 a.m. After reaching altitude, Ted welcomed them reminding Tom and Maria and their parents that this was their second time with Doug and Caroline. Doug's parents had changed their mind and did not come. Mrs. McDermott was deathly afraid of flying and he wouldn't go without her. They would be watching it on TV. Ted announced that they would be arriving at Andrews at 9:15 a.m. or so. They had a surprise awaiting them. All would be revealed soon.

Then Anne, from her station, introduced herself, and said a hello again to Doug and Caroline. She then started calling names and asked them to identify themselves by raising a hand. Tom, Maria, and Alice, Mr. and Mrs. O'Banion, Mr. and Mrs. Vitale. Then she said, 'By the way, the handsome man about halfway back on the right is my husband Sam. We managed to arrange an invitation to the ceremony and the luncheon after so we'll be with you until you leave for home this afternoon. By the way, you'll have a different crew going home. There are two bathrooms on this plane, one in the back and one up here near where I sit." She added, "We have coffee, juices, and breakfast pastries. I'll be around to serve you."

After a smooth landing at Andrews, all went inside and were met by Jonathan, the manager, who knew them all except the parents. A noise arose outside the main waiting room. Maria asked, "What is that noise?"

Doug said, "That's Marine One, the president's helicopter operated by Marine Helicopter Squadron One. This is our ride to the White House. The pilots will be in shortly to allay any concerns about this ride."

He came in and said, "Hello folks, I'm Captain Johnson, your chief pilot for Marine One. Who has not flown in a helicopter before?"

All but Doug raised their hands. Captain Johnson said, "You are in for a treat. This is a great ride and fun way to access the White House.

Very safe and we don't have to fight traffic. We'll land on the South Lawn and have a short walk in. A White House tour guide will meet you at the entry door, check you Id's. She is charged with showing you around on a short tour and will end at the room where the ceremony will be held. Does anyone need a bathroom stop before we board?" He paused. "You're all set, good! Follow me please."

When they were airborne, the co-pilot came on the PA system. "Hello everyone, I'm your copilot and landmark guide for your ride to the White House. I'll be pointing out landmarks far enough ahead of them so you can see them. If you are not into landmarks, just sit back and enjoy the ride."

After the short 'copter ride and the check-in, they only had an hour for the tour. They finished at the entrance to the press room. The ceremony was being held there so the recipients could get the media coverage and a broader group of people would get the lesson about what happens if you serve your country.

President Johnson came into applause from the audience, the media, and the invited guests. He thanked everyone who was in attendance and spoke of the importance of serving your country and of being recognized for that service.

Captain Jim Hanson took over at this point and invited Doug McDermott to join the President at the podium. He said, "Captain McDermott started his military service in the ROTC while in college. He liked the military so much that he made it a career and joined the Army. He took officers training in the Army where his special skills were noted by our intelligence agencies . He served for many years as a member of a special forces teams. This commendation, signed by President Kennedy, recognizes his long service to the country and in particular in France. He retires today with the rank of Major. He served France more often than other countries and was recognized by French President Charle de Gaulle for service to France with an award of the *Légion d'honneur*. This is the only medal that France awards to non-French, and his is one of only a few awards."

President Johnson handed it to him. No pictures were allowed during this part of the service at the request of one of the intelligence offices. Major McDermott returned to his seat beside his wife.

Aide-de-camp Hansen now asked Mr. Tom O'Banion to come to the podium along with his wife Maria, and their daughter Alice. "Inclusion of his wife Maria and their daughter Alice is at the request of President Johnson. The President will tell you about this family." He said, "Mr. President."

The President opened with, "This man, his wife, and child Alice have become special people to me. As you all know we just lost President Kennedy. He had asked me to make a temporary notification of an award to Tom and his wife for special service to their country. I met them at Andrews when they returned from France. When they entered the room where I was waiting for them, they had with them their newly adopted daughter." He put out his arms and Alice went to him and kissed him on the cheek as he did on her cheek.

"That's the way she took to me. I was thrilled to have a new friend. Now let me tell you about her new parents, Tom and Maria. They were both long-term friends of Doug McDermott. Doug and Tom, Maria as well, were part of the task force that solved the mystery of the Group of Nine who tried to take over their town, Muskegon, Michigan. Their success in solving that case led them to form their own husband and wife detective agency. Doug in the meantime had gone to France on another mission. This is all by background."

The President continued, "Tom and Maria decided to take a long-delayed honeymoon in Paris, France. Doug persuaded them to cut their honeymoon short and help him out with his protection detail for French President De Gaulle and America's Speaker of the House John W. McCormack and his entourage. They were attacked by a rogue group who had been trying to assassinate President de Gaulle. No one was hurt except one of the attackers who was shot and killed by Tom O'Banion."

"President Kennedy convinced everyone that we should commend the family with an award for their service to our country. Again as you all know, we lost President Kenedy last November, so I am following up and carrying out his wishes. I agree with him on this."

He said to Tom and Maria, "This commendation to you is for extraordinary service to our country from a grateful nation." The award was given to Tom and Maria. The three of them, thanked President Johnson, pictures were taken.

Tom said, "Thank you, President Johnson. We accept this award from a nation we love. Our Alice will become a citizen of her new country."

They all left the press room and were guided to the White House dining room. President Johnson had to leave for business of the country. All others enjoyed a White House luncheon. Sam and Anne McConnel were seated at Doug and Caroline's table. This was to be their hoped for get acquainted time. Sam had to be back to the Pentagon and Anne was scheduled for another flight. They promised to meet up as often as schedules permitted. All were flown by Marine One back to Andrews where Doug and Caroline had a rental car waiting. They were going to do some sightseeing for Caroline and close down Doug's life in the D.C. area. The rest were flown with new crew back to Muskegon and home.

64

Tom, Maria, and Alice soon settled into their studies with Amalie. The schedule they had set was Mondays and Wednesdays and would be their full teaching days working with Alice in the morning and working with Tom and Maria in the afternoons while Alice napped. Tuesdays and Thursdays would be afternoons when Amalie would teach Tom and Maria conversations *en français* so they could develop their accents and learn how to carry on with teaching Alice when their time with Amalie was done. Fridays through the weekend was scheduled time off with Tom and Maria carrying on the teaching on a more casual basis.

They soon settled into this routine watching carefully to be sure it wasn't too much for Alice. They would re-evaluate progress at the end of each month. It didn't take long to see progress.

Their extended family learned not to call during teaching time. Phone calls from others were dealt with as breaks in the routine or depending on who it was, let their answering cassette tape take the message.

This schedule was followed through the months of January through most of May 1964. It was a rigorous schedule but it paid off. When the session with Tom and Maria on Thursday, May 21st finished, Amalie said to them, "I have been tracking your progress for each of you. I think it is time to take a break. The progress for you all, but most especially for Alice is, how shall I put it, astonishing. I think it is time to stop our schedule, report to you where each of you stands, and let you proceed as planned with just the three of you following what you do now mostly on weekends. Then in a few weeks, maybe after we all return from France this June, I will retest all of you. My 90% guess is that all of you will continue to progress at about the same rate that you are experiencing now. What do you think of that?"

Maria and Tom locked eyes, nodded. Maria said, "We have been expecting you to propose something like this. We both feel that we are ready for that, what shall I call it, a pause point to let our progress become part of us."

"That's a good way to put it. You could keep going but at a slower pace than you have been doing. You may find that Alice will lead you when she is ready to speed up again. I've seen it before with the twins."

Tom said, "Well then, let's do it. When will you have your test results?"

"I think about the middle of the week, Wednesday or so."

Maria asked, "Could you and your family join us for a late lunch on Saturday May 29th? It could be timed so that Bridget and Aiden could leave early if they wish."

"We could do that. I'll check with Jerry and the twins and let you know."

65

Amalie, Jerry, and their twins joined Tom, Maria, and Alice at a late lunch Saturday the 29th of May. The occasion was the celebration of the success of Amalie's teaching. They welcomed them to handshakes and hugs. Alice made her rounds after welcoming them with, "*Bonjour Amalie et Jerry et les jumeaux* The twins, *les jumeaux*, Aiden and Bridget were introduced.

Tom said, "We'll be starting out at the dining table. We have a special appetizer, It is *baked brie en croute*, as you know, also known as *baked brie with jam and rosemary*. Alice wants to start grace today." She did so *en Français*. All smiled at her and started to clap. Alice said *en Français*, "*Un instant s'il vous plaît. J'ai d'autres choses à dire.*"

When she saw they were waiting, she said, "*Merci pour tout ce que tu as fait pour moi et maman et papa. Nous vous aimons tous le deux.*" Big applause. Jerry and Amalie said, "*Nous vous aimons tous aussi.*"

Tom teared up, brought the Kir Royales, and added, "To our new friends."

Jerry wanted to add a toast. "We have had a good life here as a bilingual family. What you are doing with Alice and yourselves has brought back good memories of when Aiden and Bridget were young. Thank you."

They clinked glasses and started on the *baked brie en croute'*

Maria laid out new plates and silver. Tom brought the beef *bourguignon, dauphinoise potato gratin,* and a very smooth Beaujolais. All enjoyed the main course. Maria confessed, "I got these recipes from Caroline who got them from her *grand-mere.* It was fun learning how to do them."

She continued, "Let's move to the living room for dessert. Alice is ready for her nap, just about asleep already. She will have her dessert later. Say goodnight Alice. "

"*Bonne nuit à tous*" she said and fell asleep.

Jerry asked, "Does she always fall asleep like that?"

"Not usually but we were up early this morning. With all she ate, it just got to her."

Bridget added, "I think Mom told me I used to do that too when I was her age."

Tom brought out the coffees and chocolate mousse. When the twins had finished theirs, they asked, "May we be excused? We have a meeting with some friends. Thank you so much for a great celebration dinner."

"Of course, these are your last few days with your friends. Who knows where you'll be next year? We'll see you again soon."

As Tom refreshed their coffee, he asked, "You said you would be bringing some test results. How did we do? Did we pass?"

Amalie laughed and took out some papers. "These are Alice's test results. You didn't need any tests but you asked for a final and I can tell you did pass. I don't often see people learn so quickly. Both of you have worked hard to get to a level that will let you lead her the rest of the way in both languages. Your accents are good but you need to listen to a lot of native French when you are over there again."

"As for Alice, she now has the vocabulary of a five plus nearing six-year-old and with you both speaking to her in French, that will begin to grow. Her English is not quite as strong but it will grow with you using both languages. I think your friends in France will be amazed at her. I'm leaving you some notes on how to proceed from here on."

Tom took out an envelope and added "If I may speak of your contract, I have a check covering through the end of the month. And we have a bonus for you." He noticed them reacting and said, "Please accept it. You two have been a godsend for us. We didn't know where to turn and you brought us to an important level for both Alice and us." He handed the envelope to Amalie.

She said, "Thank you, Maria and Tom. I had the best sabbatical I could have had. I've learned too. I have five more years to teach and we both will retire. I will be using some of what I've learned in my classroom.'

She continued, "We already have a bonus, our friendship. We both hope it lasts a long time."

Maria added, "We feel that way too. I think I heard you say that your graduation trip to France is still on."

Jerry said, "It is! The boss is giving me some extra time off. We may take a quick hop over to Ireland as well."

Tom asked, "Do you know when you are going?

"We plan to go the first or second week in June."

"Well, if we can coordinate times, I can offer you a ride at least one way and at no cost. I'm chartering a plane to bring our parents and Doug's parents to the wedding. There is room for four more."

Jerry asked, "When are you going?"

"The wedding is Saturday June 13th and we want to be there a day or two before. So maybe on the 10th or 11th . Will that fit for your dates?"

Jerry looked at Amalie, She nodded. He said, "How about the 10th?"

"Done! We'll leave at 8:00 am on June 10th. We'll be landing at Orly private so that is where you'll want your car waiting."

Amalie exclaimed, "This is terrific. Saving one fare for four will save enough that we will have some other choices, maybe Ireland. Thank you both."

Maria added, "It is going to be fun to have you on board."

"Can I help you clean up?"

"Thank you, but it is almost done. Just what's here and that will go quickly."

They said their goodnights and promised to stay in touch to keep things coordinated.

66

It was an excited crowd of fliers gathered at the Muskegon airport. There were Tom's family of three, Doug's family of two, three pairs of parents, and the McNeal clan, fifteen passengers plus the crew of three. The Captain, chief pilot, met them all in the private terminal for last minute instruction. He gave them a rundown of their path and their stops for fuel. He said, "I understand that the three sets of parents are the only passengers we'll have going back so for you, we'll see you on the Wednesday the 18th . If that changes, please let me know. Follow me please."

They were airborne at 8:00 am. There were two cabin flight hostesses. They had been appraised of one nervous passenger who had just taken a therapy course for first time flyers. When they reached altitude, one hostess started preparing breakfast, the other calling out names so they would know the 'newbie.' The one calling out names said, "We're not taking attendance. We just want to get to know you. We'll probably ask you again if we forget your names. Enjoy your flight."

The flight passed without incident. As they were taxiing into the terminal a hostess said, "This is a small terminal so it won't be long before your luggage will be inside. Thank you for taking our flight."

Tom walked with the McNeals to their rental car. "You are welcome to the wedding if you can make it. Here are maps of France, Paris, and Sucy en Brie. Here is my card with the address and phone number where we'll be staying. I hope you have a wonderful trip. If we don't cross paths, we'll see you when we get back home." Maria and Alice joined him to wave goodbye to their new friends.

Henri and Belle drove up in a passenger van just as they started back inside. They walked in and Tom said. "Gather around all! I want to introduce you to two special people. They are Henri and Belle who worked for Celeste and Etienne for some time. They are now the managers of the chateau we now own. They have been pushing decorators and carpenters to make changes that we were planning before we left. They are now bedroom suites. They are your rooms while we are here."

Henri and Belle were introduced to the families. Alice took over and said, "C'est *Grand-père et Grand-maman*" putting Tom by his parents. "*C'est Grand-papa et Grand-mere*" putting Maria by her parents. She stopped for a few seconds and continued, "*C'est Harold et Ann*," putting *Oncle* Doug et *tante* Caroline by Doug's parents.

Belle smiled through her tears, "*Tu es spécial, viens à Belle*" Alice ran to her and jumped into Belle's arms.

Belle said, "Oof! You are heavier."

To which Alice said, "I'm taller too and I'm three years old."

Belle gave her another hug. The rest stood around in amazement at Alice's level on both languages.

Henri urged, "Let's get going. The ladies will have dinner ready for us."

They made the trip quickly. The luggage was brought in and all were settled in their bedroom suites. They were told that there are elevators for those who need them. All were back and seated in *salle à manger*. The staff brought in Kir Royales. Tom asked if he could make a toast. He raised his glass, closed his eyes for a moment, then made the toast, "It is good to be here after a long but quite safe trip. We are back here in a room full of people who love each other. Maria, Alice, and I have been looking forward to this trip filled with joy that people we love are here as well. Here's to all." Here, here echoed through the room.

The staff served two charcuterie boards, identical ones for each end of the table. They also set small bowls of a wonderful smelling dip along with plates of crostini.

Tom looked at it all and inquired, "This is all new, new boards and an interesting addition."

"Yes, Tom. They are new. This is a new selection of cheeses, meats, and other goodies. They will always be served with bowls of warm pimento cheese dip and plates of crostini. We are now serving a blend of mostly French and some American delicacies. We haven't decided yet whether it will be available for all patrons or just for visiting dignitaries. We need to talk to you and Maria about all this."

"We will but I have one more question. Where did the notion of combining the dip and crostini come from?"

Belle continued, "The French think of the charcuterie board as something for a casual party or as the French call it *apéro dinatoire*. Then we thought we needed something more. We stumbled across an American travel magazine that had an article about The Biltmore in Asheville, North Carolina. The story of how it became what it is today made for fascinating reading. When it was built it combined French Renaissance style with, as they say, American creativity. So I called them, told them what we were about and how we wanted to incorporate an American appetizer for our *apéro dinatoire*. Valerie was the name of the person I spoke with. She said she had just the thing. We got the recipe for the warm pimento cheese dip. We put the crostini with it *et voila*."

"What did they want in return?

"Just some recognition that the recipe was from there."

"Belle, you and Henri did well."

"Thank you, Tom."

The table was being cleared, and the main course was being served. It *was Beef Bourguignon, Gratin Dauphinois*, and bread sliced from a *baguette* and toasted with garlic butter.

Tom smiled, then a chuckle, "This is what we had for Christmas dinner this year. Maria made it with a recipe from Caroline's grandmother."

The salad course was *salade lyonnaise* and the sauvignon blanc wine that Belle knew Tom and Maria liked. Maria finished hers and noted that Alice was just about to fall asleep. She has had a long day. Maria said, "If you will excuse me, I'll put Alice to bed and return for dessert and a *digestif* that you mentioned."

The staff served Belle's *profiteroles* with pastry cream and topped with chocolate *ganache*. There were three choices with the final topping of powdered sugar, whipped cream, or nothing but chocolate. Coffee was served for all and a digestif for some.

Some started feeling the time change more than others and said they would be going to bed. Belle said, "We'll make tomorrow morning a sleep in. We'll have breakfast a la carte. One of our staff and I will get you whatever you want starting at eight in the morning. Just relax, sleep in. We will show you around in the morning but otherwise just have a relaxing day. By Thursday, you'll be time-adjusted and we'll talk about what's coming. Goodnight to those of you who are ready now."

Soon it was only Belle and Henri, Maria and Tom, Caroline and Doug talking and catching up. Belle asked, "Caroline, you mentioned that you and Doug would be staying in Muskegon. Can you tell us how that came about?"

"It happened quickly, within a few days. I told Doug how I felt and it soon began to feel like home, as though it was meant to be. We are renting a house now and are working with Tom and Maria's realtor Jeanne Hanley. Houses began coming on the market in March and a week before we left we found just the place. We took possession in mid-May and have started looking for furniture and we'll make the final move in when we get back."

Henri asked, "How is your Papa doing? Is he going to make it to the wedding?"

"We will be going to see him tomorrow after we check in with Father Lemire and the Reverend Mother. We have talked with the staff from the nursing home but won't know if he can come until we get up there and talk in person with the staff doctors and nurses. Unfortunately, he has gotten worse so we will see for ourselves." She could feel Doug's arm coming around her, she leaned on him but fought the tears back.

Belle said, "We're so sorry he is not better and will pray that he can be here."

"We have been told that the best way he can come is in an ambulance. We'll know more about the future then. The consensus at the nursing home is that he has a year at most. We will see how he makes the trip and if that affects that time estimate."

Doug and Caroline met with Father Lemire and the Reverend Mother to discuss the wedding. After sharing events to catch up with each other, Father Lemire got down to business. He handed them each a copy of how things would happen at the wedding with the responses. He said, "I assume that you have your vows memorized."

"We do! We are ready, Father!"

"Good. Then I think we are done. The wedding is at 11:00 a.m. so you and Caroline should be here by no later than 10: 00 a.m. and the men about the same. Where are you off to next?"

"We are on our way to see *mon père*. He is not as strong as he was when we left. We talked several times from the U.S. but couldn't talk long. We'll see if he can come. If he can, is it possible to have him where he at least start me down the aisle and watch from there?"

"We'll work with his handlers, nurses, and such. Let us worry about it. Go now and enjoy your time with *votre père*. We are pleased to see you both so happy."

When they arrived at the nursing home, they talked a bit with the nurses and his doctor. The doctor said, "We better take you down. We have about an hour before his lunch comes. He usually falls asleep after lunch."

Caroline and Doug went in first. The nurses and doctor waited outside in case they were needed. Caroline said, "Good morning, Papa."

"How about a hug for me?" She hugged him carefully and kissed him on the cheek. He wanted to know everything and seemed pleased that they were going to be living in Muskegon.

She hugged him again, saying "I'm so glad you approve. I am happy there. It feels like home already. What do you think about making the trip to the wedding? Father Lemire has said they will work out how you can start my walk down the aisle."

"I would like to do that. We'll see what the doctor says about my going. And, Daughter, I won't be coming to your new hometown with you. It will be easier if I stay here. I want to be buried beside your *maman*. The arrangements are all made for that."

"I understand that *papa*."

He patted her tummy and asked, "Do you have a little one going yet?"

She said indignantly, "No, *Papa*. We wanted some time just the two of us. And we didn't feel it would be right before the full ceremony."

She continued, "When the first one comes, if it's a boy, he'll have your name and if it's a girl, she'll have *maman*'s name."

"You've made me very happy. Thank you. And this big man, he's good to you."

"Always, *Papa*."'

Lunch arrived, They said their goodbyes and said he would see them Saturday if the doctor said so.

Doug said, "Here is Father Lemire's phone number and the number where we'll be staying. I have your number so we'll see what comes. And by the way, I'll cover the expenses of the ambulance and their salaries if you make the trip."

67

Saturday morning dawned with a warm sun, a perfect day for a wedding, Everyone but Doug and Caroline were already at breakfast. When they came down, she teased Belle with, "None of your rule about not seeing him today until the wedding, right?"

They all laughed, and Belle said, "Have your breakfast together this time, enjoy my pancakes."

When they were finished having some more coffee and conversation at the table, the phone rang. Henri answered and told Caroline it was for her. She and Doug both rose and she said, "This is Caroline. It was the nursing home. They are on the way. Your papa will be there. Both a nurse and his doctor are with him."

She said, "Thank you, we'll see you all soon" She burst into tears, but they abated when Doug held her in his arms.

Belle said, "We start with good news. It's now nearly 8:30 a.m. The wedding is at 11:00 a.m. It takes 15 minutes to get to the church so you should all leave about 9:45 a.m. We'll be right behind you. Our seats are reserved but we need to move out shortly after you. Let's go to a wedding!"

Tom was waiting at the front door of the church. The ambulance pulled up at 10:35 a.m. The ambulance driver and his second rolled Caroline's *papa* out and to where he would be positioned near the head of the aisle. Tom asked, "This aisle is not very steep. Do you think you could have her walk down beside him?"

"We'll try. We may not go all the way down. But going part way will mean a lot for both of them."`

Tom hurried to his spot with Doug ready to walk out to the altar. Promptly at 11:00 a.m. Maria made her walk down. The men moved Caroline's *papa* into position. Caroline came to *Papa*'s left, put her right hand on his, Mendelssohn's Wedding Song started. People were startled but soon realized what was happening. They walked down about a third of the way, stopped, Caroline kissed *Papa* on the cheek and said, "I love you *Papa*." He did the same. There wasn't a dry eye in the chapel. They moved her *pere* back to the head of the aisle and Caroline began her walk to Doug. She saw all her nun friends lined up on both sides of the altar. When Father Lemire guided Caroline and Doug to join hands, the nuns moved to their positions on the outside aisle.

The service proceeded. After the singing of the gospel, Father Lemire started his homily. When he had finished with traditional homily, he said, "I want to deviate just a bit now. The Bishop, who is here, said it would be alright. I've known this young lady since she first came here as a novitiate in the church. She was getting close to becoming a nun with us. But God had a different plan. This young man showed up at several functions and they fell in love. Is that the right way to say that 'fell in love'? The Reverend Mother talked with Caroline a lot and I talked to Doug. By the way Doug had his own ideas of what makes a good marriage. He said use them if you wish. You heard them in the earlier part of the homily."

He continued, "Doug hadn't declared his love for her yet. The last teaching session was with them, the Reverend Mother, and I. When we let them know that they appeared to us that they belonged together, Doug was on his knees with a wedding ring asking her to marry him. He doesn't waste time. He put the ring on her finger, stood, and kissed her right in front of us. More laughter! Thanks to the persuasion by the Bishop and some of my own, they received a dispensation from the

Pope. I performed a civil ceremony a few months ago and today is the traditional one. One last comment and we'll proceed. When you all stood to watch the bride come down the aisle, she walked part way with a man on a hospital bed. As you all figured out, that is her papa. He is quite ill but made the trip from about an hour away. He has already been returned to the ambulance and once Caroline sees him again they will go back. We are so happy for both of them that he was strong enough to come. The ladies of the church are feeding them now."

"So now we'll restart the wedding with the Celebration of Matrimony, the mass starts, the questions, vows, the exchange of rings, and the prayer over their marriage.

A few minutes later, there was a final prayer and he said, "Now, to the town people, there are some newcomers here. In addition to Caroline's papa, there are three other sets of parents from America here. Please make them welcome. Let's go meet Mr. and Mrs. Douglas McDermott and have a celebration. Here they are Doug and Caroline McDermott."

After greeting all the witnesses to the marriage, Caroline and Doug went out to the ambulance to see Papa one more time before he went back to the nursing home. She asked, "How are you feeling, *Papa*?"

He replies, "I'm tired, Daughter. Will you be coming up again before you go home to Michigan?"

She said, "Yes, we will, *Papa*. You can count on it."

"Good. I would like to talk to you again before you leave."

"I love you, *Papa*. We'll see you soon and we can talk."

"I love you too." he said.

They went back in. Father Lemire was waiting for them at the door to the big dining area. He walked with them to the head table where Maria and Tom with Alice, Belle and Henri, Jean Paul and his wife, he and the Reverend Mother, and the Bishop would be seated. He asked Caroline and Doug to hold back while he got the attention of the townspeople. He said, "Ladies and gentlemen of the parish, once more, here are Doug and Caroline McDermott. Please let them know how welcome they are. Let us say grace together and we'll celebrate their new life."

Lunch was served. As they ate, the townspeople came up and welcomed them. Caroline and Doug were moved by the warmth of the town's folks. They circulated among them and thanked them for being there. Finally Doug asked for their attention. He said, "Caroline and I are moved by the welcome you have shown us. Caroline, as a novitiate, was prepared to become a nun but God told her that she had another way to demonstrate her love. I was the main beneficiary of that change. I am a blessed and lucky man. Thank you for celebrating with us. Caroline?"

Caroline said, "I've known many of you for a long time and was prepared to become a nun in your church. But God had other plans and now we will soon be back in Muskegon, Michigan. We have just bought a home there. We hope to fill it up with a passel of children. Thank you for being here to show us your love and approval of our union. Thank you for your love and your warmth. And thank you for your kindness you showed my *papa*. It was special for us that he was able to be here."

Father Lemire had a last word. "The Reverend Mother and I have come to know both of these young people as they build a new life and a family. They have already found a new parish home in Muskegon, but their promise is to remain a member of this parish and will continue to support us. Finish your lunches and tell them they are always welcome here."

\

68

———

When Caroline and Doug came downstairs the next morning, most of the others had already had breakfast. They were sitting in the living room with their last coffees, chatting away. Belle whipped up some eggs and bacon for them. When they finished, they joined the rest with their coffee. They took some good-natured teasing from Tom and Maria who said, "We didn't think you would be down so soon."

Caroline said, "We wanted to join you all and let you know how happy we are that you were all here. It was such a grand affair yesterday, but our civil ceremony will always be our wedding anniversary date."

Doug's mother said, "I'm so happy that I came. Welcome to our family, Caroline. We are looking forward to those grandchildren."

With a twinkle in her eyes, Caroline said, "We are too. We will do our part."

Maria asked, "Are you going to take another honeymoon?"

"Actually, we are anxious to get back home. First though I need to see *Papa* one more time. We'll take a ride up there sometime today to see how he stood the trip."

The phone rang. Henri answered it. He said, "Caroline, it's for you. It's the nursing home."

Her *Papa*'s nurse said, "Caroline, your *Papa* is asking for you. He has taken a bad turn this morning. He wants you to sing 'Amazing Grace' for him." Caroline burst into tears. Doug took the phone and was told that her *Papa*'s time had come. "You should get her here quickly. He wants to see her one more time."

Doug said, "Please do all you can to keep him alive. We'll leave right away."

They were on the road quickly. Henri led the way with all the parents. Tom was driving Doug's rental car with Caroline and Doug in the back seat. When they arrived, Doug and Caroline went right in. The rest held back while the two of them were taken to *papa*'s room.

Her *Papa* said, in a whispery voice, "Caroline, would you sing Amazing Grace for me now and then at my service? My time is coming, Then go back to your new home with this good man of yours."

She did so while holding his hand. Her voice was shaky but beautiful, When she finished, he gave her hand a squeeze and was gone.

She burst into tears; Doug held her.

Tom and Maria heard it all from the open door. Doug and Caroline came out. Doug asked Tom and Maria to be with Caroline while he talked to the staff about his arrangements.

He was shown the documents outlining what her Papa wanted. No service except at the graveside. Everything was firm except who the priest would be. And finally Caroline was to sing 'Amazing Grace' if she is present and able to, and bury him next to his beloved wife.

He asked them, "Can this happen tomorrow afternoon?"

The manager of the home said, "The funeral director is already on his way and should be here any minute. If he is not tied up with another service, there should be no problem for tomorrow afternoon. Here he comes now."

The funeral director said, "We will be able to do all we need to and hold the service at, let's say, 2:00 p.m.

Doug said, "It's my understanding that he has already paid for your services. Is that correct?"

"It is, Prices have risen since we made the agreement, but we will honor it."

Doug said, "We'll take care of you, and all the other details."

Doug came back to the room where Caroline, Maria, and Tom were waiting for him. He told them what arrangements had been made and the funeral director said he will be ready by 2:00 p.m. tomorrow.

Caroline said, "This is good. Will we be able to go home with the others on Wednesday?"

Doug answered, "If that's what you would like to do, we'll do it."

"I do want that. I want to go home."

"Then that's what we'll do. For now, let's head back to Sucy so I can make some phone calls."

When they were all back home and the parents were caught up on what had happened, Doug asked, "May I use the phone? I have a number of calls to make, Father Lemire, Jean Paul, and the pilots for the return trip home."

Tom contacted the pilots and let them know there would now be eleven people going back Wednesday June 17[bh].

Doug called Father Lemire, told him what had happened and asked if he and Caroline could see them that afternoon. They agreed on 3:00 p.m.

The last call, to Jean Paul, went to his answering machine. The message had all the details about the service in case he wanted to come.

Father Lemire and the Reverend Mother were waiting in the foyer of the church when Caroline and Doug arrived. When Caroline saw them, the tears came again. While the Reverend Mother comforted Caroline, Doug filled them in on the details. He said, "Monsieur Laine had all the arrangements made except who would do the service. We are asking you now if you would. It is tomorrow afternoon at 2:00 p.m."

Father Lemire said, "I would be pleased and honored to do it. I assume Monsieur Laine is a Catholic." Doug nodded yes.

Father Lemire continued, "I have two questions. One, is it a closed service? Or can the nuns come as well? I'm sure the nuns would like to be there. And does anyone else have a role in the service?"

Doug answered, "It is not closed. And if there is any way I can help to get the nuns there, please let me know. To the second question, yes, Caroline was asked by her Papa to sing 'Amazing Grace' at the gravesite. You only have to find an appropriate place in the service.'

The Reverend Mother said, "Child, why didn't you say something about your singing?"

Caroline said, "I didn't think it was my place to say anything until I was a nun."

"Will you sing it *en Français*?"

"*En Français*. That's what I did when I sang it to him in the nursing home."

"That took courage."

"Yes. And I have been praying that God gives me the courage for tomorrow."

Father Lemire, "How long does it take to get there?"

Doug answered, "About 45 minutes. Henri will be driving a rented van for the parents. Some of the nuns could ride with us if you wish. You could follow him up."

"*Papa* had it all written out. Here is a copy for you."

Doug said, "If there are no more questions, we need to get back to our home. We have loved ones there who need to know that things are all set. Thank you for doing all this."

69

———

Since there was no plan for anything other than the service, they were soon on their way home. Father Lemire's service was exactly right. Caroline sang beautifully. Belle had left instructions to have ready a light dinner and wine.

While enjoying the food and wine, their conversation was subdued at first, but they soon put things behind them and talked about what was coming.

Tom asked, "What is your pleasure for the next day and a half? What with packing and all, that is about all the time we have." The consensus seemed to be just staying put and spend the time here at the house getting to know each other better.

Tom's dad said, "We should ask Belle and Henri what they think. Can you handle us being here another two days?"

Belle smiled, saying. "We want to have more time to get to know each other. We now have staff to keep us fed so we get to join you in that."

Doug said, "Good. That is settled. Let us just enjoy our time. Another glass of wine anyone?"

They all laughed. One said, "I love this bunch."

The phone rang. Henri answered and said, "Tom, it's for you."

"Hello Tom, Jerry McNeal here. We just wanted to let you know that we are in Ireland. Yes, we made it here and we are all booked on a flight from Dublin to Muskegon on Friday of this week. We also want to say thanks again to you and Maria. Amalie is asking me how your friends there felt about Alice's progress."

"You are welcome, Jerry. Tell Amalie that they were quite surprised about how well she is speaking both languages. We'll share more when we see you at home. Thanks for the call."

Wednesday morning they were at the Orly private hanger by 7:15 a.m. After the chief pilot again told them about the route and fuel stops, he said, "The weatherman said that there is a good chance of tailwinds today. If he is right, we might be in by 7:00 or 8:00 p.m. Michigan time. We'll see. We'll feed you a brunch in about an hour and a dinner about four or five hours later."

"Let us go home.

Their hostesses welcomed them again, checked their seatbelts, and they were off for the first leg of the trip. Tom and Maria were seated near the private area with a bed where Alice could take a nap after the brunch. They were served omelets, bacon, and toast. Most of the adults had mimosas with their brunch. The exceptions were Doug's parents and Alice.

When the brunch was over, as prearranged, Tom moved up to talk to Doug while Caroline went back to sit with Maria and Alice for their talk. It didn't take long for Alice to start her nap. Maria said, "You know what we'll be doing in the immediate future. Tom and I will continue our work with Alice and ourselves so we can become a bilingual family. Tom will be focusing on getting a consulting contract with the city so he can work toward Fred's plan for Muskegon. Over time we can share more as the four of us get more time together. I would like to know more about what you and Doug are planning."

Caroline said, "Our immediate job is to get moved into our right now empty home. We're counting on your help. It will take some time to find the furniture. The kitchen and dining area, out bedroom, and the living room will be our priorities. The bedroom furniture is already just waiting for us to tell Langlois to deliver it. The kitchen is next. Doug and I are already working on a plan about the order of things, but it will take time to get it moving. I figure that we will have at least six months before we have those three rooms done. Doug will need to make one of the bedrooms his practice room for his cello studies. Eventually he wants a practice room that is just for that purpose. He is anxious to get to the performance level he needs to before he auditions for the symphony.

"How about your family plans?"

Caroline smiled saying, "We are working on that.'

"Good girl. You and Doug are going to have beautiful children."

In the meantime, Tom and Doug were catching up on future plans. Tom said, "I would guess you and Caroline will be busy setting up a home in your new house."

Doug replied, "You're right. We need at least our bedroom and the kitchen before we can move in. The basic kitchen is there but we have to make some changes to have a breakfast nook. We have some living room furniture to use until we can get new. Caroline has never furnished a house before so we want to take it slowly so we can get it the way we want. She is looking forward to tapping Maria's wisdom on room designs."

"You will get it figured out. It took us a while."

Doug continued, "I want to set up a practice room for me and my cello. I've spoken with my teacher in the DC area, and she promises to get me a list of names close by for a new teacher. I will be talking with Muskegon Community College and see if there is anything there for me."

Doug asked, "How quickly do you think we can move on getting the money accounts set up?"

"John Strahan will get that moving for you. Jean Pall will be making another trip to the US in a week or two. He will meet with John, and we'll make a trip to Chicago to set things up with you as well as take care of my move to being a silent partner with Gerald. You too if you decide to do that."

Doug added, "That takes care of my plans. How about you. I know your first focus is continuing your teaching that you and Maria will do with Alice. "

"You're right about that. Our goal is two-fold; get Alice to the level she needs to do well in whatever school we find for her. My second target is to get tight with the city council and gain a new consulting contract with them. I'll need some thinking time before I tackle that and will need more discussions with you, John Strahan, and many others to make it happen."

Tom smiled and said. "There's one more thing that both of us are doing for the first time in our lives."

"What is that, Tom?"

"We both are family men raising children, me now, and you soon will be. Who knows what these new citizens of the United States and France will do for this great country of ours."

ACKNOWLEDGMENTS

I have so many people to thank. Let me start and end with my children and grandchildren who are first, last, and always, encouraged and inspiration. Thank you all.

Thank you to all my teachers of writing craft beginning with my hometown writing group, Stirrings. Thanks to Angie Maloy who brought me in, who continued to teach and inspire, who set up the structure of the sessions so that we all got lots of feedback, both good ideas to correct problems and praise when we had done well. You all taught me so much about how to write and tell stories.

Thank you to my teachers and friends at the Bear River Writer's Conference who taught me with your praise and critiques. There's one person I especially have to thank. Laura Kasischke, you are a genius teacher. I was in your class for three straight years. You awakened the writing muse in me and look where it has taken me. When I publish my memoir, I will have more about all my teachers.

Thank you to my teachers and mentors for various aspects of the writing craft and the business of writing when I attended the University of Madison Writers Institute. Thank you, Christine DeSmet, for your Master Class in novel writing. I appreciate your 'time generosity' after the session when you critiqued my early pages and led me in a new direction. You said, "Try again and do this." I did that and it worked as you said it would.

Thank you also to my brother, Phil, and his wife, Jean, my late brother, Michael, and his wife, Cheryl, my brothers and your wives, for your unwavering support and encouragement in my writing efforts. Your big brother is taking a new step. Who knows what's next!

In a Bear River staff presentation, Keith Taylor, then director of the conference said this, "Get yourself a good editor and listen to her/him. He/she will help you make it a better book." I took his advice and did just that. My daughter, Deborah Smith Cook, was my developmental editor and as Keith said she would, made it a better story. She caught things I missed and helped me find a better way. Thank you, Deb. Of course, any errors are my own.

My self-publishing consultant is Jody of Skinner Book Services and Deborah was my coach and guide for the independent publishing side of the business. Jody will take all the parts of the third novel and work with Adrijus to make the final product. Thank you, coach Deborah, Jody, Adrijus of Rocking Book Covers, You all make my part in the process easier. Thank you all.

And finally, again, thank you to my children and grandchildren. Your constant encouragement and support helped me bring this book to reality. I love you all.

ABOUT THE AUTHOR

After a satisfying and productive career as a research physicist, Hayden Smith came home to Muskegon to be near his children. Not content with resting on his laurels, he started a new career as a physics and mathematics instructor at the local community college. Working with his students and interacting with his colleagues was one of the most fulfilling times of his life. However, he would often say at lunch with colleagues that he would like to write a novel -- that he had an idea for a story.

Two things happened to make that dream a reality. One of his daughters, who knew about his wish to write, told him about The Bear River Writers' Conference and sent him to it. At about the same time, a dear friend and former colleague remembered the lunch conversations and suggested he join the writing group that she led. He did both, attended the Bear River Writer's conference and joined the writing group in his hometown. He is so grateful for both suggestions. His life changed forever. He found a new passion that he didn't know he had. In addition to all the other writing he did along the way while learning his writing craft, his novel began to shape up. That dream was fulfilled with his debut novel in 2020, *Nine Expensive Funerals*. His second novel, *Vengeance Served Cold*, and of course, the third novel, *Intrigue in Paris* are now done. In this book, you will learn about my next project, a memoir entitled *The Fourth Quarter*. Then when I finish the memoir, I will return to the second trilogy and the adventures of Tom and Maria O'Banion..

Now he has five passions that feed and gratify him. The first and foremost passion is to stay close to his children, grandchildren, and great-grandchildren. They are his joy. What else? He is getting back to his roots in music and theatre, both performing and attending. He is passionate about travel – especially to France, Ireland, and Italy, and around this great United States. He particularly loves the wine regions in California, Oregon, and Virginia. Hayden continues doing research in physics and physics-related subjects. And of course, writing fiction and the stories of his life. He often says, "It is a great, full life!"

A SNEAK PEEK AT MY MEMOIR
THE FOURTH QUARTER

Coming Soon

I have been a dreamer all my life. At least that is what Mother and Daddy told me when l could understand what they were saying. They said my face took on a look that said to them, "Look, he's off somewhere again." In my younger years, they would just snap their fingers, and I would come back and smile at them. As I listened to Mother singing her blues and jazz, I would sway to it and would stop when she stopped singing. When I heard the Lone Ranger or Green Hornet on the radio, I dreamed about being the Lone Ranger or the Green Hornet. As I learned about things in school, latest ideas in my head took me to dreams about being a deep-sea diver or a space traveler. As Daddy said, "Something is always going on in that head of his! The doctor said don't worry, he just has a regularly active imagination that brings about dreams from new ideas that pop into his head. You'll likely see him acting them out. They will be like a bubble, as in champagne and each bubble will bring him a new adventure. A new 'here'!

What is 'here'? It is an event, a happening, at a certain place and point in time that shaped me or moved me in a different direction.

What comes now is a sample of my 'Heres' – bubbles that popped and I had a new 'here.'

Here One

What's the origin of 'here?' In August of 2023, I was attending my 14th Bear River Writer's Conference with Tom Lynch as our teacher. He had asked us to write a 500-word essay focused on *where* it was happening and *when* it happened. I did so and called each place and time, a 'here' -- a defining event that happened at a particular moment. Each of the chapters that follow will be a new 'here' for me – a defining moment of time that shaped who I am today. With each chapter in this memoir, think of each place and time as a new 'here.'

Here Two

My first 'Here' came in early childhood. Mother and Daddy grew up during the time of blues and jazz. Mother sang them to me instead of a lullaby, and Daddy went along because he adored her. This music and acting became a life passion before I knew what a passion was.

Here Three

I started Western Michigan University with the intent of teaching music in high school. When I realized how much time that would take away from my family, I switched to majoring in political science and history, two other subjects that I loved. For my degree, I had to take a science course and chose Physical Science. That course was a major turning point in my life. My teacher for that was Dr. Haim Kruglak, who aroused in me a deep interest in Physics. Because I hadn't taken math and physics in high school, I had to persuade the department head to allow me to major in Physics. I also did a major in Mathematics. I graduated with special honors in Physics. One of my heroes in Physics was Albert Einstein. In Annus Mirabilis, his magical year of 1905, Einstein published four important papers. Mass-energy equivalence or $E = mc^2$, Special Relativity, Brownian Motion, and the Photoelectric Effect, for which he received the Nobel Prize.

I would never have found Physics were it not for the music that had led me to Western and Haim Kruglak.

Here Four

As you know, I started out with intent to teach. When I graduated, I chose instead to take a research job in southeast Michigan. All my research at the Bendix Research Lab had to do with some aspect of the photoelectric effect and led to some new particle detectors that flew on satellites in outer space. I was there for 4 years while earning a Master's in theoretical Physics.

Here Five

My work at the David Sarnoff Research Center in Princeton New Jersey continued my focus on the photoelectric effect. It was now more of a theoretical investigations into the particle detectors of the day, particle detectors that are serving as detectors at such places as Fermilab and the huge detector system at CERN. During this time I was taking classes at the doctoral level at Princeton and could have been admitted into a doctoral program. When I divorced Wanda, I left the field of physics and moved back home to Muskegon.

Here Six

I got back to my original desire to teach. I taught part time at both Muskegon Community College and Grand Valley. I became a full-time teacher teaching physics and mathematics at Muskegon Community College. These were some of the most satisfying 22 years of my life. I still miss my students and often bump into them in Muskegon. They tell me that I'm missed in the Physics department.

I retired in 2005 from teaching and two years later my second wife of 35 years passed away. I felt lost as to what to do next. I was 75 years old and looking for a new life, some new 'Heres'.

While recovering from that loss, I considered many options though I soon realized I had to stay where I was. I would miss my children, my friends, and the possibility of new friends.

What follows are some samples of the kinds of things that have bubbled up and given me a full life to this point 18 years into the fourth quarter. If I am given the privilege of making it to my goal of one hundred years old in another seven years it is my hope that I do not stop finding what is in the next bubble. We will see.

Here Seven

My friend Angie Maloy remembered that I wanted to write and invited me to be part of the writers' group, Stirrings, that she led. We met once a month and critiqued each other's work. My daughter, Deborah, saw an ad for the Bear River Writers Conference. She and my son-in-law ,Joel, paid for my first year, 2009. I went home on a high and wrote a sixteen-page summary of this first year, calling it *A Life Changing Experience*.

This was a twofer, two 'Heres' at once. What joy! Learning how to write fiction at both the writers' group and the Bear River Conference.

Here Eight

In 2010 I returned to my childhood love of music. I started singing with choirs and acting in musical theatre. I was in a small group of adults who toured with Blue Lake's International Choir and Orchestra. We sang Mendelssohn's Elijah in two cities in France and one in Germany.

I started voice lessons again. Nicholas Loren, a former New York

City opera singer, voice teacher, and coach. Nicholas is a friend as well as voice teacher.

More amateur theatre roles came my way.

Finally Nicolas and I decided I was ready to show off my pipes in some solo work. Using my new writing skills and new vocal abilities, I wrote, produced, and performed in two cabaret shows. Remember the Elijah performances? There was a soloist for each voice and the soprano soloist was a woman named Sabrina Laney Warren. She and I performed two cabarets at the Frauenthal Center's Beardsley Theatre. Such a rewarding 'Here' for me.

So many 'Heres.'

Is there another 'Here' coming. Hang on!

Here Nine

Remember Angie, my friend? She also recommended me for the board of the Friends of Hackley Library. I served five years on the board, one year as president. This service was deeply satisfying for me.

Here Ten

The trip with the Blue Lake reawakened my love of travel. I've been privileged to travel back to France several times, to Ireland once, to Mexico, Yellowstone, the Grand Tetons, and Glacier National Park.

Here Eleven

And finally, I am still doing research in physics. Next year, if I finish my research, I hope to publish my first paper since my early pieces back in the 1960's. There is a big change in the theory of particle physics that has a bearing on my work. Some physicists are even proposing that there are no particles. Fields are the fundamental quantity; particles are only excited states of each particle field.

Summary

Am I done yet? I hope the adventures aren't over. And the best part, my children are with me, encourage me, and are always there at performances, and almost always with me when I travel.

My passion is to stay close to my children, grandchildren, and the great-grands. They all are my joy, my raison d'être. Five other passions vie for my attention each day. They are writing, music, theatre, physics, and travel. When you combine these with number one, I have a 'Here' that is an amazing time and place. I'm having the time of my life.

I hope you are motivated by this sampling to read the book. You will learn what always motivated me and keeps me moving. Thank you for reading. It has been a good life!

A LITTLE BIT OF FRENCH TO ENGLISH

French (**English**)

Alice, tu ne les aimais pas, n'est-ce pas (You didn't like them, did you?)

Allons à la salle à manger. (Let's go to the dining room.)

apéro dinatoire (cocktail dinner)

artichauts Hélène. (artichoke bottoms stuffed with cheese and sometimes bacon or sausage)

Avoir un peu (Have a little?)

Belle est en France (Belle is in France.)

boeuf bourguignon (beef braised or stewed in a red wine sauce with mushrooms and onions)

Bon (Good)

Bonjour Mademoiselle Alice. Bienvenue en Amérique! (Welcome, Miss Alice. Welcome to America)

Bonjour mes amis, merci d'être venus (Hello my friends. Thank you for coming.)

brie en croute (Brie wheel baked in a crust)

champignons fourrés au fromage frais (mushrooms stuffed with cheese)

Chez moi. (My home)

coq au vin (Chicken in wine sauce)

crêpes (pancakes)

dis les grâce (Say grace)

Elle est maintenant mariée à moi, alors vous pouvez l'appeler « tante Caroline » (She is now married to me so you can call her Aunt Caroline.)

en anglais (In English)

en français (In French)

Garde Républicaine (French Secret Service—before 1983)

gestionnaires de domaine (House managers)

gougère (baked savory choux pastry made of choux dough
 mixed with cheese)

haricots français beurrés (French yellow beans in butter)

j'ai faim (I'm hungry)

Je m'appelle Hayden (My name is Hayden.)

Je t'adore! Merci! Merci (I love you. Thank you. Thank you.)

Je t'aime aussi (I love you too.)

Lardon (bacon)

le dîner est servi (Dinner is served.)

le magret de canard (Duck breast)

magnifique (magnificent)

maman (Mom or Mama)

Maman arrive (Mama is coming.)

Maman, je dois faire pipi (Mama, I have to pee)

Maman, où est Belle? (Mom, where is Belle?)

Mangez (Eat!)

Merci beaucoup (Thank you very much.)

*Merci pour tout ce que tu as fait pour moi et maman et papa. Nous
 vous aimons tous* (Thank you for everything you have done
 for me and Mama and Papa. We love you all.)

mère (Mother)

mes amis (My friends)

moules marinières (mussels)

Notre maison (Our house)

nous serons de si bons amis (We will be the best of friends)

Oeufs (eggs)

papa (Dad)

père (Father)

plus s'il vous plait. (More please)

pommes de terre à la crème (Creamed potatoes)

poulet fermier (Roast chicken)

pour vous, maman (For you mom)

pour vous, oncle (For you uncle)

pour vous, papa (For you dad)

pruneaux au lard (prune wrapped with a thin slice of bacon, grilled in the oven.)

Réveille-toi, ma petite (Wake up little one.)

sophistiqué et charmant (sophisticated and charming)

soupe de poisson (Fish soup)

suis-moi dans ta chambre (Follow me to your room)

ta maman (Your mama)

ton papa (Your dad)

tout suite (Right away, immediately)

Très bien (Very well)

Un instant s'il vous plaît. J'ai d'autres choses à dire (One moment please. I have some other things to say.)

veuillez le faire (Please do it)

Voici de nombreuses années heureuses, mon chère. (Here's to many happy years, my dear.)

Vous avez bien dormi? (You slept well?)

9 781735 998350